He already ⬚⬚⬚⬚⬚⬚⬚⬚⬚⬚⬚⬚ ⬚⬚upplies, he silently sl⬚⬚⬚⬚⬚⬚⬚⬚⬚⬚⬚⬚⬚⬚ was a mailbox part⬚⬚⬚⬚⬚⬚⬚⬚⬚⬚⬚⬚s. He'd already chec⬚⬚⬚⬚⬚⬚⬚⬚⬚⬚⬚⬚vas the best place to ⬚⬚⬚⬚⬚⬚⬚⬚⬚⬚⬚⬚side of the mailbox, ⬚⬚⬚⬚⬚⬚⬚⬚ see him without walk-ing straight toward him. He would wait for his angel. Wait and she would come right into his arms.

He pretended to mail a letter, just in case anyone happened by, then slid into his hiding place.

And waited.

He heard the *flap-flap-flap* of decorated spokes before he saw her.

He counted to three, then stepped out of hiding, right into her path.

Also by Allison Brennan

THE
Kill

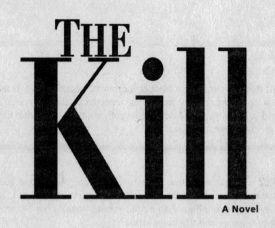

A Novel

Allison
BRENNAN

BALLANTINE BOOKS • NEW YORK

A Ballantine Books Mass Market Original

Copyright © 2006 by Allison Brennan

All rights reserved.

Published in the United States by Ballantine Books, an imprint of The Random House Publishing Group, a division of Random House, Inc., New York.

BALLANTINE and colophon are registered trademarks of Random House, Inc.

ISBN 0-345-48523-8

Cover design: Tony Greco & Associates

Printed in the United States of America

www.ballantinebooks.com

OPM 9 8

Untold innocent children whose names we will never read in any headlines continue to be saved from the horrors of child abduction through the tireless efforts of Maureen Kanka, John Walsh, Brenda van Dam, Mark and Cindy Sconce, Kim Swartz and so many others. May the good they do for our society bring peace to their lives.

ACKNOWLEDGMENTS

The act of writing is a solitary experience. Taking a tickle of an idea and seeing it blossom into a 400-page novel is exhilarating. But in the process, the writer often seeks guidance from those with knowledge beyond her scope. Several people kindly shared their time and expertise to help pull together the details of this book:

Gary Olson, public safety consultant for the California State Assembly, for helping me research California law, specifically the 1972 Supreme Court decision that abolished the death penalty, resulting in 107 criminals having their sentences changed.

Romance writers are immensely generous with their time and talent. I particularly want to thank Morag Pippin and Ann Schuessler for their information about Seattle and Vashon Island.

Once again, Wally Lind at Crime Scene Writers has been an invaluable reference, helping to bring the forensic details alive; former FBI agent and author Rae Monet graciously answered a myriad of odd questions at all hours of the day and night; and Lillian Peck, customer service representative with the Municipal Court of Seattle, answered multiple questions about their court system, prisoner housing, and transportation. Any inaccuracies are solely my domain.

For much needed emotional support, thanks to my friend Karin Tabke and our blogging partners in crime at murdershewrites.com.

Special thanks to Jan, Sharon, and Amy, who read the first chapters and asked the tough questions; my fabulous agent, Kimberly Whalen, whose excitement is contagious and who always loved Zack; and my wise editor Charlotte Herscher, who helped whip this story into shape. In addition, I want to thank the entire Ballantine team for their support and encouragement, especially Dana Isaacson, Gilly Hailparn, Kim Hovey, and Signe Pike.

Most important, I want to acknowledge the parents of murdered children who, through much personal pain and sacrifice, continue to focus the notoriety of their families' tragedies to effect reform of child predator laws nationwide.

And, the sexual assault investigators who dedicate their lives to solving crimes against the most innocent and vulnerable of our society.

PROLOGUE

Livie tilted her head toward the late-afternoon sky and frowned, wrapping her arms around her stomach. "Missy, *pul-eeze*. I wanna go home. It's gonna rain."

"You *want* to go home because it's *going* to rain," Missy said without looking up from her book.

Just because she was in fourth grade and had straight A's and was on the honor roll, Missy always corrected her words. Livie hated it, but her sister was going to be a teacher, after all, and needed to practice.

The wind came down in a gust before tapering off to a tickling breeze. "Missy, I'm *cold*."

Her sister rolled her eyes and breathed that loud sigh she had when Livie was *annoying* her. It meant Livie was being a pest.

"Ten minutes, okay? I want to finish this chapter."

"Fine." Livie pouted.

She picked up her shovel again and absently played in the sand, digging and watching as the grains fell slowly to the ground. She loved the park, but not when they were the only kids there.

The swings were her favorite. Livie always pumped her legs faster and harder to see if she could go all the way around the top, but she hadn't made it yet. Her daddy called her fearless. Missy said she was stupid. And her mother told her she'd break a leg one day and learn her lesson.

Tomorrow was Halloween. Livie was no scaredy-cat, but last week she'd watched a movie about ghosts and she didn't want to be outside after dark. The rule was they had to be in the house five minutes after the streetlights came on, but Livie wanted to go home *now*. The sun had already dipped below the Pattersons' two-story house with its pretty pink trim.

"*Missy,*" Livie begged.

Her sister ignored her and Livie threw down her shovel. She stood and walked over to the swings at the far side of the playground. She didn't feel like flying today, so she swung back and forth without effort, her arms pimpled with goosebumps as the wind gusted in bursts of anger. Red, orange, and brown leaves skittered across the ground as the wind drove them away.

Livie liked spring better, when everything was green and bright and sunny. When the fog didn't dampen every morning, sometimes not going away until lunchtime. But spring was a whole six months from now. Livie would be six next spring. She counted the months in her head. *May, June, July, August, September, October . . .* she was five and a half! Yesterday she'd turned five and a half!

She jumped off the swing and turned to run back to Missy to tell her what she had just figured out. She stopped.

Missy wasn't alone.

A man was talking to her. He was really tall,

although not as tall as Daddy, and not as old as Daddy either. He wore no coat. Didn't he know you could catch a death of a cold in this weather if you went outside without your jacket? *And* he'd colored on his arm with blue marker.

Livie started toward them, a tickle in her stomach that didn't feel quite right. Missy didn't seem scared, but then *she* hadn't watched the ghost movie last week. Livie bit her lip. She didn't want to be a cry-baby, but she wanted to go home. Right now. And if she had to cry to get her way, then she'd do it. Missy gave in when she cried.

"Missy?" she called.

The man turned and looked at her and his eyes did something funny, squinty-like. He grabbed Missy's arm. "Come on."

"No!" Missy shouted and tried to pull away.

Livie ran toward them. "Let my sister go! Let go!"

The man picked Missy up just as Livie reached them. She didn't know what she was going to do, but she knew strangers weren't always nice and this man with the blue bird on his arm was holding Missy over his shoulder.

Before Livie could grab Missy, the man hit her. Livie fell to the ground and couldn't catch her breath. Her mouth tasted funny, like when she'd lost her first tooth that summer. She tried to scream, but gagged on her spit.

She stumbled as she got up, tears blurring her vision. The man had Missy and he was running across the grass to the street. "Daddy!" Livie yelled through her sobs. "Help! Help!"

The bad man pulled open the door of a black truck and threw Missy in. When she tried to get out, he hit her with something that looked like a big stick, then ran to the driver's side and drove off.

Missy didn't try to get out again.

Livie cried as she ran all the way home.

"Daddy! Daddy!"

Her father yanked open the door, his face full of worry. "Olivia! What's wrong? Where's Melissa?"

"A m-man took her!"

Mommy screamed and Daddy grabbed Livie's arm and pulled her into the house. He pushed her at her mommy and started running out the door. "Call the police!" he shouted as Livie sank into her mommy's safe arms.

The brief hug ended.

It was the last hug she would ever receive from her mother.

CHAPTER
1

The day Olivia St. Martin's life turned upside down for the second time began like any other.

She inserted two slides onto the glass plate of the microscope and bent over the lens, adjusting the magnification until the minute carpet threads became clear. She recognized a match immediately, but went through all the points of commonality for her report and indicated them on the lab sheet. When she was done, she used the microscope's built-in camera to photograph the matched fibers, removed the evidence with latex-covered hands, and preserved it in a sealed case to prevent contamination.

She signed the report, then reviewed the file to make sure her team had finished processing all evidence in the Camero murder. Everything appeared in order, though DNA hadn't reported in yet. A foreign pubic hair had been retrieved from the victim and sent to the CODIS unit to be analyzed and run through the database. Contrary to what was implied on popular television, DNA matching was a slow, laborious process largely dependent on staff and resources.

Olivia loved her job and had been well rewarded:

last year, she'd been promoted to director of Trace Evidence and Materials Analysis at the FBI's Virginia-based laboratory.

The door opened and Olivia glanced up as Dr. Greg van Buren walked in. Her ex-husband's grim expression surprised her: Greg was generally either amused or thoughtful, rarely depressed.

She arched her eyebrow as she closed the file folder.

"Olivia." Greg cleared his throat. Beneath his wire-rimmed glasses, his clear blue eyes narrowed with concern. He shifted uneasily and glanced down. Something was wrong.

Her chest tightened. "What is it?"

"Let's go for a walk."

"Tell me."

"C'mon, Olivia."

Her legs weren't completely steady when she stood, but she kept her head up as she walked down the hall with Greg. They were on the top floor of the three-story building, but took the stairs rather than the elevator to the main level.

Outside, a wave of hot, humid air washed over Olivia. She scrunched her nose. The cotton lining of her skirt instantly stuck to her legs and she resisted the urge to adjust it. She'd never get used to these sticky East Coast summers. She'd thought once Labor Day had passed, the weather would cool; no such luck. She never thought she'd miss the San Francisco peninsula's gray mornings, but she'd trade humidity for fog any day.

She studied Greg's demeanor and posture—something was very wrong. Her stomach flipped. She was impatient for him to tell her, yet it might well be something she didn't want to know.

They walked past the stone plaque in front of the FBI laboratory, erected when the new facility opened in 2003.

BEHIND EVERY CASE IS A VICTIM—MAN, WOMAN, OR CHILD—AND THE PEOPLE WHO CARE FOR THEM. WE DEDICATE OUR EFFORTS AND THE NEW FBI LABORATORY BUILDING TO THOSE VICTIMS.

Olivia rarely allowed her emotions to surface, in public or private, but the sign never failed to move her, reminding her there was always more than one victim in every crime. That the dead left behind people who loved them. Family, friends, and often whole communities mourned, sometimes so deeply they resembled an empty shell, gutted. All the survivors had left was their hope that the guilty would be punished for their crimes.

"Liv, I don't know how to tell you this."

Greg stopped walking and they stood in the shade of the building. Two smokers loitered in the designated smoking area a few dozen feet away. A faint trail of stale cigarette smoke hung in the still air.

"I don't understand why they don't move the smoking area farther away," Olivia said, delaying the conversation.

Greg frowned. "Olivia, this is important."

His tone set Olivia's entire body on edge. She turned and stared at his aristocratic profile. His long face, chiseled nose, deep-set eyes. Greg van Buren—a distant relative of the former president—was attractive in a quiet, preppy way. He was familiar, soothing.

"All right, so tell me." She tried to disguise her tension under an air of disinterest.

Pain clouded in his eyes. And worry. "Hamilton Craig called me today."

"Why in the world would Hamilton call you?" She had seen the district attorney just three months before, when her sister's killer was up for parole, which had rightfully been denied.

Craig was growing old and had announced he'd be retiring at the end of his current term. Olivia now asked, "Is something wrong? Is he okay?"

"He's fine," Greg said. "It's about Hall."

Olivia closed her eyes. She couldn't think about Brian Harrison Hall without conflicting emotions. Pain. Sorrow. Victory. Emptiness. Satisfaction that he was in prison, where he belonged. Rage that he hadn't been put to death. Her sister was dead because of him; he should have met the same fate. But the California Supreme Court tossed out the death penalty shortly after his conviction, so every three to five years he went up for parole.

She hadn't missed even one of Hall's six parole hearings. She would do anything to keep him behind bars.

"What?" Outwardly, she was calm. Composed. Professional. Inside, her nerves vibrated at an uncomfortable pitch.

"His attorney petitioned for a DNA test. The police had preserved evidence including pubic hair samples. So there was something to compare Hall's DNA with. The court granted the request last month. The California state lab issued their report this morning." He paused, running a hand through his short-cropped hair. "I don't know how to say this except flat out. No match."

Olivia was certain she hadn't heard Greg accurately.

"I don't understand," she said slowly. "No match to what?"

"Hall's DNA does not match the pubic hair found on your sister's body."

"I don't believe you."

Her voice was reasonable. Her words were not, but she didn't care. There had to have been a mistake.

Evidence doesn't lie.

"Hall's being released tomorrow."

"No. No," she said, shaking her head. "It can't be. He killed Missy. He killed her. I saw him."

She spoke matter-of-factly. She *had* seen him. She remembered the black truck. The blue eagle tattoo. The tattoo still on his arm. His blond hair. The truck was his—the evidence had proved it.

She hadn't known anything about the investigation when it happened thirty-four years ago. But she'd read the reports multiple times since. Memorized them. Olivia knew every grisly detail of what Brian Harrison Hall had done to her sister. Fibers from the floor mats of his truck were found on Missy's body. Her blood was found on his front seat.

The murdering bastard.

"Hamilton faxed me the report. I read it carefully. I called the California state crime lab and talked to the technician who ran the comparison. There's no mistake, Liv."

"No. *NO!*"

Her shout startled both of them. She never shouted. She never raised her voice. Greg reached to touch her arm.

"Olivia, let me help—"

She jerked away. "I want to see the report."

Before Greg could dissuade her, she stormed off toward the side doors, slapping her ID card on the keypad to regain access to the building. She heard his footfall behind her as she yanked open the door to the stairwell and raced up to the third floor.

There had to be a mistake. Hall's new attorney had switched the evidence. It was corrupted. Not enough to match. The sample degenerated over time. There was a *reason* for this lie. There was always a reason. Hall was guilty. He killed Missy. He killed her, dammit!

With every step up, Olivia's fear and rage grew. Rage that justice had not been served. That Hall would be getting out on a technicality instead of rotting in prison. That he was playing the system, his miserable defense lawyer trying to make a name for himself as an advocate for murderers.

Then came fear. Deep, bone numbing fear jolted something deep inside Olivia, fear that Hall was innocent. That Missy's killer was still at large. That he was still killing girls. Destroying families. Breaking hearts.

And it was all her fault.

She faltered in her brisk stride and reached out for support, her hand shaking as it touched the wall.

Greg caught up with her in the corridor outside the DNA laboratory. "Olivia, stop."

She couldn't look at him, fearful that her eyes would expose her raw soul.

"I'm okay."

"No you're not."

"I just need to see the evidence." She spoke each word carefully, clearly, her jaw clenched.

"You're shaking."

"Show me the damn report!"

She took a deep breath and bit the inside of her cheek to control her emotions. With every ounce of willpower, she composed herself and turned a blank face to her ex-husband.

"I'm sorry," she said. "That was uncalled for. I shouldn't take out my frustration on you."

She would not break down in front of Greg. Olivia St. Martin would not break down in front of anyone.

Even herself.

He opened his mouth to say something and Olivia steeled herself to defend her position professionally. She *was* a professional after all, able to look objectively at evidence. To see the truth in the facts, and present those facts clearly, concisely, to her peers or the court.

She could do it now.

He closed his mouth and used his passkey to unlock the lab door.

"The report is on my desk."

CHAPTER
2

Detective Zack Travis pinched the bridge of his nose as if fighting back tears. But those who knew him stepped aside. The vivid pulse in his neck bespoke barely contained rage, anger simmering beneath the surface, a tangible force radiating from Zack's hard body.

Nothing was worse than the murder of a child.

The scene had been secured before his arrival. He looked everywhere but at the ground and the bright blue tarp with the small bump beneath.

The body had been dumped in a garbage-strewn, light industrial area north of Interstate 90, near Quest Field, where weathered cinder-block and steel buildings stood sentry, dark and forbidding at night. During the day their wear and disrepair was a sad reminder that this area of town wasn't going to recover anytime soon, city council platitudes, promises, and redevelopment funds notwithstanding. With clean, modern business parks popping up in recently developed neighborhoods, the dilapidated areas failed to attract new business. Half of the warehouse storefronts within Zack's sight had FOR LEASE signs.

The sparse security lighting in front of each door

turned the fog a sickly yellow. The illumination ended at five feet. The fog hung low tonight, this close to the water, the glow from the flashlights creating a dry-ice effect in the wide alley.

When Zack worked Vice, they had raided several of these warehouses over his three-year tenure. Desperate hookers foolishly strayed this far from the relatively safer streets north; Zack's first month as a homicide detective, he'd found two prostitutes dead of an overdose, walking distance from where the current victim lay.

Breathing deeply, he squatted, knowing there was no way to truly prepare himself for what he was about to see. He pulled back the tarp.

No child should die, especially in a squalid alley in a decaying section of town. But Zack immediately determined nine-year-old Jenny Benedict hadn't been killed here. There was little blood. And from the number of stab wounds, there would have been plenty.

He didn't look long. He'd face her again in the autopsy, but right now he needed to focus on finding the bastard who killed her.

"Coroner?" he asked his partner.

"On his way," Nelson Boyd said.

Zack sighed and rubbed the back of his neck. Boyd was a rookie, Zack's responsibility, and he didn't like it one bit. He'd never wanted to be a field training officer, but when Rucker up and retired, Zack had been stuck with Boyd.

The kid was as green as they came, right down to his sparkly blue eyes. Zack would be surprised if he shaved daily. But Boyd had spent five years in uniform in quiet suburbia, and now that he had his shield, he'd been transferred to the big city. The chief had assigned Boyd to him, no doubt as revenge because his ex-squeeze had hit on Zack at the Guns and Hoses football game. The chief *knew* how much Zack hated being an FTO.

"What next, sir?"

"Can the *sir,*" Zack mumbled. Boyd made him feel ancient, reminding him that his fortieth birthday was only months away. Not that he cared about the number, but his body was beginning to protest his vigorous morning workouts.

He pushed his frustrations aside and asked, "Where're the damn crime techs?"

"On their way," Boyd said, bouncing. Yes, *bouncing* on his heels. His fidgeting drove Zack crazy, and they'd only been partnered up for two weeks. How the hell was he going to last six months?

"Where's the guy who found her?"

"Officer Paul has him on ice inside the electronics company next door."

Zack raised an eyebrow. *On ice?*

"I want to talk to him. Stay here and keep everyone away until the crime techs arrive." He frowned. The fog and subpar lighting would make searching for evidence next to impossible, even if they brought in high-watt industrial lamps. They'd have to stay on scene until well after sunrise. But if this was a body dump like Zack suspected, there'd be little to find.

The witness, a young skinny guy with a long face, sat at a secretary's desk inside the nondescript building. Zack looked around. This could be any business in the lot, the same dirty chairs, stained industrial-grade carpeting, beat-up metal desks worse than Zack's back at the station. But the computers in the cubicles lining one wall looked state-of-the-art, and Zack noted a high-tech security system by the door.

"Travis," Officer Tim Paul acknowledged and crossed over to the door, out of the witness's earshot.

"Who do you have?"

"Reggie Richman, twenty, employee of Swanson and Clark Electronics. Said he was coming to run computer backups, does it twice a month after close of business. Checks out. I called his boss, verified his employment and his story. He's been with the company two years, goes to Seattle Central Community College part time."

Zack nodded, observing Reggie Richman, who looked down at his constantly moving hands. Drumming fingers, tapping pencils, flipping through papers without reading them. Nervous energy? Or guilt?

"What'd he say?"

"He almost rode his bike over her."

"A motorcycle?"

"No, the kind you pedal." Paul cracked a small smile, then grew serious again. "He lives in a walk-up a mile away, halfway between here and the college, doesn't have a driver's license though does have a Washington State ID. Says he went to class after work, grabbed a burger, and returned here, probably about 9:30. He didn't see her until she was only feet in front of him. He came in the building, called 911. The call came in at 9:42. Urbanski and I arrived on scene at 9:55. We called it in and secured the scene."

Zack glanced at his watch. Ten thirty-five. "Thanks. I'll take it from here, but I'd appreciate you covering the door."

"No problem."

Reggie glanced up as Zack approached. "Can I go?"

"Not yet." Zack sat in the metal-legged chair in front of the desk. The chair creaked, showing its age, and Zack hoped it held him. He wasn't overweight, but he was a big guy. He leaned forward more to balance in the flimsy chair than to intimidate the kid, but he was pleased with the secondary effect. He'd get the truth.

"Reggie?"

"Yes?" The kid broke a pencil in half and stared wide-eyed at the two pieces, then dropped them like they burned. He crossed his hands in front of him. "Sorry."

This kid didn't look like a killer, but Zack didn't have much faith in appearances.

"I'm Detective Zack Travis, Homicide. My officers tell me you found the body and called it in."

"Y-yes. I did."

"Could you go over what happened? When you got here, what you saw, when you called?"

"Um, sure. I told him." He motioned toward Officer Paul standing by the door a dozen feet away.

"I need to hear from you how you found the body."

"Oh. Okay." He took a deep breath and started playing with a box of paper clips. "I knew she was dead, so I didn't like, um, touch her. I wasn't supposed to, was I? I wasn't supposed to do mouth-to-mouth, was I?"

"You did fine. You say you knew she was dead."

"Yeah. Her eyes were open and they didn't look—you know, like they were alive."

"I know what you mean."

"I, um, I was riding my bike and—"

"Maybe it would be easier if you started from when you left work today. What's the deal? Why'd you come back tonight?"

"I left at four, like always. I have classes Monday, Wednesday, and Friday: Computer Engineering at five o'clock and Advanced Database Programming at 7:15. That gets over at 8:45, and I went to McDonald's after."

"What'd you eat?"

"Um, two Big Macs and a chocolate shake." He turned away.

This kid wasn't a killer. Zack felt it in his gut. He'd passed the remnants of a McDonald's meal on his way into the building. The kid must have puked at the sight of the body. Zack was glad he'd managed to get away from the crime scene before he lost it.

"Then where'd you go? Home?"

"Naw, I came here. It was getting foggier by the minute, and I wanted to finish the backup and get home before cars couldn't see me even with my light. Cars don't care much about bikes on the road. I've been hit twice."

Zack nodded. "I hear you." Most cars didn't respect motorcycles, either.

"So, I was riding down the alleyway and there she was, right in the middle. I would have hit her, but I swerved. I went back and looked and—well, that's when I knew she was dead. I came in here and called 911. And that officer came to the door and I let him in. I, um, kept it locked because I didn't know what was going on, you know?"

"You did the right thing, Reggie. You left here at four today. When do people normally leave?"

"It's Friday, people cut out early, but the boss usually stays until six. I can check if you want; the last person who leaves sets the alarm."

"It was on when you came in?"

"Yes. I can print out a report."

Zack knew he was getting into the area where he might need a warrant, but the kid had offered him the reports—Tim Paul was here to witness that, so he decided to let him.

"Great, get me the report."

The kid sighed, obviously relaxing, and his fingers whizzed over the keyboard. A couple of minutes later, the printer kicked into life and Reggie spun around, pulling a page as it came out.

He explained it to Zack. "This shows that employee 109—that's Marge, this is her desk—entered and turned off the alarm at 7:04 this morning. And here—see, Mr. Swanson set the alarm at 4:45, but he didn't leave."

"How can you tell?"

"He only turned on the outside doors. Full alarm is both internal and external sensors. He left at 6:10 and set full alarms. And this is me, employee 116, coming in at 9:40 tonight."

"What does the company do?" Zack looked around, couldn't see a business name.

"Refurbish printers. We buy them on the cheap from governments, schools, whatever, in big blocks, clean them up, replace worn or broken parts, then sell them to a wholesaler."

"And your job?"

"I'm the IT Department. I make sure everyone's computers are working, the network, run reports, things like that."

Everything Reggie said made sense. He was just the unlucky guy to come across a dead body.

"Did you see anyone? On foot or in a car? Did you see a vehicle, either moving or parked?"

Reggie shook his head. "This place is dead at night." He reddened. "Uh, I didn't mean anything by that."

"I know." Damn. The body couldn't have been here more than a couple of hours.

There was a lot of work to be done. It was Friday; few people would be working tomorrow. They'd have to track down the owners over the weekend, see what they could learn about schedules, anyone who was working after six tonight. It would be much better to interview people tomorrow, but there was no way they could track down the hundred or so employees who worked on this side of the industrial park over the weekend. Any leads one of them might have would be cold by Monday.

Swanson, Reggie's boss, would be the first, though. Then the buildings closest to where the body was dumped.

"Thanks for your time, Reggie. I'm going to ask that you hang out here a little while longer. The crime techs might have some questions for you once they inspect the scene."

"Yes, sir."

Why did everyone under thirty call him sir? "Thanks for your help."

The crime scene, about forty feet from the main door of the printer refurbishing business, now glowed with light, the fog casting a ghostly shimmer. The crime techs had arrived. Zack noted Doug Cohn, the head of the unit, had come out himself.

He approached Cohn as the tech directed his team of three to check the perimeter of the lights first. Fifty and almost completely bald, Cohn had a youthful face and calm disposition. "Thanks for taking it yourself," Zack told him.

Cohn shrugged it off. "Sleep's overrated." He paused. "I heard it's the missing kid."

"No positive ID yet, but yeah, it's her." Zack swallowed thickly. Jenny Benedict had been missing for three days, abducted late Tuesday afternoon while playing with friends in a neighborhood park.

Zack knew where he would be going when he left the scene. It was one stop he didn't want to make, but couldn't avoid.

"Witness?"

"A computer tech almost literally stumbled across the body while riding his bike."

"At night?"

"Running backup reports or something."

"What do you think?"

"Of the witness? He had nothing to do with it. But I had him stick around. He swears he didn't touch her, but I thought you should check him out."

"Will do as soon as I'm done with her." Cohn frowned as he pulled on gloves, knelt next to the tarp, and lifted it. "Sweet Jesus."

Under the lighting, the girl's skin looked far whiter than it should, the deep red stab wounds attesting to her death. Cohn's assistant took photographs, then Cohn inspected the body.

"She's been dead at least twelve hours, I'm guessing even longer. Maybe as long as twenty. We can probably get a more precise time frame from the autopsy. Appears that she bled to death, looks like one went directly into her heart chamber. Gil can give you an exact accounting of the wounds." Gil Sparks was the coroner.

Cohn lifted her skirt. She wore no panties. "External evidence of sexual assault."

He turned her head to the side. "What's this?" he said, almost to himself.

"What?" Against his will, Zack leaned closer.

"It appears that a section of her hair has been cut. A good inch, right up against the scalp, with scissors."

"He took her hair?" Zack's gut clenched. Sick bastard. And sick bastards didn't stop with one victim.

"Looks like it, unless her parents have something else to say. Maybe she cut it herself, or a friend did it . . . " Cohn's voice trailed off. He didn't believe what he was saying any more than Zack did.

"Shit," Zack said, rubbing a hand over his face. He was about to ask another question when Cohn mumbled, "What's this?"

"What?" Zack asked, thankful that Cohn had closed the girl's eyes. *Rest in peace.*

"See these marks?"

Cohn was pointing to the girl's forearm. At first, Zack couldn't see anything. Then a few small dots, like odd-shaped commas, became evident under the light. "I have no idea what made these marks," Cohn said. "I'll talk to Gil about it. There's at least a dozen small punctures, but they were definitely made postmortem. Perhaps from something used to transport her, but I'm only guessing."

At least it was something that could tie the killer to his victim.

"Anything else you can tell me before I go see her parents?"

"Only what you're thinking."

Serial killer. One victim, and already Zack feared the worst. But it was the manner of display, the stab wounds, and the missing hair that told him the killer would strike again. "I hope we're wrong."

"We're not."

Zack walked away from the scene, leaving the victim in Doug Cohn's sensitive and capable hands.

Nine-year-old Jenny Benedict had been missing for three days and her mother had feared her ex-husband had taken her. They'd found Paul Benedict yesterday, working in a steel mill in Pennsylvania, unaware that his daughter was even missing. He'd been avoiding his wife's calls because he was late on his child support.

Zack called for a counselor to meet him at the Benedict house. A kid was dead. He thought it couldn't get worse.

He was wrong.

Three weeks later another blonde girl went missing, and Zack knew for certain he had a serial killer on his hands.

CHAPTER
3

Freedom. At last. His idiot lawyer, Miles Bledsoe, actually did what he said he was going to do, and Brian was now a free man.

Brian Harrison Hall—shit, he *hated* his middle name, but that's what the dumb-asses in the press repeated in every article about him. And the judge at his sentencing.

Brian Harrison Hall, you've been found guilty by a jury of your peers and are sentenced to death in the electric chair, pursuant to . . . some stupid law.

He thought he'd never feel as good as he did three months after he was locked up. Because three months after he went in, the California court ruled the death penalty unconstitutional. Fucking *cruel and unusual punishment.* Damn straight. Especially since he was innocent.

Innocent, dammit!

But no one believed him. They believed that little bitch, that little girl who said she saw him.

And that fascist cop, the one who came to each of his parole hearings and went over how he "found" the evidence in his truck. Bull-fucking-shit. The cop couldn't have found anything in his truck unless he put it there himself. Brian hadn't killed that girl.

Brian had been at home when the girl was killed. He had nothing to do with it. And now the bitch who squealed and the cop who lied were being shown for the fucking *hypocrite liars* they were.

It felt so damn good to breathe free air.

Then why did his heart hammer so hard? Why did his hands tremble? He felt light-headed, and he didn't like it one bit. Something was wrong.

"Hey, Miles, I don't feel so good."

They were standing outside Folsom Prison. Miles Bledsoe, the latest in a long line of public defenders, had been yapping at him about something inane, which Brian ignored. He was good at that. He'd had to ignore the stupid fucks on his cell block yapping all the time, the sisters screwing each other in the dark. Blocking out the bullshit became second nature.

Miles frowned at him. "You look pale. But it's probably just relief at being out of prison after thirty-four years. I was saying the state rented you an apartment for six months. Enough time to get you back on track, time to find a job. The standard reimbursement for wrongful imprisonment is $100 a day, which I calculated to be just over $1.2 million. It'll take six to eight weeks to process the claim, then the Legislature has to approve it before they can disperse funds."

"Speak English, college boy." Brian shook his head, trying to clear the uneasy feeling that clung to him. Everything was too bright, almost like he was detached from his body and watching the exchange with his attorney. He wasn't sick. It was something . . . else.

"You'll get $1.2 million, but it might take some time," his attorney said.

"Holy shit." A million *dollars*? He'd be set for life.

"The only problem," Miles continued, "is you did lie to the police when you were arrested, and your truck—"

"Who cares? I didn't kill that girl."

"But the district attorney can still file charges if—"

"Look, Miles, just do your job and let me do mine. The D.A. won't file charges because I'm innocent. I didn't kill that girl; I didn't kill anyone. Where's my pad?"

Miles blinked, then handed Brian the notebook he held.

Brian threw it to the ground. "Shit, Miles. My pad. My *apartment*."

"Oh." He blinked again and Brian wanted to bitch-slap him. He didn't, of course. Miles was his ticket to a million bucks.

A million bucks would set him up for life and help him find that bitch who put him here.

And the cop.

And that old fucking prosecutor who stared at him with such contempt in the courtroom. *This man raped and killed a child.* Bull-fucking-shit. He didn't touch children like that. Only disgusting, sick perverts got their kicks from kids.

Payback. A million dollars would go a long way toward payback.

But somehow, it didn't seem enough for thirty-four years of his life.

* * *

DNA Evidence Frees Convicted Murderer
Brian Harrison Hall once faced death penalty; now exonerated.

Incredible. Harry was out of prison.

He'd read the article twice to make sure he had

the facts straight. Truth be told, he was surprised Harry had ever been convicted in the first place. The evidence was circumstantial at best. But Harry—being the stupid dumb-shit he was—had lied to the police.

Served the blowhard right. In his fifty-five years, he'd rarely met a blowhard, lazy-ass jerk like Brian "Harry" Hall.

"Hey, dude, come to the Bay Area with me and we'll score." By "score," Harry had meant find a couple of women to take two Vietnam vets under their wing. Console them and give them blow jobs whenever they wanted.

Harry had no comprehension of *women.* Just like he had no understanding of discipline. Cleanliness. Order.

But Harry did have a job lined up and promised to get him in. So he had joined him in California.

Neatly, he folded the newspaper along the creases and placed it at the corner of the small, glass-top table in the cottage he'd been renting on Vashon Island for the past year. He didn't need to look at the clock to know it was time to leave. The sun crested over the Sound, a lush, vivid sight of which he never tired.

He could retire here.

But he wouldn't. Settling would be foolish; moving was the only way to truly cover his tracks.

He'd be moving again soon.

For now, he had a job to do.

The cottage didn't have a dishwasher, but he didn't mind. He took care to wash his coffee mug, plate, utensils, and the single pan in which he'd prepared his bacon and eggs. He dried them completely and put them where they belonged. He folded the damp towel and hung it precisely on the rack he'd installed on the wall next to the sink. His chair was pushed in *just so*; the crumbs on his place mat carefully shaken into the garbage; then the garbage—only a quarter full—taken out to the trash can by the side of the house.

The thought of letting garbage rot in his house all day made him ill.

Another quick glance at the newspaper got him thinking again about Harry as he locked up the cottage and walked to his job at the beachside restaurant.

Stealing Harry's truck that long-ago night had been a spontaneous act. He hadn't known exactly what he was doing, just a vague idea. Then he saw *her* and knew. She'd been sent to him, to replace the Angel he'd lost. He had quickly formed a plan, and it had been almost perfect. He frowned, thinking of the spunky little brat who had tried to stop him. Then he returned the truck before Harry had even noticed its absence.

What he hadn't expected was the police finding the truck, but that discovery ended up being a blessing.

He'd learned many important lessons after Harry was convicted of murder.

Be careful. Don't leave any evidence of yourself anywhere.

Keep moving. Be patient. Don't rush. Let the sweet anticipation build, but control it. Don't let the need control you. Be smarter than the cops. Know when to move on.

It was all a matter of discipline. Something he'd been taught well.

One niggling mistake soured the otherwise pleasant day. Harry had been released because of DNA evidence, which meant the authorities had *his* DNA.

He would have to be doubly careful from now on.

CHAPTER
4

Olivia grabbed the paper as it slid off the laser printer, her eyes scanning the information, her heart beating fast as her theory solidified.

Patterns.

Missy's killer had left Redwood City after her murder, probably because Brian Hall had been arrested and was going to take the fall for Missy's death. He lay low for a couple years before resurfacing in New York, where he raped and killed four blonde girls in the Albany suburbs before disappearing.

Then two in Lawrence, Kansas. A known sex offender was arrested, tried, and convicted and was now sitting on death row for those murders. But Olivia was ninety-nine percent sure that man was innocent of those particular crimes.

Four more girls killed in Atlanta.

Four in Nashville.

The list went on. Years separated his crimes, but Olivia had uncovered twenty-nine murders in thirty-four years that fit the same pattern.

Blonde girls between the ages of nine and twelve.

Sexually assaulted. Underpants taken.

Dumped facedown in a relatively public location,

usually a rest stop off a sparsely traveled road, or an industrial park at night.

The reports she had access to were sparse. She wished she could view the autopsy reports and the lab notes, but most were not computerized. The older the crimes, the less information she had. But the key commonality, the factor that convinced Olivia she had found the link, was the missing lock of hair. The killer had been taking "souvenirs" from his victims, a piece of his victims he could see or touch to relive his crimes.

"What are you doing?"

Olivia jumped, her hand to her chest. "Greg! You startled me."

"You were deep in thought. So deep you missed the senior staff meeting."

She glanced at the clock. Noon already? How did the time escape her? "I'm sorry, I was working on . . ." She bit her cheek. She couldn't think of a convincing lie, especially on the fly.

Greg frowned and pulled the document from her hand. His scowl deepened as he opened the file folder on her desk and realized what she'd spent the last two weeks doing.

"I can explain," she began, though she had no idea what to say.

"You don't need to explain to me, Olivia. I understand you need to find out who killed your sister. But why didn't you talk to me first?"

"I don't know. It's kind of personal." More than personal; guilt sat like a lead weight on her shoulders. Her testimony against Brian Hall had enabled an evil predator to go free.

"Personal?" He sat down across from her and ran

his hands through his hair. "We were married for three years, we've been friends for ten more, and you couldn't share this with me?"

Hurting Greg was the last thing she wanted to do. "At first, I just looked at Missy's case. At the evidence, the DNA reports, the interviews. I thought, well, I don't know what I was thinking, except that maybe I'd see something that could put Brian Hall back in prison." She laughed, a hollow, sad sound.

She continued. "Then I thought, what if? What if he had a partner? There was never any indication that he worked with anyone, but he's not all that bright—if he did have an accomplice, Hall probably would have turned on him to avoid the death penalty. But what if Hall did have a partner who he was protecting for some reason? We know he didn't rape Missy, but that doesn't mean he wasn't somehow involved. But then I thought, what if Hall is really innocent?"

"So you started researching similar crimes," Greg said, holding up the paper he'd taken from her hands.

"Yes. And, well, things started falling into place. I flounder when I don't have hard science to back me up, but now—I really think I'm on to something. Will you take a look and tell me if we have enough to go to Rick?"

Rick Stockton was their boss, director of FBI Laboratory Services. He was also a friend, and Olivia wasn't afraid to capitalize on that friendship if it meant finding Missy's killer.

Greg took the folder and Olivia sighed in relief. She found herself wringing her hands as she tried to avoid staring at him while he read her compiled reports.

"I don't understand—in Kansas and Kentucky someone was convicted of the murders. In Kansas, the guy was a known sex offender. I don't see where they fit into your pattern."

"The hair," she said. "Look at the autopsy reports."

"I saw that, but—"

"Isolated, it doesn't mean anything," Olivia interrupted, anticipating Greg's objections, "but coupled with all the other similarities, my theory holds together. This guy has killed more than two dozen girls. He can wait years between attacks, but then kills two, three, four girls in a short period of time before leaving the area. Why? I don't know. Maybe he's satisfied for a time. He shows excellent self-control and discipline. Maybe the police get too close for his comfort. Or in some cases they arrest another man and our guy leaves quietly. Like Hall."

"I see your point." Greg stared at the ceiling as if reading the tiles, but his expression was familiar. Olivia grew excited—he was seriously considering her theory. Looking at it from every angle. She held her breath. Having Greg on her side would help her with Rick—not only were Greg and Rick friends, but Greg was also assistant director of CODIS, one of the largest departments in the FBI laboratory, and well respected in the building.

He finally looked at her. "What can Rick do?"

She handed him a report. "Two girls in Seattle who fit the profile are dead, one discovered just this morning. We need to get the Seattle bureau involved. Get the local cops on our page. Profile this guy—he's disciplined, methodical, and patient. But what else? His job? His family life? If we can trace his steps from Redwood City thirty-four years ago to now, we can learn his identity. Stop him before another girl dies."

"It's circumstantial, Olivia," Greg began.

"But—"

He put his hand up. "But I'll go with you to talk to Rick. I agree, it's worth pursuing."

"Olivia, Greg, come in."

Rick Stockton glanced at his designer watch, then opened his door wide and motioned for them to enter. "I have a lunch meeting in twenty minutes, but I can be late."

"Thank you." Olivia glanced at Greg, who nodded. It helped having him on her side, even if he wasn't completely convinced.

Rick closed the door behind them, then walked to his desk, sitting on the corner rather than behind it. He smiled wide, a warm smile that brightened his eyes. Rick Stockton was the talk of most of the women in the building: good-looking, sexy, and smart. Olivia didn't pay attention to the talk—she had more important things to do than ogle men—but she had to admit that her female colleagues were right about his sex appeal.

"Sit," he told them and she did, clutching her file like a lifeline. Greg stood behind her, his hand resting on the back of her chair. "What can I do for you?"

She bit the inside of her cheek. She and Greg had talked out how to approach Rick, but all her best-laid plans disappeared and she said, "I believe my sister's killer is in Seattle right now. There have been two like-crimes over the last three weeks."

Rick's left eyebrow rose as he glanced at Greg, but that was his only reaction. "How did you come to this conclusion?"

"I followed the evidence. What little there is," she admitted. "When Brian Harrison Hall was released two weeks ago, I ran a search—on my own time— for similar crimes throughout the country. I found a total of twenty-nine murders in ten states, including Missy's. I believe she may have been his first."

Rick frowned. "Ten states? And no one saw a pattern?"

"He is surprisingly patient between attacks, up to six years in one case. He goes into a community, generally a suburb of a large city, and kills up to four blonde girls before disappearing. The only time he kills fewer than four girls is when someone is arrested for the crime." She paused, handed him her folder. "It's all here."

Rick took the folder and flipped through it. "You were thorough. But what about common evidence? DNA? Witness testimony?"

"Two cases had a witness mention a tattoo on the abductor. Nashville and most recently Seattle. There has been no DNA logged in any of the cases into CODIS, except the new results from the California lab on Missy's case. But I was hoping we could offer assistance to help in the older, cold cases."

"You want me to take over cold-case files in local jurisdictions?"

Greg interjected. "If a DNA sample was preserved, or any other hard evidence, perhaps we can connect them and prove that the same man was responsible for all these crimes."

"To what end?"

Olivia blinked. "To capture him, of course."

Rick flipped through the file in silence. "You have three cases here where someone was convicted. They got the killer."

"I believe they were wrongfully convicted. The release of Hall proves it in that case."

"You want me to call the district attorney in those states and tell them they put an innocent man in jail? One of these guys is on death row." Rick shook his head. "I can see the headlines now. We have a bad enough reputation with local police that we don't need to criticize the way their criminal justice system works."

"I never thought of you as one to back down from a challenge." Olivia bit her lip. She couldn't believe she'd said that. "I—I didn't mean . . . I'm sorry."

Rick's eyes flashed first with anger, then compassion. "Olivia, I know Hall's release has been difficult for you."

"This has nothing to do with Hall."

"Doesn't it?" He held up the file. "This must have taken you a hundred hours to compile. You've found a couple of interesting threads, but it's circumstantial and these cases are old. We have a backlog of work here, and I'm sure the local authorities won't want to dig up cold cases. We have no jurisdiction, no authority to go in and take charge. There's nothing we can do at this point."

"Yes, we can!" she pleaded. "You can contact the Seattle bureau chief and have him take over the case. Or work with the local detectives." She hoped she didn't sound as desperate as she felt.

"In Seattle?"

She nodded. Rick was interested, she could tell.

She leaned forward in her seat. "Two girls have been murdered there. Jennifer Benedict three weeks ago, and Michelle Davidson's body was found this morning. It was the Benedict child that told me it's the same killer. A witness identified a tattoo on her abductor's arm.

"That's two girls," she continued. "If he follows his pattern, he'll kill two more before he moves on. This is our chance to catch him."

"Olivia." Rick stood, walked behind his desk, and looked out the window. "I'd like to help you put your sister's murder behind you, but this isn't the way. I can't tell Seattle to take over a local investigation. We are spread so thin now we can barely cover our urgent cases."

"But it's the same guy!"

Rick turned to her, a quizzical look on his face. "I can see you're passionate about this. But there is no hard evidence in this file. While the information on the surface connects the crimes, and could prove helpful when the police find a suspect, nothing leads to an individual. It's less than circumstantial. You have my permission to monitor what's going on in Seattle. If they find a suspect, I'll contact the local bureau and give them what we have. But right now we have neither the time nor the money to pursue cold cases."

"But if we use our resources to test the evidence, take apart the carpet fibers—look here." She stood and flipped the folder open to the middle, her hands shaking. "Carpet fibers from a different truck were found on virtually every victim. I think he steals the trucks, or maybe he works in a place with access to different vehicles. I didn't have time to run auto theft

reports, and because they're not in a federal database I don't have immediate access, but I can write
up a memo for local authorities to compare theft
reports to the vehicles the killer used, and then we
can—"

"Stop."

Olivia blinked. Rick's voice was quiet, but commanding.

He walked over to her and took her hand. She was
still shaking. She resisted the urge to pull away.
"Please, Rick," she said. "I know there's something
here if we just look deeper."

"There's nothing we can do until the local authorities ask us to get involved."

"But—"

He squeezed her hand. "Your research is a good
start, but it doesn't give us anything to find this guy.
I'm sorry, but we just don't have the resources for an
investigation of this magnitude without being
asked." He paused. "I need you here, on my team,
working for victims who are just as important as
those two poor girls in Seattle. You know I care
about them. In a perfect world we would have the
money and staff to pursue every investigation, cold
or not. But we don't have the time, resources, or personnel to tackle this. Leave it to Seattle. If they need
us, if they want us, they'll ask."

She looked down, afraid to meet Rick's eyes. He'd
said no. "I understand." She did, professionally. But
her heart told her to do something, anything, to find
this guy.

"Thank you for hearing us out," Greg said. "I
appreciate it."

"I'll keep my ears open. If I hear anything from

Seattle, I'll bend over backward to help them," Rick said. "But until then—" He threw up his hands.

"I understand," she repeated and stood. "Thank you."

"Olivia, do you want to take a little time off? A week, go on vacation. You haven't had a vacation in years."

"I just came back from Montana."

"You stopped at your friend's wedding on your way to Hall's parole hearing months ago. I don't consider that a vacation."

"I can't. I need to work." Working helped focus her on seeking justice by doing what she could for crime victims. Or it used to, anyway. Now, she didn't know. She couldn't stop thinking about the two girls in Seattle. She'd followed each case in the press. Seen their pictures. Olivia had looked into their eyes.

"Thanks again, Rick," Greg said as they walked out.

It was the middle of the lunch hour and the building was quiet. Olivia closed her office door and collapsed into her chair, burying her face in her arms.

How could she live with herself? Missy's killer had walked free for thirty-four years because Olivia had helped convict the wrong man. Now, she'd found evidence linking twenty-nine murders—twenty-nine!—and she could do nothing about it.

Missy's killer was in Seattle. She was as certain of that as she was of the sun rising tomorrow. And he would kill again.

What could she do to stop him? She wasn't a field agent, at least not anymore. She was a scientist. She needed more information. She needed to talk to the

Seattle detective in charge and find out if there was a DNA sample. Expedite the analysis. Figure out how and when the killer steals the trucks so that they could focus on auto thefts and perhaps catch him that way.

She couldn't do anything more from her desk three thousand miles away from the crime scene.

"Olivia, are you going to be okay?"

Greg stood in the doorway. She was definitely not okay, but she couldn't tell him that.

"I'll be fine."

Vacation.

An idea crept into her brain. It wasn't ideal, but it was the only thing she could think of that might work.

But she needed Greg's help. "Greg, I want to go to Seattle."

"*What?*"

She put up her hand, palm out. "Hear me out, please?"

He sat in the chair across from her desk and crossed his arms in silence, his face unreadable.

"Okay." She took a deep breath. "You agree that the information I pulled together is solid, right?"

He shrugged. "It's promising."

"Greg, please."

"It's good circumstantial evidence, but without opening up those cases we can't get the information we need."

"Right. I understand that. And without that information, we can't open the cases."

"Catch-22."

"But if I go to Seattle, with my experience and my access and my reports, I can help focus the investigation. I know what they're doing—all the right things to track a standard killer—but by the time they see the connection, he's going to be gone. They need to see the big picture. I can give them that edge."

"Rick said to stay out of it."

"I know, but—"

"Olivia." He took off his glasses and rubbed his eyes.

"Unofficially. I'll take a week's vacation. Go to Seattle and offer my help—unofficially," she repeated, "and we'll go from there."

"They'll never go for it. Most local cops would rather drink acid than call in the Feds. They'll laugh you right out of the police station."

"Don't underestimate my ability to persuade them."

Greg frowned and readjusted his glasses. "No, when you set your mind on something, you usually win."

"This isn't a game."

"I know."

"Well?"

He sighed, and she knew she'd won him over, at least a bit. "What do you want me to do?"

"Be my boss."

"Your boss?"

"Call ahead to Seattle and tell them I'm coming."

"I don't understand—oh, no." He stood and started pacing. "No, I won't let you put your job on the line chasing a theory. You're not an agent any-more. You gave it up nine years ago to work here. I'm not an agent, either. I can't just assign you to a case. No."

"This is important, Greg. I may not be an agent, but I know how to do the job and more important, I know evidence. I know this case better than anyone else."

She came from behind her desk, rested her hand on Greg's arm, imploring him with her eyes. "Please, Greg. I'll be careful. But I have to do anything I can to stop this killer. Please."

Greg stared at her hand. She'd surprised herself: she didn't like touching people. It had been a sore point in their marriage. She'd often jumped when Greg reached for her.

She loved him, in many ways. He was smart, very smart. Attractive, with light brown hair peppered with gray and intelligent blue eyes. Physically fit, even though he was nearly ten years her senior. They shared a love of science, a faith in facts. They were workaholics, both relishing problem solving and long days in the office. Their mutual love for science had kept their marriage intact for a time.

But Greg wanted more from her than she could give.

Why had she even married him in the first place? She often wondered. He was safe. He never pried, never questioned her, never challenged her quirky ways.

But she hated giving up her private space. Didn't like sharing a house with someone. Sex was fine, but she couldn't give herself over completely to him. Not just her body, but her mind. Her dreams.

Her nightmares.

When he'd said he wanted children, she wanted out. How could she bring another human being into such a violent world? How could she ever hope to protect her child from evil?

She would never take the risk. Never give birth to a beautiful child who could all too easily die a painful, brutal death.

She dropped her hand and turned away. She'd thought she convinced Greg to help, but maybe she really was on her own.

"All right," he whispered. "Exactly what do you want me to do?"

Her heart rate raced. He *would* help her. "Call the Seattle chief of police and tell them you have someone familiar with the case willing to come out unofficially with information that might help them catch a killer," she said quickly before he could change his mind. "They might hem and haw, but they'll take the help—they have PR problems, too. If it ever got out that the FBI offered assistance and they didn't take it, they'd get blamed for the next murder."

Greg didn't hide the surprise on his face. "That's quite—Machiavellian," he said.

"I'm willing to do whatever it takes to stop this predator."

Greg took off his glasses and rubbed his eyes. Sighing, he put his frames back on and said, "I'll do it. But don't make me regret it."

CHAPTER
5

Zack Travis slammed the phone receiver down on his desk so hard the mouthpiece broke. He stared at the chunk of plastic and blinked. Why did he let Vince Kirby get to him?

He knew why, but didn't like to think about it.

He looked up and saw a couple of the guys in the bullpen staring at him.

"Kirby," he said, and several heads bobbed in understanding. He breathed a quiet sigh of relief that he didn't have to explain further. Yeah, they all hated the reporter who portrayed their department as incompetent and overpaid (now, there was a real joke). But Zack's reasons were more personal than the newspaper's animosity toward the Seattle P.D.

Damn Kirby. Just talking to him brought back conflicting memories. Anger and deep sadness. Because every time he talked to Kirby, he thought of his dead sister. Having him reporting this case was going to poke at old wounds, but Zack was determined not to let Kirby get under his skin any more than he already had.

"What's up?" Boyd asked, jerking Zack from his thoughts.

Zack picked the broken plastic off his crowded blotter and tossed it into the trash. "Kirby's running with the damn serial killer angle."

"Oh." Boyd frowned and looked down at the pen he twirled between his fingers.

"What?"

"Maybe he's right," Boyd said.

"Hell, I *know* he's right, but the last thing we need is every friggin' mother picketing the station, or a copycat pervert snatching little girls off the street. One twisted killer is enough."

Two girls, abducted, raped, and stabbed to death. One was nine, the other eleven. Both had blonde hair. Both were playing with friends and wandered only a short distance away. He wished he could picture them alive, playing, laughing. Instead, he could only picture them under the coroner's knife.

The first, Jenny Benedict, had been in a park with neighborhood friends. She went to get water from the fountain and two girls saw her willingly walk off with "some guy."

When Zack learned the father was allowed only supervised visitation with his daughter because of a bitter and prolonged custody battle, he wanted the man to be guilty. He tried everything to get him to confess. But in the end, Paul Benedict wasn't a murderer. He was a father beyond grief, as destroyed by the news of his daughter's murder as any innocent man would be. More so, perhaps.

I should have been there. Protecting her. Benedict's words haunted Zack. Too close to the way Zack felt about his sister Amy.

I should have been there.

But what could he have done? Amy hadn't been a

little kid, and she sure as hell hadn't wanted anything to do with her brother, the cop.

The second girl, Michelle Davidson, had been riding her bike when she raced ahead of her friends, trying to beat them home. Her bike was found in the yard of her next-door neighbor. Michelle was found dead three days later.

That was early yesterday morning, thirty-six hours ago. Now the press was all over him. They didn't care that the parents were grieving or that he'd slept no more than four hours a night since the first victim was murdered three weeks ago, or that he spent two hours yesterday afternoon watching the autopsy of someone far too young to die.

"Did you run the killer's M.O. through the computer?" Zack asked Boyd. The single best thing about the young rookie was his skill with all things electronic, in particular, computers. It would have taken Zack endless hours to plug in the information with his hunt-and-peck-and-erase system, and then he'd probably have to redo it because of mistakes. But Boyd was of the next generation. He was a whiz with the damn thing and took over that end of their work.

Boyd nodded. "I printed out the report. There are several unsolved cases. Seven years ago in Austin, Texas, four blonde girls were abducted in a six-month period. No suspects, no witnesses. The bodies were displayed in the same manner."

"Fully clothed, underwear missing, hair cut," Zack mumbled.

"Ten years ago in Nashville four girls were killed who matched the M.O. An eyewitness gave a description, but it didn't lead anywhere."

"Do you have it?"

"Nashville is digging it up and said they'd fax it by the end of the day. But there wasn't enough information for a composite."

"At least it's something." Like hell it was. Zack glanced at his watch. It was already five o'clock here; there's no way Nashville would be getting them anything tonight. "What about the tattoo?"

Jenny Benedict's abductor had some sort of tattoo on his upper left arm. The two girls who watched her leave couldn't tell what it was, but a tattoo was better than nothing.

"The Nashville witness also mentioned a tattoo, but no description of it was in the file. I asked them to check on it."

"Two cases?"

"You said go back ten years. That's what I found."

Zack's instincts screamed that this guy had left a lot more than eight dead girls in his wake before hitting Seattle. He was too damn slick; he had to have had practice. And since Zack suspected that he'd been at this for a long time, the killer might have left something more of himself at the beginning of his crime spree.

Serial killers worked hard to perfect their murders. They preyed on humans for their own sick pleasure. Though they often looked normal, acted normal—even charming, like Ted Bundy, or attractive, like Paul Bernardo—beneath the surface they felt no remorse, no empathy for their fellow human beings. They were cunning, and constantly striving to commit the perfect crime.

Right now, Zack didn't have much to work with. The trace evidence they'd collected at the two crime scenes was still being analyzed. Their best bet at this point was carpet fibers collected from the victim's clothing. Unfortunately, the samples were from two different vehicles, which didn't make sense to Zack. One was a late-model Ford Expedition, the other a late-model Dodge Ram. Two very popular trucks that could belong to one of thousands of men in Seattle alone. This morning they'd run registration reports for both types of vehicles. Now, they were manually comparing the lists to see if any address had both truck types registered. Zack didn't expect the results until tomorrow. He'd been frustrated that with all the technology they had, and the ability to run instantaneous registration reports for the two vehicles, running a comparative match was impossible because the "program didn't work that way," he was told. What was the point of technology if it couldn't do what he needed?

This morning, the coroner had sent a DNA sample to the state lab. Even though Doug Cohn had asked the state to rush the analysis, it could still take weeks, maybe months. Once complete, he'd enter the information into the national DNA registry, CODIS, and see if there were any hits. Unfortunately, with tight budgets across the country, law enforcement primarily entered DNA information only in active cases. Ten years ago it wasn't a common practice, and twenty years ago—forget it. All the cold cases had to be entered manually, and unless there was funding for it, the work was done haphazardly if at all.

But DNA was only good if there was a suspect to go with it. Zack hoped that whatever Doug Cohn preserved from Michelle Davidson's body would match a known offender in the registry, though he didn't expect miracles.

Then there were the odd marks on the victims' forearms. Both Jenny and Michelle had twelve small, almost uniform, punctures made with some sort of extremely narrow, sharp object. It could be a fine-tipped knife, like a scalpel. The marks weren't made with the same knife that killed them, but the coroner said with certainty that they were intentional.

"Do you think—?" Boyd began before he was interrupted by the bellow of Chief Princeton.

Princeton wasn't really his name but he strutted around like God's gift to women, complete with a master's degree from some Ivy League school. Zack had been tired and drinking at the blue bar down the street with a bunch of the guys late one night. Earlier in the day, the chief had been playing politics with the mayor and they'd been overheard talking about their respective alma maters. Zack didn't know who had come up with the nickname "Princeton" for Chief Lance Pierson, but it had stuck.

During the two years Chief Princeton had been in charge, Zack learned to respect him. The chief was good at schmoozing with the politicos, something that needed to be done and that Zack detested, and Princeton backed up the boys in blue 110 percent. That went a long way in Zack's book, even though the chief often acted like his extra year in college and some brainy Latin award made him smarter than his men. They'd developed a good working relationship, and when the chief had learned about his nickname, he laughed it off.

"Detective Travis. My office," Pierson ordered.

Boyd jumped at the chief's call. "Yes, sir," he said.

"Down, Boyd," Pierson said. "Just your FTO."

Zack told Boyd, "Run over to the lab and see if they have any word on the trucks." Zack would have preferred to do it himself.

He crossed the bullpen. "What's up?"

"There's someone you need to meet," Pierson said.

"You're not setting me up for another glad-handing with the mayor." His chief constantly tried to get Zack to play politics.

"It's about your homicide case."

Though Zack had four active homicide cases on his docket, only one commanded his attention now.

"What?" Zack didn't want to be blindsided.

"Someone who might be able to help."

Pierson wouldn't say anything else, and Zack followed him to his office, curious but apprehensive.

Through the glass window Zack saw a slender golden-haired beauty sitting in the chair across from Pierson's desk, her profile classic and elegant, with perfectly carved features and luscious red lips. He blinked when he realized she was wearing only lip gloss, not lipstick—or if it was lipstick, it was the most natural-looking color he'd ever seen. He'd seen a lot of colors. Hell, he'd kissed a lot of lips.

As the men approached the door, she turned fully to face them, as if she didn't like having her back to anyone. *Cop.* Zack would know, he never sat with his back to the door, either.

But this little number dressed too well to be a cop, complete with an expensive-looking pale gray suit and blue silk blouse. And were those pearls around her neck? She looked nothing like the hot, flashy bimbos Chief Princeton liked to date. Far too classy. And she looked smart.

Pierson walked in, smiling solemnly at the woman. Zack leaned against the doorjamb, not stepping inside until he knew what was up.

"Agent St. Martin, I'd like you to meet the detective in charge of the case you're interested in. Detective Zack Travis is, frankly, our best cop here. He'll certainly be able to help you."

Zack vaguely heard the compliment. He was irate after hearing the first word. *Agent.*

"What's this?" he asked through clenched teeth. "You brought in the Feds without talking to me?"

He didn't have anything personal against the FBI. But every case Zack worked in which the Feds got involved, they caused more problems than their presence was worth. Not to mention they became all proprietary with evidence, kept local cops out of the loop, and generally acted like they were superior.

"Detective," Pierson said in a tone that made Zack take note. They stared at each other and Zack knew that his chief hadn't made the move. It made him feel marginally better, but with the Feds hanging around his precinct, something was up.

Pierson continued. "Agent St. Martin is here because of a similarity in your case with one she investigated, and believes her information may help us find the killer. I spoke with her boss yesterday and he assured me that they're not sending anyone officially. I agreed, after hearing what information they had, that he could send someone unofficially."

"Yesterday?" Zack repeated. Why hadn't the chief given him a heads-up?

"I don't have to remind you of the seriousness of

this matter," Pierson continued, ignoring or oblivious to Zack's implied question. "I agreed to the FBI's offer, but you'll retain total control over the investigation. Agent St. Martin is here simply to help. Think of her as—" he paused, now obviously uncomfortable "—your partner."

That didn't sit well with Zack, but he wanted any and all information that could help him find the bastard who murdered two little girls. Still, could he trust this Fed to be on the level?

"You know how they operate, Chief. All wine and roses up front, false promises to share information, then *wham*! They pull a rabbit out of the hat at the last minute, and we find out they've been keeping their cards close to the vest. We do the work, take out the bad guys, and they take the credit because they were less than forthcoming." It had happened twice in Zack's career, once with near fatal results. He wasn't going to let it happen again.

"I wouldn't think it would matter who got the credit as long as justice is served," Agent St. Martin said, her voice as smooth as twenty-year-old Scotch.

Zack glanced at her, cool and collected, making him feel like a hothead. When he was a kid, he'd had a harder time controlling his temper, especially when someone was being unfairly picked on.

"Zack," his grandmother would say, "your passion for those who can't defend themselves is admirable, and will take you far if you don't become a bully in the process."

He'd worked hard at it, mostly had his temper under control, but tonight he remembered the bad taste the Feds left in his mouth the last time they'd worked together.

He was about to explain his comments when the woman said, "What's mine is yours, Detective."

She arched her eyebrows and stared him down, her hands clasped in her lap, her hazel eyes firmly locked on to his. Almost daring him, challenging him . . .

He looked away, surprised that the little woman had such courage to attempt staring *him* down. Yet she had. He'd turned away first. He felt an unwanted jolt of admiration. "Fine," he said. "But," he continued, looking at Pierson, then at Agent St. Martin, "if I find out that you're playing games, withholding evidence, or generally jerking the department around, all deals are off."

"I don't play games, Detective," she said.

Olivia knew she was on thin ice. If Detective Travis really pushed, he might learn the truth. The threat of exposure terrified her, but also gave her the courage to stand firm, and she mentally braced herself for a confrontation.

Travis stared at her, his dark eyes taking in her entire appearance with an almost crude appraisal. She resisted the urge to straighten her spine. He reminded her of a football player, a man who worked out and liked it. She felt even smaller than her diminutive not-quite-five-foot-three. Being seated certainly didn't help.

But Olivia would not be intimidated.

"As long as we understand each other, Agent St. Martin," he said. "Ready to share?" He made a sweeping gesture with his arm toward the door.

Olivia released a pent-up breath. Slowly, so neither Chief Pierson nor Detective Travis could see her relief.

"Absolutely," she said as she stood, holding her

briefcase. She nodded to the chief and followed the detective from the office.

"I have one of the conference rooms set up for this case," Travis said. "Let's go there."

"I'm not here to cause problems," Olivia said, feeling a strong need for him to accept her.

"I'm sure you're not." Sarcastic.

"You don't like the FBI?"

"My dealings with them in the past have never been what you'd call positive."

She frowned. She knew some stories of locals and the FBI not getting along, but she'd always been two or three steps removed from the investigation. Everyone she worked with seemed to be friendly. True, her experience was often thousands of miles away in a crime lab, but she thought she would have picked up on hostilities.

Detective Travis led her through a maze of desks. A dozen men and women watched them pass. Their watchful eyes made her increasingly nervous as she crossed the brightly lit space. She kept her face impassive, determined not to let any of these people get to her. She was already playing a dangerous game; jeopardizing her career was only the beginning. But she would see it through. She had to.

She would find Missy's killer and he would pay. Justice would be served. Or she would die trying.

The thought didn't scare her—and *that* worried her. She *should* be scared. She should be terrified of the killer who—by her count—had raped and murdered no less than twenty-nine girls in thirty-four years. Thirty, counting the death of Michelle Davidson.

But she'd come this far. There was no backing out now.

Zack stopped abruptly and turned into a conference room, closing the door behind them. "Sit. We have a lot of work to do."

Olivia put her briefcase down and slid into a chair. "I said I would share everything I have. I don't think it's fair that you're judging me without even giving me a chance to prove that I have no agenda other than to capture this killer." A tickle of guilt flitted down her spine. She was withholding information from him, but not about the case.

He pulled out a chair and sat heavily, pulling a stack of files toward him. He stared at her, seeming to weigh her words. His scrutiny made her uncomfortable, but she held firm. Zack Travis was the type of cop who would see right through her if she even *thought* about lowering her shields.

"I'm glad that we could come to an agreement," he finally said, without directly responding to her comments. "Our department wants to find this guy just as bad as your agency."

Olivia nodded. *No you don't. No one wants this guy more than I do.*

Zack noticed an odd look cross Agent St. Martin's face, something he recognized but couldn't put a name to. She straightened her back, which didn't do much for her overall height. She was petite, trim, with an hourglass figure under an expensive suit.

As he stared, she tightened her jaw. He almost missed her biting the inside of her cheek, and for a brief moment she looked haunted. But he blinked and whatever he thought he saw had disappeared, and she simply looked like someone used to being in charge.

Zack said, "Do you have a first name? Or should I just call you Superagent?"

He liked the way she bristled. She would have been fun to tease if they didn't have serious business ahead of them.

"Olivia," she said.

"Do people call you Liv?"

She shrugged. "Some."

He waved a hand to the murder boards set up against the far wall. He'd watched her eyes darting toward them, obviously eager to get started.

"What do you know of my cases?"

She tucked her hair behind her ear, but it almost immediately fell forward. "Initially, I read the press reports, then I had the lab reports sent to me so I could review the evidence. But everything I have is from the Benedict murder. I haven't had time to review the Davidson file. I assume it's the same killer?"

"Yes."

"No doubt?"

"Not in my book. The director of the crime lab is taking the case himself. Doug Cohn. He concurs— same knife, same M.O., and—" he paused, then said, "You know about the hair, right?"

"The killer cut a chunk about one inch in diameter from the victim's head."

Zack nodded.

"Any differences between the two cases?"

Zack shook his head. "Nothing substantial. Jenny was nine; Michelle was eleven. Jenny was an only child whose parents are divorced; Michelle has two siblings and her parents are still married. Both were abducted in the afternoon, killed within forty-eight hours, bodies dumped in a marginally public area and discovered in less than twenty-four hours."

"Someone found the body of Jenny Benedict quickly, though," Olivia said. "Your report said possibly within two hours?"

"We tracked down every employee who works in that industrial park. The owner of Swanson and Clark Electronics left just after six o'clock Friday evening, three weeks ago. He swears he walked right past where her body was found and she wasn't there. The last employee to leave," Zack checked his notes, "Ann Wells. Works at an industrial paint supply store at the end of the row. She didn't see or hear anything unusual; her husband picked her up right at seven o'clock."

"And your witness arrived about 9:30?" Olivia prompted.

Zack nodded. "Sunset was officially 6:57, but it probably wasn't full dark until after 7:30. I'm figuring he waited until dark to dump the body as an added precaution."

"You're looking at a two-hour window?"

"I'm thinking the killer didn't expect someone to discover the body until at least Saturday morning, and possibly not until Monday. None of the businesses open over the weekend."

"I saw something about a tattoo." Olivia's heart quickened. This was what she really wanted to hear, but she didn't want to seem overeager at this point. "No details?"

"One of the girls who saw Jenny walk away with the killer saw a tattoo. It was a vague impression, and she had nothing else for us. My partner is looking into similar crimes. We've tracked down two so far—four dead girls in Austin, Texas, and four in Nashville, Tennessee. We're waiting on

Nashville's reports." He stared at her and leaned back in his chair. "You work either of those cases?"

Clearly, it was her turn to share.

Olivia opened her briefcase and took out the thick folder of information she'd compiled. "Unfortunately, I believe the man we're looking for has killed thirty girls, including Michelle Davidson."

"Thirty? And no one caught on that we have a nationwide serial killer?" Zack looked as irate as she felt.

"He's cautious. Methodical. Patient. Years of inactivity between murders. In three cases—California, Kansas, and Kentucky—someone else was arrested and tried for the crimes. There's no clear-cut pattern, and because the murders happen within weeks of each other before he stops, the cases grow cold quickly." She slid over a copy of her file.

"How did you connect these cases to mine?"

"I told you someone was tried in California for a crime I believe your Seattle killer is responsible for. The M.O. is similar. The man convicted was just released from prison because of a DNA test. He was convicted on circumstantial evidence, but it convinced the judge and jury. But he didn't rape Mel— the victim."

"He could have been involved."

"Yes. I've thought of that, but the prosecutor said the evidence after all this time is too thin to guarantee a conviction. And with all the publicity over wrongful convictions across the country—well, I think they simply didn't want to try a difficult case." She'd talked to Hamilton Craig about it when Hall was released two weeks ago. He was willing to retry

Hall, but he didn't think they'd win. There was no evidence suggesting there were two people involved. That didn't mean there weren't, but it would be harder to prove. And thirty-four years later? Virtually impossible.

"What do you think? Think my killer has a partner in crime?"

He was asking her an opinion that another cop, or an FBI agent, could offer. She didn't know. "I don't have any evidence to suggest either way—"

"What do you *think*? What's your *gut instinct* say? Or aren't you FBI types allowed to listen to your instincts?"

Instincts? She didn't know how to listen to her instincts. She needed the facts in front of her. Numbers. Statistics. Probabilities. She could compare microscopic threads and tell with certainty whether they matched or not. But her feelings about whether Missy's killer had a partner? This was unfamiliar and potentially dangerous territory, and an area she wasn't comfortable exploring.

"Well," she said, trying to buy time.

"You have an opinion. Spill it. I'm not going to hold you to it if you're wrong."

She swallowed, tucked her hair behind her ear. "Okay, I think the killer works alone. His crime is too personal, too *intimate* to share with another person. But—the California murder appears to be his first. And maybe he was still working out the bugs in his killing style. The primary evidence that convicted Hall was his truck—evidence in the truck proved that the victim had been in it." She paused when she realized she'd said Hall's name out loud. She hadn't meant to, and quickly continued her line of reasoning, hoping Zack didn't seize upon her slip. "Perhaps he drove the killer? Or maybe lent the killer his truck? But I can't see anyone keeping quiet and going to prison to protect someone."

"I agree."

She was surprised. "You do?"

"The crimes are too personal. I don't see him having a partner. But maybe early on he had help." Zack shrugged. "We won't know until we find him."

"Do you have a DNA sample? Anything like that?" Olivia asked.

"We have a sample off Michelle Davidson, but it's apparently small." He shook his head. "I'm not well-versed in DNA testing, I've left it to Cohn. He's good. But it'll still take a few weeks to get anything. Cohn's trying to push the state crime lab into rushing the test, but they have to put court-ordered DNA testing first." He ran a hand over the dark stubble on his face, then rubbed his neck.

"I—" How could she get that sample without Zack thinking she was taking over the case? She had to proceed carefully. "You know, I might be able to rush the sample through the FBI lab."

He gave her a blank stare, only the tic in his neck telling her he was suspicious of her motives. "And?" he prompted.

"We have state-of-the-art equipment there, and I sort of know the assistant director of CODIS. He'll rush it for me."

"Oh?"

She felt like she was on the hot seat. "He's my ex-husband."

"Your ex-husband works in the lab?" He grinned.

"Hell, I wouldn't be able to get my ex-wife to do me any favors."

His humor relaxed Olivia a bit. "Well, he'll do it for me. We parted friends."

"It's not easy keeping a marriage going in our line of work," Zack commented, almost to himself.

Guilt again tickled Olivia. It wasn't her line of work, but she knew enough agents and cops to know relationships were difficult for them. Ironically, work was the one thing that had brought her and Greg together, and kept them friends.

"All right," he said, standing abruptly. "If we can get answers faster by using your ex, I'm all for it. Let's go down to the lab and you and Cohn can talk about all that technical stuff. You probably picked up a lot of knowledge just being married to one of those lab guys."

He doesn't know the half of it, Olivia thought.

CHAPTER
6

Brian stomped down the three flights of stairs to the alley where his beat-up truck was parked. He was stuck until his attorney could get him some money from the damn government. You'd think they could have handed him a check on his way out the door—he was *innocent,* he'd told them he was innocent, and no one had believed him because that stupid fucking cop lied about the evidence. Planted evidence. Isn't that what happened to O.J.? Cops planted evidence.

Of course Brian didn't believe for one minute that O.J. didn't do his wife, but hey, the cops fucked it up just like they screwed up everything and so they probably planted evidence on O.J. to make themselves look good, just like they'd planted evidence in his truck.

He jerked open the tinny door of the mini-pickup, wishing he had his big Dodge, but it had been seized *as evidence.* Shit, that wasn't fair. It was probably a classic now. Worth some money.

Three tries as he pumped the clutch and gas to get the rust bucket to turn over. He'd wanted to see his mom and show her that he was fine, just fine, better than ever. He wanted to move home, eat real food, sleep in a real bed, and never again see another cock-roach.

He'd called his mom from the prison last week, the night before he was released.

"Ma, it's me. Brian."

She didn't say anything for nearly a minute, and Brian thought for sure he'd been disconnected, some lame-ass prank of the prison guards.

"Brian," she finally said, her voice old and flat. Unhappy.

Anger and a funny sort of pain clogged his throat. He swallowed with difficulty, then said, "Ma, I'm getting out. I didn't do it."

Another long pause. "I don't understand. Where are you?"

"I'm still in Folsom, but they're letting me come home tomorrow. They have new evidence, and it says I didn't kill anyone."

"Home? You're coming home?"

She sounded scared. Hadn't she heard what he'd said? That he was innocent? That the stupid fucking cops had made a mistake?

"Yeah. I'm *inn-o-cent*," he stressed. "I told you that before."

It hurt that his mother hadn't visited him. He squirmed. He really didn't know what his mother thought, what she even looked like as an old woman, or how she was coming along with his dad being dead.

He was surprised at how much it bothered him.

"I—Brian, I don't know what to say."

"Say I can come home."

"I don't know. I don't know."

His hand clutched the receiver so tight his knuckles whitened. *Stupid bitch! I told you I didn't do it!*

A familiar guilt spread through him and he hated himself for thinking so poorly of his mother. Shit, this was no good. He had to show her.

"Ma, it's okay." He took a deep breath. "The court got me an apartment and is giving me a little money, and because I was wrongfully imprisoned they're going to give me over a million dollars. So I'll call you next week, give you some time."

"Thank you. Brian, I never stopped praying for you. Not one day. I hope you'll do something good with your life now that you're being released from prison."

"Yes, Ma." He hung up, afraid he'd start yelling at her. *Something good with his life?* What'd she think he'd do, murder someone? He didn't murder that little girl, never would kill a kid. And the guy on the yard, hell, that had been an accident. And the Vietcong had been the enemy. He hadn't murdered anyone, like in cold blood. It wasn't fair, it fucking wasn't fair, that he'd been sent to prison for thirty-four years because the stupid cops screwed up their investigation.

Fucking *not fair.*

Brian wiped his brow, sweating, hot wind blowing through the open windows of his pitiful truck. It wasn't just the weather. It was this odd feeling he'd had ever since he'd walked out of Folsom Prison a free man. He didn't feel free. He didn't feel like he was in his body. He was disoriented. He'd been watching television nonstop since he'd been out. He'd taken nearly half the piddling stipend the prison handed him—like $1500 and a free apartment was supposed to last for three months until his million bucks came—and bought a fine 36-inch tube. It wasn't like he'd been living in a vacuum in prison—he'd watched the news and a few stupid shows and movies and whatnot, but he didn't realize how much he'd missed.

His mother lived in Menlo Park, in an older, middle-class neighborhood on the San Francisco peninsula. It was only ten minutes from his shit-ass apartment on the bad side of the tracks in Redwood City, where he was the only white boy in his building. But until he got the money from the government, he couldn't go anywhere.

Life sucked.

By the time he'd turned into his mom's neighborhood, he was a basket case. First, he hadn't realized how much the area had grown in the last thirty years. He almost had a heart attack on the freeway surrounded by a gazillion cars and big rigs. Shit, where did all these people live? The peninsula connecting San Francisco to San Jose wasn't that big.

A lot of the houses in his mom's neighborhood were big and opulent, well kept. Classy, he thought. Some were add-ons, little houses turned into big homes. This was not the middle-class neighborhood he'd left when he went to Vietnam. These people had money.

The trees were bigger—a lot taller. But the streets had a hint of familiarity, and there was the park where he'd played as a boy.

Tears stung his eyes and he pinched the bridge of his nose. How'd it all get so fucked? He used to walk on this exact road with the guys, Pete and Barry and Tom. Kicking rocks and jabbering. Whittling wood like his daddy had shown him. Where were the guys now? Pete had gone to Vietnam, like him, but Barry and Tom didn't go, at least not that he knew. Barry had the brains; he'd gone off to some big college. Probably made good money and married and had kids and did all the stuff they hadn't thought about as kids, but figured they'd get around to sooner or later.

Tom? Hell, he could have landed himself in prison for all Brian knew. He was always walking that line, like the time he ripped off Old Man Duncan's soda shop on El Camino Real, or when he nabbed Debbie Palmer's purse and found out she had birth control pills in her wallet. Debbie Palmer wasn't a virgin? Tom had returned the purse without her knowing, minus five bucks, and hit on her. Got her in the back of his dad's pickup one night after a ball game and they went at it like rabbits.

Brian stopped the truck in front of his mom's house and it sputtered before it died. He stared at the neat little bungalow. The same, but different.

Same red-shingled one-story, but freshly painted. The porch still had a swing, but it wasn't the one Brian remembered. This one was wooden with a red-and-white flowered cushion. Flowers lined the walk. Petunias, his mother's favorite.

"They grow like weeds but they're so colorful I can't help but love them," she'd told him many times when she planted at the first sign of spring.

What was she doing planting petunias now? She was eighty. She shouldn't be on her knees in the dirt.

As with many of the homes in the neighborhood, the garage was set back from the house. Still, a new Honda rested in the driveway. He couldn't remember a time his mother didn't garage the car. He hoped she was well.

He missed her.

He got out of the truck and walked slowly up the brick path, straightening his new Dockers. Twenty-four bucks. He couldn't believe a pair of stupid pants cost that much—and the shirt was half-price, but still fifteen dollars! But he wanted to look nice for his ma.

The door opened before he even knocked. It wasn't his ma.

Uncle Glen? Looked just like him. Full head of light gray hair, watery blue eyes, and fat nose, much too big to be on the little guy's skinny face.

Brian blinked. Couldn't be Uncle Glen, his mom's brother. He'd be ancient by now. And didn't Ma write saying that he'd croaked years ago?

"Toby?" Brian blinked again, his mouth falling open. His cousin Toby looked so old. But he was six years younger than Brian, and . . .

. . . And *he* was old. *He* was fifty-four. In his fucking fifties.

His life was gone. Over. Stolen.

"Brian." Toby made no move to open the security screen. When had Ma installed it?

"What are you doing here?" He didn't mean to sound so defensive. He used to like his little cousin. But that was three decades ago, before shit happened.

"Aunt Vi called and said you'd been released. I came down to help."

"Help with what?"

Toby shrugged.

"Let me in. I want to see my mom."

"You're not going to cause problems, Brian, are you?"

Brian fumed and wanted to slap that stern, holier-than-thou expression off Toby's rotten face. "No," he said, reining in his temper. "I wasn't released. My conviction was overturned. I didn't do it. I always said I didn't do it; now there's proof."

Toby nodded. "Yes, that's what Aunt Vi said you told her. She asked me to look into it."

His own mother didn't believe him. She didn't believe that he'd been *exonerated*. She didn't believe his word—she'd sent his lousy cousin to check up on him.

But more than the pain of his mother's belief in his guilt was the anger that she'd been subjected to this travesty in the first place.

He didn't kill that girl! His jaw trembled as he controlled his anger.

"So you know I told the truth." It was almost impossible for him to speak. He wanted to pummel Toby's stupid, gloating, idiotic face. Damn asshole, walking into *his* house and turning his own mother against him.

Toby gave a half-nod. "To an extent. But you still could have been involved."

"Bullshit!"

Toby flinched and Brian heard a gasp from somewhere in the living room, behind his cousin. His ma. Shit. He ran a hand over his face, regaining his control.

"Your mother is eighty-one years old, Brian. Her heart isn't too good. If I let you in, you have to promise not to upset her. Or I *will* have you arrested."

Brian wanted to leave and never look back. All these years, in prison for a crime he didn't commit, and now his own mother didn't believe he had nothing to do with it.

But he missed her. He had to see her. She was all he had left.

He glanced down, torn but contrite. "All right."

Toby opened the screen and Brian took a tentative step inside. As his eyes adjusted to the dim indoor lighting, he couldn't help but notice everything had changed. While the house itself hadn't, the furnishings were new, more modern. Leather. But the grandfather clock was still in the dining room. He couldn't see it, but he heard its steady tick-tock, an intimately familiar sound that soothed him as he remembered listening to it as a small boy when he couldn't sleep.

Tick. Tock. Tick. Tock. Tick. Tock. Slow and comforting.

Calmer, he searched out his mother.

She sat in a recliner, a walker perched next to her. She seemed so—small. Old. Shriveled. Three decades aged anyone, and Father Time took a middle-aged woman and made her elderly. Her hair, which she had dyed blonde for as long as he could remember, was now snow white. She was skinny and wrinkled. His mother despised wrinkles and used every lotion and potion under the sun to prevent them.

Guess they didn't work.

But her eyes—blue and clear. She hadn't lost her mind. As she turned those sharp eyes to him, he felt her disapproval, her sadness. He wanted to fall on his knees and beg her forgiveness.

Yet he had nothing to be forgiven for. He was innocent!

"Ma." His voice didn't sound right. He cleared his throat. "Ma, it's good to see you."

She nodded slowly, looked him up and down. Tears welled in her eyes and Brian's throat constricted and his eyes blurred. Her arms came up.

"Brian."

He stumbled toward her, fell to his knees and into her skeletal embrace. "Ma, I'm sorry. I'm so sorry. I never wanted to hurt you, I never did anything to hurt you."

"I know, son."

He sobbed into her lap, wanting to erase the years and make something of himself. Wishing he hadn't volunteered for Vietnam, yet wishing he'd never left the military.

He had wanted to be her hero. Just like Daddy had been.

Now he was nothing.

CHAPTER
7

Doug Cohn was no pushover, yet Zack watched Agent St. Martin quietly win him over. In less than ten minutes, they were speaking a language foreign to Zack, about DNA samples and test procedures and how they would transport the evidence found on Michelle Davidson's body to the FBI lab in Virginia.

Then he heard Olivia mention her theory about the killer stealing trucks.

"I don't have the motor vehicle records from the other jurisdictions," Olivia said, "but I think the killer steals a truck the day of the abduction, and either returns the vehicle or dumps it somewhere."

"We ran auto theft reports," Cohn said. "One Expedition in the manufacturer year we're looking for was reported stolen the day before Jennifer Benedict's abduction, but it hasn't been recovered."

"Why would he steal them?" Zack asked, almost to himself.

"Convenience," Olivia said. "Removes him from the crime scene—if it's not his vehicle, it's less likely it can be traced to him. Two different vehicles were used for two victims. It doesn't make sense that a killer smart enough to move from state to state in order to avoid detection would use his own vehicle to transport a victim."

Zack frowned, realizing Olivia was probably right. "We had no idea there was an established M.O. The little information we've received from Austin and Nashville dealt more with the victim profile."

He must have sounded defensive, because she said, "I didn't mean anything by it. I would have done exactly what you've been doing with the information you had."

Cohn nodded. "Makes sense to me. Travis, I'll go ahead and run auto theft reports daily, see if the Dodge pops or any other SUV or truck. There'll be dozens every day."

"I'll talk to the chief about alerting patrols to keep an eye out for the trucks on our list," Zack said. "Probably won't lead to anything, but maybe we'll get lucky."

"We're looking for a white male, over fifty," Olivia said. "Maybe you can add that to the watch list."

"White men over fifty driving a truck in Seattle?" Cohn laughed. "That'd fit half the population, including me."

She smiled, a wonderfully genuine grin that lit up her face, but didn't reach her eyes. She was even more beautiful when she smiled, Zack thought. *Stop it, Travis. She's not only your partner, but a Fed, too.* "True. I was thinking with regards to the stolen vehicles."

"Over fifty?" Zack asked. "I wouldn't think he'd be that old."

"The first suspected case, the one in California I mentioned, was over thirty years ago. If he was eighteen when he committed that crime, he would be fifty-two today."

"Pervert," Cohn mumbled.

Zack's cell phone rang. He frowned as he glanced at the number. It was the Sheriff's Office. He flipped open his phone. "Travis."

"Detective, Jim Rodgers here. You're working the two homicides, right? The blonde girls?"

"Yes." Every muscle in his body tightened. The sheriff would only call him directly to share bad news.

"We think we have another one."

"An abduction?"

"A body. Jillian Reynolds, age nine. She's been missing for nearly three months. And by the look of things, she's been dead that long."

"Why do you think it's related to my investigation?"

"She was blonde. Apparently stabbed to death. The body's not in real good condition due to decomposition, but it appears a chunk of hair was cut."

Zack's gut churned. "Where?"

"Vashon Island."

"I'll be there in—" he glanced at his watch. If he stepped on it he could make the ferry. Maybe. "Forty-five minutes."

"I'll have a deputy meet you at the dock."

Zack slammed his phone shut.

"Do you need me?" Cohn asked, obviously clued in by Zack's end of the conversation that there'd been a crime.

Zack shook his head. "The sheriff's people are there. But it looks like the same guy, so I'll have them send everything to our lab." The sheriff's department generally sent evidence to the state lab, but Seattle had a top-notch facility and could expedite the lab work. Whenever possible, the county used the local lab.

Cohn nodded and ran a hand over his nearly-bald head. "Rodgers's people are team players. We'll have no jurisdictional problems."

Olivia looked from Cohn to Zack, perplexed. "What happened? Another kidnapping?"

Zack glanced at Olivia and for a split second thought he saw rage in her eyes. Rage tinged with fear. Then it was gone, like an opaque shield sliding down. She grabbed her briefcase off Cohn's desk, all business, cool and detached.

"Three months ago," Zack told her. "They just found her body." He led Olivia from the lab to the parking garage.

"Three months . . ." Olivia paused in her stride and stumbled. When Zack caught her elbow to steady her, she tensed under his touch. "Thanks," she mumbled, but moved away from him. "Three months," she repeated. "That means Michelle Davidson was his third Seattle victim.

"Zack, I don't think I pointed it out when we were reviewing the cases, but he only kills four girls in each city he hits. If we don't get him now, we'll lose him."

Vince Kirby ran a hand through his short-cropped hair before hitting SEND on the e-mail to his editor.

Now, he couldn't take it back.

The Seattle Slayer? Corny. And it didn't sit well with Kirby. These were kids who were murdered. He didn't feel comfortable sensationalizing their deaths.

Well, if Bristow wanted to fire him, fine. But Kirby wouldn't stand for major editorial changes under his byline. Not anymore.

The biggest problem was Zack Travis. When he

read the paper tomorrow morning and saw the sub-headline *SPD fumbling investigation*, he'd blame Kirby, no doubt.

Why did Kirby even care? He'd tried to explain to Travis a half-dozen times that he didn't write all his stories the way they came out in print.

But Travis had been important to Amy, and that made him important to Kirby.

Kirby reached over, picked up the only picture on his cluttered desk, and stared at Amy's secretive smile. Lips together, turned slightly up, her dark eyes lit with humor and a touch of mischief.

God, he had loved her.

Bristow's door slammed open. "Kirby!" he called.

So, maybe sending the e-mail wasn't the wisest thing to do, but changing the article at the last minute when he'd been covering the crime beat for eight years—that was low, even for his editor.

He stood. "Coming," he called.

But Bristow was already crossing the floor. Most everyone had left for the day, but Kirby had a feeling the senior editor lived in the building. There wasn't a time of day or night that Kirby was here when Bristow wasn't.

"Get out to Vashon Island ASAP. There's some sort of police activity, all hush-hush on the band, but one of my contacts said the sheriff called in Detective Travis. My gut says it's the Slayer."

Kirby cringed at the killer's moniker. "Mr. Bristow, I think we need to tread lightly in this case. I—"

The editor waved his hand as he lit a cigarette. It was a nonsmoking building. Bristow took that to mean nonsmoking during business hours. Then, he smoked in his office. "I saw your e-mail. Funny. You work the beat, I'll clean your copy. Now go, before you miss the damn ferry."

Kirby stuffed his camera and notepad into his backpack and slung it over his shoulder.

He had to find another paper to work for. Nothing was keeping him in Seattle now that Amy was dead.

Except a promise.

He prided himself on his discipline.

He planned each operation precisely, from the vehicle he stole to the neighborhood he targeted to the girl he chose. Patience. Planning. Discipline.

Two or three times he'd acted on impulse. The first time, of course, but that worked out amazingly well. After all, stealing Hall's truck turned attention to someone else. It was after that he decided he would steal trucks for every operation. That took finding the least likely vehicle to be reported stolen, which was surprisingly easy. He generally picked people going on vacation. More often than not, they took a taxi or shuttle to the airport. Picking locks was child's play; virtually everyone had an extra set of car keys in the house. He had use of their truck for days and no one reported it stolen.

He preferred either American trucks or SUVs because they were big, he understood the mechanics, and they were common. If he selected a pickup, it had to have a shell over the bed for privacy; an SUV needed darkened windows and collapsible rear seats. Cars were too small and their trunks usually stuffed with the owner's junk, and cargo vans were out of the question; they immediately appeared suspicious sitting in a residential neighborhood.

Sometimes he made mistakes. Like the time in Texas when the daughter came home from college to house-sit. Close call, but he'd talked his way out of that one.

If only that bitch had known she was minutes away from dying. He'd wanted to reach out, wrap his hands around her neck, and squeeze. Squeeze until her neck snapped.

But rash actions like that could have drawn attention to him, and he had more important operations to plan.

His sweet angels waited for him to free their souls.

But three months ago he'd again acted on impulse. He'd seen his little angel running along the edge of the water, glowing. *Radiating* just for him. And he knew beyond a doubt she'd been sent to him.

He'd been on the island for a year, blending in, planning. He'd already selected a neighborhood off the island, and was looking for the right truck when the angel ran along the beach and her soul sang to him.

He brought her to his cottage. Another mistake.

There was nowhere else to take her—he couldn't remove her from the island because of surveillance cameras on the docks. And the authorities had started the search immediately, even before he'd secured her inside his house.

He kept her safe, hidden, until the search was called off well after sundown.

Everyone thought she'd drowned.

Then he freed her, and his sweet little angel became a spirit, pure and brilliant.

But it had been a mistake, an impulsive decision that he now regretted. The police were swarming the island. Would they talk to him? Perhaps. They had nothing on him, couldn't come into the cottage, had no reason to suspect him. He'd been on the island long enough to divert suspicion, and the fact that he was still here helped his case.

No one had seen him with her; otherwise they'd never have assumed she drowned when they couldn't find her. Days later, he'd put her empty shell in the middle of the island, where the woods were dense and people would be less likely to find it. He quickly dismissed the idea of burying it. That wouldn't do. Her shell was nothing; her spirit was free. To bury it would imply there was some value in emptiness, something to preserve.

He'd planned to be gone by now, but one of his little angels eluded him. It didn't happen often. He watched, waited, planned. He followed the patterns. There were always patterns. But sometimes it happens that a schedule suddenly changed, and last month he'd been waiting and she never came. So he was behind.

Not for long.

Even mishaps like changing schedules were planned for. He had more than one contingency plan.

With the angel's shell discovered and the police on the island, he'd considered leaving. But disappearing now might cast suspicion on him. A waiter not showing up at the restaurant right after the police find a dead body on the island? No, that wouldn't do. He needed to report to work. Answer questions if they were asked. Express a moderate amount of surprise. Expected sadness. Go about his business.

He would leave after freeing the next spirit. Then he would be at peace for a time. He didn't quite understand why the peace ended and he needed to find more angels, but he always knew when to act and when to hold back. His internal clock protected him.

He believed it always would.

Walking into the small cottage bedroom, he closed the door. Locked it. Crossed to the closet and retrieved his special case. It had a combination lock on it. He spun the numbers and took a deep breath.

Open.

His hands shook as he reached for a lock of hair. Long, beautiful golden curls. Reverently, he brought it to his lips. "Be free, angel. Be free."

He touched each of the thirty-two locks in turn. He saved the oldest for last. The curls had lost their luster, turned frizzy and dry. He didn't notice.

"Angel, until we meet again."

Tenderly, he put all the hair back into the case, but he didn't close it. No, he relived each death and rebirth. Remembered every one of his angels.

Especially the first.

The memories made him ache, his rigid penis straining against his shorts. He reached down, grasped himself. He stared at his collection until relief finally came.

Calmer, he locked his special case and returned it to the shelf in the closet. Unlocked his door, and stared out the kitchen window into the blackness of the island.

He had never failed in an operation.

He wouldn't fail freeing his last Seattle angel.

Then he would leave.

Wednesday night, the ferry to Vashon Island was less than half full. Zack flashed his badge and backed his car onto the ferry only minutes before its scheduled departure. Last on, first off. He shut off the engine.

"Let's get out and stretch," Zack said. The police-issue sedan felt tight, confining. He much preferred his Harley, but he couldn't very well bring Agent St. Martin to a crime scene on his bike.

They walked up the stairs to the observation deck. Olivia tilted her face to the sky. He joined her. The stars multiplied over the water, brighter and closer, the distant and low-lying Vashon Island skyline reminding him why he loved the Sound. A clear night; the fog had yet to roll in.

Olivia rubbed her arms through the thin material of her suit. Zack took off his leather bomber jacket and attempted to put it over her shoulders.

She jumped a good two feet from him.

"Hell, Superagent, you're freezing your butt off. I thought you might want a jacket. We can go up to the cabin if you want. I think it's heated." He wasn't sure. He couldn't remember ever going into the enclosed area above.

"Oh. Yes. Thank you, but I'm fine."

Prickly, but there was something—different. Not fear, but something he couldn't quite put his finger on. She was obviously distracted by something. He wondered if it was personal—she'd called her ex-husband about the DNA tests while they drove—or professional.

"So, Superagent, any theories?"

She didn't say anything for several minutes. The hum of the ferry, car doors opening and shutting on the deck below, passengers boarding, the call of crew members . . . the sounds lulled him, familiar. The cold salt air mixed with the ferry's diesel fumes grounded him.

He glanced at Olivia. The breeze tossed her golden, chin-length hair around her elegant face. She impatiently tucked it behind her ear, but the gesture did little to stop the errant strands from dancing.

He watched her closely. Big mistake.

Olivia St. Martin was all feminine softness under a spine of steel. And there was a working brain under that shiny hair. A sharp mind and hot body. But every fiber of her being screamed *don't touch*.

If there was one thing Zack Travis knew, it was women. When to touch. Where to touch. How to touch. Whether they liked soft kisses on their neck or a thorough devouring of their lips. Gentle caresses or urgent strokes. With one probing touch he discovered exactly where their erogenous zone was—not the obvious one, but their hidden sensitivities. A whisper in the ear. A kiss on the neck. A trail of warmth from under their knee down to their pinky toe.

He saw Olivia as one big erogenous zone. Her entire body begged to be held, but at the same time demanded that everyone stay away, don't get too close. It was the way she hugged herself. The delicate tilt of her head. The darkening of her eyes when someone stood too close.

There was a fiery woman under that icy exterior. Suddenly, unbidden, Zack wanted to crack her shell and watch her melt.

Why did she not like being touched? Had something happened to her? On the job . . . or before it? Why did she keep herself so contained and controlled?

He saw in Olivia something unusual. Special. He wanted to learn more about her.

He shifted his stance, uncomfortable with where his thoughts led him, and turned once again back to the water. A whistle sounded, letting passengers know they'd be leaving in two minutes. The idling ferry rumbled as the captain prepared to depart.

Olivia spoke, as if the change in the ferry beneath them prompted her to speak. "In the ten cities where we know the killer has been, he's taken up to six months between his first and last kill."

While her words were matter-of-fact and her tone calm, Olivia's entire body was on edge.

Any other woman, and Zack would have rubbed the tension from her shoulders. But he didn't dare reach out for Olivia.

Instead, he said, "If Jillian Reynolds is in fact his first victim in Seattle, why would he have laid low for three months?"

"I don't know," she said, her skin pale under the artificial light.

"Give me the facts. We didn't get a chance to run down each case before we left." He already knew he'd be spending all night going over her files just to get up to speed.

"Okay, let's say for the sake of argument he attacked here first," Olivia said. "Three months ago. What day did Jillian Reynolds go missing?"

"June thirtieth."

"June . . . then he kidnaps Jennifer Benedict the first week of September. That's about nine, ten weeks. Michelle Davidson three weeks later.

"We'll need to plot out each of the other cases," Olivia continued, "but if I remember my notes correctly, he speeds up his attacks until he hits number four, then he disappears." She frowned. "But not always. He doesn't have a clear timeline. In Colorado he killed four girls in a six-week period. First one, he waited nearly five weeks, then killed three more in ten days. It's almost like he has a sixth sense about when to kill, when to hold back, when to leave."

"Serial killers have a strong sense of self-preservation," Zack commented.

Olivia glanced at him. "You're right. Maybe I should be asking you the profiling questions."

"I learned a lot about serial killers when the Green River Killer was on the loose."

"I remember that case. I worked on—" she stopped.

"You were here? Part of the task force?" Zack asked.

She shook her head. "I just consulted. It was a long time ago, and my role was small. I never came out here."

Zack frowned. There was something odd in her voice.

The loud whistle startled Olivia and she jumped, then felt foolish when Zack said, "The ferry's heading out. It's a twenty-minute ride."

"Oh. Thanks."

Olivia gathered her wits about her. She'd almost blown it, and she'd only been working with Detective Travis for a few hours. She'd almost told him she'd processed trace evidence for the Green River investigation. If she wanted to stay on this case, she had to be more careful.

She stared out at the water, hugging herself. She wished she hadn't said no to Zack's offer of his jacket, but it wouldn't have been wise to accept. She would have felt even smaller than she was. Detective Travis had an imposing frame—he was a good foot taller than her, and wide. Not fat by any means, just *big*. Like a lumberjack, all chest and hard muscles. And the way he looked at her, as if he could see under her clothes as well as under her skin, disturbed her to no end. No one had ever studied her so closely. So obviously. As if he were trying to figure out exactly what she was thinking, what she'd done in the past, what she was likely to do in the future. Assessing her.

His scrutiny unnerved her.

All she wanted was to stop the killer she had inadvertently let go free when she fingered Brian Harrison Hall for Missy's murder. She wasn't so naïve as to believe she was solely responsible for Hall's conviction—there was enough circumstantial evidence to warrant it—but she'd read the reports and knew her identification was part of the decision. And because of that, a brutal murderer was roaming the country freely.

He crossed state lines at will, under the radar of the authorities. Four men had been suspected in some of the investigations, and three had been convicted. The last one was released for lack of evidence, but after looking at each case, Olivia knew they were all innocent. It was *him*, Missy's killer, playing the system. Missy's killer was smart. He knew what he was doing. Planned it. Reveled in it. He wouldn't stop until he was in prison. Or dead.

"Penny for your thoughts."

She jumped, almost forgetting where she was. Seattle. On a ferry. With a probing detective who wouldn't stop looking at her. She didn't know whether to be irritated, flattered, or worried.

She cleared her throat and rubbed her arms, trying to be discreet. She didn't want Detective Travis to know how chilled she really was.

"I was thinking about something that's been bothering me since I started piecing these cases together," Olivia admitted. "I mean, you know as well as I do that most serial killers don't want to be caught. They live for the hunt, they enjoy the kill, and they will do anything to avoid capture. But I was thinking about the BTK Killer, in Kansas. He slipped up and was caught. His crimes were spread over years, but he still only killed ten people. When you mentioned the Green River Killer, I was thinking about how he confessed to forty-eight killings, most of them committed nearly twenty years before he was caught."

"Most of the cops on the case think he killed far more," Zack said.

"So do I," she said. "But the thing is, he messed up. It was his semen that led to his capture—decades-old DNA. We have this killer's DNA—but it's not matching anything. He was never arrested for a sexual crime. He hasn't slipped up. He hasn't made one of those mistakes that could set us on the path to capture him. For thirty-four years, he's killed with impunity, hiding the pattern, keeping a low profile so that he can keep on killing these children."

Olivia blinked. She hadn't intended to say so much, and she took a deep breath. Zack was looking at her oddly. Had she blown it? She normally didn't become so impassioned about, well, anything. But being here, so close to Missy's killer, was doing something to her. She wasn't thinking straight, letting both the circumstances and Zack's intense perusal get under her skin. But having to keep her lies in order was far more difficult than she'd imagined.

"Why are you here?" he asked.

"I don't understand."

"Olivia." His voice was low, deep, commanding. "Why *you*? Why are *you* here unofficially and not someone else?"

She swallowed and prayed he couldn't see her raw nerves. These past weeks had been a living hell and it had become more difficult to keep her emotions in check. What could she safely tell him? She was an awful liar. She could skirt the truth—Chief Pierson hadn't asked tough questions, because Greg had paved the way with a phone call the day before—but lying was next to impossible.

She'd probably still be married to Greg if she'd been able to lie about her feelings.

"I was involved with a case years ago where this killer got away," Olivia said, carefully choosing her words. "An innocent man went to prison. I want to catch this guy. The real killer. End his reign of terror."

Zack stared at her. She stared back, determined not to break eye contact. Keep her chin up. Never back down. Never show weakness.

"Guilt."

She blinked. How could he get so close to her real feelings when she kept them so deeply buried? His inspection of her motives unnerved her. "Well, not so much—"

"Don't try to get out of it, Olivia. It's not necessarily a bad thing. Guilt can be a powerful motivator. It also has the power to destroy you. You sent an innocent guy to prison; now you want justice because of your guilt."

So close. Too close. She didn't know what to say.

"You're freezing," he said.

Once again, Zack threw Olivia off balance. He'd brought too many feelings to the surface, then dropped the subject so swiftly that she floundered.

She began to protest, but he stared into her eyes and simply shook his head, a half-smile on his lips.

Without asking, he draped his worn leather jacket over her shoulders. It was far too big, falling over her hips and hanging past her fingertips. She felt like he'd wrapped her in a bear hug, his residual warmth caressing her. His scent of raw soap and leather permeated her senses. Warm. Intimate. Too intimate.

She tore herself away from his eyes. She bit her lower lip and looked out at the water. The island was much larger than it appeared from West Seattle. She focused on it and not on Zack, but she still pictured his dark, intelligent, probing eyes.

"Why'd you join the FBI?" Zack asked after several moments of silence.

She glanced at him. Mistake. He stared at her intently. If she lied, he'd most certainly know.

"I knew someone who was killed," she said, looking away. "When an FBI recruiter visited my college campus, I felt compelled to apply after graduation." There. The truth, of sorts.

"Who was killed?"

Why had she said anything? She was inviting questions she didn't want to answer. "My sister," she said quietly, looking at her hands clutching the railing, the sleeves of Zack's jacket covering her fingers. Just thinking of Missy made her stomach clench.

"I'm sorry." He sounded sincere. "I had a sister, too."

She turned to him, surprised. "What happened?"

He paused. "She got involved with the wrong people. Ended up getting herself killed."

"That's awful. Was she young?"

"Twenty-two. In college."

His voice was both bitter and hurt. Olivia couldn't help but wonder what more there was to the story. But she wasn't going to ask. He might start up with questions of his own, harder questions she couldn't avoid.

"The young think they're invincible," she said after a moment. "Indestructible. Nothing can hurt them." She'd believed that for the first five years of her life. And from her experience since, most kids grew into adults before realizing they weren't superhuman.

Too often, they looked death in the face before coming to that conclusion. The unlucky ones didn't get a second chance at life.

They were approaching the island. At first, it hadn't looked like anything was there, just a dim sort of glow on the horizon. But as they came closer, the glow had turned to distinctive lights, and the island took shape against the dark sky.

Olivia turned her head to view the Seattle skyline to the east.

"Isn't it gorgeous?" Zack said, his voice quiet and filled with awe. "Like jewels against the night sky. This is my favorite view of the city."

Jewels against the night sky. How beautiful! Yet beauty juxtaposed against the death scene that awaited them hit her hard and she closed her eyes.

She didn't want to see the girl's body. She didn't want to be on the island deceiving anyone about her credentials. Especially a dedicated cop like Zack Travis. But there was no other way, and she admonished herself to get over her remorse.

She would do anything and everything to catch Missy's killer. Maybe this time the killer had slipped up. Maybe this victim would give them the evidence they needed to find her attacker.

Olivia hoped and prayed for something—anything—that led to the killer.

Before another girl died.

CHAPTER
9

By the time Olivia and Zack arrived on Vashon Island, the girl's body had already been taken to the morgue. The coroner would expedite the autopsy the following morning in hopes of confirming or ruling out that it was the same murderer who'd killed Jenny Benedict and Michelle Davidson.

Approximately twelve miles long and eight miles across at its widest spot, Vashon Island was a popular getaway spot for both locals and tourists. Miles of pine-edged country roads, pristine beaches, and a historic lighthouse gave the island an old-world feel. The artisans and crafters pretty much ran the place with monthly art shows, a local drama troupe, and numerous fine art galleries.

The island was a fun place. Now Zack would never be able to set foot here without thinking about a dead girl.

Jillian Reynolds had been dumped in a dense, wooded area in the middle of the island. Zack glanced at Olivia. She struggled in her pumps—certainly not made for scaling boulders or trekking through sand. But then again, neither of them had been expecting to attend a crime scene on the island in the middle of the night.

The three of them—Sheriff Rodgers, Zack, and Olivia—stood just inside the crime-scene tape, which was pulled around trees in a roughly hundred-square-foot area. High-wattage construction lights had been brought in, making the landscape harsh in the artificial brightness. Details seemed too sharp, faces almost colorless.

Olivia was thankful that it was warm under the lights. She was doing everything she could to stop her teeth from chattering. She'd returned Zack's jacket without a word—it would be unprofessional to wear his clothing to the crime scene. The fact that she hadn't brought a warm coat was her own fault—in her rushed departure from Virginia, which was enjoying an Indian summer, she hadn't thought of checking the weather in Seattle before packing. Frankly, she hadn't thought about much of anything but Missy's murder during the last weeks since Brian Harrison Hall had been released from prison, but her oversight on appropriate clothing irritated her.

Standing under the warmth of the potent lights, Olivia watched the crime-scene technicians finish collecting potential evidence and itched to join them. She followed their every movement with a sharp eye—was that woman going to forget to collect a soil sample? Good, she saw the flash of a test tube. What about the tree branches? Perhaps the killer had snagged hair or skin on a protruding limb. Good, one of the techs was inspecting the foliage. But it had been three months since the murder; any biological evidence would be gone. She tried not to feel discouraged, but time and the elements were enemies of evidence.

"My people know what they're doing," Sheriff Rodgers said.

Olivia glanced up at the cop, detecting a hint of offense in his tone. It didn't help that Zack had introduced her as "Agent St. Martin with the FBI." She'd watched the sheriff bristle and straighten. He wasn't as tall as Zack, but compared to her he was huge.

"They appear more than competent." She gave him a smile. She wasn't the villain here, but she had to tread carefully. This was uncharted territory for her, and she couldn't afford to slip up.

"Have you notified her family?" Zack asked.

"It's being done," Rodgers said. "She wasn't a local. Her family was on a weekend trip to the island when she disappeared. I remember the case. We'd conducted a search, believing she'd gotten lost. When she wasn't found, she was listed as a missing person, but her mother said she couldn't swim and she'd been last seen near the water. We all thought—well, the undertow is strong on the west side of the island." He ran a hand over his stubble, looking tired and defeated. It had been a long night.

Olivia said, "How did you identify her? Three months outdoors, decomposition would have been advanced."

"She was still wearing a medical bracelet for a penicillin allergy, which has her name on it." He took a deep breath. "You're right, there wasn't much of anything else identifiable."

Olivia had seen decomposing bodies weeks, months, and even years after death. They were difficult, emotionally, to work with. To see what death did to the human body always brought to mind one's own mortality. Or, in this case, the mortality of loved ones.

"I contacted the sheriff down in Bellevue," Sheriff Rodgers continued, "and he said he'd see the family tonight. The coroner will confirm her identity—we already have dental records as part of the missing persons case."

"No one saw anything?" Zack asked. "Back when she went missing?"

Rodgers shook his head. "She wandered down to the shoreline, promised she'd stay out of the water, and it was a quiet Sunday morning."

"Alone?" Olivia asked, incredulous.

"The island is safe, Agent St. Martin. We get a lot of families here on the weekend. Few problems. Nothing like this."

No place is safe from those who hunt children.

"Safe." She snapped out the word, the familiar tension bubbling under her skin as she fought her emotions.

Who was safe? Surely not innocent children, the most vulnerable in society, the ones we should be protecting. No one thinks that the average-looking man down the beach is a killer under that kind face. Everyone expects evil to be obvious at first sight.

Don't they know evil looks like them? That sick perverts don't have "child predator" written across their face? That killers don't have "murderer" tattooed on their forehead?

"Olivia?"

It was Zack, breathing down her neck. Why did he come so close when she was ready to explode? She took a step away from him, a small step, but she felt him shift his stance. Ever since Olivia learned Missy's killer was still at large, her emotions refused to stay contained. They fought the steel box she'd locked them in years ago, hammering away until the pounding was almost unbearable.

"Liv?" Zack's voice was low. The sheriff had turned his back to them and was giving instructions to a deputy. "Are you okay?"

She made the mistake of looking into his eyes. They were assessing her, probing her, trying to see through the layers of control she'd painstakingly built over the years. Zack had a tough edge about him, his entire body on the verge of movement even when standing still. His square jaw covered with stubble and the hard lines of his face made him look far more formidable than his dark eyes, which watched her with concern and warmth.

"I'm okay," she mumbled, tearing herself from his steady gaze. Taking stock of the crime scene, she let the emotions fade away and put her control firmly in place.

The familiar ritual of evidence collection grounded her. She took a deep breath, gathered her strength, and tried to forget that Zack was still watching her. She could feel his eyes on the back of her neck.

She watched as a woman, not much taller than she, squatted to photograph possible evidence. The flash of the lightbulb comforted her. Familiar. Though she now worked primarily in the lab, at the beginning of her career, when she'd been a field agent, she'd been assigned to the Evidence Response Team out of the San Francisco field office. She'd worked some big cases. A cross-jurisdictional serial killer her largest.

But that was ancient history. She joined the Quantico lab nine years ago, leaving the FBI and fieldwork after only a year. Sometimes she missed it, like now, watching trained professionals doing their job. She wanted to be with them.

Right. She didn't work well in a team unit, which was why she'd joined the lab. True, it could be considered a promotion, and with her Ph.D. and science background, the lab was a better fit for her anyway. But had she functioned better in the group she would never have left the FBI. She found it hard to open up to others, and when you worked closely with the same eight or ten people in a high-stress operation, you needed to be able to relax, let off steam, shoot the breeze. Not Olivia. Ever. And the stress of keeping up her defenses almost tore her apart.

Quantico was better. Less interpersonal pressure, more independence. Solitary work, just her and the evidence. That was what Olivia was best at. Depending on herself to get the job done. Not on anyone else.

Olivia realized that Zack and the sheriff had been talking to each other for the past several minutes. She focused on the conversation.

"Since the coroner is downtown, do you want me to handle the autopsy?" Zack was asking the sheriff.

"Fine," Rodgers agreed. "I'm sending my crime team to the Seattle lab with the evidence, instead of to the state lab. What's mine is yours."

"Likewise."

They shook hands in agreement.

"What's the Federal interest?" Rodgers asked Olivia, but he glanced at Zack.

"We suspect that this killer has been active in several other states for many years," she said. "It took time to connect the dots, particularly since there were suspects for some of the crimes."

"Do you—" Rodgers began, then shut his mouth as he gestured downslope at the approach of Vince Kirby.

Zack turned in the same direction. "Aw, shit," he muttered. "How the hell did he find out about this so soon?"

"Not from my unit," Rodgers said, disgusted. "But I wouldn't put it past him to have a spy somewhere inside."

The sheriff was probably right, Zack thought. The reporter had too much inside information printed in his rag to just be lucky. He had people on the inside, probably more than one. Bastard.

Kirby smiled at them, looking a little too long at Olivia, who was shivering in her heels and standing dangerously close to the searchlights. To keep warm, no doubt. Zack wanted to give her his jacket again, but he sensed she'd balk at the offer.

"This is a crime scene, Kirby," Zack said.

Kirby stopped just on the other side of the bright yellow police tape and smiled like the Cheshire Cat, his features oddly shadowed and blue under the fringe of the lamps. "That's pretty obvious."

"What are you doing here?" Zack jammed his fists into his pockets, primarily to keep from decking Kirby. Every time the condescending prick approached, Zack itched to wipe the smirk off his long, narrow face with one well-placed blow.

But every time he wanted to hit Kirby, he wondered if it was because he blamed him for Amy's death, or because he blamed himself.

"I'd think that would be obvious, too." Kirby looked beyond them to where the crime-scene techs were finishing up their job. "Same guy?"

"No comment," Sheriff Rodgers said. "I'll be issuing a statement in the morning. Feel free to come by headquarters about eleven."

"Hmm." Kirby pulled out his notepad and pencil. "Let's see—Detective Zack Travis out of his jurisdiction. Young girl's body found. Blonde, or so my sources tell me." He looked at Olivia and grinned. "Well, Travis, bringing your dates with you to murder sites. Didn't know that was in the manual. But you've obviously moved up a notch. This one looks like she can read beyond 'See Dick Run.'"

Zack pulled his hands from his pockets and took a step forward. "Get out of here, Kirby."

"I need a statement."

"I'll give you—" Zack took a deep breath when he felt a firm hand on his forearm. Almost as quickly as Olivia had touched him, she pulled back, but the quiet power of her pressure halted his momentum enough to realize Kirby was baiting him.

He couldn't let Kirby get to him. The past was the past; he couldn't see Amy's face every time he looked at her boyfriend. Sometimes, though, it was damn hard to forget and leave the past alone, especially when it made him bleed.

The sheriff stepped between him and Kirby. "I'll give you a statement away from the crime scene," Sheriff Rodgers said.

"But I think—"

"I don't care what you think, Kirby. I will not tolerate contamination of my evidence by having you here. Take it or leave it."

Kirby glanced at Zack, then Olivia. He winked. "When you're done with Detective 'Make-My-Day'

Travis, come by the paper and I'll show you how a real man treats a lady."

Zack shifted uneasily and glanced at Olivia. The last thing he wanted splashed across the front page of the paper was that the Feds were involved in the investigation. And Kirby wouldn't let it stop there. He'd lambaste the police department, the sheriff's department, and everyone else in between.

Olivia didn't say a word. She arched a single eyebrow at Kirby, her expression cool, detached, and disapproving. It was Kirby who squirmed under her visual reprimand, and Zack couldn't help but be impressed at the power Olivia wielded with a simple look.

Kirby cleared his throat. "I'll come by the station tomorrow, Travis. Still on swing shift, right?"

"Talk to the chief, Kirby. I have nothing to say to you."

"Right." He winked at Olivia. "I was just teasing you, you know. Travis's bark is worse than his bite. You could do a lot worse than him."

What the hell was that supposed to mean? Zack wondered. Kirby being *nice*?

"Let's go." Sheriff Rodgers led Kirby over the rocky ground to where they'd parked at the clearing below.

"Thanks for not saying anything," Zack told Olivia, though he was still trying to figure out if Kirby was playing some sort of game where he didn't know the rules.

"I have nothing to say to a reporter." She sounded irritated.

"What's wrong?"

She looked up at him, her face impassive. "Give

me a little credit, Detective. The last thing I want is the press to focus on my presence instead of what's important.

"And what's important now is finding this killer before another child dies."

Brian Hall stared at his reflection in the filthy, scratched mirror of his pathetic apartment. The bitches next door were going at it again, screaming at each other, using language Brian had learned only after being in prison. Bitch One, the chick who looked like a dyke, had lost her job as a busboy—busgirl?—and Bitch Two, the druggie, wanted money for her fix.

The mirror shook when something metal hit the common wall, and Brian wanted to go over there and pummel the two bitches into silence.

How could he think? How could he plan with the two of them going at it all the fucking time? At least in prison there was silence. Anything above normal conversation could get you dinged. Yeah, there were fights that broke out time and again, but at night—like now—it was usually quiet. Peaceful.

Brian put his hands on the wobbly dresser and peered closer at his face. He was old. His life was over. His face looked tired, his blue eyes too pale. Bloodshot, too, because he hadn't been sleeping so good. He ran a hand over his buzz cut. He'd gone down and paid ten bucks to the barber—ten bucks!—for the cut. He had to. His hairline was receding and the shorter his hair, the less he noticed how little he had. In prison he hadn't cared.

His mouth had turned into a perpetual scowl. He tried to smile at his reflection, but it was no more than a sneer.

He had no life. No one would hire him, except as a busboy in some greasy restaurant where the slop people actually paid for was worse than prison food.

No one gave him the time of day. It didn't matter that he'd been proven innocent. He'd been in the joint for three decades. No one really *believed* he was innocent.

He closed his eyes, and when he opened them he stared at the top of the scuffed dresser. The dull blued steel of the .38 glinted at him in the artificial lamplight. He'd bought it off the street behind his god-awful dive apartment. He was shocked at how easy the deal went.

He picked up the gun with shaky hands and stared down the barrel. "My life is over," he said, his voice hollow and tinny.

He put the gun in his mouth, the metallic taste making him cringe. Tears streamed down his face. His entire body shook as his right hand curved around the gun in order for his index finger to reach the trigger. It felt awkward. Wrong.

But slowly he depressed the trigger. He felt the hammer pull back as the trigger reached the halfway point. It resisted, as if the gun itself told him wait, don't do it, and then . . .

Click.

The gun was empty; he hadn't loaded it. Sinking to the floor, he sobbed.

His mother was scared of him, but he blamed that on his cousin Toby. He had no home, no friends. Nothing was as it had been when he went to prison.

Angry, he wiped the tears from his face. Look what that bitch had turned him into! A whiny, sniveling old man.

"Stupid cunt, I'll kill you!" Another piece of furniture hit the wall next door as the bitches continued to rant.

Pathetic. He was *pathetic*, sitting on the threadbare carpet that might have been beige years before, but was now brown from years of *pathetic* losers like him living in this *pathetic* flat.

Retribution. He had to do something to the people who'd destroyed his life. But what? What could he do to pay them back for the life they'd stolen from him?

He slowly stood and shuffled over to the lopsided Formica-topped table in the corner that passed for a kitchen with a pitiful refrigerator that didn't keep beer cold and a two-burner stove top. A journal rested on the table, a ninety-nine-cent spiral-bound pad he'd picked up at the supermarket. Ninety-nine cents for this little piece-of-crap notebook with forty pages in it.

He sat at the solitary chair and placed the gun carefully in front of him. Turning the page, he stared at the names of the people who had framed him.

Hamilton Craig. Damn attorney. Not only did he convict him, he argued six times against paroling him. Brian couldn't find his home address, but he learned the asshole was *the* district attorney for the county. Brian knew exactly where he worked, and he'd never forget what the bastard looked like.

Gary Porter. The cop was retired, and Brian couldn't find his address either, but he had an idea: First, take care of Hamilton Craig. Then follow the cop home from the funeral. If he was lucky, that bitch would be there too.

The bitch who started it all: *Olivia St. Martin.*

If it weren't for her, he'd never have gone to prison in the first place. She lied to the cops, said she'd seen him take her sister, which was bullshit because he hadn't. He didn't give a rat's ass that she was a little kid at the time; she had still lied, and that's that. She would have to pay big time, the icy bitch. For the accusations every time she came to oppose his parole—like it was his fault her stupid mother had killed herself. She even said once that he should have been dead.

"Had justice truly been served, this man wouldn't be sitting here today; he would be buried in the cold ground after receiving a lethal injection."

Oh, yes, he had plans for Ms. St. Martin.

First he'd take care of the damn attorney, then the cop.

He would save the best for last. Olivia St. Martin would be sorry she'd ever lied about him.

She would pay for her crimes.

CHAPTER
10

Olivia hated autopsies, but she'd always held her own in the few she had observed. Sheer will to control her emotions enabled her to maintain a calm demeanor while watching the coroner take apart and put back together a dead human body.

She'd never witnessed the autopsy of a child, but she would remain a professional. A scientist. She could do this for Jillian Reynolds and Missy and all the victims of whom the press now called *The Seattle Slayer*.

She took a deep breath and glanced at Zack. He stared straight ahead at the door through which the coroner would emerge. His face was all hard angles and rigid, as if he, too, were waging an internal battle.

If a man as strong and experienced as Zack Travis was having a difficult time in this room, how could she hope to observe, to be impartial?

The doors opened and a small, elderly Asian man wheeled in a stainless steel gurney. He was followed by an attractive woman, tall, with dark hair pulled back in a band. The woman nodded at Zack and gave him a half-smile. It was easier for Olivia to watch that exchange and wonder how they knew each other than it was for her to look at the white sheet draped over the small body.

The woman started laying out instruments while the man wrote in a log. The doors opened again, and a rotund, white-haired man who reminded Olivia of a short Santa Claus burst in, nodding to his staff as he crossed over to where she and Zack stood.

"Detective Travis." They shook hands. Even without smiling, the coroner looked jovial.

"Dr. Sparks, this is Agent St. Martin with the FBI."

Dr. Sparks took her small hand in both of his. "We'll get started here in a moment." He looked from her to Zack. "This isn't a pretty sight. We cleaned up the body the best we could—I sent what we've already collected to Doug at the lab—but the victim is in an advanced stage of decomposition."

"Let's get it over with," Zack said.

Olivia wanted to stay. She wanted to see what the bastard had done to Jillian Reynolds. But as soon as Dr. Sparks removed the sheet, she had to leave.

"I'm sorry," she mumbled to Zack and ran out the door.

She was almost outside the building when Zack caught up with her. "Olivia."

She couldn't look at him. What must he think of her? Wholly unprofessional. But if she had stayed, she wouldn't have been able to control her reaction, and that was simply unacceptable.

"I'm sorry," she repeated.

He clasped her shoulder, forcing her to face him. She thought she'd see frustration or anger or something in his eyes that showed he knew she was a fraud.

Instead, she saw deep compassion.

"Liv," he said softly, using her nickname. "It's okay. I understand. Take a walk. I'll meet you right here in an hour."

She nodded, afraid that if she spoke her voice would crack.

She left the building and walked briskly along the street busy with noontime traffic. All she wanted was to get away from the building, get away from death.

Don't think about it. Don't think about what Jillian now looks like.

For a brief moment she wondered if the body would haunt her for the rest of her life. How could she be a scientist—a witness to many autopsies, dead bodies, and horrid crime-scene photos—yet be derailed by one victim?

Who am I? Who have I become?

Minutes later, she slowed her pace, not knowing how far she'd walked. She stood near a fountain outside a building she suspected was City Hall. Lunchtime walkers in skirts and tennis shoes strolled briskly around her in pairs or threesomes, chatting while burning calories. It was a lovely autumn day. Perfect, warm with a light breeze and clear blue skies.

A perfect day? Hardly. A nine-year-old girl lay in a cold autopsy room down the block. A child who would never again enjoy an autumn day.

She sat on a bench in front of the fountain and stared at the dancing water.

She'd been five when Missy had been killed, and she remembered her feelings of fear and helplessness more than any details of the actual abduction.

The tattoo. She'd never forget the tattoo. The blue eagle still gave her nightmares, the way it rippled under Hall's muscles, the way it bulged as if about to take flight . . .

Not Hall. Someone else. Another killer. Had Hall known him? It seemed far too much of a coincidence that Hall's truck had been used and that he had the same tattoo as Missy's killer. A blue eagle wasn't uncommon, but still—two young men in the same town connected through Hall's truck? She wasn't convinced that Hall hadn't been involved—it was his truck, that evidence was certain. She'd reread the police report on Missy's murder several times since Hall was released. Missy's blood was definitely found in his truck. Carpet fibers from his floor mats were on her clothing.

Missy had been there. But had Hall been involved in her kidnapping? Or was he the victim of circumstance?

Her cell phone melody startled her and she groped in her purse for the phone. Greg.

"Hi. Everything okay?" she asked.

"I got the DNA sample. Thanks for putting it on a plane; it gave us another day. I'll start the tests tonight. It'll take a couple of days, but I'll get you the results as soon as possible."

Most people who watched television thought they understood DNA profiling, but in truth it was a complicated and time-consuming process. Large portions of a single person's DNA are actually the same as every other person's DNA simply because they are human beings. But certain fragments of DNA are unique to each individual, and those are what scientists needed to build a unique genetic profile.

But the genetic profile was only one small, though important, step. They still needed a suspect with whom to compare the profile.

"Run them against any DNA profiles from those old cases," she said. They had run the DNA profile from Missy's case against known offenders in CODIS as soon as they got it two weeks ago, but there were no matches. The guy had never been put into the system. But while Olivia was out in Seattle, Greg was working his own contacts to see if there were any other profiles created at the local level that hadn't, for one reason or another, been input into CODIS.

"I'd planned to."

"It'll just be one more confirmation when we finally find him. I don't want him getting off."

"I know my job, Olivia."

Greg sounded irritated. "I'm sorry," she said, feeling guilty all over again that she'd put him in this position.

He sighed. "Be careful, Liv, okay? I'm worried about you."

"I know you are, but so far it's going okay. Chief Pierson didn't bat an eye when I walked in yesterday. And I'm working directly with the detective in charge. Another body has been found, three months old." She gave Greg the brief summary of Jillian Reynolds's disappearance and discovery. "It's probably the same guy. Detective Travis is in the autopsy right now."

"How's the lab there? Competent?"

"Very. There's a state crime lab, but Seattle has its own lab as well and they've prioritized this case. I checked it out yesterday and they haven't neglected anything that I could see." Her phone beeped and she glanced at the caller-ID window, not recognizing the number but noting a Seattle area code. Was Zack already done with the autopsy? "I have to go, Greg. I'll check in when I have news."

"Be careful," he repeated, then hung up.

"Olivia St. Martin," she answered.

"Liv! It's Miranda."

Her heart quickened. Why would Miranda be calling her? Did she know she was in Seattle?

"Miranda—this is a surprise."

"Quinn and I just got back from our belated honeymoon and heard about Hall being released. I'm so sorry."

Olivia's mind processed the information. That's right. Their honeymoon had been cut short last June when Quinn had been called out on a critical investigation. She'd worked some of the blood evidence in the lab for him in a multistate shooting spree. Olivia vaguely remembered reading Miranda's e-mail about them heading to the Caribbean a couple of weeks ago.

She tensed. Quinn Peterson was assigned to the FBI's Seattle office. But he couldn't possibly know she was here. Could he? Would Chief Pierson have called to verify her credentials with the local field office, instead of relying on Greg's phone call and contact information? She didn't think so; he'd appeared cordial and seemed to believe every word she said.

"Liv? You there?"

She shook her head to clear her thoughts. "Yes, sorry, I was in the middle of something." Lying. To her best friend. Her empty stomach felt queasy. It was one thing to ask Greg to break the rules for her; it was another to put Quinn Peterson in the position of having to lie to his boss.

"Sorry to bother you, I'm sure you're busy, but I had to call and make sure you were okay. Quinn said Hall's attorney challenged the DNA and proved Hall hadn't, um . . ." Miranda's voice trailed off.

"No, he didn't rape Missy."

Olivia had a strong urge to tell Miranda where she was and what she was doing. She was in over her head. Intensely loyal, Miranda would keep her secret.

"I'm so sorry," Miranda repeated. "Do the police have any leads? What's the FBI doing?"

Her questions were to be expected, but Olivia didn't know how to answer. "Um, I don't know."

"Is the FBI doing what?" Olivia heard Quinn say in the background.

He was there. There was no way Olivia could talk about her activities now. And it wasn't fair to ask Miranda to keep such a secret from her husband, an FBI agent. No, that would be putting her in a compromising position, and the last thing Olivia wanted was to come between Quinn and Miranda. Miranda had been through so much adversity in her life, she deserved happiness with a man who so obviously loved her.

"Thanks for calling," Olivia said. "I appreciate your concern. But I'm okay. Really."

"Have you spoken with the police in California? Do they have any other leads?"

"I spoke with Hamilton Craig, the attorney who prosecuted Hall. He's of course reopening the case. But it's cold. I don't think they have the resources to pursue it." She shifted on her feet, relieved Miranda couldn't see her. She'd know she wasn't telling the whole truth.

"Ask about . . ." Quinn's voice cut out in the background.

"Quinn wants to know if the DNA from Missy's case was put into CODIS now that it's an active case and if he can do anything—hell, let me put him on and you two can talk shop."

"No, really," Olivia said quickly, "I have to get back to work. I trust the people working the case, but it's cold and I've accepted that."

"But—"

"I'll call you later, when things are less hectic."

"O-kay," Miranda said slowly. "Take care of yourself. And Liv—"

"What?"

"I love you."

The room was too cold. A deep silence permeated the atmosphere, as if the building itself were holding its breath, interrupted only by the clink of metal instruments on a metal tray.

Zack felt alternately ill and enraged during the autopsy of Jillian Reynolds. He watched without comment, his jaw tight. He'd attended many autopsies—never feeling completely comfortable, but it was part of the job and he did it without complaint. He'd never get used to the smell, but he'd normally banter with the pathologist and feign interest in what the old coot was doing.

Not now. Not with the little girl. No one spoke, not Zack, not Doc Sparks, and not his assistants.

Time dragged, but only seventy minutes had passed from beginning to end and Zack had everything he needed. Cause of death: multiple stabbings in the chest and abdomen. Death had blessedly come quickly, but not before the sexual assault.

Zack had never wanted a killer more than this one.

They had one bit of good news: a possible DNA sample. No semen, but three pubic hairs with nubs. There was no way of knowing if they had degraded to the point where the DNA was unrecognizable, but it was at least something to work with. He told Sparks that Doug Cohn would send someone over to pick them up once he had them prepared for transportation.

He hoped Olivia's ex-husband was the good guy she seemed to think he was and wouldn't balk at rushing another set of tests. He couldn't help but wonder what had happened to make him an ex-husband.

"Doc Sparks, were there any marks on her right forearm, like in the Benedict and Davidson cases?"

"There's not enough left of the skin and muscle tissue to tell. The abrasions in the other cases were shallow. There's just no way of knowing if the killer left the same marks on this victim. But I did confirm that her hair was cut. I'll write that up in the report."

"Thanks."

As Doc Sparks cleaned up, Zack left the autopsy room. He didn't find Olivia in the lobby. He ran a hand over his rough face and realized he'd neglected to shave this morning, a common occurrence, especially when he worked a difficult case.

He wished he could have said something more to Olivia to let her know that it was okay that she hadn't stayed. The pain in her eyes was unmistakable, before she got herself under control. There was no way he could blame her for her reaction, yet Olivia had such a strong backbone he was surprised she hadn't stood her ground just to prove to him that she was a tough cop.

That alone intrigued him. There was definitely more to Olivia St. Martin than a pretty face and sharp intellect.

Stop it, Zack. No sense trying to figure out Superagent. She made it perfectly clear with her body language that she didn't want anyone to get close to her. But he had to admit she was growing on him. There was so much pent-up energy in that petite body of hers; she rippled with it. He doubted she even noticed the way she constantly tucked her hair behind her ears, pulled on her lobes, or fidgeted with the single ring on her right hand.

Where was she? He was a little worried. Not that she couldn't take care of herself. He glanced at his watch. He'd give her five minutes, then try to find her. She could simply be in the ladies' room.

Movement from the front of the building caught Zack's attention, and he looked at the double glass doors that led outside. Olivia St. Martin opened one side and stepped through. She blinked, adjusting to the artificial light. Her skin was pale. Too pale. Her hand brushed against her ear, tucking her hair behind it, though immediately a few strands fell forward. As she saw him across the lobby, she straightened and steeled her jaw, her face losing the softness she'd entered with.

"I apologize for my unprofessional behavior," Olivia said as she approached. "I shouldn't have left."

The feelings simmering beneath Olivia's cool mask were almost tangible, but she fought to prevent him from seeing anything. Why did she feel the need to keep such tight control over her emotions? If he didn't release his frustration at the gym every morning, he'd be a bear all day. The job was demanding; you took release where you could get it.

"I told you I understood. You don't have to put on a tough-girl act for me." He paused, awkward. "I've known strong men to break down at the sight of a child on that table."

She sighed and attempted a smile, but avoided his comment completely when she asked, "Did the exam yield anything useful?"

"Pubic hair. Doc Sparks is preparing it to be transported. Do you think your ex-husband would rush another sample?" He tried to make light of it, but Olivia was in no mood for humor.

She turned her back to him and started toward the exit. "I'll call Greg and tell him to expect it. Have Doug send it to the same place. We have time to overnight it, because even if we put it on a plane again it wouldn't get there until late tonight." She paused, glanced at him. "It's the same guy, though." It wasn't a question.

"No doubt." Zack frowned and followed her out the door. He technically wasn't on duty until four, but he'd already put in dozens of overtime hours, half of which he hadn't logged.

He caught up with her in three strides. "What happened on the case you worked? Where the wrong guy was put in prison?"

She jerked, almost imperceptibly, but Zack was watching her very closely. Definite sore spot with her.

"The police found blood evidence in his truck that tied him to the girl's murder," she said momentarily. "He lied about his alibi—said he was at a bar, but when that didn't hold water he changed his story to being home alone sleeping off a day of drinking. He was convicted largely on circumstantial evidence, but the evidence coupled with his lies to police—it was an easy call for the jury." She rounded the corner toward where he'd parked after picking her up from her hotel.

"And then?"

"He got an attorney who learned there was a DNA sample from the killer and had his compared, which proved he hadn't . . ." She stopped talking but refused to look at him as she strode down the sidewalk. She cleared her throat. "He didn't rape the victim."

"And they let him out? Just like that?"

"The D.A. realized that their case was compromised by the new evidence. He may have been involved, but the remaining evidence was circumstantial. There was nothing that *proved* he killed her."

"Why hadn't the DNA been compared earlier? That's standard procedure."

"It's an old case."

Old case? How old? For at least the last ten years, longer in many places, DNA testing had been commonplace. Zack glanced at her profile as they crossed the street to where he'd parked his police-issue sedan. On the surface she looked young. He'd thought thirty or so when he first saw her. Soft, delicate skin, shiny hair, slender curvy frame. But now he noticed fine wrinkles around her eyes, a slight weariness to her expression. The way she held herself showed a maturity that most women never learned to possess. She must be older than he thought. Thirty-five? Older? Maybe the case was the first she'd worked on. She'd blown it, took it personally, was on a vendetta—

"You're not going to play vigilante, are you? Trying to right some wrong you think you did with the evidence in that old case? Because I'm not going to sit back and let the Feds screw up this investigation. I want this guy. Bad. But I want him by the book. I don't want the bastard to walk because of a tainted investigation."

She abruptly stopped walking and turned to him, her hands fisted at her sides. Her entire body reverberated in restrained anger. "This murderer has eluded justice for more than thirty years; I will do nothing to jeopardize a conviction. No one wants this killer more than me, Detective Travis. I'm sorry you have a problem with the FBI, but don't take it out on me!"

She stormed off, stopping only when she reached his car.

Oh, yeah. Something was definitely going on. And Zack would damn well find out what it was.

Olivia didn't know what had gotten into her. She never lashed out in anger. But her entire body felt like a tightly wound coil, ready to spring, shooting her emotions in all directions.

It had to be seeing Jillian Reynolds on the table. Just for a moment, but it had unnerved her. She had thought—for a split second—it was Missy lying there. About to be cut open by the coroner.

Then talking to Miranda—lying to her best friend—and knowing she and Quinn were in town. Why'd the killer have to strike in Seattle? The one place she actually had friends? She wouldn't be surprised if Miranda hadn't believed her when she said she was fine. After all, she was the world's worst liar. Even over the phone.

She hated the deception. She wanted to tell Zack the truth. But if she did, there was no way he'd let her be a part of the investigation. He might even call Rick Stockton and have her fired. It would be within his rights. She'd misrepresented herself, misrepresented her assignment, and if this precarious house of cards fell before they found the killer——

No. She couldn't think that way. They would find him. They had to.

Feelings of responsibility and remorse squeezed her soul until she could barely breathe. If it hadn't been for her testimony thirty-four years ago, the police wouldn't have closed the case. And maybe, just maybe, the real killer would have been caught.

CHAPTER
11

Zack didn't question Olivia about her outburst outside the coroner's office, which seemed a little too impassioned to be a lecture on justice. It was personal. He wondered exactly how personal this case was to her.

By the time they got back to the station, Zack had other things on his mind. He went to track down Boyd and find out what was going on with the trucks while Olivia excused herself to the conference room.

Boyd was still comparing the list of Expedition owners with the list of Dodge owners, but he was making progress.

"When or if you get a match, take Jan O'Neal with you to do the interviews," Zack told him.

"You want *me* to check them out?" Boyd asked.

Why did he look so shocked? This was why Zack didn't think he made a good FTO. Maybe he didn't give Boyd enough positive reinforcement. The kid had done a good job so far, and Zack saw promise in him—if he stopped second-guessing himself and lost his over-eager puppy demeanor.

"Yes," he said. "But not alone. You know what to look for, and O'Neal is a good cop." One of the most meticulous on the force. Boyd could learn from her.

He glanced at the clock on the wall. "Agent St.

Martin and I are going to talk to the two witnesses in Benedict's abduction, see if they remember anything else about the guy they saw, but I'm not holding my breath."

"Because kids start making things up," Boyd said.

"Right. But the first time we talked to them, there was a lot of emotion. Maybe time will help in this case."

"Is everything going okay with the agent?" Boyd asked.

"Better than I had hoped. We're going to review each case she brought with her and see if we can spot any additional patterns. Stop by the conference room—I'll have some follow-up work to do contacting other jurisdictions that I'll need your help with."

Zack's next stop was Doug Cohn's lab. The lab director was bent over a microscope. Zack waited, impatient but not wanting to rush him. Finally, he walked over.

Without looking up, Cohn said, "I don't have anything new, but I did get the pubic hair off to Agent St. Martin's contact at the FBI lab. Normally I wouldn't think they'd get it done any faster than us, but she seemed adamant they'd jump on it."

"Thanks. Look, I know you're swamped, but I have a favor."

"If it's about this case, anything you want." Cohn looked up from the microscope.

Zack handed him the list of cities Olivia had given him earlier. "Can you contact each of these departments and see if you can get any information about the marks on the forearm?"

"Those been bugging you, too? Was Gil able to get anything off the Reynolds body?"

Zack shook his head. "There wasn't enough soft tissue left."

"I'll see what I can do. Anything else you want me to find out?"

"Sure, the killer's name and address."

"Ha. Look, I'll feel out the labs and see what they have."

"Good, I'll be in the conference room. I'm going to call Nashville and find out why they haven't sent the information about the tattoo, then start down the list and talk to the detectives in charge and get copies of all the files.

"Maybe," Zack said over his shoulder as he left the lab, "we'll get a lucky break."

He swung open the door of the conference room and he said, "Liv, I have Cohn working—"

Olivia was standing on a chair in her stocking feet, on her tiptoes, as she wrote across the top of the white board. She startled at the sound of his voice and the chair went out from under her. She landed unceremoniously on her butt.

Zack took two strides and helped her up. At first, Olivia looked indignant, then she smiled sheepishly. "I guess standing on chairs isn't the smartest thing to do, but short people do what they must to even the scales."

She moved away from him and Zack looked at what she'd written across the top. "Dates?" he said.

Listed under the current year in neat block letters were the three Seattle victims: Jillian, Jennifer, and Michelle. Next to each girl's name was her age, date of abduction, likely time of death, and when her body was found. Olivia had apparently done the same thing for all the victims in nine other states, but there was missing information—specifically, time of death. She'd put her guess in a different color marker.

She had moved the map and the victim's photographs from the corkboard and taped everything on the white board, so all information about the case could be viewed at once.

Zack shrugged out of his blazer and tossed it across a chair in the corner. Some detectives wore ties; he wasn't one of them. Dockers and a black T-shirt was his preferred uniform. The blazer was primarily to conceal his shoulder holster.

"It appears you were right," Zack said. "His last three victims are clustered together, while the first victim is at least a month before."

She frowned.

"What?" he prompted.

"Well, I've a feeling there's something about these first victims that's different than the others. But I don't see what."

Zack looked at the dates on the wall. "Let's talk this out. The guy moves from state to state. Why? To avoid detection. How? Is he independently wealthy? In a job that moves around a lot? Sales maybe?"

Olivia shook her head. "I agree with the why, but the how? I'm thinking he doesn't need a lot of money to live on. He's single. Disciplined. Probably doesn't indulge in a lot of luxuries."

"But he's not living on the street."

"No. He's clean. Probably meticulous in his appearance. Has an honest face. That's why Jenny Benedict walked off with him. He doesn't look like he'd harm a fly."

"Maybe some sort of retail job? In a mall? Lots of

kids hang out at the mall, shop there with parents. Perfect hunting ground."

Olivia wrote notes on the board. *Occupation: Retail? Possibly mall.* "He'd be good with people, particularly women. Conversational. Probably sounds educated, can talk about a variety of subjects. Manipulative, but not obviously so."

Zack said, "If he moves every couple of years, he's probably not in a career where he'd need an established client base, like a lawyer or doctor. What about something with kids? Like a teacher?"

"Teacher. Maybe." She wrote it next to *Occupation* on the board. "Except . . ." She stopped. She didn't have any facts to back up her feelings. Maybe she was saying too much. Leading Zack down the wrong path. What if she made a mistake? What if they focused on a part of the investigation that gave them no results? What if they wasted precious time because of her feelings?

"Olivia?" Zack prompted.

"Teacher's a good idea. Kansas was the last place we know for sure he was. We can contact all the schools in Seattle, see if anyone transferred from Kansas."

"Not a bad idea, except you don't think he's a teacher."

"But maybe he is. We can't ignore your instincts."

"I'll get Boyd on it, but I want to know what you're thinking."

She bit the inside of her cheek. "I'm not a profiler, I don't know for sure—"

"Dammit, Olivia, I'm not a damn profiler either." He ran a hand through his hair and stared at the ceiling. She'd obviously said the wrong thing, but what?

"Look, stop second-guessing yourself." Zack said. "Just spill it. If it's a stupid thought, I'll forget you said it, okay? I thought we had this conversation already."

Olivia mentally slapped herself. She had to start acting like the seasoned FBI agent she'd led Zack into believing she was.

"No, I don't think he's a teacher," she said with conviction.

"Why?"

"Because I don't think he would be able to stop himself from touching the girls if he was surrounded by them every day."

Zack nodded. "Good point."

"But I think we should look into it."

"I will."

Olivia stared at the board. It was obvious now that the first victim was killed long before the remaining victims in the same city, but why?

"You might be on to something," Zack said a moment later.

"What?"

"Why he doesn't work with kids. You said it's because he wouldn't be able to keep his hands off the girls. He'd be discovered very quickly. So part of his discipline is to stay away from temptation."

"Makes sense."

"The first victim in each town is separated by time . . . what if his first kill is spontaneous? He's afraid he's made a mistake, and goes into hiding. Waits, makes sure the police don't know enough to find him. Also, look here . . ." Zack got up and grabbed the dry-erase marker from Olivia's hand. He did some math under each grouping of victims.

By the time he reached Texas, Olivia saw what he saw.

"The bodies of the first victims took longer to find." All the other victims were discovered within days. The first victims were discovered in weeks.

"He didn't hide them exactly, but he must have dumped the bodies in low-traffic areas," Zack said.

"Is there any way to get information from the other cities? Some of these cases are so old . . ."

"I'll get it." He glanced at his watch. "I didn't realize it was so late. I need to call Nashville about the tattoo—they were supposed to fax over the report." He picked up the phone.

"Can you get the entire file sent over?"

"I'll ask, but it might take a couple of days. It's been ten years."

While Zack talked to the cops in Nashville, Olivia studied the map. Jillian Reynolds's body was discovered within three miles of where she was last seen. According to Sheriff Rodgers, her mother and the police believed the girl had drowned and focused their attention on the beach areas, with only a secondary effort made to search the rest of the island. Olivia had read the report last night. The ferry videos had been monitored, with the thought that she might have run away, or just wanted to ride the ferry and maybe got lost, or that if there had been foul play, they would see her with a stranger.

None of that came to fruition, but by the next day they concluded she had likely drowned. The undertow was strong on that side of the island, and therefore she could have been dragged out to sea and her body would follow the current until she was washed ashore, miles away, or caught in a fishing net.

But the killer was methodical. He hadn't removed her from the island. He'd known about the video surveillance on the ferries and at the docks. Taking her in a private boat would have been dangerous. Especially since he'd abducted her in the morning.

"Zack," she said.

"Excuse me," he mumbled into the phone. "What?"

She shook her head. "I forgot you were on the phone."

"What?" he repeated.

"Jillian was abducted on the island and found on the island. It stands to reason she was killed on the island. It's not a big place. We need to find out if she was stabbed to death there in the woods. If not . . ."

"The killer had a place to keep her."

She nodded.

Zack finished up his conversation with Nashville and hung up the phone. "They're still looking for all the records, but will send what they have. They're faxing the reports and sending a copy of the entire file. Now let me call Doug Cohn and get him on the soil analysis ASAP. I'm going to owe him big-time when this case is over."

Jenny Benedict had lived in Sahalee, an upper-middle-class neighborhood. Ten years ago, the area was little more than open space and gentlemen's ranches; now young families seeking safety for their children and a quiet environment had built up dozens of home developments.

Olivia watched lawn after perfect lawn roll by, all identical green rectangles. Grand, two-story homes indistinguishable but for their alternating faces of brick, stone, or wood. Children rode bikes, though Olivia noted parents stood in attendance. A child had been abducted and killed from this very neighborhood that should have been safe. Parents were more vigilant. For a while, at least.

But one thing was certain: A stranger would stand out in this neighborhood. This killer didn't. He looked like one of them. Watching for the perfect opportunity to act out his sick fantasies. Waiting for the perfect opportunity to kill.

"You okay?" he asked.

Olivia glanced at him. He didn't look comfortable, but she didn't know if it was because he was too large to be comfortable in the midsized sedan or because he had to face Jenny Benedict's friends and parents.

"Olivia?" he asked again.

"I'm fine," she said.

"Really." He glanced pointedly at her hands, then back at the road.

She quickly unclasped her hands, which had been clenched together as she internalized the rage over what had happened to Jenny Benedict. She smoothed down her skirt and stared straight ahead, consciously remembering to keep her hands apart.

Zack parked in front of one of the larger homes in the subdivision, its brick-and-stucco exterior similar to that of the other houses.

"I asked that the two witnesses meet here to make it easier on the girls," he said. "I already took their statements separately, but I want to see if they remember anything else. They were both emotional at the time. After this I need to check in with Michelle Davidson's parents. They've been calling the station for updates." He ran a hand over the thick dark stubble on his face. "I don't know what to tell them. We're following up on every lead we can find, but each one is a thin thread."

Olivia reached out and lightly touched his arm with her fingertips. The gesture felt awkward. She'd never been good at consoling anyone. "You're doing everything you can. They'll see it in your eyes."

His dark eyes held hers. An unusual, strange feeling crept into her stomach. A fluttering. She swallowed involuntarily as she realized she was attracted to Zack. She'd easily put romance and sex at the bottom of her priority list. Bottom? Were they even on the list? After her amicable divorce from Greg, she no longer cared. The divorce had been a relief.

She still recognized this rare feeling. It went deeper than physical attraction. She'd noted when she first met him that Zack Travis was sexy in that dark, arrogant cop kind of way. He filled any room with the power of his personality, his mere presence, which had little to do with his build and everything to do with his raw appeal.

But the real attraction was his deep compassion for victims and dogged belief that good police work would catch the bad guys, that he was doing everything possible to bring justice for the survivors. Watching him think and question and care touched her heart.

She turned away. Unnerved, she reached for the door handle to get out of the suddenly too-small car when he grabbed her arm. She froze. She wanted to jerk away and tell him she didn't like people touching her, but something stopped her. He held her firmly, then eased up as if he sensed her fear.

His fingers caressed her bare arm, his touch surprisingly soft, sensitive, intimate. A complete contradiction to his gruff demeanor. She resisted the urge to lean into his touch and she shivered.

She didn't dare look at him, her emotions too close to the surface. He'd see how conflicted she was, how needy. How he jumbled her thoughts and feelings and confused her.

"Look at me," he said.

She shook her head ever so slightly as she swallowed, gathering every ounce of control he so easily made her lose.

"Olivia."

Taking a deep breath, she faced him. His expression had loosened somehow, lost the usual hard edge. All she could think about was burying her face in his broad chest and letting him hold her. His presence was so strong, so all-encompassing, for a brief moment she believed he could protect her not only from her nightmares, but from all the evil in the world.

Impossible. But her lip quivered, aching to taste him, and she bit it. What in the world was she thinking?

"What makes you tick?"

Her eyes widened. Where had that question come from? What did he want to know? Why?

"Justice," she whispered. She cleared her throat. Go back to business. She had to rid herself of these unwelcome thoughts about Zack Travis. He was a cop investigating a murder. That was all.

He moved his head ever so slightly back and forth, holding her gaze. His eyes were bottomless, deep and probing. "I don't think so."

She broke eye contact, unsettled by the exchange, and pulled her arm from his grasp. She opened the car door. "I don't care what you think," she snapped and jumped out, slamming the door behind her, desperate to put distance between them and regain control.

Zack watched Olivia stride to the mailbox and stop. She wasn't looking at him, but she was most certainly thinking about him. And he was thinking about her. He'd been so close to kissing her. Kissing? Hell, he would have devoured her. The way she looked at him, it wasn't simple lust. There was a complexity of feelings buried beneath the controlled posture. He wanted to unwrap her and find out why she was so uptight, why she didn't share anything about herself, why she didn't like being touched. He wanted to hold her, thaw her. The cold personality was a façade; he'd seen her wrestle with her emotions. He sensed she burned from within but kept her feelings locked up tight.

He wondered what would happen if he found the key.

He got out of the car and kicked the door shut. Olivia St. Martin was hiding something, and while he found her sexy as hell, his number-one concern was the investigation. What could she possibly be hiding? She'd seemed so forthcoming at the lab, working with him and the evidence, her methodical notes on the white board—not at all like the woman who'd just vacated the car.

When he'd first met Superagent yesterday in Pierson's office, he thought he had her all figured out. Now he had to admit he didn't know what was going on with her. He remembered her reaction outside the coroner's office. At the time he thought it was a personal issue, but while they worked together in the conference room she was all professional.

She was hiding something—but was it personal or professional? Or both?

He caught up with her at the mailbox at the end of the path leading to the house.

"If you're hiding something about this investigation, I will find out," he said, his voice low. "I won't let anyone play games with my cases, especially this one. Take all the glory; I couldn't give a shit about the press or recognition or credit. But don't mess with the case."

A flash of anger reddened her cheeks. "Glory?" Her voice was a mere whisper. "You think I care about *glory*? You bastard."

She brushed past him, her jaw tight.

He'd made her angry, and he wondered what secrets she would spill if he really pushed her. Secrets. Yes, she had secrets. And he was damn well going to find out what they were.

They walked to the door in tense silence. The house belonged to Will and Dina Adams. Their daughter, Laura, had been Jenny's best friend and a witness to her abduction.

Mr. Adams opened the door before Zack could knock. "Detective Travis," he said solemnly as he opened the door for them to enter.

Zack introduced Olivia and Adams led them down a wide, tiled floor to the family room in the back of the house.

Laura Adams was a pretty girl of ten with a short brunette bob and large blue eyes that now teared. She smiled and blinked. "Hi," she said shyly.

"Hello, Laura," Zack said. He smiled at the other girl, who sat with her back straight and hands clasped tightly between her knees. "Hello, Tanya. You doing okay?"

"Yes," Laura said while Tanya shrugged.

Tanya's mother sat across the room next to Dina Adams. "How long is this going to take? Hasn't my daughter been through enough? Why do you have to talk to her again?"

"Ms. Burgess?" Olivia inquired.

"Who are you?" Ms. Burgess said, wringing her hands.

"I'm Olivia St. Martin with the Federal Bureau of Investigation. I know this is difficult for you and your daughter, and I promise we'll be done soon."

Olivia's voice was both professional and soothing, with the cadence of a psychologist. She sat next to Tanya and smiled at Laura, who sat on her friend's other side. "You can call me Olivia," she said to the girls.

Zack would have questioned the girls, but a glance from Olivia told him she wanted to take a stab at this. He gave her the opportunity, curious. The anger she'd displayed toward him was gone or buried; her entire disposition and demeanor seemed softer, but confident.

Her quick turnaround intrigued him.

"Detective Travis told me that you saw the man who took Jenny," Olivia said, her voice calm. "That must be hard for you to think about."

"I'll never forget," Laura said, her large eyes watering. "I—I keep thinking he'll come back."

Olivia knew that feeling all too well. For years, she'd feared the exact same thing. That the mean man with the tattoo would crawl up the rose trellis outside her bedroom window and carry her away, just like he'd done with Missy.

She'd broken the trellis on Halloween, three years after Missy was killed. Her father thought it was the teenagers up the street who were known to engage in petty vandalism. She'd never told him the truth.

"I won't let anyone hurt you," Laura's father said, his voice rough with emotion. Olivia realized everyone was looking at her. How long had she been thinking about the past?

She cleared her throat. "It's normal to be scared," she told the girls. "No one blames you for being scared about what happened to Jenny. But you have parents who love you and will do everything they can to protect you."

Mr. Adams sat on the arm of the couch next to his daughter and squeezed her hand, his mouth firm and his eyes moist.

"Laura, Tanya, I know you both already told Detective Travis and the other policemen what you saw. But sometimes, you might remember a little detail that didn't seem important at the time, or you forgot because of all the scary stuff that was going on. If you think you can, I would like you to tell me what happened. In your own words. And anything you remember, no matter how little or unimportant or dumb you think it is, please share."

Laura nodded, almost eager to tell her story, but kept glancing at her father for reassurance. She'd picked up on his discomfort at having her recite the tragedy. Will Adams probably thought how easily it could have been her—and how relieved he was that it hadn't been. Then came guilt at that relief.

Olivia understood those feelings as well.

"We were playing at Brown Park, the one around the corner. We usually ride our bikes, but mine had a flat tire and I didn't want to get out the bike pump and get all dirty, so we walked. We always go there."

"The neighborhood was so safe," Mrs. Adams said. "I always thought it was safe."

Having her mother break down wouldn't do Laura any good, so Olivia said, "This is a beautiful neighborhood. Of course you felt it was safe." She turned back to Laura before a conversation could develop. "So you walked. How long did it take?"

She shrugged. "I dunno. A few minutes. I don't have a watch, and we weren't rushing to get there. We only go there because it's something to do, you know?"

"What did you see when you got there? Were there other kids there?"

"There were some older kids sitting by the pond smoking. We didn't go over there, though we'd brought bread for the ducks. But my mom always says stay away from the older kids."

Laura glanced at her mother, and Olivia instantly knew she was lying. Her heart sped up.

"Did you know these older kids?" she asked cautiously.

Laura shrugged again. "No."

"Never saw them at the park?"

"Well, sure, we saw them around. They live in the neighborhood."

"Ever talk to them?"

"No. I mean, maybe a 'hi' or something, but not talk."

Olivia raised her eyebrow and looked at Laura directly in the eye.

It was Tanya who burst into tears.

"It's my fault!" she cried.

Olivia reached out and squeezed the girl's hand. "Nothing is your fault," she said firmly. "Tell me what happened."

"J-J-Jenny said not to go t-t-to them, but Laura and I, we, we, we wanted to just t-t-try. You know, one cigarette. And, and they'd offered before and we said no, but we'd talked about it and Jenny didn't want to, but Laura and I did so we told her to wait by the fountain. We'd be right back. But, but—"

Tanya's little body heaved with sobs. Olivia wanted to pull her into her arms and tell her everything would be okay, but she had to know the rest of the story. She squeezed the girl's hand harder to get her attention, and Tanya finally looked at her, tears streaming down her face.

"No one is angry with you, Tanya. No one. Please tell me what happened next."

Tanya's bottom lip quivered. "We, um, went over to them and asked for a cigarette. I took a puff and started coughing. It tasted bad. Nothing like I thought. Laura didn't want to try after that, and the kids started laughing at us so we ran away, back to the fountain." She bit her lip.

Olivia turned to Laura, who looked stricken. "Laura?"

She nodded. "But Jenny wasn't there. Tanya was drinking water because her tongue felt yucky and I looked around, and that's when I saw Jenny talking to the guy. He had really short hair. A white T-shirt. I couldn't see Jenny's face, but she went with him. I yelled for her and waved my arms so she could see me, but I don't know if she saw me. She got into his truck."

"What did his truck look like?"

Laura glanced at Travis, then back at her. Another lie coming up? "It was big and black, but I don't know what kind it was."

That's what she'd said before, and according to the reports she'd described what they determined was a Dodge Ram because of the trademark symbol on the side.

"Anything else?"

She shook her head.

Olivia turned to Tanya. "You said you saw a tattoo on the man's arm."

"I thought it was."

"What kind?"

"I don't know. Just a blue blob. It was too far away." She wiped tears from her face and snuggled into her mother, who'd crossed over to her.

Olivia sighed. "What about the kids you were talking to? What are their names?"

"I don't know."

"I know one of them," Laura said. "Sean Miller. He's Betsy's older brother. She's a third-grader." She made it sound like Betsy was a little kid instead of the grade behind Laura and her friends.

"Where does he live?"

"Across the street from the park. I don't know the address, but they have daisies painted on their mailbox. You can't miss it."

"Good work," Zack said as he pulled up in front of the gray mailbox painted with bright yellow daisies.

He'd been as surprised as the parents when Tanya made her confession about smoking with the teenagers. Their original story—that Jenny had gone to get water at the fountain and that's where they saw her disappear with the stranger—seemed plausible. He hadn't thought to press them.

"It doesn't change anything, but maybe this Miller kid will remember seeing something. Or one of his friends."

Though her words were straightforward, she sounded defeated, while he was just kicking up a gear. Any new information was a bonus; they had a potential witness to interview, and as any detective knew, the more witnesses, the greater the chance of learning information valuable to the investigation.

"Let's see what the Miller kid has to say."

They walked up to the front door of the grand house facing the park where Jenny Benedict had been abducted. From the front of the house, the entire park could be seen. Zack wondered how long Jenny's killer had waited in the park. Had he driven around the neighborhood? Waited for the perfect opportunity? Or was it a chance meeting, a spontaneous abduction?

They'd canvassed the neighborhood after Jenny's disappearance, had even come to this house, but no one had reported seeing anything.

But they hadn't spoken to the kid Sean Miller. They hadn't told him they knew he was in the park that day.

A girl of about eight answered the door. Zack showed her his badge and handed her a business card. "Would you please get your mom or dad for me?"

She looked at the card and frowned. "They're not here. My brother is, though." She closed the door before Zack could say anything.

Zack weighed the pros and cons of talking to the kid without his parents. They could have a problem since Sean Miller was a minor, but since he wasn't a suspect, Zack would worry about potential problems if they arose. Hopefully, no one would make an issue of his interviewing the kid.

He glanced at his watch and ran a hand through his hair. What was taking the kid so long? He raised his hand to knock again and Olivia said, "Impatient?"

He dropped his hand and frowned. He was about to make a wisecrack when the door swung open.

Sean Miller looked barely old enough to shave, but his brown eyes held the defiant wariness of many teenage boys who have something to hide from the cops, from something as minor as smoking a joint once in their backyard to as major as joyriding in their neighbor's new Jag and totaling it.

"You can't come in," he said, his chin out. "My mom's not here and no one is allowed in the house."

"We don't need to come in. Sean?" Zack took a step toward him, towering over the scrawny teen.

"Yeah?"

"We need to talk."

"I haven't done anything."

"Did I say you did anything?" Damn, where'd the attitude come from? Zack couldn't help but recognize some of his own bad attitude from when he was a young punk.

"Then why are you here?"

"Why didn't you tell the police who were here last

week that you were in Brown Park when Jenny Benedict was abducted?"

He shrugged.

"That's not an answer."

"I have nothing to say."

"Maybe you'll have something to say at the police station."

"You can't make me come. I haven't done anything." But the kid crossed his arms and took a step back, fear darkening his eyes.

"Withholding information from the police is a crime."

"I didn't do anything," he said, glancing from Zack to Olivia.

Olivia glanced at Zack and nodded her head toward Sean. She turned to the kid and said, "Sean, I'm Olivia St. Martin with the Federal Bureau of Investigation." Her voice was calm and soothing. Zack could listen to her for hours. He wondered what she sounded like when she interviewed suspects. He'd bet she could make them confess without raising her voice.

"I'm sure you haven't done anything wrong," she said. "In fact, I think you're just as scared as your little sister Betsy."

"I'm not scared," he said in a tone that said anything but.

"Maybe not," she said, "but Betsy is, isn't she?"

Sean didn't say anything, and Olivia pressed.

"Jenny Benedict was taken from the park on Tuesday afternoon. About this time. Your mom works. Where was your sister while you were at the park?"

"I didn't say I was at the park."

"You didn't say you weren't."

"I—" he stopped, glanced at Zack. Zack glared at him. Olivia was definitely playing the good cop; Zack didn't mind being the big bad cop in this scenario.

"I was there," he admitted.

"What did you see?"

"Nothing," he said quickly, too quickly. Zack was about to jump down his throat when Olivia said, "You weren't supposed to go to the park without Betsy, were you?"

"She wanted to watch this stupid show, the same dumb kids' show every afternoon. And she'd rat me out about smoking if I brought the gang to the house. The park is only across the street; I can see my front door from the pond. And I was only gone thirty minutes; she didn't even notice." The kid was talking faster. "And when I heard one of the girls screaming about something, we hightailed it out of there. I didn't see anyone taking Jenny. I swear."

"You heard a kid scream and you left?" Olivia's good-cop impression was done. She sounded like she wanted to slap the kid. Zack didn't blame her, but he also didn't want to lose this kid's cooperation.

"I—I—" he glanced down, feet shuffling.

Zack asked, "What did you see before Jenny was abducted?"

Sean paused. "I don't know. It's not important."

"Try us."

He hesitated again, and Olivia said, "Sean, the man who killed Jenny will kill another little girl if we don't stop him. If it was your sister, wouldn't you want to help?"

Fear and worry crossed his face. "I—aw, fuck." He breathed heavily, then said in a rush, "I saw a guy that morning. He didn't look familiar, and my friends and I are always at the park, you know, there's nothing to do and none of us have our driver's licenses. He hadn't been around before, and he was an old guy, you know. Not that he looked that old, really, but you could see it in his face, you know? I thought he was like my dad's age, like forty, but maybe he was even older, like fifty."

"You got a good look at him?" Zack asked.

Sean shook his head. "No, it was just an impression. Really."

"Could you work with a police sketch artist?" Olivia asked.

"No, I really didn't get a good look at him."

"Where was he when you saw him?" Zack asked, changing the direction of the conversation.

"My pal Kyle and I were sitting at the pond feeding the ducks and just shooting the shit, you know? It was early; my mom hadn't even gone to work yet and I just wanted a couple minutes' peace before having to baby-sit all day. There was this guy just walking through the park."

"Why did you even notice him?"

Sean thought a long minute. "I don't know, exactly. I think it was the tattoo."

Zack felt Olivia tense and lean forward, but she didn't say anything.

"Tattoo?" Zack asked.

"Yeah. People around here don't have them, at least not those big blue designs like Popeye."

"His tattoo was of Popeye?"

Sean shook his head. "No, it's just what I thought

when I saw it. Popeye the sailor man. Popeye has an anchor, I think. This tattoo was an eagle."

"You must have been pretty close to him to notice it was an eagle."

"He walked right by the pond, but he didn't stop or anything. Kyle and I looked up, then went back to feeding the fish."

"Hair?"

"Short. Like a really short buzz cut. Maybe that's why I thought about Popeye."

"Eyes?"

"He wore sunglasses."

"Shirt?"

"White."

"Pants?"

"Jeans."

"Shoes?"

He paused. "That's why I think we really noticed him. There's a lot of walkers in the neighborhood. But he had on these big hiking boots."

"If you had to guess how tall he was, what would you say?"

"Taller than my dad, but that's not saying anything. My dad's shorter than me."

"We'll need Kyle's last name and address," Zack said when he realized he couldn't get any more details out of the kid. "And I am sending over a police artist. I think you'll remember a lot more than you think."

Kyle Bolks had nothing to add to Sean's information, and in fact didn't even remember what day
Jenny had been abducted. Olivia listened to Zack on
the phone calling his partner to accompany a sketch
artist to the Miller house. Sean's mother would have
to give her consent, but Olivia didn't think that
would be a problem. Most people wanted to help.

She stared out the window as Zack drove from the
Benedicts' new home development into the Davidsons'
more established neighborhood several miles and a
bridge away. Large maple trees lined the sidewalks,
curbside mailboxes were decorated with elegant
numbers. Long narrow walkways led to quaint, well-
maintained older homes that reminded Olivia more
of Vermont than the West Coast.

Zack had been quiet during the fifteen-minute
drive across town, but that was fine with Olivia. She
was still uncomfortable from their conversation
prior to their meeting with Laura and Tanya. But
what really unnerved her was the expression on Sean
Miller's face when he realized the man he saw in the
park earlier the day Jenny was abducted was likely
her killer. That it could have been his little sister. It
could have been someone he loved.

Olivia pictured the eagle tattoo and involuntarily shivered. There was no doubt in her mind the man Sean saw killed not only Jenny Benedict, but her sister, Missy. He was in Seattle. Readying himself to prey on another unsuspecting victim. Waiting for the right time to come in for the kill.

Stop. She had to put all her feelings aside. Zack Travis had already proven too perceptive. If he even thought she had another motive for being in Seattle, he'd send her packing. Call up her boss and have her fired. Without her job she had nothing. She'd built her entire adult life around helping other people the best way she knew how—with science. Without it, what could she do? Who would she help? Without her job, she would no longer be fighting for the rights of the victims, fighting for justice for those they left behind. But Olivia was willing to risk everything she had, everything she was, to stop this predator. When and if Zack learned the truth, she would deal with the fallout. Until then she had to keep her wits about her and stop feeling guilty. There was time enough for guilt later.

Zack stopped the car in front of a two-story Victorian-style home with a wraparound porch, complete with hanging swing. He made no move to get out. "I hate this."

Olivia glanced over at him. He stared straight ahead through the windshield, his jaw tight.

"They can see you care," Olivia said quietly, chastising herself for worrying about her own plight when there was more than her future at stake. "Sometimes that's all you can do."

Zack looked at her, and she was surprised that a man of such physical and emotional strength would allow the pain of a troubling investigation to cloud his expression. If she allowed the pain and anger to surface, she'd never be able to put it aside.

She swallowed, determined not to let him see anything but a professional sitting next to him. Inside, the weight of her deception sank her spirits lower. What right did she have to even question Laura Adams? Or Sean Miller? Or to be here outside a house full of grief?

Abruptly, Zack got out of the car before Olivia could even think of voicing her conflict. Good thing. *Focus, Olivia. Focus.* Keep the goal firmly in mind: stopping Missy's killer before he stole another life.

She would deal with the repercussions—internal and external—later.

Anyone entering the Davidsons' home would instantly think family. Pictures of three children— two girls and a boy—filled every available surface and many of the walls. Shoes in several different sizes were kicked against the wall just inside the door. A coat rack in the hall separating the entry from the kitchen boasted cubbies for lunch boxes, hooks for outerwear, and a corkboard for notes.

Olivia stared at Michelle's message board.

We love you, Michelle.

Coming here was not a good idea. She should have remained at the station reviewing the evidence logs. Focusing on the facts, the science, that would see this case through. Not talking to child witnesses, and certainly not facing the parents of one of the victims.

You're in over your head, Liv.

"Can I get you coffee?" Tall and slender, Brenda Davidson walked as if each step sent a bolt of pain up her spine.

Zack declined for both of them and Mrs. Davidson nodded, as if the effort exhausted her. Dark circles framed her large blue eyes, eyes bright with thinly concealed pain.

She led them down the hall, through the large open kitchen, and into the family room. Again, *family* was the operative word. Kids' videos overflowed from bookshelves on either side of a large-screen television. Board games filled another built-in shelving unit. And pictures. Everywhere, pictures.

Olivia picked up a silver frame and stared at a girl who could have been Missy. Same long, curly blonde hair. Same big green eyes. Olivia's lip quivered. What bastard could hurt such a sweet, innocent child?

"That was taken last year, when Michelle turned ten."

Olivia jumped, almost dropping the picture. Carefully, she placed it back on the shelf and turned to Mrs. Davidson. "She's beautiful," she said, shifting her feet. She clutched her purse with both hands.

Mrs. Davidson's swollen eyes brimmed with tears, the grief etched in every small crevice of her skin. "Did you find him?"

Zack spoke. Olivia had almost forgotten he was there. "We're working every lead, ma'am. We have a lot of good people working on the case."

Lead. What did they have? A teenager who saw an eagle tattoo and a man about fifty in sunglasses. Maybe something would come of it, but before another girl was killed? Before the predator slipped away?

Zack glanced around. "Is Mr. Davidson here?"

"He's sleeping." While her voice was a monotone, Olivia detected a hint of anger in her eyes.

Zack shot a glance at Olivia, then said, "We don't mean to bother you, but it would help us if we could review the day Michelle was kidnapped and see if you remember anything at all about the truck your neighbor saw. If you saw it in the neighborhood. Any little thing might help."

Mrs. Davidson sank into the sectional sofa and worried an afghan in her hands. "I've gone over every minute of that day, every second. Nothing. Nothing. I'll never forget it."

"It's not your fault, Mrs. Davidson," Zack said.

"I taught Michelle about strangers," she continued as if Zack hadn't spoken. "I told her what to do if a strange man approached. What to do if anyone tried to hurt her and, and . . ." She stifled a sob.

Something fluttered out of the corner of Olivia's eye. She turned her head slightly. A petite blonde child stood just inside the kitchen, about six or seven. She hung back, just outside of her mother's sight.

"My sweetheart. My perfect little angel," Mrs. Davidson mumbled into her hands.

"Mommy?" The girl's voice was a squeak. Brenda Davidson didn't seem to notice her standing in the threshold, but Olivia couldn't take her eyes off her. Inside, she was five again, watching her own mother fall apart.

"Michelle was a dancer, you know," Mrs. Davidson said. "Beautiful dancer. She had the lead in the spring recital. She would have had the lead this fall . . ." Her voice trailed off as she gazed at another picture on the wall.

"Mommy?"

Mommy? Missy isn't coming back, is she? Olivia

heard her own childlike voice in her mind, the memory of her mother clearer than ever. Her mother hadn't answered her question. When she looked at Olivia, she didn't see her. When Olivia spoke, she didn't hear her.

"Mommy?" the child whispered, her large round eyes so much like her older sister's, blinking rapidly as she fought against crying. Olivia remembered the feeling all too well, trying to keep her own tears under control because her parents didn't want to see them and she didn't want to hurt them.

"Tell me you know who he is," Mrs. Davidson said, her voice suddenly harsh. "That you'll find him. That you'll have him executed for what he did to my baby!"

"We're working every day and night to see that he's brought to justice, Mrs. Davidson," Zack said. He placed a business card on the end table. "If you think of anything, even if it doesn't seem important, please don't hesitate to call me, day or night." He sounded defeated.

Defeated, just like the little girl who took a step back into the kitchen as her lower lip quivered. *Amanda.* Olivia remembered her name from the reports. As Olivia watched, Amanda opened the door of a cabinet and crawled inside. Disappeared. Olivia stared at the cabinet, remembering hiding in her own sanctuary, her bedroom closet. She'd fallen asleep there many nights. Her parents never knew. They never checked on her.

Melissa was so good, so perfect. She didn't deserve to die.

Her mother's voice again, speaking as if she were in the room. Olivia shivered, a ghost touching her skin. Olivia loved her sister, but when she died, she'd become a saint in her mother's eyes. Perfect. An angel.

And Olivia . . . wasn't.

"Mrs. Davidson," Olivia said firmly. "Where are your other children?"

The grieving mother blinked. "What does that have to do with anything?"

"Do you know where they are?"

"Of course I do. They're upstairs."

"Are you sure?"

"Agent St. Martin, I think—" Zack attempted to interrupt, but Olivia ignored him.

"Do you care where they are? Are you so wrapped up in your grief that you can't see that there are two kids who still need you?"

"I assure you, Ms. St. Martin, that we are all thinking about Michelle. Michelle is what matters right now. You should be out finding her killer rather than accusing me of being a bad mother!"

"Let us worry about finding her killer. You have two children who need you to be a mother, not close yourself off in your grief. I'm so very sorry about what happened to Michelle, but Amanda and Peter are still alive and they need you now more than ever."

"How dare you!"

"Excuse us, Mrs. Davidson." Zack grabbed Olivia by the arm. She was shaking. She'd gone too far. She knew it, but she couldn't stop herself.

If she could save one little girl from being neglected, it will have been worth it. She should have found a way to be more professional, more diplomatic, something! But all she could see was little Amanda

Davidson crawling into the kitchen cabinet. It was like watching herself.

Zack pulled her outside. "What has gotten into you?" He didn't wait for her answer, which was good because she didn't have an answer to give. She didn't know what had possessed her to jump down the woman's throat. The way she talked about Michelle? Or the way Olivia remembered her own mother talking about Missy?

"Get in the damn car and wait for me. You'll be lucky to have your shield when this investigation is over."

He stormed back into the house.

Olivia stood by the passenger door and rested her forehead on the roof of the car. She couldn't control the shaking, and focused every molecule in her body to just *stop*. Slowly, she regained control and took a long, hiccupping breath.

Brenda Davidson was not her mother. What had she done? How in the world could she have lost control like that?

Worse, she didn't regret it. Had she become so callous in her own pain that she couldn't see the anguish of others?

Her job was already on the line, and she may have just dug her own professional grave. She almost laughed at Zack's comment about having her shield. What shield?

It would be worth losing everything she had, everything she was, if she could stop Michelle's little sister from growing up like she had.

Zack didn't know if he was more angry with Olivia for attacking a grieving mother or himself for watching it unfold and not stopping her before she crossed the line. He hadn't known Olivia for long, but antagonizing victims was the last thing he expected of her.

He couldn't speak, couldn't even look at her, as he drove too fast out of the Davidsons' neighborhood and to a nearby lake he'd frequented as a teenager. He didn't know why he was drawn there, except that it was where he used to do a lot of thinking when he was torn between going home to an empty house or getting into trouble with his friends.

He braked as soon as he pulled into the gravel parking lot and wished he had his bike. He needed a good hundred-mile-an-hour venting session.

Zack pushed the automatic gearshift into park with his right hand and hit his left on the steering wheel. "What the *fuck* was that about?"

Olivia wouldn't look at him, and that angered him more. She stared straight ahead, her hands clasped tightly in her lap, like a prim librarian. The only sign that she was even mildly disturbed was the slight tremor in her body, as if she were shaking and doing her utmost to stop.

"I'm sorry," she said quietly. Too calm. Too composed. "If you would like to file a report with my superior, I'll—"

"Oh, fuck that!"

He wrenched the car door open and slammed it shut, walking as quickly as possible to the edge of the water.

He stared out at the lone fisherman sitting in a rowboat on the far side of the small lake. The sun was beginning its descent; he'd lost track of time.

He took deep breaths, staring at the still water, regaining his composure.

Something was up with Olivia St. Martin. Everything he'd seen since she arrived yesterday afternoon told him she was a professional through and through. She'd been upfront about the information she had and didn't have. She shared more than he'd expected. He'd been so impressed with the way she handled the interviews with Laura Adams, Tanya Burgess, and Sean Miller. Everything until that tirade directed toward Mrs. Davidson.

He replayed the scene in his mind, thinking back to what had set her off. There was something, but he couldn't put his finger on it. Was it when the little girl walked into the room? But—she hadn't been there when Olivia was lecturing. Where had she gone?

"Do you know where your children are?"

"Of course I do. They're upstairs."

But the little girl wasn't. Amanda Davidson had come downstairs. And something about her appearance had upset Olivia.

Zack was determined to find out what, but first he had to control his anger.

He took a deep breath and remembered the first time he'd lost his temper on the job. He'd been a rookie, not even six months out of the Academy, a beat cop. He and his partner, an old, wise, black cop named Kip Granger, were called out on a domestic violence case in the economically depressed Central District. The guy had been pummeling his wife into the ground with a dozen bystanders gawking.

Zack reacted on instinct and rushed the guy. The husband had a knife. Zack almost got himself killed.

He rubbed his arm where he still bore a scar from

that night. He'd learned the hard way to not let his temper control his actions.

Zack sensed Olivia's presence before he heard her footfall. His anger was only part of the complex emotions that were assaulting him. While he didn't completely understand Olivia and what had happened at the Davidsons', he had a strong suspicion something very specific had set her off.

What she told him was far worse than he imagined.

"I told you last night that my sister was murdered."

Her voice was quiet, but it had lost the soothing quality from earlier, when she'd spoken to the girls. She now sounded defeated and scared.

He didn't say anything, didn't turn to face her for fear she'd not say another word, but his heart quickened as his temper cooled and his compassion warmed.

"I was five. Missy was nine. I was there when she was abducted. I couldn't stop him. He just—picked her up. I—I ran home."

Olivia's voice cracked and now Zack did turn around to look at her. For the first time he saw raw pain in her eyes, as if an invisible shield had evaporated to reveal her soul. The unspoken pain angered and moved him in ways he could only grasp ethereally. Some unknown bastard had killed her sister and affected Olivia so deeply it still haunted her. Had this pain been buried for so long, only to be brought out by this investigation? Or were her feelings always simmering beneath the surface, unknown to anyone who looked at her because she was so good at keeping up that protective guard?

"My parents never got over it."

He waited for her to say something else, but she didn't. Her silence didn't fool him. There was more, Zack thought. So much more. He could tell by the quiver in her chin, her pale complexion, the tears in her eyes. Tears. He didn't think she cried much. And they didn't spill over, just formed a light sheen to brighten her gaze.

"And?" he prompted.

"They forgot about me."

Her voice was so little, she sounded almost like a child herself.

"Olivia," he whispered as he ran a hand through his hair. He took a step toward her, desperately wanting to take her into his arms, to protect her from her personal demons. But dammit! She'd crossed the line, and no amount of understanding or compassion could make him forget what had happened at the Davidsons'.

"I'm so sorry. But just because your parents couldn't get beyond their grief doesn't mean Michelle's parents will neglect their children. You can't treat the living victims that way."

He saw a hint of understanding and guilt in her eyes.

"But who's thinking about Amanda?" she said, a lone tear sliding down her cheek. Zack watched it reach Olivia's chin, quiver, then drop. She didn't notice, and no other tears followed.

"Did you see her?" she asked urgently. "Really look at her? She tried so hard to blend into the background, her mother didn't even notice. Didn't notice she was in the room when her mom said her 'perfect angel' was gone. How did that make Amanda feel? That she isn't perfect? That it should have been her?

That she was the one who should have died instead of her *perfect* sister?

"Not one time did she acknowledge *Amanda*. Not once. Not one time did she touch her, hug her, tell her she loved her."

"You don't know that—"

"You can tell by the way she talked!" Olivia's jaw tightened, her growing anger burying the deep sadness. "The house reeked of anguish. Brenda Davidson can't see beyond her pain to those who are left. I'm sorry! I'm sorry I overstepped my bounds, but if I can spare Amanda Davidson a lifetime of neglect and guilt, then I'm glad I said something! If only someone had told my parents—"

Olivia stopped suddenly, her hands covering her mouth, her eyes wide with shock. "I didn't—I—"

"What?" Zack wanted to know everything. He took a step closer, grabbed her by the arms, and shook her once. Voice low, he said, "Is that why you're here? Because of your family? Your sister? Are you too close to this?"

He looked at her vivid eyes, her smooth complexion, her red mouth. There was so much here in this little package, so much depth and intelligence and need—she was a loner who needed someone. But dammit, he wouldn't jeopardize the case because she was too emotionally involved.

"I promise. I'll control myself. I don't—I don't know why—I never do things like that."

He believed her. She didn't do things like that because she suppressed her feelings. And it had taken six-year-old Amanda Davidson to bring it all to the surface. No, not all. There was more, and he was going to find out exactly what was going on.

She wasn't telling him everything. He took a step closer, his hands on her shoulders. He tilted her face upward to look at him.

"Olivia," he said, his voice soft but firm, "I believe you. But there's more to this than you're telling me. Right now, tell me the truth. Why—"

His cell phone rang. "We're not done with this conversation," he said as he flipped open his phone and took a step away from her. "Travis."

"It's Doug Cohn. I think I have something."

"What?"

"It's not much, but I talked to two lab directors who remembered the blonde girls. One in Austin, Texas, the other in Colorado. Both remembered the marks on the forearm. They e-mailed me photographs from the files. I think you need to see them."

"Why?"

"They're identical. I thought maybe they were made by something he used to transport the victims, something that had sharp edges. And even when Gil said it was a sharp object, I was thinking it was stationary. There didn't seem to be a different pressure in the cuts, like someone was intentionally marking the girls. But now—I think it's his signature."

"He's signing his name?"

"Not his name, but maybe his mark. Like 'Z' for Zorro. There are twelve marks. It must mean something. When I spoke to Massachusetts, the lab director told me two of the girls were marked, two they couldn't see any detail because the bodies weren't in good shape."

"I'll be right there." He hung up and turned to Olivia, but he didn't have to repeat the conversation. She'd heard enough.

Horror and disbelief in her voice, she said, "He's branding his victims."

The police were all over the woods, but they weren't knocking on doors.

Yet.

He was cautious by nature, which had served him well over the years. He seemed to have a sixth sense about when to pull back. When to move on.

That odd sense started tickling the back of his neck. Just a light touch, and when he rubbed his head, it disappeared.

He couldn't move on. He'd already seen the next angel he had to set free.

She was waiting for him.

He had work to do first. He hadn't located a truck yet, but it was only a matter of time. If the police knocked on his door, it would only be to ask questions about the day the girl disappeared. He would tell them he remembered the news about it, but didn't have any real memories of what happened on that day. He wished he could be of more help, but it was three months ago. Him? Well, he worked for a local restaurant, came here for the job well over a year ago. He'd met most of the people who lived on the island. He liked it here.

Don't talk too much, keep it conversational, a tad somber.

He'd done it before and no one suspected anything.

No, he couldn't leave. Not yet. He had one more angel to free, then he would be at peace for a time.

He readied himself for bed. It was early, not yet nine, but he had the breakfast shift tomorrow. It wouldn't do to miss a scheduled shift. Being late—because he was never late—could arouse attention. Not that he'd ever slept late. His internal clock woke him every morning at five.

His bedtime ritual was always the same. He showered. The thought of sliding into sheets with the filth of the day on his skin terrified him.

He always checked the doors and windows, even if he remembered securing them. Lights off, no nightlight, no bathroom light. Blinds down. He'd replaced the flimsy curtains in the cottage bedroom with shades that blocked all light.

He slept in boxers, his shoes next to his bed. He could slip into them instantly if necessary, a holdover from three years in the military.

In the dark, he could sleep. Sometimes.

And sometimes, like tonight, his mind couldn't rest.

Sometimes, like tonight, he thought of *her*. Angel.

The ache in his heart spread until it became almost unbearable. He missed her so much. Her breath on his face. Her smile. He missed the way she smiled *just for him*.

And like always, when he thought of Angel before he slept, he remembered far more than he wanted to.

They were moving to Los Angeles, the seventh time they'd moved in his eleven years. But this time was different.

This time they left without his mother. She was dead.

"Suck it up, boy. Stop acting like a sissy."

Bruce wasn't his father, but he didn't remember his father. His mother hadn't married him, just like she hadn't married Bruce. But, except for some isolated feelings that alternately disturbed and warmed him, he couldn't remember a time when Bruce wasn't in the house. He wanted him to leave. He wanted the time when he didn't have to share his mother with anyone. When she let him sleep next to her in her soft, warm bed.

He missed his mother. But he still had Angel.

She was so beautiful. Her blonde hair, as white as snow when she was little, now had darkened to shimmering gold, natural white highlights shining in the sun.

She was his little girl as much as she was Bruce's and his mother's little girl. He loved her more, took care of her more. Bruce and his mother argued and then did things to each other that made his mother's sheets smell funny. When she went to work and Bruce left him to go down to the bar on the corner, he would often lie on his mother's side of the bed and remember what it was like to be held by her. He'd wrap himself with her blankets and pillows.

But it didn't smell the same. It smelled fishy and dirty and more like Bruce than his mother.

Now, his mother was gone. First her scent, now her body.

On that long, long car ride to Los Angeles, Angel reached over and took his hand. Tears welled in her big green eyes. She missed their mother, too.

Or was she already scared of her father?

He leaned over and whispered in her ear. "I promise, I'll take care of you. I won't let him hurt you."

She squeezed his hand, her face too old for her seven years. "It's too late."

Three years and nine moves later, she was dead, too.

CHAPTER 13

It was after midnight and everyone in the conference room was exhausted. Zack, Olivia, Boyd, Cohn, and Detective Jan O'Neal had been reviewing every report Cohn had received from the labs in other states, plus the pages Nashville had faxed over while Zack and Olivia were talking with Mrs. Davidson.

"Okay, we all need to get some sleep," Zack said, "but let's run through what we have one more time and figure out what we're going to do tomorrow."

"We have a few more pages to go through, but we have six matches to households that own both types of trucks," Boyd said. "Jan and I are going to check them out in person first thing in the morning."

"Good work."

"I have calls in to the other labs," Cohn said. "I'll follow up tomorrow morning. I'm pulling a couple of my lab techs into researching the marks. Maybe twelve signifies something, like in mythology."

"We should contact the FBI and see if they have information about the marks," Olivia said quietly, looking at Zack.

"Who? How can we expedite this?"

Olivia swallowed. She was going to be exposed;

there was no way around it. "You should contact the Seattle bureau chief and ask for them to run the marks through the research unit, as well as the number 'twelve' to see if it means anything."

"Ask your people to come in. Officially." Zack ran a hand over his face. "You're right. This could be the break we need. I'll talk to Chief Pierson first thing in the morning."

Olivia nodded. It was the smartest thing to do. She dreaded leaving Seattle. She wanted to be here when they caught this guy. She needed to see him, face him. Confront him.

But stopping him was her number-one goal. If exposing her fraud meant getting closer to finding Missy's killer, then she would be exposed.

"I think we're getting closer," Zack said as if reading her thoughts. "There's nothing more we can do tonight; it's nearly one. Go home, get some sleep, and be back here at eight."

Curly Bear had to come. And Bessie, her Beanie cow she got for her birthday last year from Auntie Grace. A sweater because it got cold at night. Extra underwear and socks in case it took a couple of days. Oh! Don't forget money. She had eighty-six dollars in her Cinderella bank. She used to have one hundred and eleven dollars, but last month she bought Michelle a birthday present with her own money, an art set, because Michelle wanted to be an artist when she grew up.

Amanda swallowed back the lump in her throat and willed herself not to cry. If she cried her mommy might hear her and she'd never be able to find Michelle.

But last night when she cried, her mommy didn't come. Maybe Mommy wouldn't notice, no matter what Amanda did.

Amanda bit the inside of her cheek and sucked in her bottom lip. Daddy had cried. She'd never once in her entire life seen her daddy cry, but he'd cried three times since Michelle went to Heaven.

Amanda didn't know exactly where Heaven was. Whenever Mommy talked about it, she said Heaven was in the sky. When they went to church on Easter and Christmas, the preacher guy in the long dress said Jesus was *up* in Heaven.

Amanda hadn't been born when Mount St. Helens erupted, but she'd watched a show with Daddy about it one night a long time ago. She'd been scared that night and crawled into bed with Michelle.

"What if that mountain blows up and buries us?" she'd asked as she pulled Michelle's pretty pink comforter tight around her.

"It won't."

"But the guy on the show said it could."

"Only if God wants it to."

"God? Why would he want to bury us?"

"Silly, when a volcano erupts it's an act of God. That's what Mommy said. So if it happens, it happens. There's nothing you can do about it."

Amanda had to find Heaven and bring Michelle home. If she brought Michelle home, Mommy would stop crying and hug her again. Amanda feared God took Michelle because they argued about everything, like when Michelle took the biggest piece of pizza or borrowed Amanda's new bicycle she got for her sixth birthday and then crashed it into Mrs. Hendrick's rosebushes and bent the frame.

Michelle could have her bicycle and the biggest slice of pizza forever and ever. Maybe if Amanda said she was sorry for yelling at her sister, God would let her come back from Heaven.

She just had to find Heaven first. The only way she could think of getting to Heaven was to start at the place where God told the world He was mad. Mount St. Helens.

She hoped eighty-six dollars was enough money to get there.

Brenda Davidson hadn't stopped crying for more than a few minutes since her daughter had been found dead.

She hadn't cried when Michelle was missing. Certainly, she would come home safe. Bad things happened to *other* children. Not hers. Not her baby.

She sucked in a deep breath that ended on a sob.

That woman yesterday—Brenda should have her fired. How dare she accuse her of neglecting her children! Who was she to judge? Michelle had been with friends. It wasn't her fault she was stolen. It wasn't *her* fault she was killed.

But in the back of her mind, in the center of her heart, she blamed only herself.

"You have two other children, Mrs. Davidson. Have you told them you love them?"

She told her children she loved them all the time. She baked cookies and took the girls to Girl Scouts every week and Peter to soccer practice and she volunteered at their school every Friday for pizza lunch. She *showed* her love all the time.

Brenda slammed a pan on the stove. Look, she was making them pancakes! She'd lost her daughter and was cooking in the damn kitchen. She took care of her own. She'd always take care of her own.

Brenda reached into a drawer and pulled out a metal shape. She stared at it for a long time, tears streaming down her swollen face. Michelle loved her Mickey Mouse pancakes. She'd eat four of them piled high with strawberry jam. And on special occasions, Brenda would let the kids put whipped cream on top.

Brenda slid to the floor, silent sobs wracking her body. *It's all my fault*. She hadn't been diligent enough. She hadn't watched Michelle closely enough. She hadn't thought anything bad could ever happen to her baby . . .

"Mom?"

She sucked in a shaky breath, her body heavy, her movements awkward. She blinked and looked up at her son. "What?" Her voice was thick, a mere whisper.

"I can't find Amanda."

"What's she up to now?" Brenda pulled herself up, using the counter to support her weight. "Where's your father?"

"Sleeping," Peter said, his voice low.

Andy had slept away the days since Michelle's death. How dare he sleep! She hadn't been able to sleep more than a few minutes at a time, because every time she closed her eyes she saw Michelle. It wasn't fair that she had to carry this burden alone. It wasn't fair that her baby had been taken from her.

"It's not fair!" she screamed.

Out of the corner of her eye she saw Peter flinch and close in on himself, his shoulders huddling, trying to make himself smaller.

You have two other children, Mrs. Davidson. They need you now more than ever.

What was she doing? What was she doing to her own children?

"Peter—" She reached out for him, stumbled over her feet, and pulled him into her arms. "I'm sorry. I'm sorry. I'm sorry." She held him close. "I love you, Peter. I'm sorry, so sorry for everything. Please, please forgive me."

"I love you, Mom. I know you miss Michelle. I miss her too."

"I miss her terribly." She'd never get rid of the black stain on her heart. "But you need me and I haven't been here for you."

"I understand, Mom." Tears streamed down Peter's face. Had he cried yet? Certainly he was grieving, too. He adored his sisters. Even though he was thirteen, he played games with them and let them follow him around the neighborhood without too much complaint. "But Mom? I really am worried about Amanda. I don't know where she is."

Brenda's heart skipped. No, nothing was wrong with Amanda. She was a good kid. "I'm sure she's around. She's been taking to spending time in her playhouse. You look upstairs, I'll go in the backyard."

But as Brenda reached the large plastic house in the middle of the patio, she knew Amanda wasn't inside. Panic building, she searched the entire yard, calling her name.

"Amanda! Amanda!"

She didn't answer. She wasn't outside.

She wasn't inside.

She was missing.

"Andy! Dammit, Andy!" Brenda burst into the bedroom she'd shared with her husband until Michelle went missing. "Andy, Amanda's gone!"

Andy sat upright and for the first time, Brenda saw the fatigue and pain etched in his face. Maybe he hadn't been sleeping. Maybe he'd been agonizing just like her. Alone.

"Call 911. And Detective Travis." Andy jumped from the bed and pulled on a T-shirt that had been balled up on the floor. "I'll get the neighbors looking. We'll find her. We *will* find her!"

"I can't lose another child," Brenda sobbed.

At the same time, Andy and Brenda saw the note on their dresser. The painstakingly neat block printing in purple crayon:

To Mommy and Daddy.

"Dear God, Andy, did I chase her away? Where on earth would she go?"

The shrill beep of her cell phone jolted Olivia from sleep. She fumbled for the small phone and squinted in the dark to read the red digits of the hotel's clock. 6:34. She moaned. After tossing and turning most of the night, she'd managed only three hours of sleep.

"Hello," she said before the fourth ring.

"Liv? It's Greg."

She rubbed her eyes. "Sorry. I overslept."

"You probably haven't slept much at all," he said, his voice tinged with worry. "How are you holding up?"

"I'm okay. We're making headway."

"I wanted you to know I finished the DNA testing on the sample Seattle sent me and it's a 1-in-100,000 match to the sample from Missy."

Her body tensed and she stifled a sob. Her instincts told her she was right that Missy's killer was in Seattle, her experience told her she was right, but hearing the definitive proof . . . "Thank you, Greg." *Thank you* seemed wholly inadequate. Greg was risking a reprimand or worse for not only helping her deceive the Seattle Police Department into giving her full access to the case, but using government resources without authorization.

"I received the pubic hair samples this morning. I'll jump on those today and should have an answer in the morning." He paused. "Rick asked about you this morning."

"Oh?"

"I told him you were fine."

"I'm sorry I put you in the position of lying to your boss."

"I put myself in this position, Olivia. You'd never rest if you didn't do everything you could to help. But I'm still worried about you. What are you going to do if you catch this guy?"

She'd been thinking the same thing for days. What would she do? Confront him? Slap him? Tell him to go to hell? Nothing seemed adequate. Nothing she could do would right the wrongs he'd committed. Nothing she could say would take away the pain and knowledge that for thirty-four years, a violent predator walked the streets.

"I don't know, Greg," she said.

"When this is all over, Liv, you know I'll still be here for you."

"I know." Her voice was a mere whisper. Yes, she knew. Greg still loved her. She'd been an awful wife—she couldn't give him the affection he deserved. She'd been distant and uncomfortable sharing her fears, preferring solitude to companionship. But still he stood by her, and she'd never forget it.

"I'll let you know about the pubic hair when I'm done, but I'll also contact the Seattle lab director, Doug Cohn, and send him a written report. They'll need it for court down the road."

"Thank you, Greg."

She said goodbye and shut her phone, sitting on the edge of the hotel mattress, the room suddenly too sterile. How had she ended up here, three thousand miles from her job, her friends, her house?

Friends? What friends? Her closest friend was actually here in Seattle and she hadn't even told Miranda she was nearby. And Rowan, her other roommate from the FBI Academy, was taking it easy in Colorado, at peace for the first time in her life. Her ex-husband Greg was her only other close friend, and she felt like she was using him.

Her house in Virginia wasn't a home. Though more tastefully decorated than the hotel room in which she now sat, it was hardly more intimate. She spent all her time working; she didn't need anything special to come home to.

Suddenly, she felt old. She'd be forty in a few months and here she was lying and manipulating people for the first time in her life. She didn't believe in superstition or omens or any of that nonsense, but she couldn't help but think her treachery and deceit was adding to the evil in the world.

Slowly, she made her way to the bathroom and turned the shower on full hot. The water pressure was pathetic, but at least the temperature was right.

She stripped and stood under the stinging spray and willed the shower to give her the energy she needed to maintain her façade today.

As soon as she turned off the water, she heard pounding on the door. She jumped out of the tub and grabbed a towel, but it didn't cover anything. She hadn't ordered room service. Dripping water, she rushed to the bed and slid into the thin white cotton robe she'd brought from home. This wasn't a five-star hotel with complimentary terry robes and body wraps.

The pounding continued, and she heard a muffled voice call her name, but the door was too thick to distinguish it. She glanced through the keyhole.

Zack Travis.

She fumbled with the locks and opened the door. "What—"

He immediately stepped in, and she took a step back. "Jesus Christ, I thought something had happened to you. You must sleep like the dead, I was knocking for ten—" He looked her over, slowly. "Oh." He didn't avert his eyes. They darkened, turning nearly black, as he took in her wet hair and damp robe, his gaze dropping to her chest, then back to her face.

Her body reacted to his appreciative stare. Her breasts tingled, her nipples hardened, her throat suddenly tightened. She swallowed and took another step back to let him walk in, then closed the door, grateful he was no longer looking at her, though her body still betrayed her desire.

"I didn't realize I needed to call you for permission to shower." She tried to sound professional and tough, as if she hadn't noticed the way Zack had visually inspected her body. Instead, her voice came out low and throaty.

He turned to look at her again, stared at her, unmoving. She felt trapped against the door, unable to move into the room without touching him. The thought sent a shiver through her, which she couldn't dismiss as being chilled after her shower. The sensation remained, and she was more than aware that her thin cotton robe had molded too close to her wet body.

So was Zack.

He stepped toward her and she made the mistake of looking at his lips. They parted and he licked them.

Anticipation made her heart race. His hand came up and wrapped around the back of her neck. An involuntary shiver ran through her body.

She wanted to tell him to back off. She couldn't get the words out. Instead, her eyelids drooped and her lips parted, aching to taste his.

When his mouth touched hers she'd expected the warmth; she hadn't expected a lightning bolt to shoot through her, singeing her toes.

The kiss was brief but powerful. He stepped back and she opened her eyes. By the look on his face, he'd felt the same electricity sparking between them.

She didn't want to give him any time to think about the mistake they'd just made.

"Excuse me," she mumbled. She brushed past him, grabbing clothes from the closet, and stepped into the bathroom, shutting the door firmly and leaning against it. What was it about Zack Travis that got her all in a dither? She wasn't a young female who lusted after hot cops. She was a mature, responsible professional. She had far more important things to do than go all goo-goo-eyed over a man.

She'd let him kiss her. She'd wanted him to kiss her. She wanted him to kiss her *again*.

But that was out of the question.

The shrill ring of a cell phone jolted her. But the ringer was Zack's, not hers. She quickly slid into her skirt and silk camisole. She heard Zack bark his name into the phone.

Then silence. Who had called him? Did it have to do with the case? Had someone called the FBI to check on her credentials? Had Zack already talked to the bureau chief in Seattle and told him about her? She hadn't had time to prepare. What would she tell him?

Zack might understand, but she'd be cut out of the investigation, sent back to Virginia. She'd never face her sister's murderer and see justice finally done.

The information she'd gathered over the past few weeks while in Virginia had given them new leads. They had far more today than yesterday, and far more yesterday than when Jennifer Benedict was killed.

She *had* helped, even if she had broken the rules to do it. And whose damn rules were they anyway?

She didn't want to deceive Zack, but she was in this until the end—whether it was today, tomorrow, or next week.

Taking a deep breath she slid into her blazer, dabbed concealer on the dark shadows under her eyes, put on a professional face, and ran a quick brush through her damp hair. She didn't have time to bother with her appearance.

She opened the door and saw Zack standing

against the wall, head back, eyes closed, his cell phone—now closed—held up to his forehead.

"What happened?"

He looked at her, his face pained. "That was Brenda Davidson. Her daughter Amanda is missing."

Olivia's heart leapt into her throat.

"We have to find her."

CHAPTER 15

Olivia was on edge the entire drive to the Davidsons' house. Had Michelle's killer taken Amanda? Did he have a personal vendetta against the Davidson family?

In none of the cases she reviewed had the killer taken a girl from her own home. It had certainly happened with other killers, just not this one. Unless she'd missed something. Had she missed an important connection?

No, not on a matter like this, but a seed of doubt kept her on edge.

Brenda Davidson shoved the letter at them as soon as they stepped into the house.

Dear Mommy and Daddy.
I went to Heven to find Michelle. I will tell God I am sorry. I will bring Michelle home and you wont cry anymore.
Your other dawter. Amanda Lynne Davidson.

She and Zack read the letter at the same time, and she caught his eye. Was this her fault? Had she given Amanda the wrong impression yesterday? Was she just as much to blame as the parents? More so?

Dear God, if you're there, please protect her! prayed Olivia.

"Everyone is out looking for her," Andy Davidson said. "Every place she might go. But where? Why?"

"I'm so sorry," Olivia said, thinking about her harsh words to Brenda Davidson.

"You were right."

Brenda's voice was so quiet, Olivia almost missed it. Zack said, "Excuse me?"

Brenda looked Olivia square in the eye, her blue eyes bright, bloodshot, and swollen. "You."

"I was out of line yesterday—" Olivia began.

Brenda put her hand up and shook her head, her lips quivering. "N-no. You were right. I didn't see what I was doing to my other children. I didn't really *see* them, only the hole in our family. Only— Michelle." Her voice quaked, but she swallowed and stuck her chin out as she pulled her son to her side, holding him tight as she kissed his head. She clasped hands with her husband, who embraced his family in a hug. "I can't lose Amanda, too."

"We'll find her," Olivia found herself saying. She knew better than anyone not to offer false hope. But certainly fate or God or whatever damn force was out there wouldn't take Amanda away from this family. "Can we see her room?"

"The police already searched there," Mr. Davidson said.

"I want to see it. Just for a minute."

Olivia knew what Amanda must have been feeling. And if Amanda was like her, she would have left clues, hoping her mother or father would find her. While Olivia had never run away, she'd been lost her entire life.

Brenda took her upstairs, leaving Zack to talk to the uniformed officers who were coordinating the search out of the Davidsons' spacious dining room. Olivia didn't know what to say to the woman. She stopped her outside Amanda's door. "Mrs. Davidson, I am truly sorry about yesterday."

"Maybe if I'd listened, Amanda wouldn't have run away. I neglected her." Her voice caught and her hand fluttered to her lips. "I love her so much."

"My sister was killed when we were kids," Olivia found herself saying. "My—my mother." She stopped, surprised that she'd spoken out loud.

Brenda reached out and took both of her hands. For the first time Olivia could remember, she didn't flinch. Instead, she welcomed the connection. "She acted like I did," Brenda said, squeezing Olivia's hands. "I can now see what I was becoming. If you hadn't said what you did, I don't think I would have noticed what I'd been doing to my family. Thank you."

"You love them."

"Oh, yes. I'm sure your mother loved you, too. It's just, the grief swallows you up sometimes."

Olivia shook her head. "No, my mother couldn't love anyone after Missy was—gone. She committed suicide on the anniversary of Missy's murder." Five years of living with a woman who gave birth to her but didn't see her, didn't touch her, didn't acknowledge her. Olivia had wanted to disappear then, to be anyplace but home.

Brenda's mouth dropped open and she pulled Olivia into a tight embrace. The hug felt awkward and Olivia didn't return it, but Brenda didn't seem to notice. "You poor child." Child? Olivia was fast approaching forty; she was certain Brenda was younger than she. She couldn't remember anyone calling her a *child*. But if she were a child again, she'd want a woman like Brenda Davidson to be her mother.

Brenda stepped back and stared at Olivia, resolve written across her face. "We will find Amanda and bring her home. And I promise you, she will never doubt I love her with my whole heart. We will survive."

Olivia believed her.

They didn't see anything useful in Amanda's room. Brenda repeated what was missing—a couple of stuffed animals, some clothing, and money, about a hundred dollars they figured was in her piggy bank. Her bicycle was missing from the garage as well.

As they walked out of the room, Olivia spotted a computer in an alcove at the top of the stairs. Bookshelves on either side were stuffed with papers and kids' books.

"This isn't your husband's office."

"No, it's for the children. Homework and computer games."

"Does Amanda know how to use the computer?"

Brenda smiled sadly. "What kid these days doesn't?"

Olivia sat at the terminal and was about to boot up the computer when she saw that it was already on. She moved the mouse and the blank screen was replaced by a desktop photo of the Davidson children—all three of them—in Halloween costumes.

Brenda drew in a shaky breath. "God, I miss her so much."

"You always will," Olivia said quietly. She

brought up the Internet browser and looked at the history.

Mapquest, a free Internet mapping program, was accessed at 3:35 A.M. Today. Heart racing, she pulled up the last viewed map.

"Would Amanda have any reason to go to Mount St. Helens?" she asked.

"St. Helens? Good God, no." Brenda leaned over Olivia's shoulder. "Oh my God. She's scared to death of volcanoes. She wasn't born when St. Helens erupted, but we all talk about it. She said when God gets mad he'll make the mountain blow up." She jumped up. "That's over a hundred miles away! My poor baby." Brenda ran down the stairs, calling for her husband.

Olivia printed the map Amanda had with her and tried to think like a six-year-old.

Interstate 5, which led to Mount St. Helens, was two miles from the Davidsons' suburban house, but there was no way little Amanda could get her bicycle on the freeway and ride undetected. The highway patrol would certainly have spotted the child by now. Even if she were as determined as she seemed, the freeway would be too frightening. No, Amanda would stick with side streets as much as she could.

Olivia focused on the map and picked the straightest route that stayed away from the freeway. Okay, six years old on a bike. She'd start off riding fast, but she'd get tired and slow down. Maybe she'd average two miles an hour? That would put her just north of Kent.

"Olivia?" Zack ran up the stairs and looked over her shoulder. "The mom says she's going to Mount St. Helens. What's going on?"

Olivia filled him in on what she'd learned as they went back downstairs. "I think she's about here by now," she pointed to the area around Kent.

Zack nodded. "Let's go."

"I'm going with you," Brenda said.

"You should stay here in case she calls," Zack told her.

Mr. Davidson shook his head. "No, I'll stay. Go, Brenda. Bring Amanda home."

Amanda sat under the big tree and cried. Her legs hurt and she'd eaten all the food she'd brought and was still hungry. Somewhere, maybe when she stopped in the field and peed, she'd lost Bessie. The sun was hot, but she didn't dare take off her jacket because she'd forgotten sunscreen and she burned easily.

She was going to disappoint her mommy. She'd never make it to the volcano to get Michelle back. It seemed so much closer on the computer, but she couldn't even see the mountain yet. She'd never be able to make things right and have her mommy love her again. But she couldn't go home.

Maybe her mommy wouldn't notice she'd left. Maybe she'd still be crying and Amanda could sneak back in tonight.

Her breath hitched in her chest as she wiped her tears. She'd go home and hide in the garage until everyone went to bed and then she'd go inside. No one would miss her.

"Amanda!"

She looked up. Mommy? "Mommy!" She jumped up and ran as fast as her tired legs could take her. "Mommy!"

"Oh, baby." Her mother scooped her into her arms and hugged her so tight she couldn't breathe, but she didn't say anything because she'd never felt so good in her life. She cried uncontrollably.

"Mommy, I tried to get Michelle back, I tried, but Heaven's too far away and I can't find it." Her mother's tears mingled with her own. "You're still crying, Mommy. I'm sorry."

"No, baby, no. I'm crying because I'm so happy."

"But—"

"I love you. I love you so much. You scared me, Amanda. I didn't know where you were, I didn't know why you'd gone."

"I didn't think you'd notice if I left."

Her mother's body stiffened. Then she sat on the ground and pulled Amanda into her lap and kissed her all over. "Baby, I love you. I'm the one who's sorry."

"You miss Michelle."

"Yes. Yes, I miss Michelle."

"I miss her too."

"I know you do." Brenda hugged her daughter tight to her chest, running her hand up and down her back, wishing she could take away the pain and sadness that had filled their lives since Michelle died.

She'd never forget Michelle. Michelle had a private space in her heart. But more important, she'd never neglect the rest of her family again.

They needed her. And what she hadn't realized until now was that she needed them.

CHAPTER
16

Zack and Olivia didn't talk much on the ride back from the Davidsons'. By the time they'd brought Amanda and Brenda back to the house, it was after noon. They went to the station, where the sketch artist shared her work, but it was too vague for the news media to use. The man could have been anyone, and the artist wasn't confident that Sean had remembered enough detail.

The only thing Sean described well was the tattoo. When Olivia saw the sketch, she knew without a doubt that it was the same tattoo as on the man who killed Missy.

Brian Harrison Hall had the identical tattoo on his arm.

"The man in California who was just released had a tattoo just like that," Olivia said. "A witness identified him by his tattoo."

Zack looked at his copy of the sketch. "Blue eagle. California—" he glanced at the board. "That was thirty-four years ago. The first victim." He paused, looked at Olivia. "We'd talked about how this killer probably doesn't work with a partner, but what if he and this other guy—what did you say his name was? Hall?"

She nodded, not surprised that Zack remembered.

He tapped the tattoo sketch. "Okay, let's think this through. Let's assume that Hall was innocent—and I'm betting he was. If he suspected our guy, he would have said something about it, agreed?"

"Agreed."

"So Hall is innocent, but it's too damn coincidental that two men of about the same age and build, with the same tattoo, in the same town, with access to the same truck didn't know each other."

"You mean they might have known each other even if Hall had nothing to do with the murder?" It clicked. It made sense.

"Exactly." Zack stood, paced. "Let's say, because of the tattoo, that they served in Vietnam together. Hall got out when?" He grabbed a file and started flipping through it.

"April 10, 1972," Olivia said, taking the file from him. She didn't want Zack to see all the details in the file. She'd only written the victims' first names on the white board.

If he delved too deep, he'd see that the first victim shared the same last name as her.

Zack looked at her in awe. "Good memory."

She didn't comment. She'd memorized Missy's case file.

"I'd bet our killer served with Hall in Vietnam. Maybe they were released about the same time. Maybe there was bad blood between them."

"Are you suggesting that our killer set Hall up? Framed him?"

"Anything's possible at this point. But I think we have to go with the assumption that they knew each other, and that gives us something to go on." He picked up the phone and dialed an extension. "It's not going to be easy to get military records, but I think your people can probably get them faster."

Into the phone, Zack said, "Chief? Travis here. Look, I think we need to contact the Seattle bureau. I meant to call you this morning, but with looking for Amanda Davidson . . . yeah, right. . . . Two things. First, Agent St. Martin and I have a theory that our killer served in Vietnam and was discharged around April 1972—say between the end of 1971 and October 1972. Second, remember the marks on the victim's forearms? Doug Cohn talked to several labs last night and the same marks appear on their victims. Twelve punctures. We need some expert guidance to help figure out what they could mean."

Zack listened for a moment, then said, "Okay, you call and set it up, then have them contact me and Agent St. Martin and I'll debrief them on what we've uncovered so far." He hung up.

"You know," he said, "after the chief puts in the request with Seattle, you should probably work as the liaison with your people. I don't have a problem with it. I've met a lot of Feds who jerked this department around, but you've been fantastic. I wouldn't have had half this stuff if you hadn't brought it in."

"I—" What could she say to that? She took a deep breath. "Zack, I think I should explain—"

"Hold that thought—I have an idea."

"What?"

"Get Hall to cooperate."

She blinked. "I don't understand."

"The guy who was just released. I'll bet he knows exactly who we're looking for. Even if he hasn't thought of it, he'll probably come up with a name if we ask the right questions—such as, did you know anyone who served in Vietnam who was in Redwood City with you? A lot of those guys would have hung out together. The atmosphere sucked for the military back then. I'll bet he knows him, or can give us a couple of names of guys with a similar tattoo."

Olivia didn't know what to say. Yes, the idea was brilliant. Hall most certainly would have names. But the thought of her seeing him after she'd testified against him, back then and every time he came up for parole, terrified her.

But it had to be done. It was the biggest lead they had.

"I'll call the district attorney's office and ask them to get in touch with Hall's lawyer," she said.

"While you do that, I'm going to talk to Doug Cohn and see what's going on with the lab files on those twelve marks."

Zack walked by and squeezed her shoulder. The gesture was intimate as his fingers massaged her neck. "We're close, I can feel it. Keep it up, and when we catch this bastard I'm treating you to dinner overlooking Lake Union."

Then he left.

She let him go. She could have stopped him, told him exactly why she was here, but she didn't. She was simply buying time.

In her notebook, she looked up the number of the San Mateo County District Attorney's office, where Hamilton Craig was the D.A. She got passed from office to office, and finally someone told her he was unavailable and could they help her?

She didn't want to talk to someone she didn't know, so she hung up and found Gary Porter's cell phone number.

Gary was the cop, now retired, who'd investigated Missy's case and had come to every parole meeting to speak against Brian Hall's release. He'd not only supported Olivia each time she testified against Hall's parole, but had been the father figure she didn't have during the original trial. Her own parents were so grief-stricken and distraught, they barely knew she was in the same room, let alone what she'd gone through telling the prosecutors and judge what happened the day Missy disappeared.

No matter what transpired with this case, even if she lost her job or her friends or Zack's respect, she would never regret her decision if she saved Amanda Davidson from the emotional pain she'd suffered as a child.

Gary answered on the third ring.

"Gary, it's Olivia St. Martin. How are you?"

"Could be better."

"What's wrong?"

He paused. "Didn't you get my message? I left one on your home phone and at your office two days ago."

"No. I didn't. I—I'm not in Virginia right now."

"Hamilton Craig was shot and killed. The police think he surprised a burglar in his house."

"Hamilton? *He's dead?*"

She rested her forehead on her hand, her skin suddenly clammy. She couldn't imagine the vibrant district attorney who'd been larger than life to her as a child—dead. That was why she'd received the runaround at the district attorney's office.

"The funeral is this evening."

"I'm so sorry."

"If you weren't calling about Hamilton, why did you call?"

"There might be a lead in Missy's murder."

Long silence. "Oh?"

"I've been sort of unofficially helping on another case that has striking similarities to Missy's. We think maybe Hall knew Missy's killer." She explained about the tattoos, what the Seattle witness saw, and Zack's theory that the killer had served in Vietnam with Hall and perhaps had set him up, or at least knew him when he stole his truck.

Gary didn't say anything for a long time.

"Gary?"

"Are you in Seattle now?"

"Yes."

"I didn't know you'd retained your field agent status."

She didn't respond.

"You don't have to say anything. What do you want me to do?"

"I got the runaround at the district attorney's office—they didn't tell me about Hamilton—and I don't have any other contacts there. I need someone to contact Hall's attorney and see if we can interview him."

"You?"

"Either the detective I'm working with, or someone down there. Not me, not personally. I know I can't be anywhere around it. But I think Hall will cooperate, don't you? Wouldn't he want to know if someone set him up to go to prison?"

"You're right, Hall will bite. Are you coming down too?"

"I—I doubt it." She wanted to, but as soon as the

local FBI stepped in, she'd be ordered back to Virginia. "But I'm going to try. I just won't sit in on the interview."

"I'll contact Hamilton's office and pass along the information. I'm sure they'll help. How can I reach you?"

"My cell phone. Or better yet, have them call Detective Zack Travis of the Seattle Police Department." She gave him Zack's contact information, said goodbye, and hung up.

Olivia buried her face in her arms and breathed deep. Her life was spiraling out of control, but they were so much closer to finding Missy's killer. That counted for something. Even if Zack sent her back to Virginia, or Rick Stockton fired her, she couldn't discount what she'd brought to the investigation.

She had to focus on that.

The phone on the conference table rang. "Hello?" she answered.

"Liv, it's Zack. Get down to the lab. The genius Doug Cohn just figured out what the marks mean and you're not going to believe it."

Eight people crammed into the lab conference room, which was half the size of the one Zack had commandeered for the Slayer investigation. Olivia hated the moniker the press had put on the killer, but it seemed to have stuck and she'd heard more than one cop use it.

Doug Cohn stood at the front, sheepish with the audience, fidgeting with his reading glasses as he took them on and off. In addition to Doug, Zack, and Olivia, Nelson Boyd, and Jan O'Neal were in the room, two of Doug's staff introduced as Randy and Deb, and the chief of police himself, Lance Pierson.

Whereas Olivia thought she'd be nervous, the familiarity of the charts and information on the wall about science and forensics actually gave her confidence and comfort. Doug cleared his throat. "Thanks for coming. I'm going to make this as short as possible, but I think it's important that we all understand how I came to this conclusion," he said.

Zack spoke. "To catch everyone up to speed, first we focused on the trucks we know were used to transport the victim. Boyd?"

The young detective straightened. "Detective

O'Neal and I went to six households in King County where both a Ford Expedition and a Dodge Ram were registered. Everyone was helpful, allowed us to inspect their vehicles, and accounted for where each vehicle was on the days in question."

"What about the Expedition reported stolen the day before Benedict was kidnapped?" Zack asked.

"No sign of it. We've alerted all neighboring states to be on the lookout."

"I'm inclined to agree with Agent St. Martin's theory that the suspect steals a vehicle when convenient," Zack said, "and replaces it before anyone knows it's missing."

"That would mean the killer has access to these cars for up to three days where no one would know it's missing, or where he was free to use different vehicles and no one thought it was unusual," Chief Pierson said.

No one said anything for a few seconds. "We need to contact all the rental agencies, car dealerships, and long-term airport parking attendants," Zack said.

"Boyd and I can cover that," Jan O'Neal said, making notes.

"I have a search set up on the auto-theft database," Doug interjected, "so if any SUV or covered truck is stolen in King County or the surrounding area, I'm notified. There have been twenty-three reported thefts in the last two days, and Detective Travis has alerted patrols to put them on the priority list."

"He uses them for transport primarily; he doesn't kill his victims in the vehicle," Olivia said. "That amount of blood would be impossible to eliminate completely."

"But we've never found a crime scene," Zack said. "The bodies are dumped."

They glanced at each other.

"What about his own property?" Doug interjected. "He would need privacy, so it would be a large parcel. Maybe in the foothills. Someplace that has little or no foot traffic and few neighbors."

"He'd be in a house, not an apartment," Olivia said.

Doug nodded. "A place where no one could see him carry a body back and forth from a car into his house."

"Attached garage or some acreage."

"Or maybe he takes the victim to a far-off location to kill her, then dumps her body in town," Zack said.

"Either way we're looking for a private area," Pierson agreed.

"Why dump the body in town? He could leave them exposed in the mountains and few people would find them." Olivia thought about the twelve-year-long Bozeman Butcher investigation. They still hadn't recovered all the known victims, and probably never would.

"Except for the first victim," Zack reminded her. He told the room what he and Olivia had discussed about the possible spontaneous first murder, the body left in a more remote location, making a speedy discovery less likely.

No one had a good answer as to why the killer dumped the subsequent bodies in town.

Zack said, "I asked Doug to work with the labs in other jurisdictions where similar crimes occurred, thanks to the information provided by Agent St. Martin. The markings on the victim's forearm bugged both Doug and me. Neither the coroner nor a cursory search in the criminal database yielded anything close to it."

"The marks were made postmortem," Doug said. "Twelve punctures in the victim's forearm, uniform in appearance."

Chief Pierson asked, "Does the number twelve mean anything? Is it a count of his victims?"

"We considered that, except that all his victims have the same twelve punctures. Twelve can mean anything—there are twelve apostles in the Bible, twelve is a dozen, it could be the age he thinks his victims are, almost anything," Doug said.

"That's why I asked you to contact the Seattle bureau," Zack said to Pierson. "Agent St. Martin says their research department can look into it and see if it's significant."

"But we don't need to consult with them anymore," Doug said, "because we figured it out. At least, I think we did."

"You did," Zack assured him.

Doug stepped away from a corkboard where three sets of two pictures were posted. Olivia instantly recognized the second picture as being taken with a microscope camera. The cuts, which on the surface looked like punctures—almost like commas—were actually two distinct marks.

"The top pictures are from Michelle Davidson, the middle from Jennifer Benedict, the bottom from a victim in Massachusetts. As you can see, the marks are virtually identical on each victim. Clearly, this 'signature,' for lack of a better word, ties our killer with Massachusetts. And the other labs I spoke with have similar files, though many are in storage, as the cases go back twenty or thirty years."

"Doug has done a fabulous job getting this information," Zack said. "We have virtually every other jurisdiction working with us on this. We're getting more information through fax and e-mail, and boxes of evidence shipped to us. But, because of the sensitive nature in dealing with Kansas and Kentucky because they convicted someone for those crimes, we decided not to contact them until we had a suspect in custody. Then we'll share our information with those departments and they can decide what to do with the prisoners. There may be additional information we're not privy to."

"If we can keep the press at bay while we track down this guy, all the better," Pierson said. "I don't want to muddy the waters."

Olivia had been staring at the marks on the victims' forearms. They appeared to be small holes and lines. Hole, line, line, hole, line, line, hole. Then the pattern changed, if it was a pattern at all. "There are two distinctive marks," she said. "Like holes and lines, but there doesn't appear to be a pattern."

"Very good." Doug nodded his approval and picked up a metal-tipped pointer. "Actually, it was your information that tipped me off."

"Mine?"

"You told Detective Travis about the wrongful conviction in California. The guy had a tattoo— similar to the one identified by our witness Sean Miller—and he had served in Vietnam. So I called my dad. He's eighty-five, but he served in World War II and knows everything about the military. It's his obsession. We talked about the tattoo, and he said the eagle was a common tattoo for GIs. Then I asked him the question that was bugging me about the marks—that it appears it's not a pattern and though uniform, looks like dots and lines. He asked me to read off the dots and lines—just like that, 'Can you read them to me?' he asked. So I did. And he said, 'Morse code.' "

"Morse code?" Olivia said, her mouth dropping open. "He's marking his victims with Morse code?"

"Morse code was a system of dots and dashes, standard use for telegraphy in the military and other functions, but it's been phased out since 1979. It's obsolete now."

"But in Vietnam it was commonly used," Pierson said. "That makes sense."

"In Morse code, each letter is assigned dots and dashes. For example, the letter 'A' is dot-dash, the letter 'B' is dash-dot-dot-dot, and so on. Because there's no pause, no break, between the marks on our victims, it took my dad a few minutes to figure it out, but we have a word."

Doug paused. "Angel."

Angel? Olivia mouthed the word. Her heart thudded in her chest as she asked, "What does it mean? Is he *signing* the bodies? Does *angel* refer to him? Or is he saying that his victim is now an angel? Or something else entirely?"

"Bingo," Zack said. "That's the million-dollar question. Chief, have you called Seattle FBI yet?"

"The bureau chief was in court, but I left all my numbers. He'll call back. I've worked with him in the past."

"We need to find out what *angel* means," Zack said. "Whether it's his signature, the way he views himself, or whether it references the victim. We also need to get a file for all military discharges, honorable or dishonorable, up until the first murder. Olivia, what happened with your conversation on that old case?"

"The district attorney recently died, but I spoke with the detective in charge of the original investigation and he's going to track down Hall's attorney and see when you can talk to him," Olivia said. "I gave him your contact information and told him it was vital we speak with Hall as soon as possible."

Zack filled in the rest of the team on the likely connection between a wrongful conviction and the killer.

"We don't have much time," Zack told everyone. "If his pattern holds, he'll kill once more, then disappear. If we don't get him now, he may not resurface for years."

Over the years, he'd had a variety of jobs under a variety of names, but his best source of information came from working in restaurants.

When he lived in Atlanta, his name was Tom Ullman and he was a bartender. Hands down, he yielded the best personal information and found the right truck most easily when he tended bar. But he also had to listen to a lot of crap, and everyone wanted to have a conversation.

He didn't want to talk; he only wanted to listen.

He didn't work in a restaurant or bar in Colorado or Kentucky, but when he hit Massachusetts, his name was Andrew Richardson and he found employment in a large, friendly restaurant in a middle-class section of Boston. And since he was a patient man, he was able to wait for the information he needed.

Also, in restaurants he could easily and discreetly see the parking lot. When he learned what he needed to know, he watched the patrons leave. If they had the right type of vehicle, it was an omen that the time was right for action.

Now he answered to Steve Williams.

Everything was coming together perfectly, as if preordained. He'd already found the angel. Tonight, he'd found the truck.

He'd been on Vashon for well over a year and had not only come to recognize the regulars, but knew their vehicles and schedules. Karl and Flo Burgess were retired and lived in West Seattle. They came to Vashon at least once a week to eat, and usually sat in his section because he didn't have to be reminded that Mrs. Burgess liked four olives in her vodka martini.

They owned a Ford-150 with camper shell.

He placed the tray with their change on the table. "Thank you for coming. See you next week."

He was about to walk away when Mrs. Burgess said, "We're leaving tomorrow to visit our daughter. We won't be back for a couple of weeks."

His heart raced and he smiled. "Have a safe drive."

Karl Burgess shook his head. "I'm just not up to making the drive to Phoenix this year."

"His back," Mrs. Burgess said with a half-whisper. "Growing old." She smiled and patted her husband's hand.

"I'll see you when you return, then," he said and walked away.

He was so eager to complete his planning he could hardly complete his shift, but he forced himself to remain patient. Everything was coming together perfectly. Tomorrow was Friday; he knew exactly where his angel would be.

He eavesdropped on the Burgess's conversation as they finished their coffee. Their flight left early. They were driving to the airport. That meant long-term parking lot.

He'd gotten in and out of the long-term parking lot easily in Atlanta, Kansas City, and Austin. Seattle would be a piece of cake.

He'd gotten into the habit of hanging out after his shift for a few minutes because most of the servers did it. He didn't want to stand out. He knew how people thought of him—a friendly guy who liked his job, working to support his art. He had some talent, and made a point of bringing in sketches to show the crew. It gave him the necessary background so no one gave him a second thought.

He'd told them he was divorced and had moved and settled on Vashon Island for a change of pace. They also believed he had a grown daughter in college, so anytime he was late or had to disappear for a few days, he said he was visiting his daughter in Oregon. Close enough for a weekend trip, but not close enough where anyone would expect her to visit.

Success was in the details. Laying the foundation so that people believed what he wanted them to believe. And because every story in every state was similar, he never lost track of who he pretended to be.

But tonight, he said he was tired and left the restaurant as soon as he closed out; he walked to his cottage a half-mile away, and went right to his room. He took out his map and his notepad and plotted out each step for tomorrow.

Tomorrow would be the last. The thought was bittersweet. He liked the Pacific Northwest. He particularly liked living on the water. It reminded him of his early childhood, before everything changed. When it was just him and his mother, inseparable, living on the coast in a state he barely remembered. Before Bruce Carmichael came into their lives and stole their innocence and his mother's life. Before Angel.

He found himself sitting on the small cottage porch watching the sky change color. The sun had already disappeared, but it wasn't the setting sun that enticed him, it was the layers of the sky. Azure and lavender and jewel green. He watched as one color faded into another, growing darker and darker, as the Seattle skyline came to life.

Angel would have loved it here.

"Take me away, please."

He and Angel were sitting on the narrow balcony of a three-story walk-up, cramped because the balcony was barely large enough for a planter of flowers. The old lady in the apartment next door had six pots teetering on the edge of the iron railing; twice in the three months they'd lived here one of her planters had fallen and shattered on the cement walkway below.

"Where can we go?" he said.

He was scared. He hated being scared, but the fear ate at him until he couldn't think. It wasn't fear of the unknown, or fear that he would starve, or fear that he would be killed.

It was fear that he was more like Bruce than he wanted to be.

"Anywhere," she whispered, hugging her knees, her beautiful blonde hair hanging down. It shim-

mered for him, sparkling even here, on this filthy balcony above a garbage-strewn walk. He reached out and touched it. So soft. "It hurts when he touches me. It hurts so bad. Sometimes, I can escape and make up stories so I can think about something else. But sometimes I can't and then it's worse."

Angel had had her ninth birthday the weekend before. And something about that night had changed her.

Bruce had been hurting Angel in her bed for two years, ever since their mom died and Bruce took them away. But last week was worse.

"He's going to kill me," she whispered. "Just like Mama."

"I won't let him kill you."

"You can't stop him."

Anger bubbled up. She thought he couldn't protect her. That he wouldn't stand up for her. Didn't she know how much he loved her?

"I'm going to run away," she said. "If you won't help me, I'll go by myself." She sniffed.

"You can't leave me."

"I don't want to. I'm scared." She leaned into him and let him hug her. The anger was gone, but the fear was stronger than ever.

"I'll find a way. I'll find a way to keep him away from you forever."

CHAPTER
18

After Hamilton Craig's funeral, Gary Porter walked into his empty house. He missed his wife, Janet, but considering all the sacrifices she'd made during his career, he couldn't stop her from pursuing her dreams now, even though they were in their sixties. She'd been a European history major in college and was now a docent for a major travel company. Currently, she was leading a senior-citizen tour through France. She always asked him to join her, but Gary had no desire to travel. He liked being home, having a routine. For him, travel equaled stress.

While he missed Janet, when she was home their relationship was better, stronger. He liked hearing about her job and the sights and loved the slideshow she'd put together for him after each tour.

Tonight, however, he felt old and would have given anything to have Janet with him. It was Hamilton's funeral, of course, making him feel mortal. Reminding him that life was unfair, that a random act of violence could steal the life of a good man.

Gary absently flipped on lights as he made his way to the den, his steps echoing on the hardwood floors. A quick glance at the clock in the hall told him it was already too late to call Janet in Paris.

A corner floor lamp next to his reading chair—an old La-Z-Boy he'd had for twenty-some years—and a desk lamp provided the only light for the room. He sat heavily into the upholstered desk chair and booted up the computer. While he waited, he opened his bottom drawer and took out a bottle of Glenlivit. He didn't drink when Janet was home, but he'd taken to sipping a glass or two in the evenings when she was away. He missed her.

He missed the job.

Gary ran a hand over his face, feeling the whiskers that were now predominantly gray. Hamilton's funeral was the fourth he'd been to this year. Two of the deaths were heart attacks, and one was a cop killed in the line of duty. As his colleagues aged and retired, more and more funerals would be the result of natural causes.

He poured two fingers of Scotch into his glass and sipped as he logged into his e-mail account.

At least he was still able to help. He'd made contact with Ned Palmer, one of the assistant district attorneys who was familiar with the Melissa St. Martin investigation, and Ned promised to jump on getting an interview with Brian Hall. Gary passed on the Seattle contact information, worried about Olivia.

She had been a scared five-year-old when he'd met her, but she kept everything bottled up inside. Her parents had neglected her, lost in their own grief, and both he and Hamilton had taken her under their protective wings. Made sure she didn't have to testify in court, only tell the judge what she'd seen. No cross-examination. Nothing to further terrify the child.

She'd grown into a brilliant, beautiful woman, but Gary knew her sister's murder had forever changed the course of her life. He'd seen it happen many, many times. Violent death destroyed more than one life.

The room went dark.

"Shit," he muttered as he rummaged in his desk for the small Maglite he kept handy. Probably a blown fuse. Hadn't had one of those in a while.

He couldn't find the Maglite and stood, feeling his way to the door and down the hall. There was a flashlight in the kitchen, right there on the wall in a charger, because Janet was always worried about earthquakes. When the power went out, the light went on so you could see your way in the dark. Gary could see the shadows it cast as he neared the kitchen.

At the same time he crossed the threshold, the back door opened. He reached for his gun out of habit, but he no longer carried.

"Who—"

Before he finished his sentence, he recognized Brian Harrison Hall. The man raised his arm, revealing a small semiautomatic handgun. At the same time Gary turned to run, he heard the report of the firearm and fire spread across his chest. Again the sound, but the pain didn't get worse.

He knew he would die.

Gary fell, tried to get up, stumbled down the hall a few feet, then collapsed.

He couldn't catch his breath. He sensed Hall standing over him.

"Bastard," he sputtered, his voice sounding far away. Down a long tunnel.

"You made me a killer," Hall said.

Gary heard another sound, but the last thing he thought of was Janet and her beautiful, laughing brown eyes.

Zack, Olivia, and Doug Cohn worked in the main conference room mapping the abductions and evidence from the increasing pile of reports other jurisdictions had sent them. They were looking for anything, any connection, to give them another lead. Maybe something that tied in with the Morse code or the word *angel*.

Chief Pierson popped his head in at nine that night and said, "I'm leaving, but I just got off the phone with the Seattle bureau. They're going to jump on the 'angel' connection and also run all Vietnam veterans who were discharged from October 1971 through October 1972 and had a California address. It's going to be a huge list, but it's in a database. They can get it to us tomorrow afternoon."

He continued, "They're putting one of their top agents on it immediately, and he'll probably be in contact with you."

"Who?" Olivia heard herself asking.

"Quincy Peterson. Know him?"

She nodded, unable to speak. Quinn. Miranda's husband, as well as a good friend.

Out of all the agents she knew, she couldn't have asked for a better one.

But now she was going to have to admit to her closest friends that she'd been lying to them.

"Is he any good?" Zack asked her after Pierson left the room.

"The best," she said.

The phone rang and Olivia jumped as Zack answered. She needed food and sleep. She needed to get out of here. Her nerves were all over the place. Should she call Quinn tonight and explain everything? Yes, she needed to tell him exactly why she'd done what she did. He deserved it.

Quinn played by the book, but he knew when to bend the rules. She just didn't know if he was willing to break them.

"We'll be there." Zack dropped the phone on the hook as he scribbled on a notepad. "Hey Superagent, we need to hightail it down to California. That was the assistant D.A. in San Mateo County. He tracked down Hall's attorney and we have a meeting scheduled for ten A.M." He picked up the phone before Olivia could respond. "Hey, Joe, could you call the airport and get two tickets to San Francisco? Myself and Olivia St. Martin. The chief will clear it, I promise. I think this is our break."

He hung up again. "Joe says we'll need to fly out tonight. He's setting it up. Let's swing by my place and your hotel and grab a bag."

"I can't go," Olivia blurted out. She glanced at Doug Cohn and wondered how to get out of this. The day Zack was gone would buy her time to talk to Quinn.

"Why?"

"I—look, I can't ask Doug to do all this work. These are a lot of files to go through; it'll take him all night working alone. Probably all of tomorrow, too."

"Boyd and O'Neal can cover us. This is big, Olivia. You have to come; you know more about the old cases than I do. Come on, we'll talk about it on the way."

Zack had a way of running all over her arguments, and she didn't know what to say. She wanted time to talk to Quinn before he showed up, but flying to California killed that idea.

She followed Zack from the room and tried to think how she would tell him the truth about her sister's murder.

CHAPTER
19

Zack drove by his house first because Olivia's hotel was closer to the airport.

"Make yourself at home," he said as he unlocked the side door and flipped on the lights. "I'll only be a minute."

The side door opened into a window-enclosed eating area, a room that promised to be sunny and cheerful in the mornings. The table was an immaculate fifties style with red Formica top and sturdy steel legs, the kind that twenty years ago was outdated, but now was trendy. Little pots of herbs and flowers filled a window box.

Framed pictures of fruit crate labels lined the one wall, and as Olivia stepped into the kitchen she found the quaint art filling every available space. She wandered from the kitchen—which matched the table in the nook except for the modern appliances—and into a formal dining room.

The furniture was old, obviously antique, but well cared for. Lace doilies that didn't fit Zack's personality clung to the surface of the buffet and table. She left that room and found herself in the living room, and knew this was where Zack spent his time when at home.

The dark leather furniture was soft and smooth. Pictures of the Pacific Northwest and ocean scenery lined the walls. Several antique paintings in gilded frames were set off by lights. Books were crammed two-deep into floor-to-ceiling bookshelves on either side of a brick fireplace. Stacks of books lined the corners—mostly mysteries, bestsellers, and biographies. But what surprised her most were the plants—lots of them. Several hung from the ceiling; there were two large floor plants, pothos if she remembered correctly, and several small plants of all kinds on the tables, all of them thriving. She wouldn't have thought Zack Travis had such a green thumb.

The room was cluttered but not overly messy. Comfortable.

She walked over to a round table in the corner. Intermingled with the plants were a few photographs in antique silver frames. She recognized a young Zack immediately—his eyes were just as dark and intense when he was a child.

At first, Olivia thought the older woman in the photographs was his mother, but when she saw them together she realized the tall, elderly matron was his grandmother.

She wondered why he had no pictures of his mother in the house.

A girl showed up in several of the pictures, possibly ten years younger than Zack. There was no doubt they were brother and sister—Amy, he'd told her. And she was dead.

Olivia wondered what had happened to her. She'd been a beautiful child and lovely young lady.

She heard Zack's footsteps on the hardwood floors

and turned so he didn't think she was prying. "I like your house," she told him.

"Thanks. It was my grandmother's."

"She died?"

"Sixteen years ago."

"I'm sorry."

He looked over at one of the pictures on the table and smiled wistfully. "I called her Mae. Short for Margaret. She didn't like being called 'Grandma' or anything like that. She was a hoot, and I couldn't have been raised by a better woman."

"What happened to your parents?" Olivia asked, then put her hand to her mouth. "I'm sorry, I'm prying."

Zack waved off her apology. "My mother didn't want to be burdened with kids. She left me here when I was nine. I guess I was a handful. Mae took me in—she hadn't seen me since I was a baby; my mother and Mae didn't get along. But Mae never took it out on me. Then, three years later, my mother came by again, pregnant and penniless and heartbroken. She moved in and she and Mae bickered constantly, but they wanted to make it work.

"Then she had Amy, and left four weeks later with some guy she'd met the night before. We never heard from her again."

"Oh, Zack, that's awful." Olivia didn't know what was worse, to be abandoned by your mother physically like Zack, or emotionally like she'd been after Missy died.

"When I was eighteen I tried to track her down. More for Amy than anything. Amy constantly asked about her, wanted to know when she was going to visit. I think it was hard on her having an old woman for a mother and a teenager for a brother. So I did some research, looked at some public records, and I think I figured out what happened."

"What?" Olivia couldn't help but ask.

"She died in a drunk-driving accident." He laughed, but there was no humor in his voice. "She was driving, she was drunk, and she killed two innocent people in the collision."

He hoisted a bag over his shoulder. He'd showered and shaved, Olivia noted—his hair was still damp and a fresh, soapy scent surrounded him. "The police never contacted us because they didn't know who she was. I found her in a Jane Doe database with the help of a Seattle cop. They were very helpful—I wasn't the easiest kid to deal with. A lot like our witness Sean Miller. Chip on the shoulder and all that. It was after finding out about my mother that I decided I wanted to be a cop. I said goodbye to some bad influences, went to community college, and the rest is history."

"What about Amy?"

Pain and conflicting emotions clouded his face, but he looked like he wanted to tell her. She held her breath, but didn't know why. She had a feeling this was important to Zack, and sensing he wanted to share it with her opened her heart. It was as if they each had taken an emotional step closer to something she couldn't recognize or define, but a place she yearned for. Trust? Understanding? She didn't know.

"She got herself in a mess and ended up dead."

He had chosen his words carefully. There was more to the story than what he'd said, but Olivia didn't push.

Instead of elaborating, he changed the subject. "We'd better get a move on. Our flight leaves in ninety minutes."

The intimate moment was broken, but the connection didn't disappear. Olivia wondered if Zack noticed anything different between them, or if it was a figment of her imagination.

On the drive to the hotel to pick up her overnight bag, Olivia ran through every conceivable way to tell Zack about why she couldn't go with him to California. She had to. She couldn't juggle all the lies anymore.

He pulled into the parking lot and shut off the engine. He was about to open his door when she touched his arm.

"Wait."

He turned to her. "What's wrong?"

"I can't go with you."

He looked at her for a good minute, his expression unreadable. "That's what you said at the station. What's going on?"

She swallowed. *Get it over with.* "I told you my sister was killed and that's why I joined the FBI. But I didn't tell you the whole story."

He tensed beside her but didn't say anything.

Olivia took a deep breath. "Missy was nine and I was five. We were at the park and it was getting late. I wanted to go home, but Missy was reading. She always lost herself in books." She tried to smile, but it turned into a grimace.

"I wandered off to the swings. I was mad at her because I was scared, but I would get in so much trouble if I walked home alone. We had to stick together. That was the rule.

"I looked over and a man was talking to her. I yelled, ran over to them, but he hit me and grabbed her and that was the last time I saw her alive."

"Oh my God, Liv. I'm sorry. No wonder this case is so important to you." He touched her cheek. It turned into a caress. She reached up and tried to push his hand away, but he took her hand in his and held it tight. "You've done remarkably well on this case even though it hit close to home. Sometimes, our personal fears drive our goals. That's okay."

"No, no. Let me finish." Instead of making the conversation easier, his understanding tightened her heart. "Please."

He nodded, not letting go of her hand.

"I can't interview Brian Harrison Hall. I testified against him. I helped put him in prison. He was convicted of killing my sister."

Zack blinked once, twice, as he absorbed what Olivia had just told him. He couldn't have heard right.

"What?"

"I promise you, I'm objective. I'm not going to jeopardize this case."

"You lied to me." Why did it surprise him? Hadn't he just said a couple of days ago that the Feds always kept important information to themselves?

He jerked his hand from hers and ran it through his hair. "Isn't this just wonderful? Why didn't you trust me?"

"It's not that I didn't trust you. I didn't know you when I came out here. I didn't know what I was really getting into. I'd done all that research, connecting the dots *because* of that wrongful conviction. If it weren't for me, Jillian and Jenny and Michelle might still be alive today. I fingered Hall because I saw his tattoo. I testified against him. If I'd done something differently, maybe none of this would have happened today, the police would have kept open the investigation, something!"

During Olivia's impassioned speech, Zack studied her. He saw the pain on her face, the anguish and fervor. She hadn't openly shown her emotions, and except for her outburst at the lake after speaking to Brenda Davidson, she'd kept an emotional distance. Because she was too close to the case. The realization that she blamed herself for something that was clearly beyond her control further tempered his anger.

"I wish you'd told me at the beginning."

"I know, I'm sorry. I wanted to, but I thought you and everyone else would think I was too close to the case."

"Listen to me. You should have told me, because it explains a lot. Such as your outburst at the Davidsons'. If things had gone differently, we could have had a lot of problems with them. But you've been a vital part of this investigation, and I can honestly say I don't think we'd be this close without you." The cases she'd brought with her; interviewing Jenny's friends that led them to the witness, Sean Miller. And Zack had thrived when bouncing ideas and theories off her. She was a fantastic sounding board. Except when she doubted herself.

"That's what this has all been about—every time I asked you to give your opinion you hesitated. You didn't want to share your opinion because of what happened with your sister's investigation. Dammit, Olivia, you were a child! You saw what you saw. It's up to the adults to decipher the information and figure out what it means. You should know that by now."

"I do." Her voice was quiet, and she wouldn't look at him. "I know in my head I wasn't solely to blame for what happened then. There was circumstantial evidence, a prosecutor, the police force—but in my heart I think about what I could have done or said differently. All those little girls . . . gone. Like Missy."

Her words chilled him. He wanted to reassure her that everything would be all right, that they'd catch her sister's killer. That she could put the pain behind her knowing she'd done something important to right wrongs she had nothing to do with making in the first place.

He reached for her, ran the back of his hand against her creamy, delicate cheek. When he'd first met Olivia, he thought she was petite with a spine of steel. Rigid, professional, all business. For the first time, *fragile* crossed his mind. He tucked her hair behind her ear and pushed her chin up, forcing her to look at him.

Her omission still disturbed him on a different level, but he couldn't be angry with her.

"Liv," he said softly. "I can't take the years of pain from you, or the guilt since learning this Hall guy is innocent. But I can tell you that I think you're pretty incredible. You were five years old and had your life turned upside down. I can't imagine how that felt."

"You understand I can't interview Hall. I testified against him at his parole hearings. He wouldn't want to help me, not after spending thirty-four years in prison."

He nodded. "I understand. But I still need you down there. He may give us something to follow up on. Two are better than one, and we need to get back here as quickly as possible. And you know the case better than anyone. Will you observe the interview?"

She hesitated, then nodded.

"Good." He glanced at his watch.

"But—"

"No buts. You'd better run upstairs and grab your toothbrush, or we'll have to share."

As Zack said it, he realized he wouldn't mind sharing a lot more with Olivia than just a toothbrush.

Brian paced his rat-hole apartment late into the night. He didn't want to meet with his attorney and a Seattle cop in the morning.

Especially not after what he'd done.

They didn't know. They couldn't know. He'd left no fingerprints, no one saw him, there was nothing to connect him to the killings. But his skin prickled and he couldn't help but feel that his crimes were plastered all over his face.

His attorney had talked him into the meeting.

"Look, Brian," Miles had said after Brian hemmed and hawed about going down to the police station, "I understand how you feel. I got the D.A.'s office to give you immunity. Nothing you say will be used against you. And if you help them catch this killer, you'll be a hero."

"But I don't know anything! I wasn't there. I didn't know the girl. I told you I had nothing to do with it."

"I believe you, Brian. But the cops think someone

you knew may have framed you. Stolen your truck and used it in the crime. Don't you want to know who's responsible for your imprisonment?"

"The cops are," he had mumbled. But ultimately, he agreed as long as he didn't have to go to the police station. Miles arranged for them to meet at the public defender's office in the courthouse.

Brian couldn't sleep because he couldn't get the thought out of his mind that someone he knew had sent him to prison. Who hated him that much? He didn't have a lot of friends left in town when he'd come back from Vietnam. Those who didn't go to war went to college or moved away or looked down on him. He didn't hang out with the same guys anymore. Someone he worked with at the warehouse? One of the gang of vets he'd met at the club where he'd drunk too much that fateful day?

Dawn crested over the bay before he dozed off. A sick feeling ate at him throughout the night.

Had he killed two people for nothing?

CHAPTER
20

Zack drove from the hotel they'd stayed in outside the San Francisco airport thirty minutes south to Redwood City. Olivia commented that the area had changed dramatically since she'd last visited, but didn't seem inclined to talk about her childhood.

"When was the last time you were here?"

"Twelve years ago, when I graduated from Stanford."

"Stanford? Really. What was your major?"

"Criminal justice, psychology, and biology."

"Three degrees? Wow. So that makes you . . . what, thirty four? No—you'd be thirty-nine." She was five when her sister was killed.

"It's not polite to talk about a lady's age."

"Went to college late?"

"Something like that."

Zack stopped pushing. He'd hoped she'd open up and share what had been troubling her, but maybe she was reluctant just being back in the area where her sister had been killed. Remembering her parents—that her mother killed herself.

"Is your dad still here?"

She shook her head. "He sold the house and moved as soon as I left for college."

"That must have been hard on you."

"It was harder living in the house after Missy was killed."

"You don't want to talk about it."

He felt her eyes on him and he glanced over, taking in her tired eyes and pale skin before turning his attention back to the road.

She spoke after a time. "My mother never got over Missy's death. She wouldn't let us move; she wouldn't let anyone touch anything in Missy's bedroom. I tiptoed around the house so she wouldn't see me, because when she looked at me I saw hate in her eyes."

"She didn't hate you."

Olivia didn't say anything, and Zack reached over and squeezed her hand. She flinched, but didn't pull away.

"Why don't you like being touched?"

"I don't know," she said quickly. Too quickly. "I suppose—well, after Missy died I sort of disappeared. To my mom and my dad. It was easier for them that way."

"You were five!" He couldn't help but feel hostility toward the parents who'd neglected their living daughter because they were grieving for their dead one.

"When my mother committed suicide I asked my dad if we were going to move. He just shrugged. I think if I had been old enough and put the house on the market myself, he wouldn't have cared."

Olivia paused, looking down at Zack's hand wrapped over hers. Strength radiated from his body, and she was emboldened. She'd never told anyone what happened the day her mother committed suicide.

"I found her body."

"How old were you?"

"Six." She closed her eyes and pictured her mother's bloody remains. Her mother had taken sleeping pills with a vodka chaser, but may have survived that. To ensure her death, she'd put a gun in her mouth and pulled the trigger.

"She shot herself. In Missy's room, on the anniversary of her death. I heard the shot. Dad was at work. I'd just gotten home from school. There was so much blood. On the wall behind Missy's pretty white bed. All over her dolls and toys. Everywhere."

"Oh God, Liv."

Suddenly he pulled off the freeway. Olivia opened her eyes and was surprised when Zack turned off the ramp and into the parking lot of some business. He shut off the ignition.

"I'm sorry, I shouldn't have brought it up," she began.

He grabbed her chin and forced her to look at him. At first she thought he was angry with her, and maybe he was, but not for the reason she thought.

"Stop saying you're sorry." His voice was low and gruff, full of restrained emotion.

She was drawn toward Zack, his dark eyes searching hers, as if sharing his vitality, his strength.

"Liv, you've been blaming yourself for something that is simply not your fault."

"I don't blame myself."

"Don't you?"

What did she really think? "I don't know."

"Who, then? What's eating you up inside? Your father? Your mother?"

A tear leaked from an eye, the unfamiliar wetness sliding down her cheek. "I blame Missy's killer for taking her. God for creating him in the first place. I blame me for not stopping him. I blame Missy for not leaving the park when I wanted to. My father for walking around the house like a ghost. And my mother for . . . for looking at me as if I should have been the one to die!"

Zack gathered Olivia in his arms as she cried silently, her body heaving but little sound escaping, as if she were fighting each tear. God, he wanted to take her pain. He would gladly shoulder the burden of her anguish if he could.

His mother had dumped him. She'd left him because it was convenient. She left Amy because it was convenient. He'd had a hard time with it when he realized his mother loved her freedom more than her children. He'd felt abandoned by his mother, but Mae had never made him feel unwanted or unloved.

Everything became clear to him. Olivia's reaction to Brenda Davidson and little Amanda. Her obsession with the case. Her reason for joining the FBI in the first place. Justice was a powerful motivator, and while she'd believed her sister's killer had been behind bars until recently, she was fighting for the living victims as well as the dead.

She'd spent her life fighting for victims like her.

He smoothed her hair, breathed in her freshness. He kissed her temple. Then her cheek. He tilted her chin so she looked him in the eye. Her lip quivered and her cheeks were bright with emotion.

"Olivia, when this is over I'm taking you away someplace. I want time alone with you. Without this case hanging over us, where we can really talk."

Her mouth opened in protest. He put his finger to her lips.

"Shh. We deserve it, Liv. I need to know everything about you. How you grew into this incredible woman sitting right here. You're smart and sexy and I'm damn glad you came to Seattle, not only because of the investigation."

He leaned in and touched his lips to hers, remembering yesterday when he'd spontaneously kissed her in her hotel room. She'd been so enticing in that thin robe that molded to her full breasts, showing everything while hiding it at the same time.

That image had been in the back of his mind for the last twenty-four hours. Thinking about how enticing she looked then, how beautiful she was sitting beside him now, he wanted to disappear with her. The two of them together. Alone. In bed.

He intended the kiss to be light, gentle, loving. She needed affection, not passion. But one taste of Olivia wasn't enough. She brought out the passion in him, a deep longing that he hadn't felt for a long, long time. An intense need to connect with her on every level he could. To know her mind, her body, her soul.

He deepened the kiss, her lips salty from her tears.

She moaned into his lips, a small but deep sound that bespoke desire. He swallowed her need, taking the kiss deeper, his hands wrapped around her delicate neck, her silky hair entwined in his large hands. He rubbed her shoulders, his hand trailing down to the curve of her round breast.

They pulled back at the same time. He swallowed, his heart pounding. Her hazel eyes glistened, coated with emotion and desire. Her mouth was red, lush, swollen from his furious kiss.

Reluctantly, he let her go. "I definitely want more time with you."

"After we catch this guy." Her voice was rough, but she had already gathered up the strength he'd seen in her the first day they'd met in Pierson's office.

He'd thought he'd wanted the killer bad before.

He wanted him even more now.

Olivia watched the interview from a secure room next to the public defender's conference room. She wished Gary Porter had come, not only because he'd set the wheels in motion but also because he'd always been by her side when she had to face Brian Hall. Instead, a young cop stood sentry at her side, his face blank.

Of course, Hall was innocent and she shouldn't fear him. Yet she did, an irrational and very real sensation that made her heart pound and her hands wring.

She couldn't believe she'd cried in Zack's arms. She felt foolish, but comforted at the same time. And then the kiss . . . her hands fluttered to her lips. *That kiss.*

She had to put it aside, think about it later.

When was the last time she'd cried? It might have been the day Missy disappeared. She had cried herself to sleep late that night, alone. She had tried to crawl into her mother's bed, but her father told her to leave, that her mother was sleeping in Missy's room until she came home.

Missy never came home.

Stop it. Stop thinking about it.

Olivia hadn't realized until today how much internal anger she still had at her parents. And at Missy, though her frustration with her sister was more that she was gone, and that wasn't her fault. It wasn't rational, Olivia knew, but there it was, laid out for her to cautiously examine.

It had been easy to hate Brian Hall when he was the villain, the man who stole not only her sister's life, but her family and security. His release brought back the other feelings she'd suppressed for so many years, like her anger at her family, particularly toward her mother. She should have seen it coming, especially after her confrontation with Brenda Davidson, but it wasn't until Zack's question earlier that day that Olivia *knew* she'd never forgiven her mother for treating her like a pariah.

For years, Olivia had wondered whether her mother would have felt the same way toward Missy if the roles had been reversed. If Olivia had died and Missy had lived. Would their mother have ignored Missy? Would she have mourned Olivia so deeply that she couldn't function any longer?

As a child, Olivia believed her mother would rather have had Olivia die and Missy live. As an adult, Olivia knew it wasn't as simple as that. It was like being in a burning building and only able to save the life of one of your two children: who would you pick? No matter which you chose, you would be filled with guilt over the one who'd died. You would look at the one left behind and wonder if you should have made the other choice. Bitterness and grief and pain would paralyze you until you couldn't look at your child without regret.

With years of psychology classes and science behind her, Olivia intellectually knew that her mother had a psychosis and was mentally unstable. Perhaps

Missy's death triggered it, or maybe she'd always had borderline personality disorder. Intuitively, Olivia knew she shouldn't blame her mother for everything she'd said and done—or hadn't said, hadn't done. In that case it was her father who should have stepped up and done something to get her mother help. To fill the role of both parents since her mother was incapable.

But the child inside Olivia just wanted to be loved completely, without reservation, because of who she was inside.

She didn't know if there was anything left inside worth loving.

Blaming others wasn't getting her anywhere. The guilt had been eating her alive. Zack was right—she apologized for everything, whether it was her fault or not. She had to stop.

She looked through the one-way mirror and saw Brian Harrison Hall step into the room. The familiar *thump-thump-thump* of her heart thudded in her chest, increasing in tempo. Even knowing he didn't kill Missy—and she no longer believed he was even involved—he still elicited deep, numbing fear within her.

She took a deep breath and focused on Zack. He faced her, looking into the mirror as if he could see her. His face reassured her, strengthened her.

This was it.

Zack sensed Olivia's tension on the other side of the mirror, then dismissed his feelings as ridiculous. She'd been upset when they'd first arrived, so it was natural he'd think she was still unnerved by the whole thing. Coming back to her hometown. Facing the man who for thirty-four years she believed killed her sister. Dealing with her own fears.

"They're on their way in," Assistant District Attorney Ross Perdue told Zack after closing his cell phone. Zack had been so lost in thoughts about Olivia and what she'd gone through that he'd almost forgotten the man was in the room with him. Perdue was a young, slick-looking lawyer, about thirty, who wore an expensive suit and Rolex watch. Zack wondered if he was from money, because public service certainly didn't pay that well.

"As I told you on the phone, we're granting Hall immunity if he says anything that incriminates himself. The way we see it, the man served thirty-four years in prison. If he's guilty as an accessory or for obstructing justice, his sentence would have been served already."

Zack wasn't completely happy with the arrangement, but as Perdue had explained earlier, Hall had initially balked. It could have taken days and a court order to force him to talk, and by that time, the killer could have struck again. They didn't have the luxury of fighting Hall at this point. They needed information *now*.

When Hall sauntered into the room with his attorney, Zack instantly disliked him. His attitude entered first, his body swaying as if he were in charge. But his eyes showed fear, wariness, darting back and forth like those of a rodent.

Hall was guilty of something. Zack smelled it. But he reminded himself he wasn't in this room to find out what penny-ante crap the guy had been up to in the weeks since he'd been released from prison. He was here to find out who Hall knew thirty-four years ago.

"Thank you for coming in, Mr. Hall," Zack said in his most cordial voice. He extended his hand. "Detective Zack Travis, Seattle Police Department." Obviously surprised, Hall shook it.

After introductions all around, they sat and Zack spoke. "I won't keep you long, Mr. Hall. Your attorney filled you in on why we need your help."

"You think someone framed me for that girl's murder."

Zack nodded. "Exactly."

"I don't know who, but I hope you catch him and he rots in prison like I almost did." Hall glared at Perdue.

"I have some questions that might help your memory."

"Go ahead. That's why I came here." He looked at Perdue again. "And nothing I say you can use to screw me with, right?"

"I took care of that," Hall's attorney Bledsoe interjected. "I showed you the papers on the way here."

"I just want to hear him say it."

"That's correct," Perdue said. "What's said in here is inadmissible in court. You have complete immunity."

Hall crossed his arms, smug.

Zack spoke. "When were you released from Vietnam?"

"April 10, 1972. Friggin' about time, too. I only signed for a year, but they kept me sixteen fucking months. That was crap."

"And you came to California. Were you born here, in Redwood City?"

Hall shrugged. "Down in Palo Alto. My ma has a house in Menlo Park. That's where I grew up."

"It's ten minutes south," Perdue explained.

"So you essentially came home," Zack prodded.

"Yeah. I had a job, though. In a warehouse. Moving shit and stuff."

"Did any of your buddies from the Army come back with you? Friends?"

Hall shrugged. "I dunno."

"Did you know anyone you worked with who had also been in Vietnam? Maybe they didn't serve with you, but had been there about the same time you were."

"Hell, I knew a bunch of vets after I came home. Met most of them after my discharge. *Honorable*," he stressed, then grunted. "Lotta good that did me in court when you guys railroaded me for killing that girl. I'm no fucking pervert. I don't get turned on by little girls."

Zack clenched his fist under the table to keep from throttling Hall for his cocky tone.

"Do you remember any of the vets you'd worked with, hung out with, maybe a roommate or drinking buddy?" Zack asked. "Someone with a tattoo on his left arm similar to yours?"

Hall frowned and looked up to his left, a sign that he was really trying to remember something. "There were a lotta guys in 'Nam that got tattooed up. I only got this one, on my first leave. Some of the guys, they got them all over their bodies." He shook his head. "A lot of us got eagles. American bird and all that crap."

"Any of the guys you knew when you came back to California?"

"A couple of the guys in the warehouse had tattoos like mine."

"Do you remember any names?"

"Um, there was the manager. He wasn't in 'Nam, but he did some time overseas in the early sixties. George something. I don't remember his last name. We called him George. He was there when I started, and he was there when I left."

Zack made a note of the information. The files had the information about Hall's employment. He remembered the name of the manager, George Levin. Definitely worth checking him out.

"Anyone else you can think of?"

"There were some others, but I don't know their names. Shouldn't the cops have checked all this stuff out thirty fucking years ago?"

Perhaps, Zack thought, but the evidence against Hall had seemed solid at the time. Zack liked to think he would have pursued additional avenues of investigation, but he knew when confronted with a violent murder like Melissa St. Martin's, circumstantial evidence usually did the trick.

He'd already checked into the warehouse where Hall had worked all those years ago. It was not only closed, but razed. A shopping mall had been built on the property more than ten years ago.

"You said that you'd been out at a bar drinking the day Melissa St. Martin was kidnapped."

"That's right."

"Who was there with you? Anyone who might have seen you drink too much? Someone who knew what type of truck you drove?"

"No, it was just the guys, you know? A lot of them that hung out at the club were vets, from Korea or 'Nam or World War II. Those guys are too old. I—"

Hall cut himself off and slammed his fist on the

table. "That fucker! That perverted sicko bastard! He set me up!"

The sudden rage and realization that crossed Hall's face convinced Zack his reaction was real.

"Who?" he asked.

"Chris fucking Driscoll. I should have known, the bastard. I got him a fucking job, I set him up in a studio in my apartment building. I told him, hey, pal, let's go score some chicks. He never came with us when we went out. Always doing his own fucking thing. Except that day. He came to the bar, had a beer with us. Now I know why. So he could set me up. Steal my truck. He's a fucking pervert scumbag."

Every hair on Zack's neck rose. This was it. He felt it. He spoke much more calmly than he felt. "What do you know about Driscoll? Where is he from? Did he serve with you?"

"We were in the same unit for six months. He was a machine. Neat freak. Don't fucking touch his stuff. That's why he set me up. I touched his precious *stuff*. He said if I touched his stuff again he'd kill me. I didn't believe him; everyone talks tough in the jungle, you know? All talk, no action. Except when we engaged Charlie; then we acted."

"You think he didn't like you because you touched his belongings?"

"He was wound real tight, but everyone had their own ways, you know? But it's him. He got out four weeks after me. I told him, come by, we can share a pad, I'd get him in good with the warehouse. He did see me, but didn't want to room. I found him a studio in my building. I tried to get him to lighten up. He was three years in Vietnam; I think it messed with his mind. But a guy I knew there, my sarge, said

Driscoll was always like that. Cool most of the time, then *wham!* Something would set him off and he'd be ready to kill you for no fucking reason."

"Why do you think it's him and not someone else?" Though there was no doubt in Zack's mind that something had triggered Hall's memory of Driscoll and his belief that Driscoll framed him.

"'Cause I didn't keep in touch with any of the other guys. A bunch of them got themselves killed, a couple reenlisted, most went home. Driscoll didn't have a home to go to."

"Why not?"

"'Cause he was a ward of the court, or something. Foster system. Some guy his ma was living with killed her or something."

He was in the system. Zack had to get his records, but juvie records weren't easy and they wouldn't come quickly.

"Where was he from?"

Hall shrugged. "All over, he'd said. That Bruce was a sick bastard. That's probably where Driscoll got it from."

"Bruce?"

Hall paused. "He talked about Bruce all the time, and how he was going to kill him when he got out of the Army, and no one would know it was him. One of the guys asked who Bruce was, you know, like did he steal his girl or something? He said Bruce was in prison for killing his mother."

"Can you remember anything else about Bruce? Where they might have lived? Where Driscoll's mother was killed?"

Hall shook his head to every question. "Wish I could help, but I don't know. Driscoll got all uptight whenever he talked about it, so we didn't push him, you know? Except Driscoll did say once that Bruce was in San Quentin. Yeah, San Quentin."

Hall didn't have any other information about Bruce or Driscoll's activities. He'd never heard from Driscoll while he was in prison, or since he'd been released.

As Hall was getting ready to go, Zack asked one last question. "Does 'angel' mean anything to you?"

"Angel? You mean Driscoll's sister? Shit, man, we just didn't talk about her. When one of the guys in the unit found a picture under his pillow, we all thought it was weird. The kid was like nine or ten, you know? Driscoll went off about Angel this, Angel that, and we figured out she was his sister. We asked what happened and all he said was she was dead and to fuck off." Hall rolled his eyes.

"And he has a tattoo like yours, correct?"

"Exactly like mine. I should know—he took me to the same guy who did his over in Saigon."

Chris Driscoll was The Slayer. No doubt in Zack's mind.

"When was the last time you saw him?"

Hall paused, thinking. "That day at the bar. He came in, had a beer with us, left. I never saw him again after that." Hall stared at Zack. "You're going to find him, right? He'll go to prison for framing me, right?"

"He'll go to prison for killing thirty children," Zack said, his voice surprisingly calm.

"Right." Hall nodded. "I got it."

CHAPTER
21

Zack used Perdue's office to call Chief Pierson and tell him everything they'd learned. "We need an APB out on Chris Driscoll. We need his military records, his last known address, any living relatives. Maybe the Feds can help us out getting his juvie records. I'm thinking California. His stepfather is in prison in California for murder; Hall thinks he killed Driscoll's mother. And I need to have a face-to-face with his stepfather, Bruce. His last name might be Driscoll, but we can't count on it. He was probably arrested in the late sixties."

"I'll see what I can do," Pierson said. "He could be dead, he'd probably be in his seventies by now. Are you going to stay down there tonight?"

"Not if I can help it. I have a feeling Driscoll is going to act. From the patterns Doug, Olivia, and I identified, he moves quickly at the end of his killing spree." Zack glanced at his watch. "It's eleven o'clock. San Quentin is only an hour or so away, just north of San Francisco. We'll drive, then head back down to the airport. Our flight leaves at three-fifteen, I should be back there two hours later."

"I'll call the prison and set up visitation for you."

"If the guy is dead, I want to talk to anyone who

knew him—the warden, any guard he might have talked to, a prisoner who buddied up with him."

"I'll call you within the hour."

Zack hung up and looked around for Olivia. They were outside the San Mateo County Courthouse in Redwood City. Olivia stood under an oak and stared at a line of rose trees off to the side of the main steps. He didn't think she was seeing anything; she appeared lost in her own thoughts.

He hadn't had a chance to talk to her after interviewing Hall. He walked up, touched her shoulders. "Liv? How are you holding up?"

"I'm okay."

He didn't doubt she would be, but this experience was still painful for her. "I'm waiting for Pierson to call back and see if we can get into San Quentin and talk to Driscoll's stepfather. They might have had contact over the years."

When Olivia didn't say anything, Zack continued. "We have an APB on Driscoll and Pierson is getting the Feds to jump on any military benefits this guy has. He probably has a pension, or medical benefits at the minimum. Even killers need a doctor once in a while."

"I don't think he cares. He's too methodical to get trapped in the system. He's probably not using his own name. And you know as well as I do how easy it is to establish a new identity, if you know what you're doing."

"Pierson is trying to track down a photo. It'll be old, but we can get a forensic artist to extrapolate what he might look like today."

"Good. I want to see the pictures. Before and after."

"Are you sure?"

She turned to face him, her face a mask but her voice tinged with emotion. "Of course I'm sure. I need to see it. Do you think I can't handle it? I'm not going to fall apart here."

"I didn't think you would. I just want to spare you."

She looked like she wanted to argue with him; her jaw worked, then she closed her eyes. "I have to see his face," she whispered. "Maybe that's why I came to Seattle in the first place. For thirty-four years I pictured Brian Hall as the man who destroyed my family. I want to see who was really responsible."

He pulled her to him, holding her close. She tensed, then relaxed in his embrace. Would she ever be comfortable with his touch? Then her arms wrapped around his back and she held him tightly, a wealth of trust in that one small gesture. Not something she gave lightly, he realized, as he kissed the top of her head.

Then she stepped back. "Thank you, Zack. For understanding. And for letting me do what I have to do."

Furious, Brian stormed out of the courthouse. His damn attorney said it would be *at least* another month before his restitution came through. Probably three. But "definitely by January."

January! He had no money, his job paid next to nothing, and he had to get out of town. Just in case someone figured out he'd whacked the cop and the attorney.

He thought if he came down here today, did his

fucking *civic duty,* they'd at least give him a friggin' reward.

Chris Driscoll had set him up. Motherfucking asshole let him rot in prison while *he* walked away free.

It was the cops' fault. They should have asked those questions before. No one ever asked him if anyone had a reason to set him up. No, they just assumed he was guilty and wanted to know where he was, who he was with, and didn't buy that he was sleeping off a drinking binge. Who cares if he lied about where he was? Everyone *knows* the cops are lazy S.O.B.'s who don't care if you're innocent.

As he left the courthouse, he saw his half-broke pickup truck in front of the building. A yellow ticket flapped from his windshield.

Well, fuck.

He pulled off the ticket and tore it in two. No way he was going to pay it.

That's when he saw *her.*

She was standing under a tree, dressed impeccably, the cop who'd asked him about Driscoll holding her by the shoulders. Looking at her. Then he leaned over and kissed her, wrapped his arm around her, and they walked away, toward the parking garage across the street.

There she was. He didn't have his gun; he didn't dare bring it to the courthouse. He could have shot her right here, right now.

Seattle. She was in Seattle with the cop? Brian scratched his head. He'd gone through the cop's desk and found an address for Olivia St. Martin in Fairfax, Virginia. He'd planned on going on to Virginia, whack her, then maybe up to Canada and just hang low for a while. But maybe seeing her was a sign. She wasn't in Virginia; she was working with the cop from Seattle.

Maybe he should head up to Seattle. It wouldn't take him more than two days' driving. He'd swing by his rat-hole apartment and grab his stuff and go. He had enough money for gas.

But how would he find her in Seattle? He had her home address. Eventually, she had to go home, right? And he could be waiting for her. Blow her brains out as soon as she walked through the door.

But Seattle was closer. Eenie-meenie-miney-moe.

Virginia?

Or Seattle?

"Where did you grow up?" Zack asked when they were back in the car and heading toward the freeway.

Olivia waved vaguely to the west. "Not far."

"Your sister was kidnapped from your neighborhood park?"

"Yes."

"Do you want to go back?"

She had been thinking exactly that. She'd wondered if going to the park would help purge some of the pain she still felt inside. After Missy's murder, she'd never walked through the park again. She took the long way to school in the morning. She hated walking alone, so she tried to blend in with some of the older girls in the neighborhood. She'd wait just inside the front door until the girls passed her house, then she'd run out and follow them. They ignored her, but that was okay. She felt safer just because they were there.

"Do we have time?"

"We have a few minutes. Since we're here—if you want to."

She nodded and directed Zack to continue west, instead of turning north onto the freeway.

It surprised her how much things had changed, and how much they'd stayed the same. Everything seemed *more*. More houses, more stores, more businesses. But the streets were the same, and she had no doubt how to get home.

Home. She'd never thought of her house as a home, not after Missy was gone.

A couple of turns later, Olivia said, "Stop."

Zack pulled over and looked at the houses on either side of the street. "Did they build over the park or something?"

She shook her head, her chest tight, her mind thick with competing emotions. She pointed to a house directly across the street, its brick front stately even though the house wasn't large, the white shutters freshly painted, the drapes open to bring in light.

Her mother had never opened the drapes after Missy died.

"That's where we lived."

To her, the house had been lifeless, large, and forbidding, cutting off warmth and light as well as love.

She stared at the modest two-story on Eucalyptus Street. The magnolia tree in the front, a mere sapling in her youth, had matured, its trunk thicker than her embrace, the dark chunky leaves and huge white flowers arching stiffly over the freshly mowed lawn. A grouping of three white-trunked birch trees gathered at the southernmost corner of the house, partially shielding a healthy clematis that had reached the top of an eight-foot trellis. Meticulously groomed rosebushes in every shade from white to peach to vibrant red lined both sides of the property line. Her father had spent at least three hours a day tending his yard.

The new owners must have appreciated that, because they kept the garden thriving.

Her heart pounded so loudly she could hear its *thump-thump* vibrating in her ears. Her vision narrowed until the beautiful garden disappeared and all she saw was the hostile face of her childhood house. The upstairs windows glaring at her, accusing her. The shut door like pursed lips. Her mother's rage and gut-wrenching grief.

She hated coming home.

It was the house itself that terrified her. She still heard her mother's sobs, as if the walls themselves had recorded five years of maternal agony to replay every anguished cry for her.

Olivia's shaking hand reached for the door handle. "Let's walk," she said.

Zack jumped out and opened her door for her, extending his hand for support and comfort. She felt like such an invalid, an albatross. She saw the house as it was in her memory, not as it was today.

But standing there, staring, she saw that some things had changed.

There was a minivan in the driveway.

A tricycle on the front porch.

Children's laughter flitting through open windows.

As she watched the door opened and two small children, maybe four and five, ran from the house. They giggled, the sound sliding over Olivia's ears like an oasis in the desert.

The giggles brought back memories of *before*.

Before Missy died and the world changed. When they used to run down the street to the park, laughing and teasing each other. When they planned Daddy's birthday party or surprised Mommy with flowers. When they played with dolls and set up house.

The mother, an attractive brunette with wide hips and a smile on her lips, quickly followed her children.

"Hold it!" she called as she locked the door.

The kids stopped in their tracks, a boy and a girl. "Please can we get ice cream?"

"If you're good at the store," she said.

"We'll be good! Promise!"

The mother smiled wide, hoisted a large purse over her shoulder, and slid open the minivan door. The kids scrambled into the car and she buckled them into car seats. Moments later they drove away.

"Liv?" Zack said softly, using his thumb to wipe away tears she hadn't known were there.

"I'm glad the house found a family." She squeezed his hand. "Let's walk. The park is around the corner."

They rounded the corner and faced the park, the memory of Missy's abduction so vivid Olivia could feel the bruise on her face from Driscoll's assault. It had healed before they knew for certain Missy was dead.

She walked up to the memorial plaque the city council had erected a year after Missy's murder and ran her fingers over the recessed letters.

Melissa Anne St. Martin Memorial Park.

The rickety metal jungle gym had been replaced several times over the years. The current bright red-

and-yellow play structure had three slides, a bridge, and a pole to slide down. Four separate horses were cemented into the foundation under the bark so children could gallop in place.

The trees were triple the size, in height and width. Bark had replaced sand.

The swings were gone.

How many families who enjoyed this park knew who its namesake was? How many people remembered that a little girl had been abducted at this spot?

"Let's sit," Zack prompted, urging her toward a bench in the middle of the park.

Zack's presence was comforting, like being wrapped in a down blanket in the middle of winter, snow falling all around. She'd always felt so cold, so alone, but with Zack she didn't feel bleak, and her loneliness was fading.

"They took away the swings," she said. "I used to love the swings. I always wanted to go higher."

"My sister loved the swings, too. When she was a kid," Zack said.

"How did Amy die?"

Zack didn't say anything, and for a minute Olivia wondered if she'd overstepped an invisible barrier between them.

Then he said, "She was killed in a drug bust."

"She was a cop, too?"

"No. She was a recovering drug addict."

"Oh. I'm sorry."

Zack had never spoken about Amy to anyone. It hurt too much. But Olivia would understand, and it felt right to tell her everything.

"Mae died when Amy was fourteen. I was a rookie

cop and moved back to Mae's house as her guardian. Amy had a lot of built-up anger. I'd left the house when I was eighteen, a borderline hoodlum. I was hanging out with the wrong guys, didn't want to go to college or get a job or really do anything except race my bike and hang out.

"When I found out about my mother, I did a lot of soul-searching and knew I didn't want to end up like her, caring only about myself. I felt helpless to bring back the lives of the two people she killed. Alcoholism is an illness, but dammit, I felt she should have had more control over herself."

Zack looked out at the kids playing, small children because it was a school day, and the mother who watched them. Neither he nor Olivia had had a "normal" childhood, but nowadays, what was "normal"? Maybe it was a feeling, the sense of being loved and cared for, more than a structured environment. He had been loved and well cared for, even without his mother.

Olivia had not.

And in many ways, neither had Amy.

"Mae and Amy butted heads constantly. Mae didn't want Amy turning into her mother, and Amy had our mom up on this pedestal. I'd made a big mistake early on. I never told Amy what really happened with our mom; I didn't want to hurt her. I wonder if I'd been honest at the beginning if things would have been different."

"The *what if* scenario." Olivia squeezed his hand. "I know that one well."

"I finally did tell her, after she got involved with drugs. She was fifteen at the time. And I didn't handle the situation well at all. I laid on the ultimatums pretty heavy. Something like *Get your act straight or you'll wind up dead or in prison*." He shook his head, his throat tight.

"You were practically a kid yourself."

"I was an arrogant cop, and I was scared that I was going to screw up my kid sister because I didn't know the first thing about being a parent. So I played the bad cop. I imposed strict rules and curfews. Mae was strict, but she also understood something I didn't. She understood the value of trust and love. All I saw in Amy was a defiant kid who, if she wasn't reined in quickly, would turn into one of the junkies I saw every day, passed out in the gutter."

He remembered Amy at fifteen like she was standing in front of him. Spaghetti-strap tank tops, torn jeans, always smelling of pot. In less than a year, she'd turned from a good kid with almost straight A's to a drug addict who barely passed her classes.

"Anyway, this went on for a couple of years. She'd run away. I'd track her down. Impose tougher rules. Check up on her. She hated me, and I think because I was a cop she ended up not trusting the police. Which killed her in the end."

"What happened?"

What *had* happened? Even Zack wasn't completely sure he understood Amy and all the events leading up to her murder.

"After high school, one of her best friends died of a drug overdose. It hit her really hard. She'd been living with some older college kids at the time and asked if she could move home. I said yes, if she lived by my rules. She was nineteen, and I believed—by her actions—that she really wanted to get out of the life she'd made.

"For a while, things were fine between us. I got her into drug counseling, and it seemed to help. She didn't want to talk to me about anything, but she'd lost some of the anger and hostility, so I didn't push her to talk. She started taking classes at the community college. That's where she met Kirby."

"The reporter?"

Zack nodded, remembering the day Amy brought Kirby home for dinner, ostensibly to meet him. Zack already had met Kirby, a cocky reporter who'd turned up at every sensitive crime scene like a blood-hound since taking over the crime beat six months previous. Kirby knew no boundaries then, and he hadn't learned them since.

"What Amy saw in him—I don't know."

Maybe he did know. Kirby was attentive. He had seemed to really listen to Amy. He understood her in ways Zack never had. Maybe it was because they were closer in age; maybe because Zack still resented the choices Amy had made with her life. He had been proud of her for cleaning herself up; would he have felt the same had she still been doing drugs? Would he have still loved her?

"They saw each other for a long time. Couple years. I'd sort of grown to accept Kirby as part of our family, I guess. I mean, if Amy was home, Kirby was there. I wasn't home much, taking overtime wherever I could get it. We had the house free and clear from Mae, but no money, so I needed to pay off my student loans and get Amy through college and pay bills.

"Then everything changed." Changed? Was it sudden, or gradual? He didn't know; he didn't remember much about that time except work.

"I heard about an undercover drug operation at Amy's college. I was worried about her, because she'd seemed preoccupied. I feared she still had friends into that scene."

He'd never forget what he'd learned that day. When he started asking around, he was called into Chief Lewiston's office. And told in no uncertain terms to stay out of it. The sting was a joint federal–state operation to put some big players behind bars. If it was a success, they'd be able to dry up half the drug channels into the city overnight.

"How is my sister involved?" Zack had asked.

Lewiston hadn't wanted to tell him. But in the end, Zack learned that Amy was playing undercover cop. He told Olivia, "Amy knew everyone in the drug scene. They trusted her. We couldn't get any of our guys close, so when one of our narcs on campus approached her, she said she'd help."

"She didn't tell you?"

Zack shook his head. "She didn't trust me."

"She was scared."

"She should have been. She was playing a dangerous game. If I'd known, I would have stopped her. Or protected her. As it was, I could do neither."

"Did she die during the sting?"

He took a deep breath, shaking his head. "The sting went off perfectly. Took down everyone they wanted. Cut off major supplies into the Pacific Northwest.

"Amy was gunned down the next morning in a drive-by shooting."

Olivia reached for him. "Oh, Zack! That's awful."

"You know what the kicker is? Kirby knew all along. He knew and didn't tell me. He claimed he loved her, but did nothing to protect her. In fact, he wrote all the follow-up stories about the sting and Amy's murder. I can't look at him and not think that he should have done something different. That *I* should have done something different. Not just with her playing undercover cop, but raising her."

Olivia leaned her head on his shoulder. "I can't imagine what it's like to be a parent. To be responsible for the health and safety of another human being."

"You don't want kids?"

"No. Never. Though there were a lot of little problems between Greg and me, we divorced because he wanted children and I didn't. I refused to bring a child into the world. A child who could be raped or killed or hurt. I've seen too much pain, too much anguish. My mother killed herself because she lost a child. Brenda Davidson was in deep depression. I don't blame either of them, really. How can a mother survive when she's lost part of herself? And how can a mother protect her child every minute of every day?"

"Our line of work can make us jaded," Zack said. "And your childhood didn't help. But there's good out there, Olivia. There are things to enjoy, to celebrate. I was raised in Seattle and couldn't think of a more beautiful place to live. The entire Pacific Northwest is incredible. To see the mountains on the first clear day after a snowstorm. To take a sailboat through Puget Sound. Go up to one of a hundred lakes and fish for hours." He paused, ran a hand through his hair. "I don't know. The world is dangerous, but there's so much to live for."

"Yes, I suppose there is."

They sat in silence watching the young children play.

Zack's phone rang several minutes later and he glanced at the number. "Chief Pierson," he told Olivia, then answered the call. A minute later he hung up.

"Bruce Carmichael is the man we're looking for. He died of prostate cancer three years ago. But the warden agreed to let us see his records and talk to some of the guards who knew him. He's expecting us at one. We'd better jump on it."

CHAPTER
22

Zack and Olivia spent their first hour at San Quentin reviewing Bruce Carmichael's prison file.

In 1960 he killed his common-law wife, Miriam Driscoll, a cocktail waitress in New Jersey. He disappeared with his two minor children, Christopher Adam Driscoll, eleven, a child from Miriam's previous marriage, and Angel Lee Carmichael, six, his own daughter.

He avoided capture for nearly three years until Chris Driscoll called the police from a low-rent apartment in Los Angeles, saying his stepfather killed his sister and claiming to have killed his stepfather. LAPD responded and found Carmichael and Driscoll both covered in blood. Carmichael had been knocked unconscious, but he wasn't dead. The nine-year-old girl had been stabbed to death. An autopsy revealed that she'd been repeatedly sexually assaulted. After a forensic investigation, evidence proved her own father had molested her.

The fourteen-year-old Driscoll told police that he heard his sister scream and called the operator before going into the bedroom, where he saw Carmichael stabbing her. He tried to stop him, but Carmichael turned the knife on him. They wrestled and the knife was lost under the bed. Driscoll then hit Carmichael over the head with a lamp and he was knocked unconscious. A blood test at the hospital confirmed that Carmichael had been drinking, his blood alcohol level at point-two-five.

Driscoll told police he and his sister had been planning on running away because of the physical abuse, but Carmichael found out about their plans and killed Angel.

Carmichael had a completely different story. He claimed he walked into the apartment and saw Driscoll sitting on the edge of Angel's bed. He was holding a knife and Angel was dead. Carmichael fought with his stepson over the knife, but he'd been drinking and slipped, and Driscoll knocked him out with a lamp.

Time of death could have supported either story, but the prosecutor believed Driscoll. Not only had Angel been sexually assaulted by her father, but Carmichael had stabbed Miriam Driscoll to death with the same knife.

The teenage boy was distraught that he'd been unable to protect his sister. He was under suicide watch in the county hospital during most of Carmichael's trial. The jury was unmoved by Carmichael's claim that his stepson had killed Angel. He was sentenced to life, then extradited to New Jersey to stand trial for Miriam Driscoll's murder, but he pled guilty to avoid the death penalty.

If he hadn't died of cancer, next year he would have been shipped to New Jersey to serve out his second life sentence.

"What a bastard!" Zack said, flipping through the pages quickly. "I heard a phrase once, can't remem-

ber where, that monsters are created. Chris Driscoll
is a product of his upbringing. Doesn't make him any
less guilty, but dammit, I hate that the cycle contin-
ues."

"When his father killed his sister, he could have
snapped," Olivia said. "Just like my mother did
when Missy died. He probably blamed himself,
thought he was weak because he couldn't protect
her. To survive, he absorbed the force of his stepfather's personality. He ended up being just like him.
But far worse. He's more methodical, more disciplined. He's had years to perfect his crimes. He
learned early in life how to move from state to state,
create identities, hide in plain sight—all because his
stepfather did it to avoid being arrested."

"His background might explain why the first murder in each state seems spontaneous and distinct
from the others," Zack said. "Maybe he doesn't plan
it, or at least not as meticulously as the others, but
sees a victim who reminds him of his sister and takes
her. Consider Jillian Reynolds. She was abducted,
then dumped only a couple of miles away."

"And in a secluded location," Olivia said. "Perhaps
so her body wouldn't be found as quickly?"

"Could be." He gathered up the files and
motioned to the guard who'd been left with them in
the room. "Officer, I need to speak to the warden
about getting a copy of these files sent to Seattle."

"I'll take you to his office."

Zack leaned over to Olivia. "Let's get the important stuff copied and faxed to the department and
see if it helps your people put together a profile of
where we can find this guy before he strikes
again."

* * *

Chris Driscoll drove his small SUV into Seattle International Airport's long-term parking, extracting a ticket from the machine and placing it precisely in his wallet. He drove slowly up and down the aisles, looking for Karl and Flo Burgess's large white pick-up truck.

Ten rows in he found it.

He stopped his car down the aisle, left it running, and took the extra set of keys he'd stolen from the Burgess's kitchen drawer. He pulled the truck out, left it running, and pulled his own car into the slot. He'd return the truck precisely where he'd found it.

Upon leaving, he handed the attendant the ticket he'd just received. "Forgot my medication," he said sheepishly in case the attendant thought it was odd that he had entered the facility only twenty minutes before.

"It happens," the guy said without really looking at him, "but I have to charge you a dollar."

"I understand." He gave him a dollar and left.

Thirty minutes later he was parked down the street from the angel's house. He was running a little late; she rode her bike home from gymnastics every afternoon, rounding the corner between 4:45 and 4:55. It was already after 4:30. He didn't want to miss her. He couldn't miss her.

He closed his eyes for a moment, just a moment, to strengthen his resolve. Angel came to him. A memory, a nightmare.

She'd planned to betray him.

"I'm going to talk to Mrs. Thompson tomorrow."

They were sitting on the balcony again, two weeks after her birthday, and Chris had been thinking about where they could run, how he would pay for food and clothes and rent. How he would take care of Angel.

He was also planning how best to kill Bruce. Because the only sure way they could escape Bruce was to make sure he was dead.

"What?" *Certainly he had misunderstood Angel. He'd been lost in thought.* "Talk to her about what?"

"What Daddy does to me. She's very nice. She'll help. I know she will. And you can come with me."

"No. No. I told you I'd find a way."

She shook her head, her big green eyes far older than her years, too sad for a child. "I can't wait. I can't wait anymore. I hurt all the time. I don't want to feel this way anymore. I don't want to be scared anymore."

"No."

Chris opened his eyes, startled. Ten minutes had passed. It was nearly 4:45. He had to get into place.

He already wore gloves. Gathering his supplies, he silently slipped out of the truck. There was a mailbox partially covered by ivy and bushes. He'd already checked her route and knew this was the best place to take her. If he stood on the far side of the mailbox, no one would see him without walking straight toward him. He would wait for his angel. Wait and she would come right into his arms.

He pretended to mail a letter, just in case anyone happened by, then slid into his hiding place.

And waited.

He heard the *flap-flap-flap* of decorated spokes before he saw her.

He counted to three, then stepped out of hiding, right into her path.

CHAPTER
23

As soon as Zack pulled out of the airport parking lot, his cell phone rang.

"Travis."

"It's Pierson. He has another one. Nina Markow, ten."

"When?"

"Forty-five minutes ago, in the county. As soon as the first officers arrived and realized that the victim fit our profile, they contacted me."

"Where? I'm already in the car."

"Come back to the station. We have two witnesses and I have them working with different sketch artists. And we have a partial license plate on the truck that we're running and should have a list within the hour."

"I'll be there in twenty minutes." He hung up.

"Another?"

"Forty-five minutes ago."

Olivia closed her eyes. "I'd hoped we had more time."

"Me, too. But now we have a name and there are two witnesses. A partial on the truck. Everyone's working on this."

"But can we find him before he kills her? Before he disappears?"

"I'm not going to let her die, Olivia. We'll find her."

We have to.

When Olivia and Zack walked into the police station, she felt like the world had stopped spinning on its axis, that time stood still, just for a moment.

FBI Special Agent Quinn Peterson sat at Zack's desk talking to an elderly man while a sketch artist worked next to them.

Quinn looked up and caught her eye. He didn't seem surprised to see her, but he didn't seem happy, either. He said something to the man, then stood and walked over to them. As always, he was dressed impeccably.

"You must be Detective Travis," Quinn said and extended his hand. "I'm Special Agent Quincy Peterson, Seattle FBI."

They shook hands. "Zack Travis. My chief fill you in on the case?"

Quinn nodded. "I talked to him last night and again when I arrived this morning. He's on the phone taking care of the politicians. So far the media hasn't caught wind, so we don't have that zoo yet. I have a bureau sketch artist working with Henry Jorge, Nina's neighbor, who saw the abduction and got the partial off the truck. Your own sketch artist is waiting in a conference room for Nina's friend to arrive with her parents. They should be here any minute."

"What happened?"

"Nina Markow was riding her bike home from gymnastics. She practices every day after school. She turned onto her street and, according to Mr. Jorge, a man stepped out of the bushes right into the path of her bike. She swerved and fell. The man helped her up, then dragged her over to a white truck half a block away. He put his hand over her mouth and she couldn't scream. Mr. Jorge ran after them, but he's eighty-three. He couldn't catch up before the truck drove off, though his eyesight was good enough to get a partial number off the rear plate and we're running it now."

"Pierson tell you we identified the killer? Christopher Driscoll."

Quinn nodded. "Our people are pulling every string to get his military records, but it's not easy. I did get his original military ID photo and the artist can take that with the descriptions from Mr. Jorge and Abby Vail, Nina's friend who also witnessed the abduction, and come up with a good composite of what he looks like. We've brought in a couple of agents to help your team cover the car dealerships, rental agencies, airports, anyplace this guy could get a truck without suspicion."

"Where're the victim's parents?"

"Her mother is single, a widow. She works out in the county, and a—" Quinn glanced at his notepad "—Detective Jan O'Neal went out to inform her and bring her down here. But with commuter traffic I don't expect them for another thirty or so minutes."

Quinn glanced at Olivia, then said, "Detective, do you mind if I have a word with Agent St. Martin? It won't take long."

"Use the conference room. I need to check in with my chief and I'll get you when the witness comes in. Call me Zack."

Quinn nodded. "Thanks. I'm Quinn."

He put his hand in the small of Olivia's back as he steered her toward the conference room, shutting the door behind them.

"What the *hell* have you been doing?" Quinn said, obviously trying to temper long-simmering anger. "Have you lost your mind?"

"I can explain."

"You'd better start talking. When I came here this morning and found out that *Agent* St. Martin had been a vital part of this investigation, I couldn't imagine it was you. 'Olivia St. Martin?' I asked. Chief Pierson sang your praises and told me you were in Redwood City interviewing Brian Hall!"

"I didn't—I told Zack about Missy. I told him I couldn't be in the room with Hall, he probably wouldn't take my presence very well, and I didn't want to jeopardize the case."

"Jeopardize the case! Hell, Olivia, you're not an agent! You've already jeopardized the case."

"Like hell I have!" Olivia swallowed, surprised at her outburst. "Quinn," she said, trying to remain calm, but her frustration and anger were closer to the surface than she thought. "I went through the proper channels. I went to Rick Stockton and showed him what I'd put together on these cases. Yes, I knew it was circumstantial, but there was so much of it! I couldn't just not do anything! And when he said his hands were tied, there was nothing he could do, he couldn't send a team out to help, I didn't have a choice."

"You've always had a choice. You could have called *me*. You know I would bend over backward to help you. Anytime, anyplace."

She took a deep breath, her heart tight. "I know. I

know you would have. But don't you understand? My testimony put an innocent man behind bars."

"You don't know Hall wasn't involved."

"No, I don't *know*, but I believe he wasn't. Zack and I talked it through and neither of us thinks Driscoll has a partner. The attacks are too personal, too intimate." She paused. "And Hall is too stupid."

"Olivia—"

"Hear me out. I *had* to do something. I had to get the information about Driscoll's killing spree in the right hands. I had to talk to someone on the case, walk them through the evidence. They wouldn't have listened to me; I'm a lab scientist!"

"This is serious, Olivia. You could get fired."

"Don't you think I know it's serious? Do you think I care about getting fired?" Olivia clasped her hands together to stop them from shaking. "I put an innocent man in prison, leaving a killer free to prey on little girls. He's killed at least thirty children. Because of me. *Me!* There was no way I could sit back and not do something—I know him. I know the way he works. I spent weeks studying every similar crime in the country. There are two men sitting in prison right now who I think are innocent because they were framed for Driscoll's crimes. This guy is smart. Wily. Methodical. Disciplined." She took a deep breath.

"He has control most of the time," she continued. "He preys on the innocent. Waits until they're alone before going in for the kill. And when things get too hot, when the police start to close in, he sets someone else up or just walks away. Leaves the jurisdiction. Controls his sick urges just long enough to establish a home base somewhere else. Then he starts all over again."

"Liv, it's not your fault. You were five years old when Missy died," Quinn said.

"It's not just about Missy. It's about all the other children. It's about Chris Driscoll and the families he has destroyed. I don't care if I get fired as long as we catch him. You think my job is that important to me?" She shook her head.

"Dammit, Olivia." Quinn ran a hand through his hair and paced the conference room. He stared at the white board, recognizing Olivia's small, perfect printing. He read the timeline, looked at the photos, saw the time and effort and dedication she had put into the case. "Who knows the truth?"

"No one. No one here. Greg knows."

"Greg," he repeated, shaking his head.

"Quinn, please. Please let me stay. I have to see this through."

The door opened and Zack Travis filled the opening. "Abby Vail is here with her parents. Ready?"

Olivia looked at Quinn. "I am," she said.

"Let's go," Quinn said, turning away from Olivia's stare.

She breathed an inaudible sigh of relief.

For now, she was okay.

Thank you, Quinn.

Olivia, Quinn, and Zack went into another conference room to speak with Abby Vail, the ten-year-old neighbor and friend of Nina. *The victim.*

What was going to happen to Abby if Nina died? Would she feel guilty for the rest of her life? That she didn't, couldn't, do anything to stop the bad man from taking her friend? Would the memory of Nina being abducted haunt her forever?

Abby Vail was small for a ten-year-old, skinny with short blonde hair, big brown eyes, and dimples that deepened when she talked.

"Did you find Nina?" she asked as soon as they walked through the door.

"Everyone is looking for her," Zack said. He nodded to the parents. "Thank you for bringing Abby down. I'm Detective Travis, this is Special Agent Quinn Peterson and Olivia St. Martin with the FBI."

The mother, a larger version of Abby, nodded, her eyes red and swollen. "Anything we can do. It—it could have been—" she didn't finish her thought, but glanced at her husband over Abby's head, her chin quivering. Her husband reached around Abby's back and squeezed his wife's shoulder, while his free hand grasped Abby's.

Zack began. "Abby, I know you talked to the police officer who came to your house, but if it's okay with you, I'd like you to start at the beginning and tell me everything you saw or heard."

Abby nodded and took a deep breath. "Nina lives down the street from me and I was waiting for her to get home." She paused.

"Were you going to get together and play?" Zack prompted.

Abby looked sheepish. "Not exactly. We had an argument yesterday and we were both still mad. Well, I wasn't really mad anymore, but I didn't want to say sorry first. I thought that maybe if I went outside when she was coming home, we could just sort of, I don't know, forget about the fight."

Olivia didn't know she was nodding until Abby looked at her and shrugged. "It sounds stupid, but it always works," Abby said. "So I was looking for her and saw her come around the corner on her bike. I went outside."

Quinn spoke. "Abby, where were you exactly when you first saw Nina?"

"Looking out the kitchen window."

"Did you see the white truck?"

Abby scrunched up her nose. "I didn't notice it. I didn't notice it until that man put Nina in it."

"I did!" Mrs. Vail started sobbing. "It's my fault. I saw the truck, but didn't think anything of it."

"Mrs. Vail," Zack said, his voice calm and gentle, a complete contradiction to his hard exterior. "Don't blame yourself. When did you first notice the truck?"

"When I left for the grocery store, about four thirty, a little later. The truck was there, but no one was inside. I would have noticed if someone was just sitting there." She paused. "At least, I think I would have noticed."

"The truck probably looked like it was supposed to be in the neighborhood," Quinn suggested. "Clean? Newer?"

Mrs. Vail nodded. "It looked fine. I just didn't think about it."

Abby's lip quivered. "The fight was so stupid. Mr. Benjamin picked Nina to be on the advanced team. I was so jealous. I really wanted to be on the advanced team, and I'm as good as Nina, but she's so good at the parallel bars, really good, and—" Suddenly, tears streamed down her face. "I'm next in line, but I don't want it. I don't want it like this." She turned and buried her face in her father's chest.

Olivia's chest heaved and Zack caught her eye. He stared at her, sharing his strength again, while Abby's father murmured reassurances into his daughter's hair.

She nodded, unable to smile but wanting him to know that his presence both comforted and emboldened her. She didn't care what happened to her after they caught Chris Driscoll. She'd probably lose her job, might cost Greg his career, and her friends might very well never speak to her again. But for the first time, she believed she had the stamina to see this investigation through.

Please God, listen to me for once. Protect Nina. Let us find her abductor and allow justice to finally be served.

She tore her eyes from Zack's and rested her hands on the table in front of her. Her movement caught Abby's eye and the child looked at her, sniffling.

"Hi, Abby. You can call me Olivia, okay? Do you think you can finish telling us what you saw? If you need more time, that's okay, but you know that it is really important we know everything if we're going to find Nina, right?"

Abby nodded and swallowed, her chin quivering. "I'm sorry."

Olivia shook her head. "Don't be sorry. Nothing that happened is your fault. Okay? This bad man has been hurting girls for a long time and you have nothing to do with that. Only he is responsible."

Abby nodded and wiped her face with the back of her hand. Her father handed her a crumpled tissue from his pocket and she took it, tearing it in her fingers.

"You left your house to meet Nina as she was riding her bike up the street. Then what happened?"

"She was still way down the block. I sat on my

front porch with a book so she wouldn't think I was waiting for her, but I wasn't reading. Then a man just stepped out in front of her and she swerved her bike to avoid hitting him, and rode into the bushes."

"Where was the man before he stood in front of Nina's bike?"

Abby frowned. "Gosh, I don't really know," she said as she closed her eyes. Olivia gave her time. "It wasn't the street," Abby said. "The mailbox. The mailbox!" She opened her eyes. "That's it! He was at the mailbox and then stepped in front of Nina. She swerved, into the bushes behind the mailbox."

"Then what happened?" Olivia prompted.

"He leaned over to help her up. At least, that's what I thought. But she didn't take his hand, and stumbled over her bike, trying to get up. I started to go over to see if she was hurt."

"Dear Lord," Mrs. Vail said, stifling a sob.

Abby bit her lip. "I—I didn't think anything bad was going to happen, really. I mean, nothing bad happens on our street."

"It's okay, Abby. Then what happened?"

"He picked her up and she started kicking and I yelled at him to put her down. I think I yelled for help, too. I—I sort of don't remember."

Mr. Vail squeezed her hand. "You did, honey. You did the right thing. I was working in my home office when I heard Abby cry for help. I ran outside and saw Nina's next-door neighbor, Henry Jorge, running down the street. I didn't know what I was thinking, except maybe the teenager up the street who just got his license had hit one of the younger kids. We'd talked to his mother twice about his fast driving." Mr. Vail shook his head. "Sorry."

"That's okay," Olivia said, too familiar with the urge to think and act like everything was normal.

"Abby, what do you remember about the man who took Nina?" Quinn asked.

"I told the policeman who came."

"I know, but I'd like you to tell us, too."

"He was tall."

"Taller than your father?"

Abby shook her head. "No."

"How tall are you, Mr. Vail?"

"Six foot two."

"What else did you notice?" Quinn prompted.

"He was kinda old."

"How old?"

Abby shrugged. All adults seemed old to kids.

"What specifically made you think he was old?"

"He didn't have a lot of hair."

"Bald?"

She shook her head, rubbing her nose with the back of her hand. "Short, like a buzz cut, but there was a shiny spot in the back. Grandpa cuts his hair really short because it's falling out and it doesn't make him look so old."

"Could you tell what color?"

She shrugged again. "I don't really know, there wasn't a lot of hair. It wasn't dark, like black or brown, though."

"What was he wearing?"

She thought. "Jeans. White T-shirt."

Olivia's heart pounded. "Did you see anything else that seemed different to you?"

Abby shook her head.

"What about his arms? Were they bare?"

"Yeah, but he had on—" she stopped. "No, it

wasn't a shirt. He had some weird blue thing on his arm."

"A tattoo?" Olivia asked, hitting herself for leading the girl, but unable to help herself.

"Yeah, it could have been, but it was like smudged."

"Old tattoos can look that way."

Olivia's hands trembled and she put them in her lap. Any doubt that Chris Driscoll was Nina's abductor vanished.

"Do you know who this man is?" Mr. Vail asked.

Zack and Quinn exchanged looks. Quinn spoke, "We have a couple of good leads."

"Which means what?"

"Mr. Vail, I'd like to tell you everything we have," Quinn said, "but in the interest of safety, we can't say. I will tell you that we have a suspect and between the FBI and Seattle PD, we're doing everything humanly possible to track him down."

"Abby, would you be able to describe what you saw to an artist?" Zack asked. "Someone who'll draw a picture of what you say, so you can help us get a good idea of what he looks like."

"I don't remember much."

"But Mr. Jorge remembers some, and you remember some. Together, I think we'll have a good idea of what this man looks like."

"I'll try."

"Thank you, Abby."

Zack stood. "The artist will be in momentarily. Can I get you water? Soda?"

The Vails shook their heads. "Just find Nina. Lydia's world revolves around her."

* * *

A foul smell awakened her.

Nina coughed, her voice sounding far away, then tasted a mixture of car fumes and dirt. A low, steady hum surrounded her, lulling her as she drifted between sleep and alert, but a sudden *ping-ping* beneath her jolted her awake.

Something was wrong.

Nina's entire head felt thick, like when her mother woke her in the middle of the night last year to tell her that Grandma had died. But this was different. It hurt. She shivered in the cold, goosebumps rising on her skin.

Go to sleep. You're dreaming.

No, it wasn't a dream. Nina tried to open her eyes, but something held them shut. Like a blindfold. She tried to touch the sore lump on the back of her head, but she couldn't move her arms. She squirmed. Her hands were bound behind her as she lay on her side.

Then she remembered.

Imprinted in her memory was the face of the man who'd stepped in front of her bike and made her crash.

She was turning the corner from Third to Harrison Drive, her street, when a man was suddenly there in front of her. She swerved to miss hitting him and rode into the bushes, falling from her bike.

"I'm sorry, sweetheart," he had said, rushing to her.

"I'm fine." She tried to stand, but her ankle twisted between the bike pedal and frame and she stumbled.

He caught her and she sucked in her breath, staring into very pale eyes, eyes that almost didn't look real. They didn't show any feelings and they didn't look sorry.

Something was wrong with this man, with the way he looked at her. As if he *knew* her. She drew in a breath to scream and his left hand covered her mouth while he turned her around so his right arm could pin her body against his.

It had happened so fast. One minute she was stumbling from her bike; the next he was moving with her across the sidewalk to a big truck she hadn't even noticed was there.

"Nina!"

It was her friend Abby, who lived down the street.

She bit the man's hand and he said a bad word in her ear, but didn't let go. She kicked backward, trying to hit his private parts, which her mother told her would hurt a lot.

If anyone tries to touch you, scream and kick them in their privates. They'll let go and you run and run fast.

But she couldn't connect her foot with him, and suddenly her feet were no longer on the ground as he pulled her up, half carrying her, half shoving her toward the big, white truck. Her arms were pinned to her sides and she wildly kicked her legs in the air.

"Let her go! Help! Someone, help! Help!" Abby started screaming and Nina prayed someone, anyone, was around to help her.

The man pushed her through the door of the truck and slammed her head on the dashboard. Tears streamed down her face from the sharp sting, but she still struggled to free herself.

"Stop!" It was a man's voice and sounded far away. "You! Stop! I've already called the police."

Nina recognized the man—Mr. Jorge, her next-door neighbor, the one who always complained when Scrappy her orange tabby slept in his daisy bushes. He was going to help her!

Then something hit her hard on the head and she remembered nothing until now, when she woke up to the awful smell of car fumes.

How long had she been sleeping? Where was she? She couldn't see. She squirmed and found that she could move a little. Though her hands were tied, her feet were free. She wiggled around and realized she could sit up.

The awful stench of exhaust. The bouncing, the low hum of the engine . . . she was in the back of the truck. The man with the light eyes had taken her, and Mr. Jorge and Abby hadn't been able to stop him. He was going to do something bad to her. Her mom said if a man took her he'd hurt her, and so she had to run. But she hadn't run, she hadn't been able to, and nothing she'd been taught had worked.

She sucked back tears, her fear growing with each ping of rocks on the undercarriage. The pings were coming more frequently. Where was he taking her? What was he going to do? Was he . . . was he going to kill her like those other girls she'd heard her mother talking to Mrs. Vail about?

This was so bad. All the stuff her mother told her, her teachers told her, didn't seem important at the time. Her mother worried all the time. "Yes, Mom," she'd say after listening to another lecture about being careful and to watch out for strange men.

And she'd run her bike right into one.

She stifled a cry. She wanted her mommy so bad right now, but she didn't want the man to hear her. She had to find a way to get out. She was all her mom had, ever since Daddy died. Nina didn't even remember him, she'd only been two. Her mom was her only family.

Her mom did everything for her. They weren't rich; in fact, they were always broke and they couldn't do things like Abby's family, like going to the movies or vacationing every summer at Disney World or some other fun place. Nina sometimes resented that Abby's family had money to do things and Nina's mom didn't, but Nina knew her mom worked hard to make sure she had a college savings account and she took gymnastic lessons, which cost a lot of money. Nina loved gymnastics and she knew she was good. Her mom said she loved watching her, and her coach said she'd be able to try out for the state team next year.

The state team was one step closer to the Olympic team. Nina wanted that more than anything in the world.

Well, now she wanted something even more. She had to find a way to escape.

Nina stifled a sob. She tugged at the ropes that bound her hands. They were tight, and her fingers were numb. How—wait. She just might be able to— yes! It was just like the rings.

Though it hurt her wrists so much tears streamed down her face, Nina pushed herself up with the palms of her hands and pushed her body backward through the hole her arms made. She eased down, not wanting to make a sound, then worked her arms under her legs until they were now in front of her.

Yes!

She reached up and tore off the blindfold and blinked. She saw nothing. No light coming from streetlamps. No light from the cab of the truck. She was locked away in a camper shell, far from her mom, far from help. Her heart pounded. How would she get home? Even if she got away from the man, where was she? Where would she go?

Stop it, Nina! She couldn't think like that. Just get away. Get away. She could figure everything else out later.

Just run away.

She used her teeth on the ropes binding her wrists, the rough fiber making her lips and gums raw. But it was working. They were loosening.

Suddenly, the truck started driving up a steep hill and she toppled over and couldn't stop herself from crying out when her sore head hit the back gate. She righted herself and felt around for a handle on the camper shell. She couldn't find one. She was trapped.

She continued working on the ropes as the truck slowed, winding around sharply. The air became noticeably colder.

She had to get out. As soon as he opened the gate, she had to run. As fast as she could.

And not look back.

Assistant District Attorney Ross Perdue was working late Friday night. He had no wife, no children, and lived for his job. Everyone in the courthouse predicted he'd be appointed to fill Hamilton Craig's remaining term as district attorney and could very well be the youngest elected D.A. in county history if he ran in the next election.

Most people thought Ross was a ladder-climber, but those who knew him well—which weren't many—knew he was motivated by far more than a title. Eight years ago, when he was a law student, his young pregnant wife was gunned down on their first wedding anniversary.

The next semester he changed his focus from corporate law to criminal law and he'd never looked back.

The nature of Hamilton Craig's death bothered him, but he couldn't figure out why. Maybe it was the randomness of it, that it was too much like Becky's. There seemed to be no *reason*, and random violence seemed so unfair, like a tornado falling out of the sky and obliterating only one house in a neighborhood of thousands.

The knock on his door came after six, long after most attorneys had left for the weekend.

"Come in."

It was the Redwood City Chief of Police, Bill Tuttle. Ross stood and extended his hand. "Chief. What can I do for you?"

He didn't sit. "Gary Porter was killed sometime last night in his house."

"Gary Porter? Do I know him?"

"Probably not. He was a detective, retired a few years ago."

"And?" Ross prompted.

"We checked out his house this morning when his wife called from her trip to Paris and said she couldn't reach him. He's been on heart medication for a few years, so she was worried about him. We found him in his kitchen, shot to death.

"From what we could see, Gary came home after Hamilton Craig's funeral. Turned on the lights. Went to his den. Poured himself a Scotch. Drank about half before the power went out. He went to the kitchen—probably to get a flashlight to check the fuse box—and someone shot him in the chest. Then they shot him at close range when he was already down."

"Shit." Ross's hands tensed. "Do you have a suspect? Do you need a warrant?"

Tuttle paused. "I cajoled the crime lab into working overtime to analyze the bullet. They just came back with their report. It matches the gun that killed Hamilton Craig."

"No coincidence. You thinking maybe they worked on the same case? Vengeance murders? I can run released prisoners, see if they match up—"

"There's one I want to check out right away."

"Who?"

"Brian Harrison Hall."

"Hall? I just met him this morning. He gave Seattle PD some valuable information on the murders up there. Why in the world would he kill Hamilton and a retired cop?"

"Because he went to prison for thirty-four years?" Tuttle leaned over Ross's desk. "Ross, let me tell you straight. My twenty years of experience tells me that it's no coincidence that Hall was released less than a month ago and now Hamilton and Gary are dead. He lives in town. He has a motive. I just want to talk to him. But I need a warrant to search his apartment."

"Aw shit." Ross weighed the pros and cons. If Hall was innocent, they'd be in for a rocky ride with the press. They'd had so much PR trouble since his overturned conviction. It would look like they were railroading him.

But if he was guilty . . . "Is there anyone else you think he would go after?"

"Hell if I know. The judge? That was Clive Dunn. He died years ago. Same with Porter's partner. Maybe the parole board members? The arresting officer? That gal who testified against him? I don't know."

"I don't know if we have probable cause," Ross muttered. "But—" he looked at his blotter to see what judge was on duty tonight. "Okay, luck is on our side. Faith Hayes has the night docket. She'll give us a warrant. Probably limited, but it'll get us in his apartment. Agreed?"

"Agreed."

CHAPTER
24

An hour later the two sketch artists had worked together to create a realistic picture of Chris Driscoll based on his Army photo and the descriptions of Henry Jorge and Abby Vail.

"I'll get this out through federal channels," Quinn said, taking a copy.

"Do we release it to the press?" Zack asked, almost to himself.

"I say yes," Quinn said. "He's been around Seattle for months, perhaps longer. Somebody will have seen him. If we can put it on the news stations—" He glanced at his watch. "—we can get it out to the ten o'clock and eleven o'clock news. Can we set up a hotline here to take calls?"

"Absolutely," Zack said.

"We need to copy and distribute the picture to all car rental agencies, dealerships, anywhere he can pick up a car easily," Olivia said. "And I think we should blanket Vashon Island."

"Vashon?" Quinn asked.

"The first victim was kidnapped and killed on Vashon. We think it might have been spontaneous." Olivia walked over to the map. "See how both Michelle and Jennifer were dumped more than twenty miles from where they were abducted? Not Jillian. Two miles. And we mapped out the other crimes—the first victim was always found in a secluded area within five miles of where she was last seen. The other bodies were dumped ten to fifty miles away, in a more public place."

"He could live or work on the island," Zack said.

"Exactly."

"Let's split this up," Zack said. "Quinn, you handle the federal channels. I'll have my chief deal with the media. Boyd and O'Neal can take the car dealerships. Liv, you and I will head out to Vashon as soon as we talk to Ms. Markow." He glanced at his watch. "She should have been here by now."

"Let me jump on this." Quinn scribbled some numbers down and handed them to Zack. "Here are my contact numbers. Call me, day or night. I already have your info from Pierson."

"Thanks."

Quinn looked at Olivia. "Miranda says hello. You should call her."

Olivia's heart sank. "I will. I meant to."

Quinn didn't say anything to that, but walked out.

"What was that about?"

"Quinn's wife is a good friend of mine. We were in the Academy together. I didn't call her when I came to town. I should have."

"We haven't had much down time since you got here. She'll understand."

"Yeah. I'm sure she will." Except that she'd lied to Miranda on the phone the other day. *I hope you understand, Miranda. I really do.*

Zack left the room to get enough copies of the

sketch and send teams to different parts of the city. Olivia stared at the detailed drawing in front of her.

Chris Driscoll looked so normal. Almost kind. Perhaps it was because none of the witnesses had seen his eyes. They looked bland, almost blank. Emotionless. Hollow. His face was lean, with mildly chiseled features and a slight cleft chin.

She compared the sketch with the Army photo of Driscoll, taken when he enlisted at the age of nineteen. Except for the same general appearance—close-cropped hair, pale blue eyes, height—he didn't really look like Hall. But when she was five, that was all she'd had—a general impression of the person. It was the tattoo that stuck out, and it was the tattoo that was identical.

And what did she really remember then? Ever since, she'd seen Hall as he appeared when she faced him at parole hearings. Photographs from the press. Not as the young man who'd killed Missy.

Chris Driscoll had had a miserable childhood. Mother murdered, her killer taking him and his half-sister all over the country to avoid detection. She could have some sympathy with the boy. She could see how he'd snap.

But she didn't understand how he could hurt and kill so many innocent girls. Not all kids raised by abusive fathers turned into killing machines. She imagined that it was something in his internal make-up, something that turned him into a killer when exposed to the rage of another.

Whatever or whoever created this monster, he had to be stopped. Before Nina Markow died.

A knock on the door, then Jan O'Neal popped her head in, saw Olivia, and entered. Quietly she

said, "I have Lydia Markow here. I put her in the
other conference room, gave her some water.
Where's Travis?"

"With Chief Pierson. I'll sit with her if you want to
go get him."

"Thanks. I don't want to leave her alone for too
long. She seems to be doing okay, but you never
know."

Jan held up a photograph. "We swung by her
house to pick up a recent picture of the victim."

Nina Markow was a beautiful girl, small-boned
and delicate-looking, with a wide, engaging grin.
Her white-blonde hair was pulled into a bun that
rested tight on her head, glimmering as if reflecting
all the light in the room. It was a full-body shot of
Nina in a red, white, and blue body suit, barefoot, in
a complicated pose. So much life and energy radiated
from the still shot. It overwhelmed Olivia; she found
her hand rubbing her eyes, as if willing Nina to walk
into the room right now.

"I'm going to take the photo to be copied and dis-
tributed," Jan said. She looked at the sketch in front
of Olivia. "Is that Driscoll?"

Olivia nodded.

"Damn bastard."

Jan escorted Olivia to where Nina's mother waited.
Olivia looked through the glass window in the
door. Lydia Markow looked just like her daughter,
with the same blonde hair, pulled back; she was
attractive, wearing a simple and inexpensive navy
business suit. She was playing with two thin gold
bands on her left hand.

Olivia took a deep breath and hoped Zack came
quickly. She didn't know what to say to the mother,

but she did know if she were in Lydia Markow's shoes, she'd want someone to simply be there with her.

Lydia looked up when she entered the room. Her eyes were red, but dry. She gave Olivia an awkward smile. "Have you found her?"

Olivia shook her head and sat down. Lydia closed her eyes and crossed herself.

"We're doing everything possible."

"Do you know who did it?"

Olivia hesitated. She didn't know what to tell her. "We have a suspect," she finally said. She wouldn't lie to this woman.

"It's the same man who killed those other girls, isn't it?"

Olivia didn't answer. Maybe she shouldn't have said anything. She'd never worked with survivors before. What was she supposed to say? How much was she supposed to reveal?

"I thought so." Silent tears streamed down Lydia's cheeks. "I can't lose her. My husband—he died when Nina was two. She was the light of his life. She's mine, too. I don't know how—no, God won't take her from me. He'll protect her."

Lydia tugged on a necklace that was buried under her blouse. It was a small, gold crucifix. Her lips moved in silent prayer, her eyes downcast.

Zack came into the room and Olivia turned to him, tears in her own eyes. He rested a hand on her shoulder and squeezed.

He said, "Mrs. Markow, I want you to know that we are doing everything to find Nina. Everything. Every officer in Seattle is looking for her. We have a sketch of the man who took her. Would you mind looking at it?"

She held out her hand for the paper.

She stared at the sketch for a long minute. "I've never seen him," she said. "I'm sorry."

"That's not a problem. Abby Vail and Henry Jorge both gave good descriptions. We have several leads."

Zack told her what they believed happened that afternoon.

"Do you have any questions?"

"How—how long—I mean, I read in the newspaper that he doesn't kill them right away. So we have time, right? We have time to find her, right?"

Zack swallowed and Olivia could feel the frustration and tension radiating from his body.

"We believe we have some time. We also have a lot of information we never had before. We have a partial license plate and right now six pairs of police officers are working through the list, talking to all twenty-two owners of late-model white trucks with that partial plate in King County. We'll expand to the surrounding counties next. We have a sketch of the suspect we're distributing in key locations, and the media has agreed to run the picture on the news. An Amber Alert has been issued. The FBI is involved. I promise, we will do everything in our power to find Nina and bring her home safe."

Lydia squeezed her eyes shut, tears leaking. "Thank you," she managed.

"Your neighbor, Mr. Jorge, is still here. He wanted to wait for you to see if you needed a ride home," Zack said.

"Henry is a kind man. I'll have him take me to church. If you hear anything, you'll find me at St. Stephen's."

* * *

Normally, Zack enjoyed riding the ferry from Flauteroy to Vashon Island. Tonight, the twenty-minute ride seemed ten times as long, and he paced the observation deck as he and Olivia planned out their time.

"Say he lives here or works here. That means he would probably buy groceries? Eat in restaurants? Fill his car with gas?" Zack threw out ideas.

"Let's start here. Ask the ferry workers if they recognize him." Olivia put out her hand to stop Zack from pacing. "You take the crew below, I'll take the crew on the observation deck, and we'll meet back at the car when we dock."

"You're right. I should have thought of it." He ran a hand through his hair, intensely frustrated that Driscoll had taken another girl when they were so close to finding him.

They split up, and Zack went down where the passenger cars waited. Most of the people had headed up to the observation deck; a few mingled outside, huddled in jackets. The air was distinctly colder on the water than in the city, and now that fall had taken firm hold, temperatures would continue to drop.

Zack started with the security crew. He asked all four on the car deck and none recognized Driscoll. Two barely glanced at the picture. What good was security if they didn't see anything?

Ten minutes later, when the first whistle blew, Zack was ready to go to the transportation authority over the idiots they hired.

Until he met Stan Macker.

Stan Macker was nearing retirement, bald, with the leathery face of a man who'd worked outdoors most of his life. He looked like he would prefer to die working the lines and be buried at sea. His post was at the gate.

Zack approached him, not expecting anything.

"Detective," the old man nodded.

"How do you know I'm a cop?"

"Name's Stan Macker. I've worked ferries forty-two years. I've been watching you since you came on board. You and that cute little filly. Saw that you asked all the security guards and half my crew to look at a picture. I suspect you want me to look at the picture."

Zack held out the sketch.

Stan stared at it, nodding, handed it back. "Dark green Ford Ranger. Late nineties' model. He was here today."

"When?"

"Took the one-ten across to Flauteroy. Hasn't returned."

"Why do you remember him? You must see thousands of people and cars every day."

"I've been here so long, I remember cars. People. There's a woman who lives on Vashon who's been taking the ferry every weekday for sixteen years. She didn't show up one day. I was surprised. I called over to the Vashon substation, described her and her car, said she hadn't been sick a day in sixteen years, maybe something happened. Something did. She'd had a seizure that morning. The medics saved her life." He shrugged. "I just remember."

"What makes this man memorable? Does he commute?"

Stan shook his head. "Naw. Very irregular. But he stays in his truck. Every time. No music. Doesn't get out and stretch his legs. Doesn't read—we get a lot of people who'll read a book or newspaper while they sit in their cars. Not this one. He stares straight ahead. That's why he stands out."

"Do you have security tapes? I need to see his truck, get a license plate."

"Talk to the head of security. He can get them for you."

"Have you ever seen him in another vehicle? Perhaps a large truck or SUV?" Zack didn't want to lead him, but he needed to know if Driscoll brought his victims to the island.

"No. Only the Ranger. But I'm not on duty 24/7."

"Thanks for your help. I'll talk to the security head. What's his name?"

"Ned Jergens."

"He was a cop." Zack hadn't known him well, but he recognized the name.

"Yep. Good guy. He's stationed on Flauteroy, but here's his direct number. They give it to us in case we have some trouble."

"Thanks a lot, Stan. I appreciate it."

"The guy's bad news, isn't he?"

"The worst. If you see him, call Jergens immediately. And me." Zack handed him his card.

As soon as Zack and Olivia disembarked, he called Chief Pierson and told him what Stan Macker had said. Pierson would contact the Seattle Port Authority and Ned Jergens and get all security tapes since Jennifer Benedict's abduction last month.

The shopping district on Vashon was lively at night, and Zack and Olivia split the street. Thirty minutes later, Olivia walked into a restaurant at the end of the pier. The scent of good food made her stomach growl; her only meal that day had been a prepackaged sandwich at the San Francisco Airport.

She asked to see the manager. A few minutes later a young twenty-something Asian girl came bouncing out of the kitchen. "Hi! I'm Denise Tam. Can I help you?"

Olivia introduced herself and showed her FBI ID. "We're looking for a man we believe lives on the island. He drives a dark green Ford Ranger." She handed Denise the sketch. "Have you seen him? Perhaps he's been in to eat?"

"Ohmigod," she said, her hand covering her mouth. "That's Steve."

Olivia's heart leapt to her throat. "Steve? Does he have a last name?"

"Steve Williams. He's been a server here for nearly two years. Ohmigod. What happened? He's not in trouble?"

Olivia glanced around the restaurant, trying to spot Driscoll. "Is he working tonight?"

She shook her head. "No, he swapped shifts. He has a daughter who goes to college in Oregon and went down to visit her."

Daughter? There was nothing in his records that indicated he had any children or had ever been married. It could be the truth, or a ploy.

"Do you know his daughter's name?"

"Angel."

Olivia sucked in her breath, but quickly recovered. "I need to see his employment records right now."

"I—I don't know if I'm supposed to do that."

"I can get a warrant and come back in an hour, but in the time it takes me to return someone might die. Do you want that on your conscience?"

Denise looked like she was ready to cry. "I'm sorry. I'm sorry. Come to the office."

"One second." She flipped open her phone and dialed Zack. "Bingo. Restaurant at the pier . . . the Crab Shack. I'll be in the back office with the manager."

Thirty minutes later, Zack and four sheriff deputies from the Vashon Island substation had the cottage rented by Steve Williams, a.k.a. Chris Driscoll, surrounded.

The small house sat on the edge of the woods where Jillian Reynolds's body had been discovered less than a mile away. The property felt empty, but Zack didn't take any chances. He had the deputies do a complete perimeter check, then knock on the door. When there was no answer, they entered the house.

Chris Driscoll had lived on Vashon Island for well over a year, but the cottage reflected nothing personal. No photographs. No pictures on the walls. When Zack had called the landlord about the property, he'd learned that it had been rented partially furnished. Driscoll paid cash rent and told the landlord it was from his tips. He never paid late.

The cottage was sterile, immaculate, without personality.

The garbage had been emptied. No dishes on the counter or sink. No plants in the window box. The glass-topped table had two chairs perfectly aligned.

The bedroom didn't look slept in except that the bed had white sheets and two blankets tucked tightly in, military style. Zack feared Driscoll had already escaped, that he had no intention of returning after Nina Markow.

He checked the drawers, relieved to find clothing. Three sets of uniform clothes for the restaurant—black slacks and black polo shirt—were stiffly folded. Even Driscoll's underwear and socks were orderly. There were no dirty clothes in the hamper; no clothes in the washer or dryer.

Because the room was devoid of everything personal, the lone picture stood out like a beacon.

Gloved, Zack picked it up.

The boy was Driscoll, age nine or ten. Blond hair cut in a short buzz popular in the fifties and early sixties. The girl was four or five, a beautiful little girl. A little girl who at nine would look remarkably like Michelle Davidson or Nina Markow. There was a woman kneeling between the two children, her arms around their shoulders. Smiling for the camera.

Zack turned it over.

Mama and Angel. February 10, 1960.

It had been taken six months before Bruce Carmichael killed Miriam Driscoll.

Oddly disturbed, Zack put the picture down and went to the closet. Inside was a briefcase of sorts, more like a large black box that one might see a traveling salesman use.

It was locked.

Could Driscoll have rigged the cottage with some sort of explosives? Zack didn't have the tools to defuse them, and it would take the bomb squad at least thirty minutes to get to the island, even if they used the Coast Guard.

He called Doug Cohn. "Doug, I need you and your team out to Vashon ASAP. Bring George Franz with you."

"Bomb?"

"Probably not, but I don't want to take the chance of not seeing your ugly face in the morning."

"Got it."

Zack gave him the directions, then instructed the sheriff's deputies to secure the cottage and let no one in until the crime scene investigators arrived. Then he looked for Olivia.

Where in the world had she disappeared to?

Had she seen something? She wasn't stupid—she wouldn't have gone off after Driscoll on her own! Would she? Had he read her wrong the entire time? Her heart and mind were so wrapped up in this case, between her parents and her sister and what had happened with the Davidson family.

No. She was a professional first.

But his heart beat rapidly and he drew his gun, holding it at his side as he circled the cottage.

He saw her in the moonlight, kneeling in the dirt on the edge of the woods. Relief flooded his body and he reholstered his weapon.

Olivia knelt on the ground, her legs unable to support her any longer, the beam from the flashlight dancing over the gray stone in front of her.

It looked like a gravestone.

The now-familiar dots and dashes had been carved deeply into the stone, as if the craftsman had spent hours and hours at work, then polished it until it was as smooth as river rock.

"Olivia!"

She heard Zack's voice, but it seemed to come at a distance. Instead, she heard Missy's voice, loud and clear.

"Just let me finish this chapter."

The names and faces of thirty similar victims

flashed through Olivia's mind until she felt nauseated. Lives cut short, girls who didn't have the chance to grow and learn and love and be loved.

Nor had Olivia ever learned to truly love. She had never accepted anyone's love because she'd been trapped in the past, her heart dead.

No longer would she allow Missy's murder to stop her from living. No longer would she be a prisoner of her regret and guilt.

Zack knelt on the ground beside her. "Liv, what's wrong?"

He sounded worried. She pointed to the stone.

"It looks like a gravestone, but there's no disturbed earth." She shined her light on the garden that surrounded them. In the daylight, the area would seem to burst with color.

"It's a shrine," she said, "to his dead sister."

Zack nodded. "I called in Doug Cohn's people. They'll be here shortly. I'll point this out."

"For so long I've let the past control me. The career choices I made, the friendships I fostered, my relationships with people." She stared into Zack's eyes, imploring him to understand her. She didn't know how to express the revelation that had come to her as she stared at the sad stone half-buried in the earth.

"My father's indifference, my mother's grief, my own feelings of guilt. I'll be forty next year and I feel like I haven't led my own life."

She stood and looked down at Zack squatting next to the marker. "No longer. My decisions are my own. My *feelings* are my own." She touched his head, her fingers brushing against his ear, his rough cheek, her fingers skimming across his lips. He kissed her thumb, took hold of her hand, and stood.

"You know what I think?" he said, his voice low and smooth, sending shivers across her skin. He took her hands in his, his thumbs skimming along her palms. "I think every choice you made in your career has led you here to this place and time. To me. You can't think about the past, what might have been. What is, is. What you've done, you've done. So many things are out of our control, Liv. Too many things. But the choices we've made, to be on the right side of justice, balance the scales."

He kissed her lightly, all too briefly. "Let's go meet Cohn at the docks. I hate waiting around, but until we have more information, we can't do anything else."

They walked away from the garden shrine.

"Thank you, Zack."

"For what?"

"For helping me find myself."

He shook his head. "You were never lost."

CHAPTER
25

Chris stopped the truck halfway up the Cascade Mountains, ninety minutes east of Seattle. The temperature had already dipped into the forties, and he had to set up camp. He'd checked out the area many times and had never seen hikers or campers here. He'd gone through the surrounding area, up and down the road, on foot and never seen recent tire treads or evidence of people. He suspected it was used primarily by rangers, and he'd hear them coming long before they reached him.

Being in the military had served him well; years of preparation and planning made setting up camp painless and easy. He'd leave nothing of himself behind. And any mess that was left when he freed the angel would within months be buried under snow. The ground would soak up her life, and he'd dispose of her shell.

She would be free, living without pain and sadness.

He sat on the ground, closed his eyes. Prepared.

It started when Mama died. Chris didn't know how she'd died, not then, because Bruce took him and Angel from school and they left New Jersey.

"Your ma died in an accident. I have to find work."

They never went home. Never collected his bug collection or books or toys. Angel wept for her teddy bear until Bruce slapped her.

They first went to Texas, a long way off. It took days and days to get there.

They had a one-room apartment where Chris could hear the people next door fighting. Bruce slept in the bed with Angel. Chris slept on the floor. Angel cried all night.

Bruce hurt her.

It didn't take long for Chris to know what Bruce was doing to Angel, but he didn't stop him. He was small for an eleven-year-old. His mother told him he'd grow big and strong, but he hadn't. Bruce was so big and mean and Chris didn't want to be hurt, too. But he took care of Angel when Bruce left. He cleaned her up and hugged her and bought her a new teddy bear with money he'd stolen from Bruce's wallet.

He had loved her and taken care of her for three years, and now she wanted to leave him.

He couldn't let her. He would be lost without her. Angel could never leave.

Chris rose from his spot and crossed to the truck. He unlocked the back and reached in for his angel.

A sudden, sharp jolt across his chest startled him. He reached out blindly in the dark, his fingers brushing against hair, but he was falling down.

He jumped up immediately, sensing rather than seeing his angel leap from the back of the truck and start running.

Anger burned deep and hot in his veins. She was trying to run away. Leave him.

He would never allow that.

* * *

Zack and Olivia met the Coast Guard at the docks. Doug Cohn and his team disembarked. Zack filled him in on what they'd discovered, then went back across the Sound with the Coast Guard.

"Detective Travis? You have a radio call," one of the officers said and handed him a walkie-talkie.

"Travis here."

"It's Quinn Peterson. We have an Amber Alert call. Two sightings of the truck in question on Highway 90 heading east into the Cascades. One guy swears he saw a white truck turn off onto Road 56, which crisscrosses the middle north fork of the Anchor River."

"The Cascades are huge, and Road 56 is virtually impassable in places."

"That should make it easier for us to find him. I've called the forest rangers to increase patrols; we have a helicopter standing by. The sheriff's department has already called in all off-duty personnel to start a manhunt."

"It'll take us two hours to get there," Zack said, discouraged. Two hours could be the difference between Nina living or dying.

"Thirty minutes, tops. I have a helicopter waiting for you at the Coast Guard station, with a search-and-rescue expert already on board."

"Who?"

"My wife, Miranda. And if anything happens to her, I'll hold you personally responsible."

Nina ran faster than she'd ever run before. Even when she was exhausted and didn't think she could take another step, she kept going. Or stumbled.

Sometimes she crawled. But she was too terrified to stop moving.

She was in the mountains, that much she knew, so she focused on running down, down, staying off the road. Couldn't chance that he would see her, hear her. It was really dark up here, too dark.

Nina hated the dark.

There were so many sounds competing with her rapid breath and occasional cries. Hooting owls. Scurrying rodents. The call of larger animals. Rushing water, a river.

None were as fearsome as the man she'd seen.

He looked normal. But one glance into his hateful eyes told this little girl that if she didn't find the strength to run, he'd hurt her bad.

How long had she been running? Was he still coming? Would he catch her? Could he hear her?

She was in the middle of nowhere, but she didn't stop. She didn't wait and try to hear him. She prayed and pleaded with God to help her. The moon came and went behind clouds, alternately guiding her and hiding her.

Out of the corner of her eye, she saw movement even before she heard the rustling of a body moving through trees. Her heart pounded so hard it hurt.

A sliver of moonlight reflected off two eyes.

He was there. Right there. Feet away.

He would kill her.

She stifled a scream, and the body—covered in fur—ran past her so close she felt the animal's terror. Or was that her own fear?

It was a deer. A deer, not a man.

She sank to the damp earth and cried. No one would find her. She didn't know where she was, how close she was to Seattle, if she was even in Washington State.

Get up, Nina.

No. I don't want to. I'm tired.

But the voice was persistent. *Get up, get moving, keep running. Be smart, Nina. Start marking your trail.*

She found a thick branch on the ground and started marking trees by either breaking a small branch or scratching the trunk with the branch she held. She didn't know if it would do any good, but doing *something* actually calmed her down.

She didn't hear him following. She heard nothing but four-legged predators. They were far less scary to her than the bad man. Like the deer, they feared her more than she feared them.

What was that?

She stopped. Listened. Faint, in the distance, a motor. Lights suddenly cut through the woods, then as the vehicle bounced, the light cut high and low.

Had help arrived?

She listened, her fear growing. No, not help. It sounded like the same as the truck the bad man drove. It was *him*.

She hunkered down.

A screech and an inhuman cry.

Thud. Crunch.

Silence. Dead silence.

She ran. Ran as fast as she could along a narrow trail, then suddenly she was falling . . .

Zack had told Olivia that Miranda was coming with them on the helicopter search, but seeing her was still a pleasant surprise. Miranda gave her a big bear hug and asked, "How are you?" then glanced at Zack, who was talking to the pilot. "Quinn told me everything," Miranda whispered. "Your secret is safe with me."

Olivia relaxed. "Thank you. We're so close. I don't want to blow it now and not be here when we find him."

"I know, Liv. I know exactly how you feel."

Out of everyone, Miranda did understand. Having her friend here, not only to find Nina but as support, grounded Olivia. "I'm sorry I didn't tell you I was in Seattle when you called the other day."

"We'll talk about that later. Now," she looked over at Zack, "I assume that's Detective Travis?"

"Yes."

"He's umm, well, as sexy as Viggo Mortensen in *Lord of the Rings*."

Olivia blushed. Miranda knew Olivia loved Tolkien's trilogy. "Miranda! I hadn't noticed." Of course she had, the minute she saw him.

"Then you're blind." Miranda glanced at the sky.

"We need to get a move on. The fog is creeping in."

Zack approached. "Miranda Peterson?"

"Yes." She shook his hand. "Let's get going and I'll tell you my plan on the way." She handed both him and Olivia copies of a map of the central-west section of the Cascade Mountains.

"I just got word from my partner," Zack said as he put on headphones and adjusted the equipment in the front of the helicopter to fit his long legs. "They found the owner of the truck. It's registered to Karl Burgess. He and his wife left on vacation early this morning. Their neighbor said they drove themselves to the airport. Boyd is on his way to find Driscoll's vehicle. We have a warrant and will tow it to the lab, plus have a twenty-four-hour stakeout at the airport in case he returns for his car."

"I hope he doesn't come back," Olivia said. Miranda and Zack both looked at her skeptically.

"If he returns, Nina is dead."

Zack coordinated with the sheriff's department from the helicopter and listened to Miranda lay out her plan. They spoke through microphones attached to the headphones they all wore, their voices competing with the helicopter noise.

"Until the sheriff's department says otherwise, we're assuming the witness is accurate about the white truck he saw turning onto Road 56. That puts us . . . here." She pointed to where Road 56 was accessible from the main highway. "In here are homes and cabins, spread out. Within a mile or so, the mountain starts a steep climb up. Here is the middle north fork of the Anchor River; you can see how Road 56 crosses it here and . . . here."

"All the way up the mountain," Zack said. "I've been up there. Beautiful in the summer, impassable in the winter."

"There are two places we can land other than this field near the turnoff. We can go up three miles to a lodge which has a flat, wide meadow. I talked to them already and cleared it. If we need it, it's there. Or, we can land here." She pointed about a mile farther up the mountain. "It's a campground owned by the Boy Scouts."

"He won't be anywhere people might see or hear."

"Agreed. He wants privacy, but he also wants accessibility. I'm thinking he's already staked out a site."

"He doesn't need a lot to survive," Olivia interjected. "His house was bare bones. Nothing extraneous. He won't need a fire. He'll plan ahead with a sleeping bag maybe, a space blanket. Water. Rations."

"I agree," Miranda said. "He was in the military; he knows how to live with minimal supplies. But he's also going to want an escape route. He's not going to isolate himself so much that he can be trapped."

"But he's been killing for years. He's not going to think we're on to him," Olivia said. "We only learned his identity this morning."

This morning? It had been a long day, Olivia realized. She rubbed her temples, suddenly weary. She was surprised when Zack reached over and massaged her neck with one hand.

She caught his eye.

"It's almost over, Liv," he said as if she were the only one in the copter. "We're going to get him. Tonight."

Miranda glanced from Olivia to Zack, then

cleared her throat. "So, I've marked out grids on the map. The sheriff's department is checking every trail off Road 56 to see if a truck has recently driven up it. They're going in on horseback, vehicle, and foot. We have stations set up here—at the lodge where we can land—at this ranger's station, and here, at the sheriff's substation at the base of the mountain."

"What if he sees the activity and kills her immediately?" Olivia asked.

"What else can we do?" Zack said. "If we do nothing, he'll certainly kill her. But I assume, Miranda, you have a plan to minimize our activity."

She nodded. "They're radio silent. All conversation is via secure channels. If he's monitoring commercial radio or television, then he'll know we've identified him. We have his picture going up on all the networks throughout western Washington, and the Amber Alert is out, which puts his face and description on thousands of websites in the country. He's not getting away. We just have to find him before he kills Nina."

Zack studied the map. "Your husband said you were in search-and-rescue. Liv, I thought you said you two went to the FBI Academy together?"

"We did," Miranda said. "I left before graduation. Long story." She glanced at Olivia, and Olivia felt awful that her friend was covering for her. "I was the director of Search and Rescue in Montana before Quinn and I got married last June."

"Oh." Zack's face darkened as he remembered. "*Oh*. The Bozeman Butcher."

"Yeah, well, that's over." A cloud fell over Miranda's face and Olivia reached for her.

"I didn't mean to bring it up," Zack said.

"I'm fine. Now we have The Seattle Slayer on our hands. Don't you just hate the crap the press comes up with?"

The pilot said, "I have a transmission coming in from Special Agent Quincy Peterson."

"Put him through," Zack said.

They all heard Quinn's voice through the headphones.

"The sheriff's department has found the truck 1.6 miles off of Road 56, well past the Boy Scout campground. They'll meet you at the camp and take you there."

"Nina?" Olivia asked, leaning forward.

"There's no sign of Nina or Driscoll. The truck was in an accident—hit a deer. Air bags deployed, but there's some blood in the cab. None in the back of the truck. What's your ETA?"

"Four minutes to camp," the pilot said.

"I'm about fifty minutes out. Doug Cohn and his assistant are with me. I have two agents following. And Travis, your partner Boyd found Driscoll's car in the long-term parking lot at Sea-Tac. He'll be in contact if there's anything of use in the cab."

"Thanks, Peterson. Out."

Zack stared at the truck slammed against a redwood tree, one tire in a deep gully so the back tire didn't even rest on the ground. In the middle of the road, a deer lay dead. It had barely been alive when the first sheriff deputies arrived on the scene; a park ranger had been summoned and he put the animal down just before Zack, Miranda, and Olivia arrived. Zack didn't even have to look at the skid marks to surmise what had happened.

Deer crossed road, truck hit deer, and the impact forced the truck off the road, into a gully, and up against the tree.

"Why couldn't the bastard be dead behind the wheel?" Zack muttered under his breath.

The deputy gave him a half-smile. "That'd be too easy."

Zack didn't want to disturb any evidence, but he needed as much information as he could get to figure out what had happened. Why Nina was not in the truck and where Driscoll had gone. Did he still have Nina? Was she alive? The sheriff's department was bringing in additional lighting, but all they had now were a few heavy-duty flashlights.

The air bag had deployed and there was blood on it, as if Driscoll had hurt himself or perhaps got a bloody nose on impact. When Doug Cohn arrived, he would process the entire vehicle.

With gloved hands to avoid contaminating evidence, Zack went through the cab. He found maps, registration for Karl Burgess, some books on tape, a pair of movie ticket stubs. All appeared to be old, and likely left by the owners of the truck.

In the camper shell, Zack found ropes. Loops were still in them, and he held them, wondering what had happened.

Had Driscoll untied her? Had Nina freed herself? Had he heard the news reports and dumped her in the mountains—dead or alive—in order to escape?

Where had he gone?

Zack walked around to the front of the truck and put his hand on the hood. A hint of warmth. The accident probably happened an hour to ninety minutes ago.

He slowly circled the truck, sweeping his light back and forth. The third time around, something caught his eye.

He squatted, knees cracking, and picked up a shell casing. Was it new? There was no hunting allowed in this area of the Cascades, but that didn't mean hunters hadn't crossed the unmarked boundary.

He put it back where he'd found it, marking the spot with an evidence flag he'd taken from the deputy's kit.

Standing, he looked around with his light. He saw it. Disturbed earth, footprints.

Driscoll's flight path.

"Hey, Deputy." Zack waited for the young cop to reach him. "This looks like a path of some sort. Where does it go?"

The deputy consulted a detailed map of the area. "Okay—the Boy Scouts use this area a lot, but primarily in the summer. The weather is too unpredictable in the fall. The main camp was where you landed . . . here. Two miles away. The Scouts mark off trails every year as part of their program. This path looks like one of theirs—it's not on the map."

"You don't know where it goes?"

"Their program has the kids making paths with the goal to reach the main camp. There're a lot of requirements; it's been a long time since I was in the Scouts. But . . . less than half a mile from here is a fork of the Anchor River. He'd be able to follow the river all the way down the mountain. There's enough foliage to hide. The spruce is pretty thick all through this region."

"Okay, let's assume he's uninjured. On foot, it's still going to take him hours to get down the mountain. We need a team of trackers to head to a lower part of the river and start working their way up; another set starting from here and trying to track him. We might be able to intercept him. He can only follow the river or come back up to this trail. From what I remember of the map, there are some sheer drop-offs west of the river."

"Correct. How far down?"

Zack called, "Miranda? Miranda!" Quinn's wife seemed to have an intuitive grasp of the terrain, though apparently she'd lived in Seattle only for a few months. She might have a good idea of how far Driscoll could get down the mountain with his lead time.

She didn't answer, and he pulled out his walkie-talkie. "Travis here. I'm trying to locate Miranda Peterson and Olivia St. Martin."

Crackle. "Travis? Miranda here. Liv and I are checking out something up the road. It looks like there was a scuffle. Hold."

Hold? Dammit, he didn't like the idea of two women—no matter how well trained—off tracking in the middle of the night when a killer was on the loose.

"Where are you?"

"About point-six miles up the trail from your location."

"I'll meet you there. Stay visible."

"Got it."

Zack turned to the deputy. "Keep the area secure. I'm heading up the trail to see what they discovered. Keep the channel open—if there's any trouble, let me know."

With all the men in the woods, Zack didn't think

Driscoll was around. He was probably hoofing it down the mountain as quickly as possible, hoping he could get to the main road and disappear before they caught up with him.

His cell phone didn't work up here, so he used his radio on the secure channel to call into the sheriff's substation and relay the information he'd picked up from the crime scene. Before he hung up, twelve rangers and deputies were on their way to the base of the mountain to follow the middle north fork of the Anchor River up in the hopes of apprehending Driscoll as he made his way down. Another six were on their way to the Boy Scout camp, where a makeshift checkpoint had already been established.

Zack hoped he wasn't wrong about Driscoll's flight, but he had a bad feeling it wasn't close to being over.

Please, God, if you're listening, please make her okay.

Careful not to trample the evidence, Olivia ran through the scenario in her head.

A small camp had been set up. No fire, but a sleeping bag, backpack with rations and water, and a slick plastic tarp.

Olivia suspected that Driscoll used the tarp to transport the bodies back to town to dump. She wondered why he didn't leave them in the wilderness. It would take much longer to find them. That was a question for the psychology experts in the Bureau. If she had to hazard a guess, either he wanted their bodies to be found for burial or closure, or he had a subconscious wish to get caught.

Or maybe something less profound: maybe he simply wanted to prove he was smarter than everyone, that he could get away with the "perfect" crime.

The ground was moist up here, littered with pine needles and pebbles and lots of wet dirt. The foot impressions were excellent—she and Miranda had flagged several she thought would make good casts.

The smaller set of footprints led down the mountain, but with the fog growing thicker and her flashlight not providing enough illumination, she wasn't sure if they belonged to Nina.

"Miranda, come over here," she called, wanting her friend's expert advice.

"I just got off the radio with your detective. He's on his way up."

"He's not *my* detective," Olivia said.

"Hmm."

"What's that supposed to mean?" Olivia shook her head. "Save it. Look at these." She shined her light on obvious footprints that headed down the mountain.

"Someone was running, but the ground is moist and they slid here . . . and down here," Miranda said.

"They look small."

"Small for a man."

"I'm thinking Nina escaped," Olivia said, hope bubbling. "What if she got away somehow? What if she ran and ran and got away from him? We need to go after her."

"I agree, but you need to prepare yourself that she might already be dead."

"No. Why? Why do I have to? She could just as easily be alive. I can't be too late."

"This isn't all on your shoulders, Liv."

Olivia shook her head. "You don't understand."

Silence.

"I'm sorry," Olivia said. "I didn't mean that. You understand better than anyone."

"It's okay, Liv, but I just want you to be prepared for the worst and hope for the best. Look here—" Miranda parted two spruce saplings and pointed to deeper impressions in the earth. "He pursued her. He may have caught up with her."

"Or she could have got away," Olivia said stubbornly.

"Yes, she could have. Or she ran and he caught up to her and killed her. Or he thought it would be easier to find her in the truck. Or maybe he wanted to escape." Miranda's eyes were filled with compassion. "Liv, prepare yourself, okay?"

Olivia closed her eyes, pictured Nina dead. Nina's face turned into Michelle Davidson, then Missy.

"No. She's alive. I feel it."

"Olivia!"

Zack's voice cut through the still fog.

"Over here!" she called, and watched as his shadow emerged. The quality of light was surreal with the flashlight beams bouncing off the mist.

"What did you find?"

Olivia walked him through the evidence. "Zack, I think she escaped. She's probably scared to death, terrified, and cold. We have to go after her. Miranda has extensive experience tracking." She glanced at Miranda, hoping she wouldn't contradict her. Olivia knew she was putting her friend on the spot, but right now finding Nina was the most important thing.

She *had* to be alive.

"I agree," Zack said.

Olivia was about to protest when she realized Zack was on her side.

"The three of us will go, stay in sight of one another. I'm going to call in our location."

When he spoke to the deputy, he learned that Quinn Peterson and Doug Cohn were only fifteen minutes out.

It was surprisingly easy to follow the tracks, even in the dark. The beams from the flashlight made each impression stand out, and they proceeded at a steady pace. At first, the ground dropped away and Olivia feared Nina had fallen down the steep slope to her peril; there were several long, sliding impressions. But only a hundred feet downslope the ground leveled out. In the dark mist, the smell of spruce and pine and damp dirt overpowered all other scents.

Nina had to have been terrified. Running at night from a man who wanted to kill her for no reason her ten-year-old mind could fathom. But what impressed Olivia more than anything was that Nina had the wherewithal to escape in the first place. She was an amazing girl, and though Olivia didn't know her, she was immensely proud of her.

Nina had zigzagged down the slope for several hundred yards. Even with a down vest over her sweater, Olivia was chilled. Nina had no warm jacket and would be freezing.

A flash of yellow to Olivia's left had her stopping. Miranda was leading, focused on the ground, while Olivia took the middle and Zack the rear. "Stop," she called.

"What do you see?"

"Look." She pointed to a bright yellow spot on the ground. Her heart leapt into her throat.

Nina was last seen wearing a bright yellow windbreaker.

"Stay here," Zack commanded.

He sidestepped over to the jacket, cautious. He squatted, then came up with the jacket and brought it back.

It was ripped to shreds. From the looks of it, by a sharp knife.

Miranda held out an evidence bag and Zack placed the windbreaker in it, then marked the spot with a red flag.

"Oh no, oh no. You were right Miranda," Olivia began, her hands shaking.

"She's not here."

"But—"

"There's no blood on the jacket."

Olivia blinked, looked at the shredded material through the clear bag. "I don't understand. What happened?"

They were silent for a minute, then Olivia spoke up, tentatively at first. "What if she removed her jacket? What if she realized the color would attract him in the dark?"

"And placed it in an obvious spot. Then went in the opposite direction," Miranda said, nodding. "I think you're right."

"Why is it shredded?" Olivia asked.

"He was enraged," Zack said. "She'd outmaneuvered him. That would explain why he didn't pay attention to the road. The marks on the trail indicate he'd been driving way too fast for the soft ground.

He overcorrected when he saw the deer, hit it, then slammed into the tree."

"Makes sense to me," Miranda said. "Let's fan out, figure out which way she went."

Ten minutes later, Zack called Miranda and Olivia to his location. "Look." He pointed to a mark on a tree.

N.M.

It was faint, low on the tree, and looked like it had been made by her thumbnail or a small branch. "She may have been marking her path in the hopes of retracing her steps in daylight," Zack said.

"Maybe she's hiding. Laying low until it's safe," Miranda said.

Olivia called, "Nina!" Zack and Miranda joined her.

"Nina!"

Their voices had an odd, hollow sound in the mist. The entire mountain seemed to hold its breath, waiting.

A bright light cut through the trees and Olivia stifled a scream. Zack took two strides and got in front of her, gun drawn.

"It's the trail we drove in on," Miranda whispered.

A Jeep passed slowly only ten feet from them as they hid in the trees. It then stopped.

Zack put his finger up to tell them to stay quiet, and walked along the edge of the trees to the vehicle up ahead. Voices trickled down.

"That's Quinn!" Miranda said, and emerged from the woods.

Less than twenty feet away, the white truck was still up against a tree.

Olivia stayed back from the group, watching

Quinn and Doug Cohn and three others emerge from the Jeep and start talking. Quinn gave Miranda a brief hug, and Zack explained what they'd learned and what they believed happened to Nina.

"Did you find anything useful at his house?" Zack asked Cohn.

"More than enough for a conviction," Cohn said. "That case you found? Both the underwear and the hair was stored inside, among other things. Maps, old notebooks detailing his plans, fake identifications in dozens of names."

"What about the stone in the garden? With *angel* in Morse code engraved on top."

Cohn's jaw tightened. "Buried two feet under the stone was a blood-soaked tarp and sheet. Considering the location, I'll bet we'll find the blood matches Jillian Reynolds. We also used Luminol in the bedroom and discovered traces of blood under Driscoll's bed."

Olivia put her hand to her mouth and walked away. Though the police had done a basic search of the island, they didn't go into any homes because they thought they knew what happened to Jillian. She couldn't swim, so they figured she must have drowned. Driscoll had kidnapped her, hidden her away until the search was called off. Then he killed her and dumped her far into the woods so no one would find her for a long time.

She walked off the side of the trail.

Then she saw it.

"Zack!" she called.

Zack, Quinn, and Miranda came running down the trail. "What happened?" Zack asked. "Are you okay?"

"I'm okay. Look."

Small footprints followed the edge of the trail, then disappeared down the slope opposite from where they'd emerged when they saw Quinn's car.

"When we drove up, we must have passed her. But she didn't know if it was safe to come out. She's hiding here someplace. We have to find her."

The four of them started jogging back down the trail, calling for Nina.

"Nina! The police are here. We're all over the mountain. Please come out. Your mother is waiting."

Over and over. Olivia called until she was hoarse.

They paused for a minute to drink water that Miranda had brought in her sack.

"Help!"

Olivia held her hand up to stop everyone from talking. Was it her imagination? Had she really heard a cry for help?

"Help! Help, please!"

"Nina?" Olivia called.

"I'm stuck! Please help me!"

"We're coming!" Zack shouted, and started in the direction of the voice.

Nina had slid off the trail and fallen down a steep slope. They shined all their lights down to see where she was.

"Thank you! Thank you!" They heard her but couldn't see her.

"Where are you? Nina?"

"My leg is stuck. I fell into this hole. I can't get out. Please help me."

"I have rope," Miranda said, and opened her pack. "We can't go down this way. We'll fall down the slope as well."

The sharp drop-off was obvious in the light, but Nina wouldn't have been able to see it running in the dark. She was stuck in a crevice. Looking carefully, Olivia saw her head poking out.

"We're going to lower down a rope," Miranda called to the girl. "There's a loop on one end. Pull it over your head and tighten it under your arms. Then hold on to it."

"But my leg. I can't move it."

"I'll go down and free her leg," Zack said.

"You're too big," Quinn said. "I'm thinner."

"You're both too big," Olivia said. "Look at that crevice. It's too narrow for either of you. I'm going."

"Olivia," Miranda began, then stopped and nodded. "I agree. But we have to find another way down."

They told Nina to stay put and someone would come down to help her. Olivia walked with Miranda several hundred feet down the trail until they found a safe place to rappel down the slope. "This is what we'll do," she told Olivia. "You free her leg and we'll pull her up. Then, I'll send the rope back for you. You cinch it under your arms, just like I told Nina, and we'll pull you up."

"Why can't I just come back this way? It's not as steep."

"This ground isn't stable. That crevice—I don't trust it. I think it's deeper than it looks from here. You need to step carefully. The earth could give way anywhere and you'll be in the middle of a rock slide. The entire Cascade Mountain range isn't stable. Remember, Mount St. Helens is part of it."

"You're not saying we're sitting on a volcano." Olivia tried to make light of it, but saw Miranda was serious.

"If you mean is the mountain going to explode tonight, no. But there's continual seismic activity that's too sensitive for us to feel. The constant minute shifts underground loosen the rocks and earth, making the ground itself dangerous in steep areas like this. The crevice Nina is stuck in is actually a split in the mountain caused by repeated earth movements."

"Miranda, I have a Ph.D. and I barely understand you."

"Okay, more than you wanted to know. But you have to be careful. As soon as I saw the terrain I knew we had a problem, but I didn't want to scare Nina, and I doubt Quinn or Zack would allow you to do this. Seriously, Liv, their weight wouldn't have held. You're light enough; I think you'll be okay. But please, *please*, be careful. Especially until you get that rope around you."

"I promise."

Miranda explained to Olivia the best way to navigate the slope and approach the crevice. The ground was much rockier here, and Olivia lost her foothold several times, sliding partway down until she flattened her body enough to scoot down like a crab. Finally, she reached the rocky crevice and slowly made her way back up the narrow opening to Nina.

Miranda was right. The space was deep. Olivia couldn't touch the bottom, and had to use the sides of the crevice to balance and move forward.

"Thank you thank you thank you!" Nina cried when she saw Olivia. "I was so scared. First of him, then—I thought I'd die stuck here, no one would find me."

Olivia hugged her, as much to soothe herself as

the girl. "I am so proud of you, Nina. You beat him."

"You got him, right? I saw his truck crash. He wasn't moving, but I didn't go back there."

"You did the right thing."

"Is he—is he dead?"

Olivia wouldn't lie to her. "He's not in the truck."

Nina shook his head. "No. No! I saw the crash. I—ohmygod, he's going to come after me!"

"No, I won't—"

Nina started to flail and pull at her leg. Rocks started falling from farther up the slope.

"Nina, stop moving," Olivia commanded.

"What's going on down there?" Zack called from above.

"It's okay!" Olivia yelled. To Nina, she said, "There are dozens of cops all over this mountain. He's not going to get you. I promise. You have to remain still and let me get your leg free. This ground is not stable. We have to be careful."

Nina nodded, her entire body shaking not only from the cold, but from fright.

Olivia knelt in the crevice, bracing herself against the sides, feeling cool air rise up from underneath her. Vertigo overwhelmed her and she paused, taking deep breaths to gather her bearings.

She felt around for Nina's foot. Her ankle was wedged in between rocks. Using her fingers, Olivia tried to scrape away dirt and loosen one of the rocks, but it was stuck. She started wiggling Nina's ankle back and forth, back and forth until she could move it to the side and up, out of the hole. Nina whimpered, but she kept her cries silent.

"It hurts," she finally said when Olivia stood.

"It could be broken, or sprained." Olivia held Nina's cheeks. "Are you ready? Hold on to the rope tightly, but let them pull you up. Stay as still as possible. It'll be slow work, but you can do it. Okay?"

"Okay. I can do it."

"I know you can." Olivia called up. "She's ready!"

There was a lot more noise up the slope, car doors slamming. More deputies must have arrived. Flashing red lights cut through the growth. An ambulance, most likely. They'd had one ready at the lodge in case they needed it.

Olivia braced herself in the crevice and awaited her turn.

Zack didn't like Olivia going down the slope herself, but Miranda was right—she had the best build for the job, considering the terrain. He was antsy and knew he wouldn't be at ease until Olivia was back up the mountain. Safe.

He and Quinn took brisk orders from Miranda as they prepared to bring Nina up. "We're going to use this tree as a pulley of sorts," she said as she wrapped the rope around it. "Put those gloves on, Quinn. That rope will leave some nasty burns if it gets away from you."

"Yes, ma'am."

"Can it, Peterson," she said.

Though the banter seemed light, Miranda's face showed strain and worry.

"What's wrong?" Zack asked.

"Nothing," she said. "We're just trying to get two people up a steep slope at one o'clock in the morning with a killer wandering loose in the woods. What could be wrong?"

"Miranda," Quinn said, "you're not telling us something. Is Olivia okay?"

"She's fine," Miranda snapped.

"What she's not telling you," Doug Cohn interjected, "is that this slope is unstable. That's why we had that little rock slide a few minutes ago."

"Unstable? How?"

Doug explained how this side of the mountain experienced regular rock slides, and that the continuing seismic activity made any treks off established trails dangerous.

"Why'd we let her go down there in the first place?" Zack demanded. "We should have waited until we had a team in place."

"Because a ten-year-old girl was trapped in that crevice," Miranda said, "and neither you nor I nor Olivia would have wanted her to wait hours for rescue after what she's been through."

Zack sighed. "You're right."

"Do we have lights yet?" Quinn asked. The sheriff's department had hauled a high-wattage construction light to the scene.

"Just about," someone called. A few minutes later, the bright light not only lit up the side of the mountain, but provided warmth as well.

"Okay, let's get Nina out of there," Miranda said. "Start pulling on the rope. I'm going to watch her ascent. Listen to my orders."

"Always," Quinn said.

Miranda rolled her eyes, but gave a half-grin.

Zack saw something in the newlywed couple that he never remembered having with his ex-wife, or any of the women he'd dated. Solid respect, playfulness, and deep affection. From the silent looks to the discreet touches, Quinn and Miranda obviously had something special between them.

Something that Zack wanted for himself.

He'd never thought that way before. He'd been content with casually dating. He was a cop—the job came first.

But the job was important to Quinn Peterson, and his wife not only knew it, but relished it. At the same time, there was no doubt in Zack's mind that Peterson would drop the world to be with his wife.

That kind of support and love was hard to come by.

He and Quinn slowly pulled Nina up. Hand over hand, they developed a rhythm that worked. He glanced down the slope, saw Nina, and then Olivia farther down, hunkered in the crevice, holding on to a young tree that seemed to be growing precariously on the slope.

There was something about Olivia—something more than her brains and beauty, her dedication to her job. Something he wanted to explore more fully.

Like he'd told her this morning, he wanted to spend time with her. When this was over. When Driscoll was behind bars.

The thought of having Olivia all to himself for a week or two, to learn everything about her, thrilled him.

"Hold it!" Miranda suddenly called, and both Zack and Quinn halted their movements.

Zack heard rocks rolling. He thought they would stop. They didn't.

"Nina! Stay still!" Miranda called down.

Nina cried out, then Olivia screamed.

"What happened?" Zack looked down and couldn't see Olivia.

"She's okay. She slipped."

"I can't see her!"

"I see her hand. Get Nina up. Fast."

Miranda didn't have to say it twice. Quinn and Zack worked double time to bring the girl up the slope. They handed her off to the EMTs who were waiting, and Miranda tossed the rope down to Olivia.

"Olivia! I'm sending down the rope. Grab it."

The earth was still moving, rocks bumping down. It wasn't an earthquake, Zack realized; it was the disturbance of people on this steep, unstable slope that was causing the loose ground to fall away.

"Why isn't she taking the rope?" Zack asked, fear evident in his voice.

"She can't see it." Miranda's lips were tight. She called down. "Olivia! The rope is three feet to your right. You'll need to let go of the tree."

"No!" Olivia's voice was faint, but she sounded petrified.

"You have to!" Miranda called.

"I'll be okay. Give me a minute."

"Dammit!" Miranda said, running a hand through her hair and yanking on the dark ponytail hanging down her back. "She doesn't have a minute," she mumbled.

Rocks continued to fall, and Olivia cried out.

Zack's heart beat double time. He shouted, "Olivia St. Martin! Grab the damn rope *now*!"

He saw her hand let go of the tree and for a split second, Zack thought she'd fallen deeper into the crevice. Then he saw both her hands reach up, feeling for the rope.

"Six inches," Miranda called. "Right there. Yes!

Pull it over your head, under your arms, right now. Now. Okay. Good."

She turned to Quinn and Zack. "Get her up. Fast."

As they pulled, a huge chunk of ground gave way, and they scrambled for a foothold. They felt additional weight on the rope, and Miranda grabbed the end and helped pull. Hand over hand. Hand over hand.

Olivia scrambled up the last twenty feet herself. A huge gash had sliced her forehead open, and blood was dripping down her face. Zack pulled the rope off her and looked down the slope.

He wished he hadn't.

The rock slide had widened the crevice. He couldn't see the bottom, even with the industrial lighting. The thought that Olivia could have fallen to her death terrified him.

He wrapped his arms around her and held her tight. She breathed heavily in his arms, her entire body shaking violently.

"It's okay, you're okay," Zack repeated. "You're okay."

He murmured words of reassurance in her ear, for himself as well as Olivia. He didn't want to let her go.

He kissed her hair, her cheek, her neck. She held him tightly, her arms wrapped around his back, under his jacket, trying to be as close to him as possible. Her shaking subsided and he tilted her face to look at him, wincing at the gash on her head.

"You need to let the EMT take a look at your head."

"Later." She leaned up and kissed him.

He returned the kiss with fervor. Needing to taste

her, to feel her response, that she was fully alive and breathing in his arms. "Liv," he whispered into her lips. "I was so scared."

"Me too," she murmured. He pulled back and looked at her, wanting to understand where they were going because these intense feelings scared him, almost as much as her falling. The thought of Olivia walking away at the end of the case filled him with a terrible sense of loss.

In her eyes he saw relief and desire, the same yearning he had for her.

She buried her face in his chest. "Hold me. Just for another minute."

He would have been happy to hold her forever.

But Chris Driscoll was still on the loose.

In the military, Chris Driscoll had learned that a backup plan was necessary for survival. Without a plan, you die.

The little bitch got away. She wasn't an angel at all, but a demon sent to trap him. He hadn't been thinking when he pursued her. If he had waited, she would have returned. If he had listened better, he would have found her.

He was so angry and surprised when she attacked him that he'd chased her, then lost her. She eluded him. She sent that deer into his path and he crashed.

But he'd prepared for failure, like any good soldier. He just needed a car.

He knew exactly where to get one.

CHAPTER
27

Zack and Quinn spread open the map of the Cascades on the desk in Zack's room at the North Fork Lodge.

The lodge owners, middle-aged sisters Kristy and Beth Krause, had opened their bed-and-breakfast to the police earlier in the evening, so when Zack and the others arrived at two in the morning, they already had several rooms prepared.

"The fog was too thick for the sheriff's search teams to attempt a manhunt tonight," Quinn said. He pointed to an area near the base of the mountain and the Anchor River. "They'll be starting here at daybreak with dogs and at least a dozen men. We'll have men with dogs coming from the other side." He pointed to the place near the Boy Scout camp where Driscoll had crashed the truck.

"He could elude our men at night," Zack said. "If he goes at a steady pace, he'll be at the base of the mountain by morning."

"Miranda said this area is almost impossible to navigate. He either has to follow Road 56—and we have men discreetly stationed at several places along the road—or wind around to the river and follow it out.

"There is a chance," Quinn continued, "that he could cross Road 56 at one point, and that would put him on this side of the mountain. There are several vacation homes and public campgrounds. It's a little late in the season, but the sheriff's department is sending deputies to each residence to first warn anyone there, as well as inspect any vacant houses. They've called in support from neighboring counties as well as the forest rangers."

"This lodge is in that area. If Driscoll crosses Road 56 he could end up here."

"That's why the sheriff assigned two deputies to these grounds."

Zack ran a hand over his face. "I should have been doing all this."

"Why? That's why you have a good team around you. You've been going practically 24/7 for the last week." Quinn slapped his hand on Zack's back. "Get some sleep. Everything that can be covered in the four hours between now and dawn has been."

Quinn's cell phone rang and Zack tensed. Bad news? Or had they captured Driscoll?

"Agent Peterson," Quinn answered. He visibly relaxed. "I'll be right there. Love you too." He shut his phone. "Miranda told me to come to bed."

"She's a good woman."

"You don't know the half of it. To think of all the time I wasted . . . " his voice trailed off. "Um, I've known Olivia for a long time. She's very important to Miranda and me."

What was that supposed to mean? Zack frowned.

Quinn held his hand up to stop whatever he thought Zack was going to say. Hell, Zack didn't know what he was going to say, but he felt distinctly uncomfortable, as if he were a teenager facing his girlfriend's father after breaking curfew.

"What I should say is, Olivia has taken the world on her shoulders and doesn't leave much time for herself. She deserves a little happiness. Especially after this."

Zack agreed. "After we wrap this up, we're going away for a few days."

"Good." Quinn nodded. He looked like he wanted to say something else, then, "You know when you're on a tough case and you're faced with an ultimatum and no decision is perfect? That no matter what you choose to do, there are consequences?"

"There are always consequences, Peterson. You have to do what is the most right."

"Exactly. Good. Well. Get some rest. Tomorrow is going to be another long day."

Quinn left and Zack frowned. What was that all about? He yawned and rubbed his face. He was exhausted, but there was no way he could sleep right now. His mind was working overtime. They'd rescued Nina, but Driscoll was still out there.

He needed a shower, so he turned on the water, stripped, and stepped under the spray.

When Olivia had slipped down the crevice, he'd thought she'd fallen to her death. He'd been terrified he'd lost her. When Zack saw her alive he could at least breathe again. When he held her in his arms, he didn't ever want to let her go. Cold fear had turned into something hot and needy. He'd never felt so close, so connected, with anyone.

She'd reached out for him, her adrenaline-induced passion pulling him over the edge. He had wanted to make love to her, right then. The fact that they were in the middle of the woods with an audience hadn't entered his mind.

Now he wanted her twice as bad.

What was Olivia doing right now? Was she sleeping? Or, like his, was her mind too active to shut down?

He shut off the water and dried off, pulling on his boxers and pacing. He was semi-hard thinking about Olivia and her lips. Remembering her full breasts under the damp robe she'd worn in the hotel room the other morning. Remembering the way her long, soft fingers drew trails of electricity wherever they touched his skin.

He wasn't going to get any sleep tonight until he kissed her again.

He pulled on his jeans, grabbed his holster, and left.

Olivia couldn't sleep either.

For the first time in her life, she wanted to go to a man. She wanted to slide into bed next to Zack Travis and ask him to make love to her.

When she'd been married, not once had she initiated sex. Greg had always suggested they have a romantic dinner, which was his way of starting a romantic evening that ended in bed.

She knew why—it was being touched. It had taken a long time to get comfortable with Greg, a long time to accept his touch. But already, after mere days, she didn't flinch at the thought of Zack touching her. She didn't hesitate to reach out for him, even to just casually pat his arm.

She'd have to be comatose not to recognize the change happening within. And it had as much to do with the way Zack had treated her, talked to her, respected and pushed her, as with her own internal growth.

But would she have become as strong and accepting of the past, putting it behind her, if Zack hadn't come into her life? The two events were linked.

She slid out of bed and crossed to the large picture window that overlooked a valley. She couldn't see much except shadows and the suggestion of a meadow. She wore a long flannel gown Kristy Krause had loaned her when the kind woman had taken her soiled clothes to wash. She'd showered and her short hair was still damp, but she wasn't cold.

What should she do? Should she simply walk across the hall and knock on Zack's door and throw herself into his arms? That's what she wanted. Needed.

But what if she was mistaken about him? She *thought* he had some feelings for her beyond professional interest, but considering she hadn't dated since Greg, she didn't know if she was reading things right. And considering they had spent the last five days on the edge, working this case nonstop, maybe it was that intensity she was picking up on and not any personal feelings between them.

Still, it wasn't just the embrace tonight after rescuing Nina. What about the kiss in the car when they were in California? He'd opened up her heart in a way she hadn't believed possible.

She hadn't told him the complete truth. She bit her lip, battling with herself. She had to tell him; he deserved to know she wasn't who she'd been pretending to be. But that could wait. It had to. As soon as Driscoll was caught, the case wrapped up, she would tell him. Explain exactly what she'd done and why.

Certainly he would understand. He had to.

The knock on her door made her jump, but she knew it was Zack. She almost tripped over her feet to open the door, feeling like a foolish teenager.

"Hi," she said, taking a step back.

"Hi." He took a step toward her and closed the door behind him.

He was shirtless, his bare, hard chest at her eye level. Her mouth went dry, her lips parted. She licked them, took a step forward and put her mouth on his pectoral, breathed in his clean, damp skin.

His arms wrapped around her, pulling her up to his mouth.

The kiss wasn't light or even kind. It was powerful, hungry, and Olivia responded with just as much passion and hunger for Zack as he showed her.

He moaned into her lips, kissing her with such urgency she almost lost her breath.

"Olivia, I was so scared I'd lost you. Lost you before I really found you."

"Zack—"

Suddenly her feet were off the ground as he swooped her up into his arms. Her head felt light and amazingly empty. All her senses prickled with the need to be touched.

She'd never wanted to be touched, intimately touched, by anyone. Now she couldn't imagine his hands anywhere but on her body, his eyes anywhere but locked with hers, his breath anywhere but on her neck.

Zack's skin was hot to the touch. She was amazed at how much heat he generated. She'd never need a flannel nightgown again, let alone a blanket, if Zack slept next to her every night.

He laid her on the bed and removed his jeans, leaving him in boxers, his large, firm body hovering over hers. She swallowed, reached for him, and he came to her.

His hands reached under her nightgown and clasped her breasts, his thumbs circling her nipples, teasing them into hard nubs. The cold that had filled her soul most of her life melted away at his insistent, probing caress.

She gasped and wrapped her arms around his neck, pulling his face to hers. She lost herself in his searching kiss.

The fire building within was unlike anything she'd ever experienced. No leisurely kisses and patient seduction. Zack focused on her entire body at once, every pore of her skin craving his attention. She rubbed her body against him, wanton and free like she'd never been before.

Zack brought out a passion within her that she'd never thought she was capable of achieving.

His mouth scorched her where his lips trod. His tongue trailed hot paths down her neck, behind her ear, teasing her lobe. She'd never known her neck, her ears, her shoulders were so sensitive, that hot kisses and urgent moans could send little shock waves of pulsing heat throughout her body.

The gown was frustrating her. She wanted to feel Zack's hot body against her bare skin. She fumbled to rid herself of the gown.

When Zack noticed Olivia was trying to remove her flannel nightgown, he reached down and with one swift movement pulled it over her head.

He stared at her body in the dim night light. She wore nothing underneath, and he found her perfect.

She was petite but curvy, with full breasts and wide hips. Her hourglass figure had been merely hinted at beneath those functional business suits. Naked, Olivia was a sexy dream.

He ran his hands down her sides, molding her, relishing the contact. He'd never forget this moment, the first time he touched her nude body, the first time he had her in bed.

He planned on many more times.

He put his arms on either side of her head and watched her expression. Eyes closed, her creamy skin flushed with desire. He leaned down to kiss her. Softly. So slowly. She was too special to rush, too enticing to wait. He wanted it all right now, yet craved time to savor every touch, every kiss, every need.

Her breasts rose with each breath. Her heart pulsated in her chest, *thump-thump, thump-thump,* matching his own heavy ache. He kissed the spot where Olivia's heart throbbed, then circled his tongue along her breast, enjoying her reaction. Her hands reached for him, grasped his shoulders and squeezed. She moaned as his tongue skimmed over her taut nipple.

He reached for the back of her neck, twisted her silky hair between his hands and sucked her nipples, first one, then the other. Time stopped; it was only the two of them, and his only goal was to please her.

He wanted her. He needed her. He paced himself, her pleasure most important to him. She responded to every caress, moaned when his mouth found an unkissed spot to devour. Slow, feathery kisses turned urgent; urgent kisses became tender whispers.

Olivia's entire body vibrated with heat and anticipation. Zack's passionate assault, which started soft and sweet, was now hard and spicy. But it wasn't enough. She wanted more. She felt out of control, lustful, hungry.

His hands never stopped moving, touching her hair, her neck, her shoulders, trailing a light caress down her arm, then taking her hands and squeezing tight as he sucked her breast, his body hard against hers.

He trailed kisses back up her neck and found her mouth. She put her hands on his face, holding him to her. Kissing him as passionately as he assaulted her. She couldn't get enough of him, his body, his strength, his lips. She found her hands roaming, pulling Zack's body closer, feeling his rock hard muscles pressed against her softer flesh.

"Olivia," he breathed into her ear, then nibbled the lobe. She gasped, the hot sensation in her ear sending even hotter tingles throughout her body.

"Make love to me," she whispered, her voice husky.

He released her arms and slid down her body, kissing and tasting until she squirmed with sweet discomfort, wanting him to finish what he'd started and stop torturing her.

"Zack," she murmured, unable to voice another word as his mouth found her inner thigh. She gasped, nerves tingling, feeling alternately hot and cold. His hot tongue circled down, down until he kissed her knee. Her calf. Her foot. Never before had

Olivia thought the leg such a beacon of erotic energy. But the more attention he lavished on her legs, the more she wanted him to make love to her.

No man had ever paid so much attention to just *kissing* her. But these were not simple kisses. Zack left no inch of skin untouched. He kissed, rubbed, licked, breathed on, every pore of her body. She couldn't see, couldn't hear, all her senses gone except for *touch*. She'd never had such a tactile experience, where the simplest whisper on her skin could make her hot and gasping for air.

Zack's mouth found her ear again. "I want to make love to you."

"Yes," she breathed. "Are you—um, prepared?" She hated to ask, but she wasn't on the pill anymore. She hadn't been with anyone since her divorce.

"I am," he whispered.

Olivia watched as Zack took off his boxers and slid a condom on his rigid penis. She'd never watched a man enter her and she licked her lips, feeling alternately embarrassed and intensely excited.

Zack stared at Olivia, her flushed skin, peaked nipples, swollen lips. He could watch her all night, hold her forever. She reached for him and he leaned down, kissed her softly, but her lips pressed harder, drew him in, urged him on. Her hands skimmed down his back, her light touch almost unbearable.

He needed to be inside her.

He gently spread her legs and touched her wet core. She gasped and squirmed against his finger. He replaced his finger with his cock and slowly began to enter her, one arm wrapped around her back, the other around her bottom.

Her body tightened and he stopped moving.

"Are you okay?" The last thing he wanted to do was hurt her.

"It's been a while," she breathed into his ear.

"I won't hurt you, Liv. I would never hurt you."

"You're not." She kissed his neck, little gasps coming from her throat as he readjusted his body, pulling out of her enough to bring his arms to either side of her head.

He looked at Olivia's beautiful face, kissed her red lips, and said, "Open your eyes, sweetheart."

She did, slowly, as if in a deep, pleasurable dream.

"I want to watch you," he said, and kissed her again.

This time, he pushed into her and didn't pull back. Slow and steady. She was hot and tight, and the thought that he was the first man she'd trusted with her body in years moved and excited him.

He pushed himself fully inside her and she gasped again. He stopped to let her body grow accustomed to his. Her eyes searched his face. What was she looking for? What did she see in him?

Did she see that he cared for her in a way he hadn't known he was capable of? Did she see a need he filled? He kissed her lips, wanted to tell her this wasn't going to be the last time. But the kiss would have to show her, his touch would have to convince her.

Olivia held her breath as Zack filled her. She looked into his face and saw raw intensity, every thought and action focused on her. Every nerve ending under her skin wanted to mate with Zack. He brought sexual desire to a higher level.

She moved slightly, and he took it to mean she was ready. She didn't know if she was ready. All she wanted was to feel him move inside her.

Slowly, he withdrew, then pushed back deep inside, the tip of his penis dancing against her cervix, creating a completely new sensation. She gasped. He did it again. Pulled slowly out, then eased back in, dancing until she drew in a long, unsteady breath.

She started moving along with him. Tentative, unsure of herself at first. She'd never been the instigator. She'd never wanted sex badly enough to push it. Now, she couldn't get enough. She reached for his hands and squeezed as a wave of sensation flooded her. Sweat coated her body and his. She could no longer tell where he ended and she began. They clasped hands and he held them on either side of her head, holding her to the bed, all attention focused on his penis in her body, in and out, slowly, unhurried.

The quiet, deliberate lovemaking didn't last. Zack moved faster on top of her, the groans deep in his chest making her even hotter. She matched his rhythm, a tornado whirling within her until her gasps came faster and her body spun out of control.

"Oh. My. God." She was parched, sweating, drained.

"Olivia," he breathed into her hair, thrusting deep inside her and holding it.

Together, they drew out the peak of their lovemaking until they were drenched, satiated. Zack rolled onto his side, taking Olivia with him, peppering her face with slow, languid kisses until he reached her mouth.

His mouth devoured hers, leaving her nearly as breathless as the orgasm.

She sighed and relaxed in his arms. At peace.

Zack hugged Olivia, holding her tight, close. He didn't want to let her go.

Something more than sex had happened between them. How much did this woman mean to him? Much, much more than he'd thought before they fell into bed together.

Her breathing grew even, unlabored, and he realized she'd fallen asleep.

He stared at her in the faint light. In sleep, she looked vulnerable—not a word he normally associated with Olivia.

His heart fluttered just a bit, but enough that he questioned his own feelings.

Love. It was not a word he normally associated with women.

But he definitely associated it with this woman.

CHAPTER
28

The sky turned an incredible shade of dark blue moments before a hint of light outlined the mountains behind the North Fork Lodge.

Chris Driscoll took a minute to watch the sunrise from his hiding place in the trees on the northwest side of the property. A year after Bruce killed their mother, before Chris had learned he'd stabbed her to death, they'd moved to a trailer on the outskirts of Grand Junction, Colorado. The trailer was filthy and had a distinct moldy smell, but the mountains outside framed their hovel, the air so crisp and clean and cold that Chris and Angel had spent as much time outside as Bruce allowed.

Often, while Bruce slept off a drinking binge, Chris would take Angel to the far end of the trailer park and they'd watch the sunrise.

A sunrise much like this one.

Angel, I'm so sorry. I loved you more than anything, more than myself.

A brief flicker of light turned Chris's attention from the sunrise to the porch of the lodge. The two deputies had met up and were sharing a smoke.

He glanced at his watch. They appeared to be doing thirty-minute rotations. He waited as they smoked. Five minutes later one deputy went south, to check out the road and the far meadow. The other went around back to check the rear perimeter and outbuildings.

Good. They were on schedule. He'd wait for one more rotation, verify their route, and then get into position.

Olivia rolled over and into something very warm and hard.

Zack Travis.

She smiled. Last night had been incredible. That was an understatement. She'd never had an orgasm like that, had never been so wanton or turned on in her life.

Sex had never been important to her. Now it was at the top of her list. *If* it was always like last night.

She watched Zack sleep, his day's growth of beard making him look more like a pirate than a cop. He slept with only the sheet, though the room was chilled. He had his own internal thermostat. She felt the heat coming off his body.

A smile touched her lips. She was *happy*. The thought startled her.

Silently, she slid out of bed and found her nightgown on the floor. She slipped it over her head and barefoot, left the room in search of the Krause sisters so she could retrieve her clothes.

Dawn had already crested the mountain. A glance at her watch told her it was after seven. The search for Driscoll had already started. The sheriff would be arriving at seven thirty to pick up her and Zack.

The scent of rich coffee drew her into the kitchen,

located in the rear of the lodge. The North Fork Lodge was more like an oversized house than a commercial hotel. She liked it and wondered if, when this was all over, she and Zack could come back for a long, leisurely weekend.

The idea warmed her.

One of the Krause sisters was busy at the counter when Olivia walked in. The helicopter pilot—Josh?—sat at the large round oak table with a cup of coffee and a huge blueberry muffin.

"Sit down," Ms. Krause said, waving her toward the table.

"Um, I was wondering if my clothes were done? The sheriff will be here soon and I want to be ready."

"Oh, of course. Follow me. They're in the laundry room. There's a bathroom you can change in as well."

Olivia followed Ms. Krause down a short hall. Her clothes were neatly folded on a table across from an industrial-sized washer-and-dryer unit, her shoes, scrubbed clean, on top.

"The pants were torn, and my sewing skills are lacking, but the seam should hold until you get to a tailor in town."

"Thank you so much for going to the trouble."

"It was no trouble at all. Really. I just thank God that poor little girl is all right." She glanced out the window and frowned. "That poor deputy."

Olivia followed Ms. Krause's gaze out the window. She'd met Deputy Will Jeffries last night when he'd arrived to guard the Lodge. Olivia didn't think Driscoll was stupid enough to show up where there were people, but Quinn and Zack had insisted.

"What's wrong?" she asked. Jeffries was on the far side of the property, near the barn. He appeared to be just fine and walking the perimeter, as instructed.

"He's been patrolling the grounds all night. I'll fix him a thermos of coffee and take it out to him."

"Um, excuse me, Ms. Krause?"

A tall, elderly man stood a the threshold of the laundry room.

Ms. Krause slapped the side of her head with her hand. "Oh, Mr. Crenshaw, I'm so sorry I forgot you and Mrs. Crenshaw had an early flight. With everything going on . . ." she waved her hand. "I'll get your breakfast as soon as I take care of the deputy out there."

"I'd be happy to take Deputy Jeffries the thermos, Ms. Krause," Olivia said. "I'll just get dressed and meet you in the kitchen."

"You're a sweetheart, dear. Thank you."

Ms. Krause ushered her guest down the hall. Olivia used the bathroom to change, then folded the borrowed nightgown and left it on the table in the laundry room. She finger-combed her hair as she walked back to the kitchen.

With a broad smile, Ms. Krause handed her a thermos and said, "I'll have breakfast for you and your people in just a few minutes, dear."

"That's not necessary," Olivia said, though the smells of sizzling bacon and oranges made her stomach growl. Food had been her lowest priority since she'd arrived in Seattle.

"Nonsense. It'll be ready. Beth already went upstairs to inform your partner and that nice-looking married couple. Oh, and I saw the deputy go into the barn a minute ago."

"Thank you, Ms. Krause." Olivia wasn't about to

argue with food. She needed it. She took the thermos and stepped out onto the porch.

Zack rolled over to pull Olivia to him, but his arm felt only a warm spot on the sheets. He opened his eyes and frowned. "Liv?"

He got up and pulled on his boxers, then his jeans. Olivia wasn't in the room, but he figured she'd gone down to get her clothes or meet with her friend Miranda.

He heard knocking across the hall. He opened the door and saw Quinn outside his room. Quinn looked at him for a moment, his face unreadable.

"What's going on?" Zack asked, shutting Olivia's door behind him and crossing the hall to his room.

Quinn followed him inside. "I just spoke with the sheriff."

"Is he here?"

"He's fifteen minutes out. The search team found Driscoll's trail and they think he's on his way here."

"To the lodge?"

"Yes. He alerted his deputies who are outside, and another team is on its way up to secure the house. I wanted to brief you, then head down and talk to the Krauses and guests."

"Why would he come here?" Zack went into the bathroom, where he'd rinsed out his T-shirt the night before. It hung stiffly over the shower bar, but he pulled it on, rolling his shoulders to stretch it.

"If I were him? To steal a vehicle. He might assume the police will be tracking him, not securing property in the area. This is the closest occupied residence to where he crashed the truck."

"Which means he's been here."

"Reconnaissance," Quinn said. "He would have surveyed the area before he brought any of the girls up here. My guess? He killed Jennifer and Michelle around here as well. Possibly in the same place he took Nina."

"I'll send Doug Cohn and his crew back up there when the lodge is secure. Let's go."

"Where's Olivia?"

"I think she went downstairs."

"Hmm."

"You don't have a problem with me and Liv, do you?"

"No problem."

Zack couldn't read the Fed, so he gave up. They went downstairs and walked into the kitchen, joining Miranda and Beth Krause on the way. Doug Cohn, his assistant, and Josh Fields sat around the table. In the adjoining dining room, an elderly couple and a young couple with a child sat at the table.

"Where's Olivia?" Zack asked.

Kristy Krause smiled brightly as she poured fresh-squeezed orange juice into glasses. "She went to take Deputy Jeffries some coffee."

Zack tensed. "When? Where?"

"About five minutes ago, in the barn."

Zack and Quinn glanced at each other. "Doug, Josh, secure the house," Zack said. "No one leaves until we get back."

The barn door was ajar. Olivia walked in, the smell of hay and ripe manure predominant. "Deputy Jeffries?" she called. "It's Olivia St. Martin." She didn't want him to think she was an intruder.

Where was he? Had she missed him leaving the barn? Had Ms. Krause been mistaken?

On the far side of the barn was another door, and it was also open. A horse nickered softly to her right. She turned, smiling at the animal, reached out and stroked its nose. "Hey, boy, how are you doing this morning? I wish I had something for you, but I think caffeine is off your diet."

The horse whinnied in response to her voice. There were six horses in the stalls, all clean and well kept. She definitely wanted to return to the lodge with Zack. She hadn't been horseback riding in years, but she used to enjoy it.

She hurried through the barn toward the far door, wishing she hadn't offered to deliver the coffee. It was chilly, and she had no jacket on.

She smelled death before she saw it.

Slowly, she turned. Just inside the door, in a stall, a naked body lay sprawled on the ground. She sucked in her breath, realizing three things at once.

Deputy Jeffries was dead—his head had been crushed with a large, heavy object.

Whoever killed him was wearing his uniform.

The killer was most likely Chris Driscoll.

She had to warn everyone in the house. The Krauses wouldn't think twice about opening the door to a man in uniform.

She ran two steps out the door when a strong arm grabbed her, pulled her into a solid chest, and held a gun to her head.

"Don't say a word."

Zack and Quinn left the house and surveyed the barn from a distance. There appeared to be no activity. Silence.

"Maybe they're chatting it up," Quinn offered.

Neither he nor Zack believed it.

"You take the east entrance, I'll take west," Zack said, checking the ammunition in his gun, then chambered a round.

They didn't get more than twenty feet when Zack saw them.

Chris Driscoll had Olivia at gunpoint. He forced her toward the deputy's car parked in the driveway. Driscoll looked neither scared nor hurried. He walked confidently, Olivia's struggling form an easy burden.

Driscoll and Olivia spotted Zack at the same time. Olivia's eyes widened. Driscoll's expression didn't change, but he pressed the barrel of the gun firmly to her head and stared dead on at Zack: a warning. He walked around to the passenger's door and shoved Olivia over to the driver's seat, then climbed into the passenger's seat.

Moments later the engine turned and Olivia drove slowly down the drive.

Zack ran toward Quinn's car. "You'd better have

the keys on you," he called to the Fed. He suppressed his fear for Olivia's life. If he thought about her as the woman he loved, he wouldn't be as effective at the job of saving her life.

It was excruciatingly difficult to bury his feelings.

"I'll drive." Quinn unlocked the trunk.

"What are you doing?" Zack opened the passenger door. They had no time.

Quinn tossed him a .30-06 sniper rifle. "It's loaded," he said. Quinn grabbed two handguns and slammed down the trunk.

The stolen police car, with Olivia at the wheel, suddenly sped up as it rounded the turn in the driveway, its tires momentarily spinning in the pea gravel before hitting the packed dirt road.

Quinn started the ignition before he shut the door. A second later he peeled out of the driveway and pursued Driscoll.

"He's not going to let her live once he's clear," Zack said, his entire chest tight.

"He's not going to kill her yet," Quinn said. "She's a hostage. No one is going to be shooting at him with a hostage."

Olivia. A hostage. The realization first made Zack ill, then furious. His fists tightened on the rifle. Though Quinn had told him it was loaded, he checked the ammunition and slid the bolt back to chamber a round.

"What's the plan?" he asked.

"Hell if I know. Look for an opportunity. Olivia's smart, she'll be thinking of a way to get out. Then we act."

"Keep them in sight, Peterson. Don't lose them."

Quinn glanced at Zack. "Olivia's a hostage. Let your training take over."

Zack had been telling himself the same thing, but it didn't help. "It's hard. Damn, it's hard."

"I know."

Olivia's knuckles were white on the steering wheel, her entire body rigid as she assessed the situation.

Driscoll held the gun inches from her head, his finger calmly on the trigger. He seemed not at all fazed that they were being followed. His eyes were on the dirt road, though every few minutes he'd reach for the steering wheel and she'd flinch. He kept her in the center of the wide, one-lane road. If she slowed, he said calmly, "Keep moving."

He would kill her as soon as he didn't need her. He'd only grabbed her because she happened to be there—a shield, in case someone came from the house. Maybe he'd intended to take one of the Krause sisters once he realized the police were all over the mountain. Or maybe he simply planned on killing the deputy and escaping in his car. And she'd had the misfortune of walking right up to him.

In the back of her mind she couldn't help but think he might have made a clean getaway if she hadn't walked into the barn this morning. Driscoll would have disappeared, resurfacing in another city to kill more innocent children.

A quick glance in the rearview mirror told her Zack and Quinn were still following. Olivia took a deep breath and tried to remain calm, focused on her situation. Not only did she need a way out, she had to delay Driscoll enough that Zack and Quinn could nail the bastard.

Missy's killer sat next to her.

The thought made her foot ease up on the gas.

"Keep moving," he said again, glancing in the side mirror at the car behind.

She jerked when he put his left hand on her knee, pushing her leg down on the accelerator. This was the hand that brutally murdered her sister. The car swerved and she came within a foot of going off the edge. He reached over and steadied the wheel. She could barely breathe, barely even *think* with Missy's killer so close.

The winding road had a steep drop-off on the right and a rock-strewn gully on the left. If she aimed the car into the shallow gully, the impact wouldn't kill them, but his gun would end her life. If she aimed the car off the cliff, they would both die. Even if they quickly hit one of the many redwood or fir trees, the steep slope and violent crash would leave them both dead. Driscoll wouldn't kill again.

Fear pressed tight against every nerve ending. She was scared, no doubt about it, but anger boiled hot inside as she thought about this evil man's horrid crimes. The children he'd killed, the families he'd destroyed.

But instead of seeing the pictures of dead children, she envisioned little Amanda Davidson.

And Olivia came back to herself.

It would end today. She didn't want to lose her life, but there was no way she would allow Driscoll to escape. A master of changing identity, of blending in, he could disappear and they wouldn't know where he was until another blonde girl was found stabbed to death.

For the victims—living and dead—Olivia would stop him. She worked to control her fear and her anger, because both threatened to overwhelm her and she wouldn't be able to act if she lost control of her emotions.

She almost laughed. For years she'd worked to suppress her feelings, to live in neutral. But ever since the day she learned Brian Harrison Hall was innocent, all her decisions had been guided by emotion. Instinct. Fear. Rage.

She slowed to round a sharp turn, glancing again in the rearview mirror. Her heart skipped a beat when she lost sight of Quinn's white sedan, then steadied when the car came back into view.

Not that they could help her.

"Speed up!" Driscoll commanded, a new edge to his voice.

"Do you want me to drive off the cliff?" she countered. Her voice quivered but at least it was audible.

"Shut up."

No conversation. Fine with her. More time to think.

She glanced at the mass of equipment built under the dashboard of the police car, trying to find something to grab as a weapon. Nothing. Driscoll had seized the shotgun as soon as they got into the car. It lay across his legs, its barrel facing her. His right hand rested on his lap, gripping the handgun, which was still pointed at her. He had turned on the police radio and appeared to be listening to the static. Did he think they were so stupid as to broadcast their plans when he had access to the radio? Perhaps.

He probably thought he was smarter than everyone.

He was looking in the side mirror again, distracted, the gun not pointing right at her, but more at the steering wheel.

If she was going to do anything to save herself and

give Quinn and Zack the chance to capture or kill him, now was the time to act.

She slammed on the brakes. Her forehead hit the steering wheel at the same time that Driscoll reached up with his hands to brace himself. She heard the gun hit the floor as she grabbed at the door handle.

She pulled and the door opened, but Driscoll grabbed her arm. "Fucking bitch!"

She screamed as her left foot touched the ground, and at the same time he pulled her against him. With all her strength she resisted, trying to break his grip. The car started to roll as her right foot left the brake in her effort to throw herself from the vehicle.

With a loud grunt, Driscoll pulled her back into the car and she heard a click. Cold metal pressed against her neck. Something ran down her throat. It wasn't until she glanced down that she saw it was blood.

The edge of a knife had cut into her neck. It burned. As the car rolled, Olivia instinctively braked. Slowly, so the knife didn't dig deeper.

His voice was low, rough, pure rage as he whispered in her ear, "Shut the fucking door."

Mouth dry, unable to swallow, she complied. She fought to control her shaking body, fearing any movement might kill her.

His breath touched her cheek, his voice an evil caress. "Try something like that again, I'll cut your heart out."

He withdrew the knife from her neck, twisted it in his hand, and plunged it toward her chest.

She screamed before she knew she'd opened her mouth, her arms instinctively coming up in a defensive move.

He stopped the knife, but not before it cut through her blouse. A sharp knick of the blade on her skin stung.

Uncontrollably shaking, she watched a rivulet of blood spread slowly down her blouse. Her heart beat visibly through her shirt. He'd actually cut her.

Driscoll stared at the blood, transfixed. For a moment, she was certain he'd stab her again, this time without restraint. The knife would tear open her heart and she'd last a full three minutes as her blood circulated through her body and out the hole in her heart, drenching her, her mind slowing but fully aware that she was dying.

She closed her eyes, waiting for the inevitable, hoping that Zack would shoot the bastard.

Dammit, she didn't want to die! Especially at the hands of a psychopath like Christopher Driscoll. She didn't want to die now that she finally had hope restored in her life, that she'd found a man she loved.

She didn't want to lose Zack.

"Drive."

She couldn't have heard right. She opened her eyes.

"Drive!" he shouted, moving the knife to his left hand and pressing the tip into her side enough to cause sharp pain. Would he nick her to death? Slowly drain her of blood until she was too weak to fight?

She let her foot up off the brake and the car rolled forward.

"Faster! And don't be an idiot."

Pressing the accelerator, she chanced a glance in the rearview mirror. Quinn and Zack were right behind them, Zack partially out of the car, his face all hard lines, his jaw clenched. His rifle was aimed at Driscoll's head. But as Olivia gathered speed, Zack jumped back into the car.

"You won't get away," she said, her voice cracking. She swallowed, the cut in her neck throbbing painfully. "Kill me, it doesn't matter. Cops are all over this mountain. They'll shoot you dead."

He said nothing. With the knife still near her side, he reached to the floor and felt around. His hand came back with the gun, but he put it under his leg. He liked holding the knife. His fingers turned it around and around. He wanted to use it.

On her.

Focus, Olivia. Don't think about the knife. Don't think about the gun. Get him talking.

Olivia didn't remember much of her criminal psychology training, but one thing she *did* remember: get them talking.

She swallowed the terror remaining from her failed escape and said the first thing that came to mind.

"You killed my sister."

His body stiffened, as if he hadn't expected her to speak again, let alone announce that he'd killed Missy.

Olivia continued, emboldened by his silence. "In California. You framed Brian Harrison Hall for Missy's murder. But you know he was released from prison."

"I read about Harry's release." His voice was well modulated, intelligent. Gone was the hoarse, dark whisper. It sounded like they were having a regular conversation.

"Why Missy?"

He didn't answer.

"I was there, you know."

He looked at her closely. She forced herself to

glance at him. If he got off on fear, she would bury it. Not give him the satisfaction that he had truly frightened her, that he still scared her, that she believed he would kill her without remorse or hesitation.

His pale blue eyes were cold, but his face was smooth, calm, *normal.* It didn't surprise her that little girls had walked off with him; he didn't look like a killer. He didn't look like the monster Olivia knew he was.

"You?" he said. "*You* were that little brat?"

She nodded, shaking, and refocused on the road, trying to maintain a steady speed. They were twisting down, around the mountain, but Road 56 was only a mile or two ahead of them. Road 56 was paved. There he'd make her drive faster, and any hope of her escape would then be futile.

She didn't think she'd live through another attempt.

"You hit me across the face," she said, the sting of that long ago blow still vivid.

"You tried to stop me from taking what was mine."

Olivia shivered at his matter-of-fact tone.

"Do you remember Missy?"

"My angel." He said *angel* with such reverence it chilled her.

"You killed her." Her voice was far harsher than she'd intended. She held her breath, awaiting a physical blow. Or worse, the knife cutting deep into her flesh.

He didn't touch her. Instead, he said, "I didn't kill her."

What was he doing, going for an insanity plea? Or claiming innocence?

"Yes you did," she said, forcing her voice to remain calm. "I saw you."

"You *said* you saw Brian Hall." His voice was mocking, almost laughing, and Olivia suppressed the kernel of doubt that tried to surface.

"We have your DNA."

He was quiet. She continued slowly down the mountain. Spiraling down, down, getting closer to Road 56, which would bring them to the interstate.

Would he still need a hostage then? She hoped he'd keep her alive as long as he was being pursued but she couldn't count on it. She needed a plan.

"She was suffering," he said.

His voice was calm, almost surreal, and he was no longer looking at her. He stared out the window, lost in thought.

"What?!" She couldn't have heard him right.

"Angels suffer, you know. So much pain. I freed her from her shell, gave her eternal life. Spirits live forever. There is no pain when you're a pure soul. You should thank me for freeing your sister's soul. You should be sad that I didn't free yours, too."

Dear God, his words terrified her but his voice was so ordinary. Reasoned.

"You killed Missy and all those other girls so they wouldn't suffer." She matched his tone: clinical and composed. She had to keep him talking. She didn't dare hope she could talk him into surrendering, but she would damn well try.

"Yes. To relieve their suffering."

"I think the court would consider that." She hated the words, but hoped to convince him the system would be lenient.

"No one understands! No one sees other people's pain."

"Didn't you know raping those girls hurt them?"

He didn't respond, and Olivia mentally hit herself. She'd blown it. She should have pursued the other line of questioning. Dammit, she didn't know what she was doing! She wasn't a psychologist.

The police were all over the mountain. Quinn and Zack had certainly called in reinforcements. They'd be waiting at Road 56, as well as down the mountain. Would there be a roadblock? She didn't know much about hostage negotiations, but logically, they would try and stop the car and talk to him. Reason with him. Promise him whatever he wanted, then find a way to take him down.

The fifteen minutes she'd been in the car seemed like forever; she certainly didn't want to be a hostage for hours. She had to find a way to escape the car as soon as possible, before they reached Road 56, where jumping would be suicide.

She had only minutes to figure a way out. Where he *wouldn't* kill her.

She had to get him talking again. Distract him. What did she really know about him other than he was a cruel, vicious child murderer? His mother had been murdered. His sister Angel. The man in his life, Bruce.

"Bruce is dead," she said.

His fist tightened around the knife that was only inches from her side. *Good move, St. Martin.*

"*Don't,*" he warned.

Too late to back out now. "He was bad news, wasn't he? He hurt your sister. I saw her picture. She was beautiful."

"He violated her." Driscoll's voice was quiet, almost childlike. "He raped her all the time and I couldn't stop him."

Olivia glanced at Driscoll. He had a faraway look

on his face. Remembering Angel? What he did or
didn't do?

His hand gripping the knife fell into his lap. He
stared out the windshield, not focused on her or the
car behind them. Carefully, cautiously, she slid her
left hand to the bottom of the steering wheel. He
didn't notice.

"When he hurt Angel, it must have made you
angry. Frustrated."

"I wanted to kill him." He glanced at her and
Olivia held her breath. "I would have killed him. I
would have killed him if I had the chance."

"I know. To protect Angel."

He nodded, his eyes brightening. Did he think she
understood him? That she agreed with him? If that's
what it took to get him to let his guard down, she'd
follow that path.

"She was a beautiful girl," Olivia repeated.
Driscoll turned to her. "Bruce was a bad man to hurt
her." She sounded like she was speaking to a child,
but Driscoll seemed responsive.

"Bruce was mean. He touched her and made her
cry. I dried her tears. I kissed her bruises and made
the pain go away."

His gaze drifted out the front window once again.

Olivia braced herself. She would have only one
shot at escape. She needed a sharp turn that veered
right. No hesitation.

"Angel must have loved you a lot for taking care
of her."

"I wanted to protect her, but I couldn't."

"You were just a kid yourself," she said.

"I would have killed him. I would have," he
repeated, defiant.

Through the trees ahead she saw the turn she'd been waiting for.

Olivia dropped her left hand from the steering wheel and placed it on her lap. The knife was more than a foot from her.

"Why didn't you kill him?"

Silence. The turn was seconds away. Now or never. Without braking, she flung open the door and threw herself from the car, rolling. Her first impact with the rocky dirt road knocked the wind out of her and she couldn't catch her breath. Gunshots echoed around her as she rolled down into the shallow gully.

A sickening crash of metal vibrated in her head.

Zack watched in horror as Olivia fell from the car and hit the ground violently, rolling away. Had Driscoll killed her and thrown her from the car? After her failed escape attempt ten minutes ago, Zack feared the worst.

"Travis!" Quinn shouted.

Zack raised the rifle and aimed at Driscoll's tires. From the passenger seat, Driscoll was trying to both control the vehicle and move over into the driver's seat. Quinn drove right on his tail, feet from the bumper. Zack fired, threw back the bolt, fired again. Driscoll's car swerved left as he overcompensated and drove hard into the gully. The rear end of the police car lifted from the ground, then slammed down.

Zack dropped the rifle and drew his .45. He opened the passenger door and knelt behind the steel shielding, waiting for gunfire.

Had Driscoll been injured? He probably wasn't dead, but Zack could hope.

He pushed aside the sickening thought that Olivia lay dead up the road.

She wasn't dead. She *couldn't* be dead.

"Travis!" Quinn, in the same position as Zack but behind the driver's-side door, nodded his head toward Driscoll's vehicle.

Movement.

Driscoll opened fired through the shattered rear window. Zack and Quinn ducked, then returned fire, but Driscoll was already on the move. He ran down the road, away from them, toward the steep slope to the north. He could lose himself in the woods too easily.

Zack ran after him.

Driscoll ran fast, but Zack ran faster, the image of Olivia slamming into the road burned into his mind. Driscoll suddenly stopped, turned, and raised his gun in one slick move.

Zack was right behind him. He body-slammed Driscoll, knocking the gun from his hand. They rolled down the embankment.

Raw rage flooded Zack's senses. When they stopped tumbling, Driscoll lay on his stomach. Zack flipped him and held him down with his left hand while he pummeled his face.

No killer had angered and scared him more than this bastard. What he had done to those girls, to their families.

He pictured Jenny Benedict's small, lifeless body.

Jillian Reynolds's decomposed body on the coroner's table.

Olivia held hostage.

Driscoll struggled and Zack used both fists and pounded into the killer's face, his chest, his stomach. Zack's breath came out in harsh, ragged gasps. He grunted and swore, but didn't know what he was saying. He heard someone shout, but didn't hear the words through the river of bloody rage that flowed in his veins.

He'd never hated anyone more than Driscoll. He didn't see a man; he saw a monster.

"Dammit, Travis!"

Quinn pushed Zack off Driscoll and he hit the ground with a thud, a rock scraping his back.

He blinked, remembering where he was.

The Cascades. The car chase. Chasing Driscoll.

Driscoll moaned, half conscious. Quinn handcuffed the killer.

"Shit, Zack, you could have killed him."

Zack stared at his bloody fists. His blood mixed with the killer's. He rubbed his hands on his jeans over and over, hating what he'd done. The anger that still embraced him had almost turned him into a killer himself.

Making him no better than Chris Driscoll.

He could barely catch his breath.

"I'm sorry," he mumbled.

Olivia.

He jumped up, stumbling as he scurried up the slope.

"Olivia!" he called, running back up the road.

Inner rage turned to bone-numbing fear. If anything had happened to her . . . no. *No.* If Driscoll had killed Olivia, Zack would never recover. He loved her. He needed her in his life.

He retraced his steps, passing the crashed police car, Quinn's sedan. "Olivia!"

He ran around the sharp bend. She lay by the side of the road. Blood soaked her white blouse. Her throat . . . dear God, he'd slit her throat. Blood smeared her neck, her collar.

Stumbling, he half ran, half crawled to where she lay, not noticing the tears streaming down his cheeks.

"Liv, oh God, Liv."

Then he saw her chest rise and fall. Rise and fall. Gently, he gathered her into his lap.

"Liv?"

He stroked her cheek and her eyes fluttered open.

"Hi."

Her voice was faint, but a smile curved her lips.

Zack kissed those lips, his tears falling on her face. "Olivia, I thought you were dead. The blood." He stared at her neck.

"It's not deep. I'm okay." She reached up and cupped his face in her hand.

He kissed her again, urgently. She was alive. Whole. He shuddered as his heart rate finally began to slow, holding her tightly in his arms. He didn't want to let her go.

"Did you get him?" Olivia asked.

"Yes. He won't hurt anyone else."

"It's over," she murmured into his chest. "Missy can rest in peace."

"And so can her sister." Zack stroked her hair, closed his eyes. Olivia was alive. Safe.

The past could finally be buried.

Zack and Olivia went back to the lodge while Quinn stayed at the crash site to help the sheriff process evidence; then he would pick Zack up and take him to the Cascades sheriff's substation, where they would interview Driscoll.

An ambulance was already at the lodge and Zack brought Olivia to the EMT to be checked out, since she'd refused to go to the clinic herself.

"You should go to the hospital," the EMT, a burly guy named Trent, told her. "Just to be on the safe side."

"See, I told you," Zack said.

"I'm fine," Olivia said. "Just clean the cuts."

Zack winced as Trent sanitized the cut on her neck and applied a bandage.

"Um, do you want to unbutton your blouse?" Trent asked, glancing from Zack to Olivia.

Olivia frowned and looked at Zack. "Are you sure you don't want to check in with Quinn?"

Zack looked at her, his heart thudding. She was worse off than she'd told him. "Unbutton your blouse, Liv. Or I'll do it."

She hesitated, then complied, wincing as she pulled the material from the dried wound on her chest.

Zack stared, feeling the rage building again. Her left breast had been stabbed, the cut at least an inch wide. The blood had dried, but in pulling the blouse off the wound had restarted a light flow.

Saying nothing, the EMT efficiently and discreetly cleaned and dressed the wound. He then turned to the cut in her side, shook his head, and took care of it.

Zack stared at Olivia. That he'd come so close to losing her affected him a million different ways. He wasn't comfortable examining his feelings under such circumstances. He wanted to step back, think logically about what had happened, accept it, and move on. But he was stymied, unable to rid his memory of the image of Olivia jumping from the car, and now the obvious signs of violence on her body.

"Trent, could you give us a minute?" she said quietly, not turning her eyes from Zack's.

Trent said, "Ms. St. Martin, you need to see a doctor when you get to town, okay?"

"I will," she said.

The EMT left and she took Zack's hand. He brought her hand to his lips and kissed the scraped knuckles.

"I'm fine, Zack. Really. I'm fine."

Zack ran a hand through his hair. "I thought he'd killed you," he said quietly.

"I know. I'm sorry. I'm sore, but I'll be okay."

He nodded, unable to speak, and sat heavily next to her on the bumper.

"Don't. Don't think about it," Olivia said.

"I love you, Liv. I don't want to lose you." He choked up and closed his eyes, bending his forehead to hers.

"Oh, Zack." She touched his cheek. "I need to tell you something. It's important."

He opened his eyes and looked at her. Something was wrong, but he had no idea what. He rubbed the back of her neck, kissed her lips, her cheek.

"What, Liv?"

"I'm not an FBI agent."

He blinked, his body tensing. "I don't understand."

"I'm a scientist. I used to be a field agent, nearly ten years ago. But now I'm director of the Material Analysis and Trace Evidence lab."

Zack dropped his hands. *What?!* Conflicting emotions battled within him, raw from the turmoil he'd just gone through.

She'd been lying to him since the minute they met? He found that hard to believe, but she'd just said it.

"You're not an FBI agent," he repeated.

"Please listen. Try to understand," she began, speaking quickly. "When I found out Brian Hall was being released, my entire world fell apart. I couldn't think, I couldn't do anything. I had helped put him in prison. I had testified against his parole six times! I called him evil to his face. But the evidence proved years later that he hadn't raped Missy.

"So I used every resource at my disposal. I spent two weeks putting together similar cases from around the country. And when I read about Jenny Benedict's murder, then Michelle's abduction, I went straight to my boss."

"And he told you to lie about your identity?" Zack felt sucker-punched. He found it hard to breathe.

She shook her head. "He said the evidence was circumstantial and until we were asked to help, his hands were tied. But," she said before he could open his mouth, "I couldn't stand back and do nothing! So I brought the evidence to you. I knew that if you had the information it would help. And it did, didn't it? I know it did."

"You haven't heard of a fax machine?"

Tears welled in her eyes, but Zack shut off his feelings. To protect himself, he had to. He would not allow her past the wall he was building inside. She had deceived and lied to him, manipulating him from the minute they met.

"You know as well as I do that my familiarity with these cases helped. The raw data wouldn't have given you as much as my interpretation."

"You could have told me any time, Olivia. Why didn't you? Why didn't you come clean when you told me about your sister?"

"I—I—don't know. I was scared I'd be removed from the case."

He barked a humorless laugh. "Removed from a case you were never assigned to? You've started believing your own lies. Have you had a lot of practice? Because you sure had me fooled."

She looked stricken, as if he had slapped her, and he had to force his attention away from her.

God, he thought he'd loved this woman. But she hadn't trusted him. She'd slept with him, but didn't trust him with the simple truth.

He'd been betrayed.

"Zack, believe me, I struggled with this. I didn't want to lie, but I had no choice."

"We all have choices, Olivia. No one held a gun to

your head forcing you to deceive me. Not only me, but my boss, my partner, my colleagues. You lied to everyone. You're a master of deception."

He looked her straight in the eye. "You made the wrong choice. And now you'll have to live with it."

"Travis, Olivia, we need to get down to the substation," Quinn said as he approached them. He stopped. "What happened?"

Zack shoved Quinn in the chest. He had liked the Fed, but Quinn Peterson was as much a liar as Olivia. "You knew and didn't say anything. You're just as much of a fraud as she is."

He walked away before completely losing it.

Tears rolled down Olivia's cheeks. "Oh, God, Quinn. I really screwed this up."

Quinn touched her chin. "Liv, how did he find out?"

"I had to tell him. I'm in love with him."

"He just needs time. He's angry, but he'll get over it."

She shook her head. "It's not his anger that I'm worried about. I hurt him badly, and I don't think he'll ever forgive me."

Quinn looked at her bandages and frowned. "Are you okay? You really should go to the hospital and get checked out."

She shook her head. "I'll be fine."

"What are you going to do?"

"Go home." She looked at her friend, blinked back the tears. "I have nothing else."

Zack paced the interrogation room, waiting for Driscoll to be brought in.

He'd skipped riding with Peterson to the substation, tagging along with one of the deputies. He needed to push Olivia from his mind. Otherwise he wouldn't be able to finish his job.

Damn, her betrayal hurt. Out of all the people he'd met, he'd never have pegged her as a liar.

The first day or two, he sensed she was holding back something. When she told him about her sister, he believed that was it. He hadn't expected more lies, additional revelations.

He slammed his fist on the table and sat, taking deep breaths. *Focus, Travis. You have a killer coming in five minutes and you need to do this right.*

He had a list of questions for Driscoll, and he needed to get his mind wrapped around the case, not around the woman he'd mistakenly fallen in love with. The woman who would bear the scars of a killer on her body.

But he'd bare the scars of their brief relationship on his heart.

He took a deep breath and focused on Driscoll. He wanted answers to his questions, but didn't hold out hope that this monster would cooperate. Still, the question *why* burned in him, not that any answer would be satisfying. But he had to try to understand.

He wanted to know how Driscoll had picked his first victim.

He wanted to know how he selected the cities he stalked.

He needed to know why he marked each victim with Angel.

The door opened and Quinn Peterson walked in. Zack tensed, but nodded to the Fed. He would put his animosity aside for the Driscoll interview.

It wasn't like he'd have to see Peterson after this case was wrapped up.

The sheriff came in with a deputy escorting Chris Driscoll, who was in wrist and ankle chains. He moved slowly from the beating, not just because of the restraints. The deputy secured the killer by cuffing his leg chains to the hook on the floor and forcing him to sit in a chair.

Driscoll looked like an average, physically fit middle-aged guy. Except for his black eye, bruised jaw, and the bandage that covered his cheek.

Zack felt no remorse for bashing the killer's face in. Though he deserved it, Zack was relieved he hadn't killed him. Washington had the death penalty, but Zack hoped Driscoll didn't make it the average ten years it took for death-row prisoners to be killed.

Child predators didn't fare well in prison.

The only thing about Driscoll's otherwise average appearance that stood out was his eyes: a clear, icy blue. In his eyes, Zack saw the killer. But he could see how another might see kindness in his face.

The sheriff had read Driscoll his rights when he was first arrested, then stayed with him while the doctor from the local clinic came over to bandage his injuries. Driscoll hadn't asked for an attorney then, nor when he was formally booked, but Quinn as a federal officer had to extend the same rights.

"Go to hell," Driscoll said, his expression unchanged.

"We have everything we need to put you on death row, Mr. Driscoll," Quinn said. "So this interview is really just for us to get to know each other, have some questions answered, before they lock you up."

Driscoll said nothing.

Zack and Quinn exchanged glances, and Quinn nodded. Driscoll wasn't going to cooperate, but they didn't need him to. What they wanted was an explanation.

"We know how you set up Brian Hall thirty-four years ago," Zack said.

Driscoll stared straight ahead, but Zack detected a hint of satisfaction in his static grin.

"Pretty smart of you. You and he were in Vietnam together, fought side by side. He wouldn't think his good pal would set him up."

Driscoll shook his head. "Hall's an idiot. He was never my friend."

Zack didn't disagree with that statement, but said, "He knows. He led us to you. He's out of prison and knows you set him up."

Driscoll shrugged.

"We've tracked down thirty-one victims in ten states," Quinn said. "Have we missed anyone?"

Driscoll remained silent and unmoving.

"It would show the judge you have remorse if you help ease the minds of families who don't know the fate of their children."

Again, silence.

Zack slammed his fist on the table, then took a deep breath. He wanted to strangle Driscoll into talking, but that wouldn't do anyone any good.

Besides, based on the evidence Doug Cohn extracted from Driscoll's cottage, there appeared to be a total of thirty-two victims. An FBI profiler Quinn had talked to out in Virginia felt that the first lock of hair Driscoll kept was of his half sister, Angel. It appeared Olivia's preliminary work had in fact identified all thirty-one other victims.

The profiler had a wild theory about Angel's murder based on the trial transcript and the fact that

Driscoll kept her hair, a fact that was left out of the police report but Quinn Peterson had dug up through the original autopsy report.

Zack glanced at Quinn, who nodded.

"We know about Angel."

At the mention of her name, Driscoll tensed.

"You know nothing about her. Don't say her name."

"We know your stepfather raped her."

"Bruce was not my stepfather. He never married my mother. His blood does not run through my veins. His name is not my name." Driscoll's fists clenched and unclenched.

"He hurt her, didn't he?"

Silence.

"You couldn't protect her."

The chains that bound Driscoll's feet rattled.

"Maybe you tried to protect her. You were older. A teenager. But he still raped her. Bruce raped Angel like you rape girls who look like her."

Driscoll grunted, his face pained.

"You wanted to touch her."

"No."

"You hated Bruce for hurting her because you wanted her for yourself."

"I am not Bruce!"

Quinn tapped his finger once on the table in a pre-arranged signal. "No, you're not Bruce Carmichael," Quinn said. "Bruce killed your mother. Stabbed her to death. With this knife."

Quinn put the sealed evidence bag in front of Driscoll. The killer's hands were restrained, but his shoulders jerked as if trying to reach it. Quinn had moved heaven and earth to get the evidence from

Angel Carmichael's murder flown in from Los Angeles this morning. He'd had another agent drive it up to the Cascades substation.

Quinn laid pictures one by one in front of Driscoll. They were crime-scene photos of Angel's murder. The black-and-white photos of the child's death disturbed Zack, reminding him that no matter what Chris Driscoll had suffered at the hands of Bruce Carmichael, nothing justified his actions now or then.

Driscoll whimpered, turned his head from the photographs.

"This knife also killed Angel."

Quinn tapped the knife. Driscoll's fingers moved, as if aching to hold the weapon. Quinn picked it up, turned it over and over in his hands, then laid it on top of one of the photos.

It was a close-up of Angel's face, her eyes glassy and unseeing, blood splatters almost black in the aged gray-toned photograph, seeming to split her face in half.

Tears streamed down the killer's face.

"You know this knife killed Angel because you stabbed her to death."

Driscoll shook his head. "Bruce killed her. He killed my mother, then killed Angel."

"Were you with Bruce when he killed your mother?"

Driscoll shook his head again. "He picked me up from school. He already had Angel. He picked me up and we drove for days. He said Mama was dead. An accident . . . " His voice trailed off.

"How did you find out he killed your mother?"

"Angel."

Again, silence.

"Angel knew?" Zack prompted.

"She was there." His voice was a whisper.

"Angel saw Bruce kill your mother?"

Driscoll's voice took on a childlike, asexual quality as he voiced his sister's words: "'I told Mama that Daddy was touching me down there and I didn't like it. Mama packed a suitcase and we were going to leave, but Daddy came home and saw. He saw and he got a big knife in the kitchen and hurt Mama. He hurt her and there was blood and she was dead.'"

"Bruce killed your mother and took you and Angel away from New Jersey. You ended up in Los Angeles."

"We lived in nine states. Nine states in three years. Angel . . . she wanted a real home. Real homes don't exist, I told her. I was her home. I would take care of her."

"But you couldn't."

Driscoll's chained hands slammed into the table. "I was going to kill him!" he shouted at the top of his lungs.

The placid face twisted in monstrous rage, his eyes wild and glassy.

Every cop in the room froze, ready to jump on Driscoll if he tried anything. He didn't move.

Zack asked, "Why didn't you kill Bruce?"

Driscoll's eyes locked on Zack's. "That's what *she* said."

"Angel?"

"The bitch. The bitch in the car. Before she fucked everything up and tricked me."

Olivia?

"I would have killed him. I would have! I needed time, and Angel didn't want to give me time.

Planning. We needed to plan. But she didn't give me the time to plan. She was scared. I protected her the best I could. I did everything for her. I cleaned her up. I took care of her. I kissed her bruises. I would have taken care of her. She wanted to run away, but how would I feed her? How could I take care of her?"

Zack glanced at Quinn, then said, "Why did you kill Angel when you loved her so much?"

A strangled cry escaped Driscoll's throat. "She was going to run away. Leave me. I couldn't protect her." He heaved out a mournful sigh and stared at the picture, unmoving. "I wanted to protect her. I wanted to stop Bruce from hurting her. She told me she wanted to be free. But then—she wanted to run away. Run away *from me.*

"Angel, sweet Angel, I had to free your soul. You're free. You're happy. I know you're happy now and no one will ever hurt you again."

Driscoll stared at Zack, but his eyes were unfocused.

"Spirits don't die," he whispered, almost pleading with them. "Souls feel no pain. Angel doesn't hurt anymore. She has eternal life."

Quinn cleared his throat and asked softly, "Why the other girls?"

"My angels—they're all my angels. They all hurt. Because that's what people are—in pain. Constant, torturous pain.

"I had to free their souls, give them a painless life forever and ever. They're at peace now. They're with my Angel."

CHAPTER
31

Olivia sat at Miranda's kitchen table holding an empty coffee mug and staring out the window.

Miranda sat across from her. "Liv, give him some time. Zack is one of the good guys. He'll come around. He'll understand. He just needs to work through his feelings."

She shook her head. "You weren't there, Miranda. I explained everything. I really thought he would understand. And he's right: I should have told him sooner. When did I become such a good liar?"

"You're not. You're the worst liar in the world."

"Not anymore. I'm a master deceiver." Zack's words had felt like a physical assault. The more she tried to explain, the angrier—and more hurt—he became.

Olivia's cell phone rang, but she didn't make a move to get it. Miranda glanced at the number. "It's someone in Virginia," she said.

Olivia reluctantly picked up the phone. "Olivia St. Martin."

"Olivia, it's Rick Stockton."

She sighed and braced herself. "Hello."

"I know everything."

She closed her eyes. "I'm sorry, I knew it'd come out, but I wanted to explain—" She rubbed her eyes.

Her excuses were already sounding lame. Last week, she couldn't think of any other options. Today? She wished she'd done everything differently.

Not because she might lose her job, but because she'd lost Zack.

"We'll talk about that later. We have more serious issues to deal with."

She sat up straighter. "What happened?"

"I got a call from the deputy district attorney in San Mateo County, California, this morning. Two prominent people from the Hall investigation were murdered in their homes this week. Hamilton Craig, the district attorney; and Gary Porter, the detective originally in charge of the Hall investigation thirty-four years ago."

"Gary? Dead? I just talked to him earlier this week. He was going to Hamilton's funeral—I thought it was an intruder, a robbery gone bad." Olivia's heart rate increased.

"The bullets from both victims came from the same .38."

"Oh no." Her hand drifted to her mouth. Both Hamilton and Gary gone. Murdered. "Who did it? Do they have a suspect?"

Rick paused. "They got a warrant to search Brian Harrison Hall's apartment. They found blood evidence that he killed both men, and ammunition that matches the fatal bullets."

"Hall?" Her voice cracked. She could barely speak.

"That's how I learned about your activities this week. When I spoke with the attorney, he told me that an 'Agent Olivia St. Martin' had been in Redwood City just yesterday morning. I called Greg. He told me everything."

"I'm sorry, Rick. I—I didn't have a choice." As she said it, she knew it was true. She really hadn't had a choice. She'd never have been able to live with herself if she'd done nothing and more girls died.

She'd helped save Nina Markow. She'd helped put Christopher Driscoll behind bars. She would do it again if faced with the same choice. She hadn't known Zack when this started. And while she regretted not telling him the truth sooner, she didn't regret coming to Seattle.

She had to explain it to him. Again. And again. Until he forgave her.

He had to forgive her. She loved him.

"So Hall's in prison again?" she asked.

"They can't find him."

Olivia tensed. "What?"

"They found a vehicle registered in his name at the San Francisco International Airport. The time stamp indicates that he parked at 4:30 yesterday afternoon. We're reviewing all security tapes and airline records to figure out where he went. He may have fled the country.

"Or," Rick continued, "he may be trying to find you."

"Me?"

"You testified against him, not only when he was convicted, but when he was up for parole. He killed a sixty-nine-year-old prosecutor and a sixty-year-old retired cop. Two men who simply did their job thirty-four years ago.

"I talked to Vigo, our profiler, right before I called you. Vigo thinks if Hall knows where you are, he'll go after you. Where are you in Seattle?"

"Right now? I'm at Quincy and Miranda Peterson's house."

"Agent Peterson? Stay there until you hear from me. That's an order, *Dr.* St. Martin. And I expect you to obey this time." He hung up the phone.

"What happened?" Miranda asked, worried.

"The police think Brian Hall killed two men who were involved in his prosecution.

"My boss thinks I'm next."

Again, Zack couldn't sleep.

Quinn had driven him back to Seattle, but they didn't talk much, other than to take care of jurisdictional issues. The sheriff's department would be transporting Driscoll to the county jail in the morning, and on Monday he'd be arraigned. The powers that be—meaning the county prosecutor and the U.S. Attorney—would work out the legalities of prosecution.

Zack didn't care what they decided, as long as Driscoll never saw the light of day. Driscoll's interview had disturbed him deeply. He'd interviewed dozens of killers, but none had been as disconcerting as Driscoll. He'd felt chills listening to him.

Quinn tried once to talk about Olivia when he dropped Zack off at his house after midnight.

"Olivia did what she thought she had to do," Quinn had said.

"Don't talk to me about her. The case is over. We're all going our separate ways."

Now, physically and emotionally drained after the most stressful week of his career, he wanted to stop thinking about her. He couldn't.

What would he have done in Olivia's position? If

he could have, would he have lied to be part of the sting operation that ended his sister's killer's life? Would he have manipulated people to find the gunman who'd shot her?

His phone rang. Pierson had given him three days of comp time, so who the hell would be calling him at one in the morning?

"Travis," he answered, his voice gruff.

"It's Olivia."

He didn't say anything.

"I'm sorry I lied to you."

"Liars are always sorry when they're caught."

"I told you myself. I didn't want you hearing it from someone else."

"And that's supposed to make me feel better? I tell you I love you, and you tell me you've been lying to me since the beginning?"

He could almost feel her anger vibrating over the phone lines. What right did she have to be angry? She wasn't the one manipulated and betrayed.

"I'm not sorry I came to Seattle. I helped with this investigation, however much you want to deny it. You may never forgive me, but you know what? That's okay. Because I did what was right at the time. I'm sorry I hurt you in the process. Do you think I planned it like this? I didn't want to hurt you. I didn't want to fall in love with you!"

She sucked in her breath and Zack stared at his empty bed.

Could he ever trust her again?

"Olivia, I don't know anything anymore. I'm tired." Weary. He didn't know what he believed, or how he could get over the pain in his heart.

"I know something, Zack. I know that I love you.

I know that I'm sorry for hurting you. And I know one more thing. I helped put Christopher Driscoll behind bars and he will never destroy another family again. And if that's all I have when I leave Seattle, I can live with that."

She hung up.

Zack stared at the phone.

Clearly, the ball was in his court. He just didn't know if he wanted to play anymore.

CHAPTER
32

Freedom comes at a price.

The only sign of Paul Benedict's shaky nerves was his sweaty palms. He stood military straight in the cold fog outside the back entrance of Seattle Justice Center. Justice! He'd laugh if he had an ounce of humor left in his soul. What did the court know about justice? What did anyone?

Justice was reserved for the criminals. Never for the victims.

And certainly not for the children. Certainly not for his daughter, Jenny. Sweet, sweet Jenny, who would never hurt anyone.

Hinder not the children.

Paul sucked in his breath as he swallowed salty tears. If the dam burst, he couldn't do what he'd come to do. What he had to do. If he broke down now, justice wouldn't be served. Clear mind, steady hand.

There was time enough for pain tomorrow. And every day after tomorrow that Jenny should be alive.

He closed his eyes just for a moment, but that was worse. He saw Rachel holding the infant Jenny in her arms. They were both so beautiful, their golden blonde hair halos. Then Jenny taking her first, tentative steps toward him, smiling, arms outstretched. Then Jenny on her first bicycle, wobbling back and forth, scared but excited. He'd wanted to reach out and catch her when she fell that first time, but his daughter would never have learned to ride if he didn't let her fall.

She'd never have a chance to fail again. She'd never have a chance to succeed.

If only he'd been here. Home, where he should have been. What had happened over the years that had torn him and Rachel apart? They used to be happy. Yeah, they'd struggled. And when he lost his job three years ago he'd been in a hell of a depression.

Why hadn't Rachel stood by him? Not that he'd made it easy. He'd been a bastard. He could see it now, in the cold light of reality. He hated that Rachel had to go back to work to support the family. That he'd been a failure, couldn't provide for his own wife and child.

His beautiful, perfect little girl.

When he got the job in Pennsylvania, Rachel refused to move with him. And one thing led to another—the divorce was final last year.

Had he been here, could he have protected his daughter? Kept her from being hurt? Kept her safe and alive?

He'd never know. He'd never know what might have been different.

But if it wasn't for that bastard Christopher Driscoll, Jenny would be alive today.

Two police cars pulled into the secure lot of the Justice Center, where the courthouse stood next to the jail. This was his only opportunity to find justice for his daughter. After this morning, Driscoll would be escorted to and from the jail through the sky bridge.

A sheriff's van pulled into the drive behind the police cars, followed by a pair of motorcycle cops.

He'd loaded the nine-millimeter with glazers to maximize internal damage and prevent the bullet from exiting the body and hitting an innocent person.

He was not a murderer. No, he wouldn't kill a person. But Driscoll wasn't human, he was an animal. A sick, deranged animal who attacked little girls.

Paul slowly drew in his breath, the steel warming in his grasp.

The cocky bastard emerged from the van, handcuffed, two cops on either side.

Jenny was in Heaven. *Hinder not the children.*

Benedict aimed his gun. Driscoll was going to Hell.

Early Sunday morning, Zack found himself at the cemetery, which wasn't a place he normally visited. He felt compelled to see his sister's grave site and sit and try to figure out why the thought of letting Olivia slip out of his life terrified him as much as the thought of her betraying his trust again.

A man sat next to Amy's headstone, a blanket spread before him. As Zack came closer, he recognized Vince Kirby. Tense, he stalked over.

"What are you doing here?"

Kirby looked up at him and sipped a can of cola.

"I should be asking you that question. I come here every Sunday."

Zack hadn't known that. He swallowed uneasily, shifted on his feet.

"Want a soda?"

"No," he snapped. He'd wanted time alone with Amy's memory. He certainly didn't want to stand around and chat with her lover, a man he didn't even like.

"Good work catching Driscoll. I was impressed."

Zack grunted. "You're not going to get me to comment on the case, Kirby."

"I don't want you to. I have enough stuff to write a different article every day for a month." Kirby drained his soda and put the empty can in a bag. "Maybe this was fate, or divine intervention, or something. That we're both here at the same time."

Zack rolled his eyes. "Just my dumb luck."

"You didn't like me because I dated your baby sister."

"I didn't like you because you were a cocky reporter who made cops look incompetent. And," he added reluctantly, "because you dated my baby sister."

Zack sat down on the other side of the headstone. "And, because you knew what she was up to and didn't tell me."

"I promised Amy I wouldn't."

"And she ended up dead."

"You don't have to remind me of that, Travis. I've thought about it every day of the last six years. I loved Amy and I miss her terribly. But there's something you need to understand."

Zack looked at Kirby. Saw the anger and sadness in his eyes, emotions that mirrored his own feelings whenever he thought about Amy.

"What do I need to understand?"

"Amy believed in what she was doing. She didn't

want you to know. She pleaded with me to keep her secret. She thought you wouldn't let her see it through.

"When her best friend died of a drug overdose, it changed Amy in ways I don't think you ever fully understood. Maybe because you were her big brother, the cop who always saw the world in black and white, maybe because you tried to protect her from not only others but herself, I don't know. But Amy made it her mission to get kids off drugs. She worked as a drug counselor for years."

"She had to for her probation after being arrested for dealing."

"That sentence was five hundred hours' community service. She became a certified counselor and put in thousands of free hours helping kids get off and stay off drugs." Kirby paused, ran a hand over her name. "Amy learned that one of her mentors, a woman she trusted implicitly, was dealing at the same time she was counseling. She went to the local DEA office. I went with her. After several months of investigation, they couldn't get anywhere, so they agreed with Amy's plan that she would infiltrate the organization and see what she could learn. Amy and I staged a public breakup and she went to this woman in tears, threatening suicide, a bunch of stuff. This woman offered her some heroin to 'take the edge off.' Knowing full well that if Amy started up again, it would be twice as hard—maybe impossible—to quit.

"I didn't like everything Amy was doing, but I stood by her because stopping this drug pusher was important to her. And the more she learned about the Seattle drug trade, the more she wanted to put a big hole in it."

"She never told me," Zack said. And it hurt. "She didn't trust me." And that hurt even more.

"I don't think it was a matter of trust."

"What else could it be? I was a cop, dammit! I could have protected her!"

"Protected her, perhaps. But they would have smelled something rotten if you started hanging around."

"I'm better than that."

"You're not discreet, Travis."

"Dammit, this was my sister's life you were playing with!"

"It was *her* choice. Her decision. She knew the risks, but she was willing to take them on herself." Kirby paused, looked Zack in the eye. "Maybe it was a matter of trust. Not that she didn't trust you, but she knew you didn't trust her."

"That's not true."

"You didn't give her many chances. One screwup and she was walking on hot coals around you."

"She was arrested for dealing drugs, Kirby. It wasn't a little screwup."

"Before that. When you first found out she was on drugs, you laid down the law. Because Zack Travis makes no mistakes."

"Dammit, that's not true. I made a hell of a lot of mistakes when I was a teenager. I didn't want Amy to fall into the same traps. I got out, but other people don't."

"And she was weaker than you."

"I didn't say that."

"No? You could 'get out' of the gutter, but Amy couldn't? Not without the big macho cop throwing his weight around?"

Kirby stood and packed up what had obviously been a picnic.

"Travis, I promised Amy that I would help get you to understand. She died before she had a chance to explain herself. To convince you she was worthy of your love and respect."

"I always loved her." Zack pinched the bridge of his nose, his eyes hot with unshed tears.

"Yeah," Kirby said softly. "I know you did. Deep down so did Amy."

"God, I hope so." He swallowed the hot sting of tears. What if Amy didn't know how much he loved her? He'd just wanted to protect her.

"I tried to talk to you after Amy died, but you never wanted to listen."

"I blamed you for what happened." Zack paused. "And myself. I was more to blame than anyone."

"The *killer* was the one to blame. The drug dealers were to blame. Not me, and certainly not you, Travis." Kirby slung his backpack over his shoulder and stared at Zack. "Amy credited you with her life turnaround. Yeah, she gave you a rough time, but she loved you. If it weren't for you, she would never have had the courage to get off drugs. You were there when she really needed you."

As Kirby walked away, he said, "By the way, I gave my notice to the *Times*. I hate my editor. Everything you think I wrote about you, I didn't. I just wanted you to know that before I left Seattle."

Zack turned to Amy's grave. He sat in the spot Kirby had vacated and stared. He ran his hand over the engraved name.

Amy Elizabeth Forster.

Amy had their mother's maiden name. She never

knew her mother, or her father. Zack was all she had, and he'd failed her in so many ways. But maybe not in the ways he'd always thought.

Now alone, he let the tears fall.

"Amy, I'm sorry we never talked. Really talked. I'm sorry I was such a domineering jackass that you thought I didn't trust you. Maybe—maybe I didn't. But I was wrong. I'm proud of you, sweetheart. I'm so proud of you."

He pictured Olivia falling down the crevice, jumping from a moving vehicle. The cut on her neck; the wound over her heart.

If something happened to Olivia, he would feel just as lost and alone as he did now. With her, he'd felt complete. She was smart and sexy and wise.

And he loved her.

Was he a fool to hold her deception against her? To use her lie as an excuse to force her from his life?

Could he forgive her?

He envisioned Olivia as she was on Friday, looking at the house she'd grown up in, a house full of grief. *I'm glad the house finally found a real family.*

He wanted a real family. He wanted the life he'd been denied by a selfish mother.

He wanted his family to start with Olivia.

CHAPTER
33

Miranda and Olivia were glued to the news while Quinn was on the phone with his boss getting the details.

Jennifer Benedict's father had shot and killed Chris Driscoll as he was being transported from the sheriff's substation to the county jail. The Slayer was dead.

Olivia certainly didn't feel sorry for Driscoll, but she ached for the man who'd lost his daughter, and now his freedom.

But perhaps his freedom meant nothing with his only child dead.

The doorbell rang, and Olivia jumped. After learning about Hall last night, she was on edge. The late-night phone call with Zack hadn't calmed her nerves. She kept replaying the conversation in her mind, wondering what she should have said. What she *could have* said to make Zack understand.

Maybe he never would. And she would have to live with that.

Quinn was well aware of the Hall threat, and he hung up the phone, looking through the peephole, gun in hand, before opening the door.

"Travis," Quinn said.

Olivia whipped her head around. *Zack!*

He looked tired, like he'd slept about as much as she had the night before. He hadn't shaved, and he wore jeans and his leather bomber jacket.

But when he caught her eye, she saw hope.

"Liv, we need to talk."

She nodded. "Excuse me," she mumbled to Miranda. For privacy, she took Zack upstairs to the guest room.

He stared at her bed. She followed his gaze to the open suitcase. She'd been packing when Miranda had called her downstairs to watch the news.

"You heard about Driscoll," Zack said.

She nodded. "We were watching the news."

"He's dead."

"I know."

"I'm glad."

She paused. "So am I."

"When are you leaving?"

"Tomorrow morning."

He didn't say anything. Olivia couldn't stand the silence.

"I meant what I said last night."

"I know."

Tears welled in her eyes. Why was he here if he wasn't going to say anything?

"What more can I say, Zack?" Her voice cracked and she wished she were stronger. "Do you want me to get down on my knees and beg your forgiveness?"

Olivia ran her hands through her hair and paced. "I was eaten up with guilt. I felt responsible for every one of those girls who died. If I hadn't been so positive Hall was guilty, maybe the police would have looked harder."

Zack was about to interrupt, but Olivia held up her hand to silence him. "I know now it wasn't just me. It was all the evidence together that strongly suggested Hall was guilty. But when he was first released, all I could think about was my own culpability.

"So I came out here to help. All I wanted to do was give you the information I had and see the face of the man who murdered my sister. I got so wrapped up in the case, I probably did things that would have gotten both of us in trouble, or killed. And for that I'm sorry, too.

"But mostly, I'm sorry I betrayed your trust. I never wanted to do that, Zack. Especially now. Especially now that I realize that I love you."

"You love me, so it's okay you lied."

She spun around, glared at him. "Are you here to torture me? To show me what I can't have? That's cruel, Zack. I made a mistake, but not the one you're blaming me for. If I had to do it over again, I would still have found a way to be here."

"I know." He looked pained, like he didn't know what he wanted to say. "Liv, I'm trying. That's why I'm here. I'm trying to understand."

"Are you?"

He crossed to the window. It was late Sunday afternoon. Zack wondered why he had come.

"I don't want to lose you, Olivia."

"Zack." She was behind him. Tentatively, she wrapped her arms around his waist. Her face pressed against his back. "I don't want to lose you, either." Her voice was soft, sweet.

They stood like that for several moments.

Zack spoke first. "I was so angry when you told

me the truth. It hurt. You didn't trust me, just like my sister hadn't trusted me. You expected the worst—that I would somehow stop you from avenging your sister's murder. Amy also thought I would stop her from doing what she thought was right.

"Were you right? Hell, I don't know. I've made decisions every day of my life, and I wonder whether some of them were right. I might not agree with your reasoning, but I understand why you got involved. And if it weren't for you breaking the rules, Nina Markow could be dead right now."

He turned around to face her. Tears shone in her eyes. He didn't want to make her cry. The thought of Olivia sad made him ache. "We would never have learned Driscoll's identity without your information on Brian Hall. You were a vital part of this investigation, and whether you have a gold shield or not, you've earned one as far as I'm concerned."

Olivia closed her eyes, a tight smile on her face. "Thank you for that."

"Open your eyes, sweetheart." He pushed up her chin so she had to look at him. "I love you, Liv. I'm not going to let you walk away because of your misplaced guilt, or my misplaced anger. There's something incredible between us, and I want to explore it. Fully. Intimately. Starting now."

He kissed her. She wrapped her arms around his neck and held on, and he ravished her lips, her neck, her ear. He'd missed Olivia last night, missed her and needed her. All his pent-up frustrations, his love, his desire, poured from him into her. He couldn't get close enough, he wanted to touch her all at once.

She entwined his hair in her hands, holding on tight.

"Make love to me, Zack," she whispered in his ear.

He pushed the suitcase to the floor and they fell on the bed, urgent. His lips clasped onto hers while his fingers fumbled with the buttons on her blouse. One popped off, but he didn't care. He needed to touch all of her, see all of her.

The sight of her injuries gave him pause.

"Zack?" she asked, frowning.

He lightly kissed her neck, the bandage on her chest. "I almost lost you forever. The thought of his hands on you, the knife cutting your delicate skin." He cleared his throat. "Liv, I—".

"Shh," she said, and kissed him.

"Are you okay?" he murmured into her lips. "I don't want to hurt you."

She shook her head. "I'm really fine, Zack. I promise. Don't hold back. Make love to me. *Now.*"

She kissed him long and hard, her passion edging him further down the dark spiral. The hope he'd thought was gone came back in a rush. The trust he thought he'd lost flooded him. This woman was his life. Olivia gave him everything he'd thought he lost when his mother abandoned him and when his sister died.

Olivia wanted Zack, needed to reconnect with what they'd had two nights ago. And it was there, everything she'd thought they had was still there, and stronger.

Their tongues battled and she moaned as his hands reached under her bra and gently massaged her breasts as he kissed her, his knee spreading her legs. He was cautious, avoiding her wounds.

Zack unclasped her bra and put his mouth to her breasts, his rough cheeks and hot mouth creating a wondrous sensation she savored. She held his head to her, urging him to continue. Urging him to move farther down to where she was already hot between her legs.

Zack's forgiveness, his love, his need, spurred Olivia on. She pulled off her blouse and bra, reached for Zack's shirt and pulled it over his head. His hard, sizzling chest pressed against her breasts. She reveled in her newfound sexuality, a side of her brought out only by this man.

In this highly-charged moment neither wanted slow and sweet. Zack stripped off her pants and kissed her between the legs. She gasped.

"Your skin is so soft," he murmured against her thigh.

As he spoke, his coarse stubble rubbed against her clit and she moaned.

"Zack," she gasped, her mouth dry.

His breath and his tongue teased and tantalized her. The kisses were warm and wet as his tongue ran along the sides of her labia, around and around, lapping her everywhere except that one spot that craved attention.

Then he hit the spot and she grabbed the bedspread in her hands as her back spontaneously arched to give him full access. She heard nothing, saw nothing, her entire body responding to Zack's ministrations.

She was on the verge, gasping and wanting him to stop and continue at the same time. But when he pulled back, she shivered at the lost connection. He kissed her stomach, her breasts, kneading and massaging her, her intense heat tempered as he slowed the pace.

"Zack, make love to me."

He stood and stripped off his pants. His body was hard, lean; Zack was the poster boy for tall, dark, and handsome. Handsome? Try to-die-for sexy.

She wriggled in anticipation. She wanted more.

He lay on her and she moved beneath, his chest pressing against hers a powerful sensation.

"I want you, Olivia." He spread her legs and plunged in. She bit down a startled cry as an orgasm surprised her.

He didn't go slow. He kissed her hard as he urgently made love to her, faster and harder until a second orgasm spiraled up, up, ready to take her away.

"Livia, I love you. Oh God I love you." He strained and they were coming together, hot and sweaty, hands clenched together, souls entwined.

Her body trembled beneath his.

"I take it we're okay now?" she asked, tentatively.

"Okay? I thought that was better than okay." He smiled and kissed her. "Yes, we're okay." He touched her hair, her lips. "I love you, Liv. We're going to make this work."

Her lips trailed from his mouth, across his rough face, to his ears. Her hands fisted in his hair, hair nearly as long as hers. She kissed his neck, her tongue feeling his pulse beating a rhythm.

Now that the urgency was over, they could take the time to fully explore each other.

Zack matched her exploration, his kisses coming harder, his mouth sucking her neck, her chest, down to her breasts. She gasped when he drew a firm nipple into his mouth, her entire body on fire. She thought she wouldn't be ready to make love so soon, but she found herself craving him again.

Zack rolled over and she found herself on the top. "What's wrong?" she asked.

"Wrong? Nothing. I thought you might enjoy being in charge."

She hesitated. She'd never done anything like this before. She'd never been wild and playful in bed. She didn't know quite where to start.

Zack must have sensed her insecurity because he said, "Kiss me, Liv."

She did, and her nervousness faded away.

She explored with her hands, her breasts teasing his nipples, her hips rocking against his. She didn't feel as petite while sitting on top; she became empowered.

His hands never stopped, roaming up and down her back, massaging, touching, molding her bottom, her thighs, her hips. She gasped when his penis jerked against her, hard and long, and she reached down and touched it, its velvety softness over the firm length quite erotic.

Every touch made her hotter, more desperate to make love. She kissed him long, tasting his lips, his tongue, his neck. He tasted salty and rich, deliciously hot and spicy.

She looked down and saw his hardened length reach for her, as if it had a mind of its own. On instinct—because she'd never been on top before—she tilted her pelvis up and with her hand, guided him into her. She watched him enter her, gasping from the erotic sight as well as the feeling of him moving within her.

He moaned, reaching up and grasping her hair.

She eased down slowly. She was small, tight, and he—wasn't. He filled her. But she was ready for him, ready to make love, and finally pushed all the way down, gasping as he jerked inside her, sending electric shocks through her body.

He grasped her hands and squeezed. She was the novice here, but he was letting her take the lead. She found a rhythm that seemed to please him as much as her. He moaned, his neck muscles taut.

"You're driving me crazy," he whispered. "I'm not going to last if you keep doing that."

"You want me to stop?" she teased.

"No."

"Good, I wasn't going to."

Never in her life had she felt more feminine, more like a real, whole woman than she did now, entwined with Zack. She moved up and down, faster. Hot, sweating, she wanted release.

Zack couldn't take his eyes off Olivia as she enjoyed her newfound sexuality. Her head tilted forward as she concentrated on the sensations they created together. Her little gasps when she rubbed her clit into him on the downstroke.

He wanted to urge her on, faster, but he loved watching her experience something so new and powerful for her. Every muscle in his body tightened as he fought to maintain control. He wanted to give her the power, to show her how much he loved and trusted her.

She began moving faster, up and down, her head falling backward, revealing her neck. Zack had to force himself not to stare at the bandage. He'd almost lost her. But here she was, alive and free and all his. He'd give her the world if he could. He would keep her safe forever. Never allow her to be hurt again.

With Olivia, Zack had the right woman, the woman who completed him, who freely gave her passion and her love.

She moaned, her body slick with sweat and desire, his body vibrating with passion. He placed his hands on her hips and pushed her fully down on him, his cock reaching her cervix, her body hot and tight around him.

"Oh Liv," he moaned.

Her gasps took on a higher tone and her body shook from head to toe, vibrating with an orgasm that rocked him into his own release. He held her tight as their shared spiral reached a fevered pitch, then her body melted onto his, her skin hot to the touch, her breathing heavy and satisfied.

"Zack." Her voice was a mere whisper as she kissed his chest with hot, feather kisses. "That was . . . well. I can't begin to describe it."

"You don't have to." He cleared his throat. "We'll have a lot of time to practice as you find the words."

"There are no words in the dictionary that come close to describing how I feel right now."

He rolled her off him and only then realized they hadn't used a condom. He wasn't usually that careless, but the thought disturbed him only briefly.

He planned to spend the rest of his life making Olivia happy. He had no intention of letting her go. So whatever happened, they were in it together.

Kissing her all over her face, he said, "Come home with me. Take some time off."

She tensed next to him and he propped his head on his hand. "What's wrong?"

"I'm going to Virginia tomorrow."

"But—Liv, we worked it out, didn't we? You know I want you with me."

Olivia wanted nothing more than to stay with Zack. She didn't even want to get out of bed again. But she owed it to Greg for helping her, and Rick for standing up for her, to face the disciplinary board and answer their questions.

She had broken the rules, and while Rick was doing everything he could to protect her job, she still had to stand up for what she'd done.

"I have to go back. I broke the rules; I have to face the music. I owe it to Greg, who also has to face the disciplinary board."

"I'll write a letter about how valuable you were to the investigation."

She smiled. "Quinn told me that Chief Pierson was giving me a commendation, and Bureau Chief Clark has written a letter for me. But I still need to be there; you understand that, don't you?"

"Yes," he said, obviously not happy about it.

"I'll be back when I can."

"I may end up in Virginia faster than that." He held her tight. "I'm not going to lose you, Liv. You know that, right?"

"I know," she whispered. "You'd really come out to Virginia?"

"I promised you a vacation. I've never been to the East Coast except for a training conference years ago."

"I can show you the sights. Autumn is beautiful out there."

"And then we can really talk, okay?"

She nodded. "Okay."

He kissed her once, twice, three times. "We'll work

everything out, Liv." He kissed her again. "I promise."

> *"In Seattle this morning a man police suspect of brutally murdering thirty-two children was shot and killed by the father of one of his alleged victims. Fifty-four-year-old Christopher Adam Driscoll was pronounced dead at the scene, and Paul Benedict, father of murdered nine-year-old Jennifer Benedict, was arrested.*
>
> *"Police Chief Lance Pierson said . . . "*

Brian sat on the park bench that Sunday afternoon, listening to the news on a handheld radio, awestruck.

That bastard Driscoll was dead.

Brian couldn't feel an ounce of remorse for the asshole who'd framed him for that girl's murder. He deserved to die, though Brian would have liked to see how Driscoll would have fared in prison.

At least that was one loose end tied up. He'd seriously considered offing Driscoll as repayment for stealing thirty-four years of his life.

He looked up at the house. *Her house.*

She hadn't come home yet, but that was okay. The two days he'd had since arriving in Virginia gave him time to plan. Not only how to kill the bitch who'd helped imprison him, but to figure out where he would go once she was dead.

Canada was relatively close, but he'd be better able to lose himself in Mexico. Cheaper to live there, too. And he had street smarts. It'd be easier to make it in Mexico. Not to mention it snowed in Canada. He hated the cold.

The whole thing was making him nervous. Not so much killing Olivia St. Martin, but being responsible for his own life. In prison, he didn't have to think about earning money to eat, paying rent, or working.

He'd realized much too late that he should have waited to kill the cop and prosecutor until *after* he got his restitution money. He'd been mentally berating himself for the past two days.

A million dollars, thrown away, just like that. Gone. There was no way he could go back to California now; he'd made too many mistakes. For one, he'd used the same gun on both men. What was he thinking?

He hadn't been thinking. The story of his fucking life, right? The reason Driscoll got away with framing him. Brian should have thought about who else could have killed that girl. If the cops had asked the questions the Seattle cop had asked, Brian would have figured out about Driscoll years ago.

One last debt to pay and he would truly be free. But while freedom was alluring, he'd begun to miss the structure and security he had in prison.

A fancy car pulled into St. Martin's driveway. Brian shut off the radio and pretended to read the book he held while he watched a tall, skinny guy walk up to the front door with two bags of groceries in his arms.

This was it. His chance to get inside the house.

He crossed the street and approached the house. He hadn't broken in when he'd first staked out the place yesterday morning because of the alarm system, but this guy entered and so must know the code.

Would he have locked the door? Brian hoped not.

He didn't want to kill the guy, but he'd do what he had to do.

Cautiously, he tried the front door. Unlocked. He glanced from left to right to make sure no one was watching him. The houses were set far apart, and with the park directly across the street, Brian felt safe enough to enter.

He listened in the doorway. His heart skipped a beat at the sound of rustling in the kitchen down the hall.

Directly in front of him was a staircase. The bedrooms would most likely be upstairs, but he'd inspect the entire house once the guy in the kitchen left. Find the best place to hide. Where she would least expect him.

Walking as silently as possible up the staircase, Brian Hall finished forming his plan.

He'd wait until Olivia St. Martin came home.

Then he'd kill her.

CHAPTER
34

Zack stayed the night, and early Monday morning he joined Olivia for a light breakfast with Quinn and Miranda Peterson.

"I'll take you to the airport," Zack said.

"I can't let you do that," Quinn said.

"Excuse me?" Zack glared at him. What was Quinn's problem?

"She's under federal protection; I'm flying out with her."

Zack looked from Quinn to Olivia and said slowly, "What's going on?"

"Oh," Quinn said. "Miranda, I think we should step out of the room."

"What's going on?" Zack repeated as the Petersons left.

"I didn't think to tell you—I'm sorry. It's Hall."

"Hall?"

"The police believe he killed two men involved with his prosecution in California. They think he's coming after me."

"Shit, Olivia!" He slammed his fist down. "You've been threatened and you didn't tell me?"

"This all just happened. We don't know where he is—he could have fled the country. His car was found at the San Francisco airport. It's just—the FBI profiler believes he is seeking vengeance for being incarcerated. Hamilton, Gary Porter, now me. Federal protection is just a precaution. Hall has hardly any money, he has a record, and his photograph and description has been disseminated to all law enforcement agencies. It's only a matter of time before he's caught."

"Before or after he tries to kill you?"

Zack yanked her from her chair. She was startled, but he didn't care. "In the last seventy-two hours, you almost fell to your death in the Cascades, you were held hostage by a serial killer, and now a suspected murderer might be after you for revenge? And you think I'm letting you out of my sight for one minute?"

"I—"

He kissed her. Full on, open mouth. He pulled back, his heart racing.

"I don't care what Quinn Peterson ends up doing, but where you go, I go, federal protection or not."

By the time they reached Virginia, it was after six in the evening. Agent Tim Daly greeted them at the airport and took over from Quinn; Zack seemed to take the situation in stride. Daly drove them to Olivia's small but elegant two-story house in Fairfax.

Olivia was embarrassed showing Zack her home. While the house was stylish, and the furniture expensive, it was empty. Barren. It wasn't a *home*—it had no living plants, no photographs, nothing that said a content, fulfilled human being lived there. Even her bookshelves were tidy with a few, mostly decorative, books. The manuals she used for work were in her office. Model homes in new housing developments had more personality than Olivia's, though she'd lived here for three years.

Agent Daly walked through the house. "Okay, the house is secure," he said as he came down the stairs. "Director Stockton said to take it easy today, but plan on being at the lab tomorrow at oh-eight-hundred for debriefing."

"Director Stockton?" Zack questioned.

"He's in charge of the FBI laboratory," Olivia explained, though she felt uncomfortable bringing it up with Zack. They hadn't really talked about *what* she did for the FBI.

"Coffee, Tim?" she asked.

"That would be great, Dr. St. Martin."

"It'll just take a couple of minutes."

"Don't rush," he said, and sat down.

She walked down the short hall to the kitchen and started coffee. Then she noticed the note on the refrigerator.

She frowned, until she recognized the small, perfect block letters on the front. *Greg.*

She opened the note and read it.

"What's that?" Zack asked.

"A note from Greg."

"Your ex-husband Greg?"

"Yes." She smiled. "He brought over some groceries yesterday when Rick told him I was coming back."

"He has a key to your house?"

Olivia looked at Zack. The tone of his voice was odd—but his face was blank.

"I don't understand," she said.

"This is the same Greg who ran DNA tests off-hours and who knew what you were doing from the beginning?"

"I explained that," she said slowly. She'd thought they'd gotten beyond her lie.

Suddenly, she felt extremely weary and sank down into a chair, her head in her hands. "I can't live like this."

"Like what?"

"With you doubting and questioning me."

"I wasn't."

"Weren't you?" She looked at Zack. "Why does it bother you that Greg knew what I was doing in Seattle?"

Zack shuffled his feet and looked sheepish. "Liv, if you think I don't trust you, you're wrong."

"Then what?"

He didn't say anything. Olivia replayed his comments in her mind. "Is it because Greg has a key to my house?"

Zack sighed. "I didn't realize you were *that* close to your ex-husband."

She almost laughed, but Zack looked so uncomfortable she didn't have the heart. She stood up and kissed him on the cheek. "Zack, Greg and I are friends. We're always going to be friends. But I love *you*."

Zack pulled her close, kissed her, held her. "A lot of marriages don't end in friendship. I haven't talked to my ex-wife in years—she's living in Los Angeles, last I heard. On her third husband."

"I'm sorry."

"I'm not. It was a mistake. We both knew it before our first anniversary." He looked at her. "What happened with your marriage?"

"We wanted different things."

"Do you still love him?"

Tension radiated from Zack's body. This was important to him, Olivia realized.

"Not like I love you."

"That's not an answer."

"Don't be jealous, Zack. Greg and I were friends before we got married, and we're still friends. I love him in the sense that he's been a reliable part of my life for years. Plus, we have a lot in common.

"But," she continued, "I mistook friendship and mutual respect for love. In fact, I don't think I was truly capable of loving anyone then. I didn't want anyone in my life, but I felt comfortable with Greg and I thought that was reason enough to marry him. It wasn't."

"I didn't mean to sound jealous, Liv. There's just so much I still need to learn about you." He kissed her. "But I'm looking forward to it."

A sound from the doorway made Olivia jump.

Tim Daly cleared his throat. "Uh, sorry, Dr. St. Martin. I was just going to help myself to the coffee."

Olivia blushed and waved him away. "I'll get it."

While she poured coffee for the three of them, Zack commented, "Nice house."

"Now that I look at it, it needs some sprucing up," she said.

"You don't spend much time here," Zack said.

She shook her head and looked at him. "This house looks like me."

"No, Liv, it doesn't."

She turned to him. "Yes, it was me—cold, sterile, and unemotional—until you came into my life."

He reached out for her and she sank into his embrace.

Being in Zack's arms, *this* was home.

It was after ten and another FBI agent, Pete Hoge, had replaced Tim Daly.

"I'm going to check the perimeter," Hoge said. "Keep the door locked until I return."

Olivia glanced at Zack, who seemed amused. He locked and bolted the door behind Hoge and pulled Olivia into his arms. "As soon as we get that guy settled, I'm taking you upstairs and making love to you." He kissed her.

She smiled. "Again, Detective? I can hardly wait."

Five minutes later, Hoge knocked on the door and Zack let him in, locking the door behind him.

"Everything looks good," Hoge said.

"Help yourself to anything you need in the kitchen," Olivia told him.

"Thank you, Dr. St. Martin." He nodded to Zack, then walked down the hall to the kitchen.

"Almost alone," Zack whispered in her ear. "Let's go upstairs."

They took the stairs two at a time and Olivia opened the door at the end of the hall. Zack picked her up and carried her across the threshold, laying her on the bed.

Zack stared at Olivia for a long minute. He'd almost lost her—twice. First to a killer. Involuntarily, his eyes dropped to the large, flesh-colored bandage on her neck and his heart tightened. She'd been so close to death, sitting in that car with Christopher Driscoll.

And then he'd also almost lost her to his own stupid pride. Thinking back to the last week and everything that had happened on the case and between them, Olivia had been a team player. She'd been an asset, and he should have been the first to admit it, instead of feeling betrayed because she'd misrepresented herself.

If he had walked away from her forever, he would be half a man today. She completed him in a way he didn't know he needed until she came into his life.

He lay down next to her and rested his head on his hand. Tenderly, he brushed her hair off her forehead, kissed her soft, creamy skin. He ran a finger lightly over the small bandage on her chest. "How are you doing?"

"Stop worrying about me. I'm fine. A little sore, but really, I'm fine."

"You know, I'm glad you're not an FBI agent. I don't think I could handle you being in the line of fire every day."

She laughed. "Most agents aren't in the line of fire *every* day."

"Once in a lifetime is enough."

"I agree. Besides, I like my job in the lab."

"What exactly do you do?" He played with her hair. He couldn't keep his hands off her. He didn't want to.

"I analyze trace evidence, among other things. For example, in a case I worked on before I went to Seattle I compared carpet fibers found on three dumped bodies in Minnesota and confirmed that the victims were all wrapped in the same industrial-style carpet, down to the lot number and manufacturer. A lot of what I do is build evidence for trial."

"Sounds interesting, but tedious." He kissed her cheek.

"It can be, but it's absolutely exhilarating when everything comes together."

Olivia's house phone rang and she reached over to answer it. "Hello?"

Zack heard a male voice on the other end.

"Olivia, it's Greg. I didn't wake you, did I?"

She sat up and said, "No, not at all. Thank you for the groceries."

Zack stood. While he knew there wasn't anything going on between Olivia and her ex-husband, he didn't feel comfortable listening to their private conversation. "I'm going to check downstairs and talk to Hoge," he whispered.

She nodded and he left.

Okay, maybe he was still a *little* jealous, but he'd get over it.

Olivia frowned as Zack closed the bedroom door. She hoped he wasn't still insecure about her relationship with Greg.

"Olivia? Are you there?"

"Sorry, Greg. Will you be at the meeting with Rick tomorrow?" They needed to formally report their activities to their boss and hope for nothing more serious than a reprimand. However, any punishment wasn't Rick's decision. The investigation would ultimately go to a review board for action.

"I already gave my report this morning. Are you well enough?"

"What makes you think I'm not?"

"Maybe being thrown from a moving car or stabbed, pick one."

Olivia sighed. "I'm definitely not cut out for fieldwork. But really, I'm in one piece and am barely sore." That wasn't completely true, but she wasn't going to let on to Greg or Zack that she felt more than a little battered.

"I can come by, maybe pick you up in the morning."

"That's all right. Rick assigned security and they'll drive me to the office."

"Rick said that a Seattle cop came out with you."

Word travels fast, Olivia thought. "Yes."

"Isn't that unusual?"

"Not really."

Silence. Olivia felt distinctly uncomfortable, but she didn't want to explain to Greg about Zack over the phone. She'd tell him tomorrow, in person.

"I'm tired. I think it's time I go to bed," she told Greg. "Thank you again for sending over the groceries."

"Anytime, Olivia."

She clicked the OFF button and rested the phone on its charger, then yawned. She was exhausted. She wouldn't mind a hot bath, though. Maybe Zack would join her. She smiled at the thought and walked over to the adjoining bathroom. She turned on the water, added some bath salts, then crossed over to her bedroom closet for her robe.

She brushed past the bed and something grabbed her ankle.

She fell hard on the carpet, her brief scream silenced when her breath was knocked out of her.

Someone scrambled from under the bed, pinning her body to the ground with his. Out of the corner of her eye she saw a hand clutching a gun.

Hall.

She pounded on the floor with her fists, hoping Zack could hear, though the carpeted floors muffled the sound.

"Stop that!" Hall ordered in a low whisper. "Stop it right now. Make another sound and I'll shoot you."

Through her terror, Olivia detected a hint of fear in Hall's voice. He had to know there were cops in the house. He'd been hiding under the bed while she and Zack were talking.

She shivered, feeling violated and uncomfortable at the thought of Hall spying on their intimate moment.

"What do you want?" she asked.

"It's your fault." Hall rolled off her, but still aimed the gun at her. "You fucking bitch. You made me a killer. You did this to me!"

She wouldn't have to make noise to alert Zack, she realized. Hall's voice was getting louder.

She slowly sat up, moving away from him at the same time.

"You don't want to kill me," she said. She catalogued the items in her room. Nothing lethal. Her gun, which she rarely used, was still packed in her suitcase.

Dumb move, St. Martin. She'd relied on Zack and the agents to protect her. She needed to protect herself.

"Brian, you need to be smart right now."

He ignored her. "Okay, this is what we're going to do," Hall said. "We're going to walk out of here and you'll take me to your bank. Then we're done."

Olivia shuddered. He was going to kill her after getting some money. And she wasn't about to be a hostage again. Once in a lifetime was more than enough.

Hall glanced around the room. "Your boyfriend is going to be back. How can we get out of here?"

Olivia would have found it hard to take Hall seriously as they sat on the floor facing each other but for the fact that he had a gun pointed at her.

And he *had* killed Gary and Hamilton.

"You don't want to do this," she said. "You don't want to go back to prison."

"I dunno. Maybe I do," he countered. "Free food, movies, little work. Why shouldn't I go back to prison? I have no life outside."

"All right. Well, I can arrange it." If she weren't so scared, she would have laughed. She didn't need to *arrange* anything. Hall had already killed two people. "I work for the federal government. I have a lot of friends in high places. Hand me the gun and we can talk about which prison you'd like to go to."

He shook his head. "You don't get it. My life is over. *You* stole it from me. I got out and had nothing. I'm too old to do anything. My own ma thinks I'm guilty. But I'm not!"

Regardless of the recent crimes Hall had committed, Olivia felt sorry for him. He'd been in prison well over half his life and no longer knew how to function in the real world.

"Brian," she said softly, "I really feel awful about what happened after my sister was killed. I hope you understand that I was just a little kid. I only saw the tattoo. Everything else was based on the evidence."

Hall's lips tightened. "It was all made up."

"No, it wasn't made up. But you're right. They should have pursued other suspects. They weren't thorough enough." They didn't have the tools thirty-four years ago to be as thorough as law enforcement was in the twenty-first century. But still, Hall had created part of his problem by lying to the police about his whereabouts the night of Missy's kidnapping.

Olivia wasn't about to remind him of that, though.

"Brian, listen. You did a good thing back in California. You helped us catch Driscoll. You helped save a girl's life. That's worth something. That's worth a lot."

Hall's back was to the door, but Olivia saw it slowly inch open.

Zack was on the other side.

"That asshole Chris Driscoll! How could he do that? How could he set me up like that?"

"Driscoll was a sick killer, and he definitely set you up. But you might not have heard the news. He's dead. He was shot and killed outside the courthouse today."

Hall nodded. "I heard it on the news. He deserved it, the fucking pervert. I'm not like him. I'm not a killer."

"You're nothing like Driscoll," she agreed. As she said it, she realized the difference between the two killers. Driscoll took intense pleasure in killing. Hall had killed Hamilton and Gary quickly and quietly, and in relative darkness.

She wasn't out of the woods yet. Hall had traveled three thousand miles to kill her. But the longer she kept him talking, the better her chances of surviving.

Out of the corner of her eye, she watched Zack step silently into the room.

"I'll tell you what. Put the gun down, and I'll do everything I can to get you in any prison you want. Any prison in the whole country. You know where the good prisons are, right? New facilities, comfortable beds, good weather."

"I heard about this one down in Texas. One of the transfers was talking about it."

"Exactly."

"Though I got pals in Folsom."

"Whatever you want."

Zack caught Olivia's eye. Even though he had a gun aimed at Hall's head, if Zack fired Hall could easily get a round off.

"I don't believe you," Hall said. "You can't do that. You can't set me up in a federal prison. You're trying to fool me."

Olivia had thought she'd had Hall ready to acquiesce. So close!

"Brian, what can I do or say for you to believe me?"

"Nothing. You'd lie in a heartbeat. How do you think I got here? I didn't kill no one and no one believed me—my own mother, even now, even after evidence proved I didn't do nothing wrong."

He sniffled, his body shook.

He used his gun arm to wipe his nose.

Olivia tilted her head to the right and Zack nodded. He was just two feet from Hall. Ten minutes ago, Olivia had cursed the carpeted floors; now she was grateful for them.

"I don't know what to do." Hall looked defeated.

Olivia moved quickly to the right and Zack tackled Hall from behind, grabbing his gun hand and slamming it against the nightstand.

"Oww!" Hall cried, and his gun fell to the floor.

Olivia hurriedly crawled over and snatched Hall's gun while Zack threw him on his stomach and knelt on his back, handcuffing him.

"It's not fair!" Hall cried. "You lied to me again." He sounded like a petulant child.

"What is it you want?" Olivia asked.

"Don't talk to him, Olivia. He's not worth it."

She shook her head. "No, I want to know."

Hall looked skeptical, but asked, "Can you really help me get into a decent prison? One that has good food and television and maybe video games?"

"Yeah, I really can," Olivia said. "I know the people who can make it happen. I'll make it right for you, Brian."

Pete Hoge came into the room and hauled Hall up by his arms. "I'll take him into federal custody," he said, "while they work on extradition to California."

"Federal custody?" Hall's face lit up. "Hey, do you really think I can get into a federal prison? They're even better than the place down in Texas my pal told me about. I hear the food's really good."

Hoge looked ready to hit Hall over the head. Zack clapped him on the back. "Take him away."

Olivia watched Hoge take Brian Hall out of her room, and she sank onto her bed. She didn't know how she would ever sleep again without checking under her bed, just like a child.

Zack took Hall's gun from her and put it in his waistband. She'd forgotten she was holding it.

He sat next to her, wrapping his arms around her. "Are you okay?"

She nodded. "You know, I feel kind of sorry for him. I mean, I hate him for what he did to Gary and Hamilton, but . . ." She shook her head. How could she explain? "I can't help but wonder if he would have been capable of killing if he had never gone to prison in the first place."

"He was caught up in someone else's game. I hate the thought that the taxpayers are going to be footing his bill for the next twenty to thirty years, until he croaks."

"He killed a cop, Zack. He could get the death penalty."

"He helped us find Driscoll. A good attorney could probably get him life without parole."

"Which is what he wants." Olivia rested her head on Zack's shoulder.

"You seem to attract danger like a magnet," Zack said, kissing the top of her head.

"Me?" She laughed, and the release made her feel a thousand times lighter. "Oh, Zack, I'm actually a boring person."

"Is that supposed to be a selling point?" he teased.

Olivia smiled into his chest, then heard something that sounded like running water. She jumped up.

"What's wrong?"

"My bath!" She ran to the bathroom. The overflow drain was working, but water still poured from the tub. She shut it off, standing in half an inch of warm water.

Zack came up and wrapped his arms around her. "You were taking a bath without me?"

"I'd planned on inviting you to join me."

"Good." He spun her around and kissed her forehead, her nose, her lips. She sighed and leaned into him.

"We're still going to have a vacation, darling," Zack told her. "I'm not counting today."

"Let's hope the rest of our vacation is less eventful," she said, smiling.

They looked down at the water all over the bathroom floor and laughed.

A siren cut into the night and Zack sighed. "We're going to have to hold off on that bath for a while."

Olivia unbuttoned her shirt and dropped it to the wet floor.

"You deal with it. I've had enough of Hall for tonight." Olivia slid out of her clothing and stepped into the full tub. "I'll wait here for you, if you don't mind."

Careful to keep the bandage on her chest dry, she sank into the warm water and sighed.

"Hold that thought. I'll be back as soon as I kick everyone out of the house."

Olivia smiled as Zack fled the room.

Twenty minutes later he was back. He entered the room naked.

Now they could officially begin their vacation.

CHAPTER
28

"Where's Olivia?" In the chapel, Zack checked his watch for the third time in as many minutes.

"I'm sure she's on her way," Quinn assured him.

"She's late." Zack had worried that Olivia would get cold feet on their wedding day. She'd already changed her entire life for him. Moved across the country. Taken a job with the State Crime Lab at a reduced salary. When they returned from their honeymoon, he was moving from swing to the day shift so they would be working the same hours.

He planned on spending every free hour with his wonderful bride.

He had considered quitting his job, intending to find a position in Virginia. He had a good résumé, good references. What mattered was that they were together.

She wouldn't let him leave the force. She'd told him she wanted to move to Seattle and start fresh. They talked about it that week after Hall broke into her house, and together decided that they would make a home together in Seattle.

That was three months ago. But the last couple of days, she'd started distancing herself from him. This morning he hadn't even seen her before leaving for the church—she'd left early for Miranda's house to get dressed for their wedding.

He was worried she'd changed her mind. Regretted the sacrifices they'd made to be together.

He'd find a way to fix it. He had to. He wasn't about to let Olivia be unhappy.

Ten minutes late.

Quinn's cell phone rang and he smiled sheepishly at the small group of people who'd assembled for the wedding. "Excuse me," he said to Zack. A minute later he hung up. "Zack, that was Miranda. Olivia won't come out of her room."

Zack's chest tightened on the five-minute drive to Quinn's house.

What was wrong? Was she scared? Did she regret her choices? Didn't she love him?

They each had a failed marriage, but at least for Zack, he knew what he'd done wrong. He'd been young, stupid, and arrogant. His job had been first and foremost, and his ex-wife had been a distant second. He'd learned from his mistakes, and he wasn't about to make the same mistakes with Olivia.

When Zack had met Greg, he had liked him. Well, if he was being perfectly honest with himself, he had been a tad jealous. But Olivia explained that she had married Greg because it was comfortable, they were friends, and she enjoyed his company. Love hadn't entered into the equation—"Not the kind of deep love I feel for you. A different love, maybe."

That had tempered the jealousy.

Minutes later, he parked in front of Quinn Peterson's house. Zack strode up the front walk but before he could ring the bell, Miranda opened the door. If he hadn't been so worried about Olivia, he

would have complimented her—she looked beautiful.

"Where is she?"

"Upstairs. In the guest room."

Zack didn't knock; he just walked in.

"Olivia, what's wrong?"

She wasn't dressed. Her gown hung on the back of
the bathroom door. Her hair and makeup were
done—or they had been. Now streaks of color ran
down her face. She had wiped most of it away with
tissue.

He took a tentative step forward. "Liv—whatever
I did, I'm sorry."

She burst into tears, and Zack gathered her into his
arms and held her.

"Liv, honey. Tell me what's wrong. We can face
anything together. You know that."

She shook her head.

"Please, Liv?"

Since they'd decided to marry, Olivia had planned
for today. But two days ago her life had turned
upside down and she no longer knew how to cope.
She didn't know how to tell Zack.

"Is it Seattle? Do you regret leaving Virginia?"

She shook her head. How could he even think
that? They'd talked about it for days before deciding
she had no roots in Virginia. The few friends she had
she could visit on vacation.

"Is it the crime lab? Do you hate your new job?"

"No," she croaked out, sniffing. She actually loved
her new position. Some of the equipment wasn't as
good as the FBI's, but her position was challenging,
she was in the field often, and she enjoyed her colleagues.

"Is it me?"

"No, Zack. It's me. I'm pregnant."

Zack's face said it all: he was astounded.

"That's okay," he said slowly. "It's fine. We haven't talked about having kids, but I love them. I mean, I haven't had one of my own, but we'll learn together." He paused, touched her cheek. "I'm okay with it, Liv. Were you worried I would be mad? Honey, it takes two to make a baby. This little guy is as much my responsibility as yours. He's *ours*. I can't think of anything better."

She shook her head and more tears streamed down her face. "I can't—"

"I don't understand."

"What if something happens to her? I can't protect her every minute of every day. Children are killed all the time. They're abducted out of their own beds! How can I bring a child into the world knowing she could die?"

"Oh, Liv." Zack pulled her into his arms and she clung to him, her body shaking.

"Olivia, Olivia. All I can promise is to love this child with all my heart. To do everything in my power to protect her and keep her safe. It's all any parent can do."

"I'm petrified. I don't see how I can function."

"You're not— Are you thinking of not going through with the pregnancy?"

She shook her head. "No, no, not that. I just don't know what to do, Zack. I'm scared."

He kissed her forehead and pulled her chin up. "Olivia, you will make an incredible mother. Your capacity to love is infinite. And every step of the way we will be together. We will love and protect this child." He laughed suddenly. "We're going to be a family."

Olivia tried to calm her nerves. She didn't know if she could make this work. She didn't know how to handle the many emotions battling within.

Zack rested his hand on her stomach. For the first time since she had learned about her condition, she felt peace wash over her. She took a deep breath.

She was still scared. She knew too much about evil and what could happen. But with Zack, just maybe she had the strength to take it one day at a time.

"I do love you, Zack."

He kissed her, embracing her tightly. "I love you, Liv. You and the little guy inside you. Forever."

"Forever," she repeated, holding him close. Her fears faded just a bit. With Zack, she could do this.

"Now will you marry me?" he asked.

"Right now?"

He glanced at his watch. "Right now."

"Can I get dressed?" She stifled a combination giggle and sob.

"Absolutely. But I'm not letting you out of my sight. Do you need help?"

She wiped away tears. "No, but you can watch."

He sat back in the chair and smiled. "This should be fun."